TALES OF THE
SHADOWMEN

Volume 5: The Vampires of Paris

TALES OF THE
SHADOWMEN

Volume 5: The Vampires of Paris

edited by
Jean-Marc & Randy Lofficier

stories by
**Matthew Baugh, Michelle Bigot,
Christopher Paul Carey & Win Scott Eckert,
G.L. Gick, Micah Harris, Tom Kane,
Lovern Kindzierski, Rick Lai, Roman Leary,
Alain le Bussy, Jean-Marc Lofficier, Randy Lofficier,
Xavier Mauméjean, Jess Nevins, John Peel,
Frank Schildiner, Stuart Shiffman,
Brian Stableford** and **David L. Vineyard**

cover by
Alan Weiss

A Black Coat Press Book

ISBN 978-1-934543-50-4. First Printing. January 2009. Published by Black Coat Press, an imprint of Hollywood Comics.com, LLC, P.O. Box 17270, Encino, CA 91416. All rights reserved. Except for review purposes, no part of this book may be reproduced or transmitted in any form or by any means, electronic or mechanical, including photocopying, recording or by any information storage and retrieval system, without permission in writing from the publisher. The stories and characters depicted in this anthology are entirely fictional. Printed in the United States of America.

Table of Contents

Alan Weiss' cover rough (2008)

Death of a Shadowman

This is the story of a carpenter, who was also a Shadowman. It also happens to be a true story, passed down through several generations of the same family.

As each French village used to have its baker, its butcher, its cobbler, etc., it also had its carpenter, whose job generally included that of a joiner, a furniture maker, a woodsman and a roofer. The job of a carpenter was serious business, dutifully handed from father to son.

Our carpenter, however, in addition to his usual tradesman skills, had a most unusual talent, which was also inherited.

He could predict who was about to die.

For among the carpenter's many duties–and not the least important!–was making the coffins for those who died. Now, most village carpenters, being relatively poor, did not have the money to order and store vast quantities of wood in advance. So, if someone died, more often than not, they had to order wood from a sawmill, and then make the coffin, cutting the planks to the proper size, which would delay the funeral for some days.

But not our carpenter!

On New Year's Day, he would go door to door, as custom required, to pay his respects to the other villagers. And as he shook hands and looked people in the eye, he would know, just by like that, who would die during the year.

One might argue that an observant eye might be able to predict the incipient demise of the old and sick, especially in a time when doctors and medicine were both rare and expensive, and, in any event, only available in larger towns and cities. But our carpenter could predict even the deaths of people unlikely to die, those who would accidentally drown, or fall from a tree, or perish from some other entirely accidental cause.

Our carpenter was not rash. He would discreetly revisit the persons in question, look at them again, weighing whatever insubstantial evidence he had gathered. But, eventually, when his mind was made up, he would order the wood. And, yes, the person would die during the year, and the carpenter would cut the wood, and make the coffin speedily.

Understandably, the carpenter never shared the nature of his gift with anyone, except for his son, who would someday take over his trade. Either no one in the village ever wondered how the carpenter always happened to have the right amount of wood required to make a coffin–or no one dared to ask.

But that is not the strangest part of the story.

According to the carpenter, a few days before the person in question was about to die, *the wood purchased for his or her coffin would start creaking*–and he would ready his tools.

World War I, and the exodus from villages towards the cities, spelled the end of artisan trades. No one in that family has been a carpenter for a century now, but they still tell the story as they heard it from their grandfather, whose father was the last carpenter...

Progress and technology changed our societies and put an end to our beloved Shadowmen just as they did away with our carpenter. There is no room today for Sherlock Holmes and Arsène Lupin, Judex and the Shadow, Doc Savage and Zephyrin Xirdal. The vampires who haunted the rooftops of Paris have been displaced by satellite dishes. The exotic hidden lands have become fodder for CNN's breaking news.

But, just as we remember the story of the carpenter, we should strive to preserve those of our heroes. This fifth anthology brings together Dracula and Josephine Balsamo, Lord Ruthven and the Count of Monte Cristo, the Nyctalope and Hercule Poirot, Arsène Lupin and Hanoi Shan, Doctor Omega and Professor Moriarty, Sherlock Holmes and Tevye the Milkman, and more...

Long live the Shadowmen!

Jean-Marc Lofficier

We open this fifth volume of Tales of the Shadowmen *with a unique art portfolio. Michelle Bigot is a talented artist and a major contributor to French publisher Les Moutons Electriques' imprint,* La Bibliothèque Rouge, *devoted to heroes and villains of popular literature. As such, she has illustrated a variety of characters, including Arsène Lupin, Hercule Poirot, Sherlock Holmes, Dracula, James Bond, and many more.* Tales of the Shadowmen *has always welcomed artists' portfolios in its pages in the past (such as Fernando Calvi's in Volume 2). Here, we asked Michelle to gather some of her best pieces, plus half-a-dozen more created especially for this book, and have arranged them in a collection centered around the theme of the Tarot–but a uniquely different Tarot...*

Michelle Bigot: *The Tarot of the Shadowmen*

I. *Le Bateleur* (The Juggler, or The Magician) – THE FAMOUS FIVE.
The first Arcana symbolizes initiative, throwing caution to the winds, perhaps even immaturity. This is the card of the Apprentice. That's why I chose Enid Blyton's Famous Five–Julian, Dick, Anne, George and their dog Timothy–who are four headstrong young heroes, full of boldness and promise for tomorrow, Jugglers amongst the Shadowmen.

II. *La Papesse* (The High Priestess) – ANTINEA, QUEEN OF ATLANTIS.
The second Arcana symbolizes wisdom, mysticism and learning; it is a passive card, well suited to the High Priestess of Atlantis, content to sit and wait in her forgotten citadel in the Hoggar Mountains, occasionally distracting herself with lovers from the outside world.

III. *L'Impératrice* (The Empress) – IRMA VEP.
The third Arcana symbolizes action, enterprise, derring-do, but in a female context. Irma Vep, the black-clad mistress of the Vampires gang, casts her shadow over the whole of Paris, like an Empress of Evil; she is the only woman who is sufficiently empowered to stand her own in a world of male villains.

IIII. *L'Empereur* (The Emperor) – FANTÔMAS.
The fourth Arcana counterpoints the third and symbolizes absolute male power and authority. While the card may sometimes be good, all too often a monarch becomes a tyrant and uses power for evil. It suits Fantômas, Emperor of Evil, who, like no other, stands for raw, unchecked power over all.

V. *Le Pape* (The Hierophant) – SAR DUBNOTAL.
Unlike the fourth Arcana, the power and wisdom evoked by the fifth Arcana are always associated with good and benevolence. Who better to be associated with it than the powerful mystic Sâr Dubnotal, a Hierophant who uses his great powers for the protection of the weak and helpless.

VI. *L'Amoureux* (The Lovers) – JAMES BOND.
The sixth Arcana is not only a symbol of Love, but it also stands for the transition from inexperience to mastery. Whether we are talking about seducing women or earning the right to kill villains, none do it better than James Bond, and this is why 007, the Lover *par excellence*, is associated with this card.

VII. *Le Chariot* (The Chariot) – NERO WOLFE.
The seventh Arcana symbolizes triumph, pride, success, but reached only through slowness and perseverance. All these characteristics, and more, fit the prodigious talents of Nero Wolfe, for this is not a card befitting someone who moves fast, but rather one who moves at chariot-like speed–decisively and successfully.

VIII. *La Justice* (Justice) – HARRY DICKSON.
The eighth Arcana symbolizes, as its name indicates, implacable Justice, even if it is delayed. Amongst the many heroes who were selected by Fate to become its avengers, none are so relentless and merciless in tracking down and exterminating monstrous evils as Harry Dickson, the so-called "American Sherlock Holmes," who often incarnates the merciless sword of Justice.

VIIII. *L'Ermite* (The Hermit) – HERCULE POIROT.
Patience, solitude and reflection are associated with the ninth Arcana. This is the card of a man of learned knowledge and patient wisdom, one who knows how to wait for results to manifest themselves. Only one figure has come to embody these virtues: the man with the little grey cells, Belgian detective Hercule Poirot, a resolute bachelor, our Hermit.

X. *La Roue de Fortune* (The Wheel of Fortune) – JOSEPH ROULETABILLE.
The tenth Arcana is about speed and movement. The wheel turns and old problems vanish, only to be replaced by new ones. Life goes on, endlessly. This is why it is well represented by the young and energetic journalist Joseph Joséphin, a.k.a. Rouletabille, who ever rides the Wheel of Life, bringing about changes to all around him, without ever stopping to think about himself.

XI. *La Force* (Strength) – TARZAN (LORD GREYSTOKE).
The eleventh Arcana is not just about strength or power; it also embodies confrontation and clash. Of all the Shadowmen, Lord Greystoke, the savage Lord of the Jungle known as Tarzan, strength personified, best symbolizes the concept of violent conflagration between powerful forces or adversaries.

XII. *Le Pendu* (The Hanged Man) – REGINALD JEEVES.
The concept usually associated with the twelfth Arcana is that of immobility and inaction; thus, some may see it as a negative card, but the omniscient manservant Jeeves is a perfect example of constructive inertia, how to triumph while being seemingly hamstrung by one's position in life. Our Hanged Man only appears to be trapped by his social position; in reality, he is the true master behind the scenes.

XIII. *La Mort* (Death) – MADAME ATOMOS.
Tarot experts claim that the thirteenth Arcana isn't just about Death. That may well be so, but it is called Death, and when it comes to Death (including its figurative concept of brutal and unforeseen change), none can beat the deadly Madame Atomos, who has slaughtered millions in her defiant battle against the United States of America.

XIIII. *La Tempérence* (Temperance) – JULES MAIGRET.
The fourteenth Arcana is a card of moderation, of slow transformation, sometimes associated with spiritual insight, which is why this card belongs to French Police Commissioner Jules Maigret, a symbol of Temperance in all things, and a deep well of empathy for all those whom he investigates.

XV. *Le Diable* (The Devil) – DRACULA.
Betrayal, illusion, power and sex. The fifteenth Arcana is best represented by the one monster who embodies all of these characteristics, and more: the Lord of the Undead, the vampire lord Count Dracula, wealthy, powerful, seducing and as deadly as the Devil himself.

XVI. *La Maison-Dieu* (The House of God, or The Tower) – DOC ARDAN / DOC SAVAGE.
The sixteenth Arcana usually stands for collapse, disillusion and loss, and yet it can also mean a hard, physical confrontation with reality, one that invariably results in material consequences that can be positive. It is represented here by scientist-adventurer Doc Savage (or, as he is known in France, Doc Ardan), whose exploits have brought much catastrophic change to the world, and who lives in a Tower of sorts at the top of the world.

XVII. *Les Etoiles* (The Stars) – DOCTOR OMEGA.
The seventeenth Arcana symbolizes Destiny, Fate, sometimes godlike, yet always benevolent. It represents a calculated celestial intervention for good, something best embodied by the mysterious traveler in the aether known as Doctor Omega, a man whose origin is written amongst the Stars themselves.

XVIII. *La Lune* (The Moon) – THE NYCTALOPE (LEO SAINT-CLAIR).
The Moon symbolizes the eclipse of the Sun, a time of darkness, of anxiety... but also given to phantasmagoria and romance. There is one colorful, extravagant hero who thrives in the dark and fights to restore the light: The Nyctalope. Always ready to fall in love, always prepared to face down monstrous villains, when the full Moon is bright, the Nyctalope is here!

XVIIII. *Le Soleil* (The Sun) – SHERLOCK HOLMES.
The Sun is the supreme star of the Heavens, which sees all, casts its light upon everyone, and symbolizes truth, success and power. This is why the nineteenth Arcana has been allocated to the greatest of all detectives, the incomparable Sherlock Holmes, a true Sun in the firmament of Heroes.

XX. *Le Jugement* (The Judgment) – JUDEX (JACQUES DE TRÉMEUSE).
The twentieth Arcana is Karma manifest, immanent justice made real, the end of the road for the villains, the time of Judgment. There is only one champion whose very name means The Judge who owns this card: Judex.

XXI. *Le Monde* (The World) – ARSENE LUPIN.
The twenty-first Arcana symbolizes overwhelming wealth, success, fame and glory. Who better than the legendary gentleman-burglar Arsène Lupin, who has it all, fame, women and wealth–the World itself may not be enough for him, ever–to epitomize it?

0. *Le Mat* (The Fool) – NESTOR BURMA.
A complex Arcana, which symbolizes in turn foolishness, nonchalance and indifference. The changes it heralds are deceptively subtle, but just as profound as those signified by Death. It has been allocated to the seemingly bumbling detective Nestor Burma, often mistaken for a Fool, and yet, whose wits and luck always unravel the deepest mysteries.

II

LA PAPESSE

III

L'IMPERATRICE

V

LE PAPE

VII

LE CHARIOT

VIII

LA JUSTICE

michelleBigot 2007

VIIII

L'ERMITE

X

LA ROUE DE FORTUNE

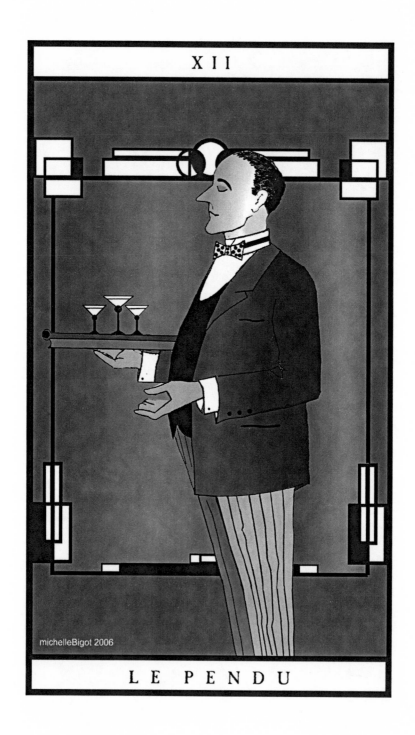

XII

LE PENDU

michelleBigot 2006

XIII

LA MORT

XIIII

LA TEMPERENCE

michelleBigot 2006

XVI

LA MAISON-DIEU

LA LUNE

XVIIII

LE SOLEIL

XX

LE JUGEMENT

LE MAT

This story was initially written for the French Madame Atomos reprint omnibus series published by our sister imprint, Rivière Blanche; others in the series include "Au Vent Mauvais...," "A Day in the Life of Madame Atomos" and "The Butterfly Files" published in Tales of the Shadowmen 3, *and "The Atomos Affair" and "Madame Atomos' XMas" in* Tales of the Shadowmen 4. *The Madame Atomos saga, created by French writer André Caroff, began on the morning of August 9, 1945, at 11:02 a.m., when Nagasaki was obliterated by the world's second atomic bomb, which killed Madame Atomos' husband and children. Some of the rubble has been left standing as a memorial, including a one-legged* torii *gate and a stone arch near ground zero. Twenty-one years later, on August 4 and 5, 1966, Scientists against A- and H-bombs held their first meeting in Hiroshima, whose city council had decided to preserve and develop the* Genbaku Dome, *a structure originally built in 1915 that had survived the blast. This passionate plea for peace, mercy and forgiveness, penned by our regular contributor Matthew Baugh, shows the deadly Madame Atomos confronting another nuclear holocaust survivor, who has chosen a starkly different path from hers...*

Matthew Baugh: *The Way of the Crane*

Hiroshima, 1966

Kato stepped into the sunlight, a small urn in his hand. He paused to watch the people pass. The park had been built to commemorate the darkest day of Hiroshima's history, but it was still a park. There were mourners, young couples, even children playing in the beautiful weather.

He moved to the statue of a young girl holding a stylized crane. Hundreds of origami birds sat sheltered beneath it. He took a square of paper from his pocket and folded his own crane. He held it as he pressed his palms together in a reverent gesture.

"Prayers for peace will not comfort the dead."

Kato turned. The speaker was a woman in her 50s, stern and regal.

"Excuse me, Ma'am," he said. "I don't understand."

"Only the weak beg for peace," the woman answered. "The strong find a way to take revenge."

Kato felt his cheeks flush.

"I'm afraid we disagree, Ma'am," he said. "Please excuse me."

He picked up the urn to go.

"Do I upset you, Hayashi-san?"

Kato turned back.

"How do you know my name?"

"When the ashes of your grandfather were identified, I knew that you would come to take them from this place."

"Do I know you, Ma'am?"

"You were not yet born the last time I saw your grandparents," she replied, "but the Kato and Yoshimuta families have been friends for many generations."

"Yoshimuta?" Kato's eyes widened at the name. He glanced around warily.

"There is no need to be alarmed," she said. "I have not come to harm you. My wrath is for the Americans."

"How can you be here?" he demanded. "You're wanted by the *Tokkoka*!"

"Madame Atomos goes where she pleases."

"Why have you come?"

"To pay my respects to your grandfather. Also, I hoped to recruit you for my organization. I understand that you are a resourceful man, and there is the connection of our families."

Kato was speechless.

"Don't act so shocked, Hayashi-san," she continued. "I have investigated you. I know that you work for the criminal organization of the Green Hornet. I offer you the chance to use your skills in a nobler cause."

"I am not a murderer!" Kato protested.

"Nor am I," she replied. "I am an avenger. I mete out justice for the angry spirits of all who died here and in Nagasaki."

"This is no place to talk of revenge." Kato gestured to the paper cranes. "Each of those is a prayer for peace. The statue of the little girl is..."

"I know the story of Sadako-san," she interrupted. "She believed that if she made a thousand paper cranes, the gods would cure her. But childish superstitions are useless in the face of evil. That little girl died of leukemia from the radiation of the American bomb."

"Her prayer wasn't just for herself," Kato replied. "She prayed for peace so that no other child would suffer so."

"My aims are the same," Madame Atomos replied. "When I am done, no child will ever again suffer at the hands of the Americans."

"What of the American children you have killed?"

"An unfortunate necessity."

"That sounds like what the Americans must have said when they dropped their bombs."

"Do you think to compare me with them?" Madame Atomos snapped. "How many innocents died? Was it 100,000, 200,000? How many more need to die before people like you understand that such an act must be punished?"

"I don't defend the actions of the Americans, but is punishing atrocities with more atrocities the answer?" Kato shook his head. "The cycle of vengeance will never end."

"It will–when I have crushed them," she retorted. "I will not leave the survivors the strength to rise against me."

"There have been many who have tried to do that," he countered. "Have any of them ever succeeded?"

"I will succeed!"

"Please reconsider," Kato said. "Revenge is like sugar. The first taste is sweet, but it gives no nourishment and leaves you craving more. If that is what you live on, it will rot you from within."

"You sound more like a monk than a gangster!" There was contempt in her voice. "Do you honestly believe they deserve my forgiveness?"

"Forgiveness is not for those who deserve it," he replied. "If we were all virtuous, there would be no need for it."

"To forgive is to excuse the guilty!" Madame Atomos shot back. "It is a denial of reality."

"I do not excuse them," Kato said. "It was a terrible thing that we cannot forget. But in remembering, we must let go of hate. That is the only way that healing is possible."

They had been moving through the park; now, they paused near a statue of a young girl with a fawn.

"I am disappointed, Hayashi-san," Madame Atomos said. "Your grandfather deserves better. For his sake, I ask you one more time: join me."

"For his sake, I ask you to seek another way." Kato held out the crane he carried.

She snatched the folded paper from his hand, and tossed it away. It landed at the base of the statue.

"For the sake of the friendship our families once shared, I will not have you killed," she hissed. "Do not try to stop me. I have snipers around the park. You might evade them, but they would kill others."

Kato's eyes widened. There were dozens of people around them, unaware of the danger. He was silent as Madame Atomos crossed to a limousine that bore her away.

When she had gone, Kato moved to the statue. There was a poem inscribed on the base.

"O god of evil, do not come this way again.
This place is reserved for those who pray for peace."

Kato picked up the crumpled paper and smoothed it until it was a crane once more, then he placed it at the foot of the statue.

There are a number of parallels between the great Belgian science fiction author J.-H. Rosny Aîné (1856-1940) and Philip José Farmer.[1] Both brought a mature, adult perspective into the genre; both tackled biological, sexual and moral issues in ground-breaking fashion and, finally, both were masters of the "Lost World" genre. It was therefore particularly fitting that Farmer adapted and retold Rosny's L'Etonnant Voyage d'Hareton Ironcastle *(1922) into English in 1976. Our regular contributor Win Scott Eckert, teaming up with fellow Farmerphile Christopher Paul Carey, drew from these prestigious sources to create another wonderful Lost World saga which brings together a bevy of characters from unexpected sources...*

Christopher Paul Carey & Win Scott Eckert: *Iron and Bronze*

Sub-Saharan Africa, November 1929

A dark form, silhouetted against the backdrop of a million brilliantly scintillating stars, loomed above Hareton Ironcastle. The shadowy shape might have been the same monstrous dreamworld being that had just startled him awake. But no. The sheen on the form's exterior was just starlight glancing off skin. Human skin.

Unnerved, but also irritated, Hareton's pulse raced. He wanted to shout at the man who stood over him, demand what the Hell he was doing staring down at him like some fiendish ghoul. Instead, Hareton feigned a yawn, ran his fingers through his straw yellow hair, and said calmly, "Having problems sleeping, N'desi?"

N'desi's only answer was to remove from a pouch at his hip a small stone, which with slow, graceful strokes, he began grating against the sharp edge of his strange square-ended, slightly curving sword. The iron weapon gleamed hideously in the starlight.

Hareton sighed. The man had been acting queerly since they had picked up the telegram in Fort Lamy that sent them on their new mission, refusing to leave Hareton's side for even a moment. This despite the fact that N'desi was no longer technically in the American's employ. Stranger still, the man had begun uttering strange pronouncements in his native Bantu dialect whenever he caught a glimpse of the glittering ax which, less than a month ago, they had recovered from the forbidden ruins in the high reaches of the Tibesti. Perhaps the fellow was taking *taduki* again. He had seen N'desi light a blue flame in the desert a

---

[1] See our article "Farmer and Rosny: Kindred Souls," in *Farmerphile* No. 2 (2005).

fortnight before they had come upon the ruins, and the unmistakable sweet aroma of that rare herb had drifted to Hareton upon the cool arid breeze.

Time seemed to shatter like a brittle stone and the strange dream from the night N'desi took *taduki* settled over Hareton. A dream of the same nightmare creature that had just now visited his sleeping spirit—a towering being, with a roughly human-shaped body, with rippling plantlike skin mottled with many deposits of sparkling silicate crystal, and thick trunk-like limbs that shot into the ground like tree roots. In the dream, the creature led him on a secret way through the mountains, its body stretching from its lower torso, twisting over the seemingly unending desertscape, while its legs remained rooted beneath the sand miles behind. When Hareton awoke the next morning, he had followed the dream path and discovered an old hermit watching over the crumbling foundations of a primordial mountainside settlement. To the protests of the hermit, Hareton, as if possessed by some feverish delirium, had with his bare hands unearthed a stone altar in the ruins, long buried by the dust of time; and upon the altar found the very prize he had come to Africa to obtain: the ax known as the Reaver of Worlds.

Had the *taduki* Hareton so faintly inhaled given him a vision, as it was so reputed to do? And if so, by what strange mechanism did the herb open up the doors of time and space and bring him to his goal? And for what sublime intent?

He felt the bulge of the ax in the pack at his side. Yes—it was still there. Feeling its hard substantiality somehow seemed to mend time and return him to the present.

"It is *xanigew*." N'desi's deep voice, so rarely used, startled Hareton.

"What? You mean the ax? It's what, did you say?" Hareton took care to impart an air of indifference. He did not want to egg on the man's superstitions, which ran thick in his bloodline. After all, N'desi's grandfather, Mavovo, had been a pupil of the great Zulu witchdoctor Zikali.

N'desi remained silent for nigh a minute. Then he said, "The glittering stone you carry disturbs your sleep. As it does mine."

Getting up from his sandy bed, Hareton shot the man an accusatory look. "The ax is cursed," he said flatly, "that's what you're saying. Or *xanigew* or whatever you called it. But I don't think it's that at all. You know something more than you've been letting on." A shiver seized Hareton, which he disguised by rubbing his arms as if chilled by the early desert morning. But an uncanny realization now came over him: meeting N'desi in the bazaar in Marrakech had been no coincidence. The man must have sought him out when he heard the famed American explorer was searching for the Reaver of Worlds.

The ax. It all seemed to come back to the ax. The stories of the natives in eastern Niger said the glittering, iron-headed weapon had been crafted from a splinter of a much larger one. The latter was reputed to have been cast to the Earth by the natives' gods, the Sky People, and wielded by a giant who, in his great anger, had smashed the ax into the Earth countless generations ago, giving rise to the Tibesti Mountains and unleashing a cataclysmic torrent that gushed from the belly of the Great Mother goddess and consumed the world. The legend of the ax, and a tip off from the wise and trusted old mystic Hâjî Abdû that the Reaver of Worlds was in truth a very real artifact, is what had launched Hareton on his recent quest.

N'desi, half a head taller than the six-foot-two American, looked down at Hareton, his dark eyes glowing dimly in the sand-reflected starlight. "The search for your countryman is noble. But it will lead to the rise of a great evil. Leave him to die in the Hoggar."

"Is that what the *taduki* has told you? That I should let the son of my greatest friend die, and place my faith in your depraved addiction to that mind-numbing herb?"

So that explained the man's odd behavior since Hareton had received the telegram from New York. Partaking of the herb had caused some errant signal in N'desi's brain to connect two unrelated events–the finding of the ax, and the search for the son of Hareton's friend, whose plane was last sighted two weeks ago by French military intelligence on a precise course for the Hoggar's Mount Tahat. Now, because of the herb's rewiring of the Zulu's gray matter, N'desi believed the ax had somehow cursed Hareton's new mission.

"Your heart knows the truth." N'desi placed his sharpening stone back in its pouch and returned the long iron sword to its wooden scabbard. "Do not forget the dream which led you to the ax you sought."

Hareton guffawed. "Coincidence! That smoke of yours fouled up my mind and sent it spinning backwards. The local hearsay brought me into the general vicinity of the ruins. It was luck we found it, I'll say, but the herb only tricked me into thinking I knew the route to the ax ahead of time. That's how the psychologists explain déjà vu, you know–the mind working backwards to solve a problem that's already been solved?"

N'desi lips stretched into a rare smile. "And what of the old hermit seizing up and dying at the very moment you raised the ax from the dirt?"

Hareton said nothing, but his own grin faded. N'desi, perhaps sensing he had won the battle but lost the war, began breaking camp. Already in the east the desert night's sable blanket faded. Soon the blood-red orb of the Sun would again bake the sands and Hareton would welcome the shadows of the Hoggar, curses or no.

Harry Killer was not dead.

He reclined on the throne, padded with luxurious gold-laced pillows, and snapped his fingers. A man shambled over bearing a jewel-encrusted bowl filled with olives and cheeses. The servant was hunched over, back and arms bent at almost simian-like angles. The dim light provided by elaborate copper oil lamps suspended from the cavern ceiling shadowed the man's face.

Killer waved the servant away and pointed him toward the cavern's other occupant.

Queen Antinea was on her knees at the base of her throne. Black circlets of metal banded her wrists in front of her, as well as her ankles. Thick chain links connected her manacles.

The servant loped toward Antinea and shoved the bowl under her face. Her lustrous dark hair waved and she shook her head in apparent disgust. Killer knew the revulsion she must feel at the man's fetid breath, his heavy, fur-covered brow, his protruding yellowed teeth.

The juxtaposition of the young chained beauty and the panting beast-man amused Killer. He admired her, the curve of her hip, the swell of her breasts under the thin gown he allowed her.

But most of all he admired her youth. He wanted it.

By rights, Harry Killer should have been dead. He should have been killed when Blackland, his criminal outpost in the Sahara, was blown to bits almost 30 years ago.

Instead, he had awoken deep in the rubble and foundations of the City in the Sahara, buried in dirt and grit and concrete. There had been a shimmering glow in the darkness where none should have been, an almost crystalline light. When he had reached out and grasped this beacon, time swirled and space inverted. The glittering light expanded and enveloped him, and he saw a vast and hidden underground realm buried in a rocky and barren mountain range.

And Killer saw the nude woman, the raven-haired queen of indescribable beauty, with haunted green eyes and a lush red mouth. This woman, posing with nonchalance and shaking her head, as if to say to him, "No, you cannot have this, Harry Killer, this is not for you."

Then time righted itself, and the crystal light was solid. It wrapped around his legs like a sea-birthed tentacle, dragging him gasping through the sand, until it thrust him upward into the air. Killer had hacked and spit up dirt and grit, and lay there on the ground for what seemed like hours, chest heaving. Then, gathering his wits, he was finally able to sit up and look around him.

The smoldering ruins of Blackland were nowhere to be seen.

Harry Killer crawled out of the desert and headed south, holing up for half a year at a native village. Scars and burns pulled his face into a ghastly skull-like visage, and his previously bushy eyebrows, burned in the explosions, were now thin and sparse. As he healed, the Wantso villagers who had initially taken in this broken and burned husk of a white man grew to be more and more afraid of him. More strength flowed into his massive frame with every passing day. And with every passing day, he took more and more liberties, eating their food, using their women.

Finally, one day, he heard some of the men complaining about him. Killer was not a linguistic expert, but he was sharp enough to pick up much of the villager's language within the six months of his stay with them. The native men spoke unthinkingly in front of him, while Killer grinned his death's head grin and bobbed his head like an idiot, and listened intently.

They planned to kill him. Dismemberment, preferably while he was still alive, was not too good for him.

Though huge and muscular, Killer was no match for a whole village of men, and he knew it. When he stole away in the dead of night, he thought about razing the village, but decided that would give any survivors even more reason to seek vengeance and come after him. If he left quietly, they might just leave him alone and not give chase.

Finally Killer made his way to the coast and from there to Europe. He traveled the globe and rebuilt his criminal enterprises, this time choosing to remain mobile rather than once again banking all his resources on one base which could be destroyed. He diversified.

There was one other thing.

Harry Killer did not age. When Blackland had gone up in flames, he had been in his mid-forties. A decade later, he felt as he had when he was 30.

War to end all wars came and went, the trenches of Europe filled with lost souls while Killer got rich dealing in the weapons of German scientists like Herr Doktor Krueger.

Another decade later, and he still felt the same. The crystal light, he realized, in the bowels of Blackland, must have saved him, even rejuvenated him.

But the effects were not permanent. By 1926, he was almost a cripple, dying.

It was chance that gave him a clue. Boredom had led Killer to the ship's library on the *Ile-de-France*, a steamer on Compagnie Générale Transatlantique's New York-Le Havre route, and thus to the fantastical memoirs of Lieutenant Ferrières, of the 3rd Spahis. As Killer read Ferrières' account of Queen Antinea's hidden lair buried in the Hoggar Mountain range of Africa–so close to the Saharan location of Blackland!–and the Queen's apparent everlasting youth, he became convinced there was a connection to his experiences and the visions he had experienced in the wake of Blackland's destruction.

Within a month, he had mounted and fully stocked an African expedition. He planned a detour to a hidden valley he had discovered in his post-Blackland wanderings, there to recruit some local "muscle:" degenerate para-anthropoids of a lost race who called themselves the Wandarobo.

With the Wandarobo beast-men in tow–or rather with him in tow, borne through the jungle and then the rocky desert in a covered litter, as he became increasingly weak–Killer descended upon Hoggar. Antinea's hideaway was ridiculously easy to find. Benoit, the editor of Ferrières' memoirs, had not taken the pains to alter names and places, trusting that the Lieutenant's account was so fantastic it would be viewed as complete fiction–as it likely would have been if not for Killer's visions.

As simple as it was for Killer to locate the decaying empire in the volcanic landscape, Mount Tahat looming in distance, it was even easier to conquer and secure. Antinea's highlands realm, the Mountain of Evil Spirits, once a flourishing community, was reduced from its former glory. Many faithful servants, handmaidens, farmers, and Arabian guards remained, but not nearly enough to repel Killer's swarming Wandarobo.

And so Harry Killer sat upon the plush throne of Antinea's Hoggar sanctuary, while the Queen knelt defiantly before him in chains.

Antinea swung her chained fists at the beast-man, sending the bowl of olives and cheese flying. She spat at Killer, her eyes cold with fury.

"Now, now, my Queen," Killer said. His dried skin pulled tightly about his skull as he forced a smile. "That will get you nowhere. You know what I want. You're older than I am; you must be much older, in fact. Yet you don't look a day over 20. I've been here two weeks. I've been gentle with you so far, but my patience wears thin. I won't wait forever."

"Gentle? Ah…You have thrown me in a cell in my own dungeon. I've no pillows to rest upon and no coverlets to warm me at night. My bath is a cold bucket of unscented water, dumped on me in the morning as I sleep. And you dare cast your treatment as gentle?"

"A little hardship in life does us all good, my Queen. It builds character."

"Then, indeed, your life to this point must have been one of unparalleled luxury."

"I'd revel in this banter with you, draw it out for days, weeks, my Queen, if I had time." A dry rattling cough wracked his body, and he recovered. "I promise you, if you don't tell me what I want to know, and soon, I may die, but if I do, the Wandarobo will tear you limb from limb while you still live. You'll beg for them to dispatch you cleanly before they're done with you."

At this threat, Antinea's imperious anger evaporated. Killer watched her smile serenely at him, then turn her gaze to the three Wandarobo guards crouched at the entrance of her cavernous throne chamber. She stood, her movements slow, sinuous. Then she reached up to her neck, unfastened the gown, and at a leisurely pace drew it down her body, like honey flowing down a spoon.

Antinea stood nude before the panting Wandarobo. They stared, hypnotized as one, at her magnificent, uplifted breasts. She continued to smile at Killer.

He was transfixed, just like the primitives who served him. Antinea appeared just as she had in the crystalline vision years ago.

Antinea's voice punched through the memory. "I think there will be no tearing limb from limb any time soon."

Killer saw red, and yelled at the Wandarobo. "Get her out of here. Back to her cell!"

He watched Antinea continue to smile. The guards didn't move. Then she nodded slightly at them in acquiescence. Or was it command? Rough Wanda-robo hands eagerly grasped her slender, pale arms and drew her away.

The beautiful Antinea, who reminded them so much of their own ruler before their exile to the squalid outpost where Killer had found them, was once again locked away in her cell. They had stood gazing dumbly at her for minutes, which would have dragged into hours, if she hadn't finally dismissed them with promises of more delights, visual and otherwise, later.

Now the three tramped through the dank caverns, grunting and bragging and arguing about which of them had captured Antinea's green-eyed gaze the longest.

As they rounded a darkened bend, a bronzed and heavily sinewed arm reached out and encircled the latter Wandarobo's neck, pulling the beast-man silently into the shadows.

His two companions lumbered onward, oblivious.

"Well, my Queen, how are you doing it?"

"Doing what?" Antinea responded to Harry Killer's question. Her ever-serene smile belied her innocence.

"You know what!" he practically shrieked. He inhaled deeply to calm himself, and, not for the first time, wished he hadn't become a teetotaler after the destruction of Blackland. He could use a snort right now, but alcohol had never tasted quite the same after he'd seen the crystalline light.

More calmly, Killer continued: "Over the past three days, half of my men have disappeared without a trace. The first, right after I sent you back to your cell following your burlesque display."

"I have no idea of what you speak."

"Never mind!" He took another deep breath. He really could use that drink. This woman was getting to him. "My men are disappearing, and they're all whispering that the *ilhinen* have come to get them."

As Killer spoke the word *ilhinen*, the Wandarobo guards in the chamber stirred and rocked back and forth, howling and making signs to ward off evil spirits.

Killer glared at them, and when they quieted somewhat, Antinea remarked, "*Ilhinen*. That is not good."

"Of course it's not good, you traitorous bitch!"

"Traitorous? I owe you no allegiance. I'll see you in the Hall of Red Marble before this is over."

Killer would have stomped his feet on the stone floor, if he had had the strength. But his energy was fast fading.

"I have no plan to become one of your lovers, or rather your victims, my Queen. Tell me what I want to know, and I'll leave."

Antinea smiled faintly.

"I'll give you one more day," Killer said. "I have no more time to play with you. Tomorrow, we start removing fingers. Then toes. Then the other extremities. I guarantee the Wandarobo won't pant at you after that. But it doesn't have to come to that. Tell me the secret of rejuvenation. We've searched everywhere. It must be here. Where is it?"

The Queen continued to gaze at him in silence, resolve showing in her cold eyes.

"Take her away," he ordered the guards, gesturing to the cavern entrance, and buried his head in his hands, exhausted.

Antinea went willingly. Before she stepped into the carved entryway, she paused and looked back.

"Ah, Monsieur Killer?"

He looked up.

"*Ilhinen!*"

The Wandarobo started howling and jumping again, and Killer plugged his ears, screaming in frustration.

Deep in the bowels of the Mountain of Evil Spirits, a group of Killer's Wandarobo guards sat at a long table with wooden benches running along each side. They slurped watery gruel from Antinea's scullery and grunted back and forth about their rapidly disappearing comrades.

One of Antinea's Arab servants, a larger man in hooded robes, set down a large tray at the end of the table, handed out fresh bowls, and began to load up the empties. Despite what must have been long years spent laboring in the dim cavern complex, the muscular hands extending from the robe's sleeves appeared to be dusky and tanned.

The beast-men ignored him, their faces pressed in their bowls, long tongues scouring for every last drop.

When they looked up, a few of them sensed something was amiss. Were their numbers fewer? Perhaps one or two had left to relieve themselves...

One Wandarobo, a shade more intelligent than his companions, whispered, "*Ilhinen...*"

Antinea was face down on a stone pedestal, held on the left by one of Killer's beast-men, her right arm extended straight out and held down at the wrist by another. Killer held a long sword poised above her splayed fingers.

"Last chance, my Queen."

Antinea sighed. "Very well."

"What?"

"I said, very well. I will show you."

45

Killer signaled and the Wandarobo let her loose. Antinea sat up, rubbing her wrist. She wrinkled her nose at the stink of the nearby beast-men. "Would it hurt for them to bathe occasionally?"

"Quit stalling."

"As you wish." Antinea rose to her feet–still chained, as were her wrists– and shambled toward her throne.

"What do you think you're doing?" Killer asked.

"Getting you what you want. Shall I stop?"

"No, get on with it."

Killer watched as Antinea stood before the throne and uplifted her arms, as if praying to an altar. The throne began to rise, stone scraping on stone. The base then slid backward on unseen mechanisms, revealing a staircase below. She began to descend but Killer shoved her aside and went first. He heard her follow him down, as best as her chains would allow.

At the base of the stairs was a small, cubicle chamber carved into the stone. Killer saw a small stone dais, upon which rested a simple metal bowl. A single item lay within the bowl. It resembled a broken and lifeless tree branch, or root, peppered with dulled silicate crystal.

That was all.

He turned to the smiling Antinea, enraged. "This? This is the mighty secret of everlasting life?"

"It is," Antinea replied.

Her calm infuriated him even more. He turned back to the branch, his frustration mounting. "It's not working. It looks nothing like what I saw years ago."

"What did you see?"

"Glowing light. Crystalline. These mountains. You."

Antinea raised and lowered her shoulders. "You said yourself there is no way I could be so youthful. I sit above this every day, on my throne, to ensure my exposure to it. It is the secret you seek, I assure you."

Harry Killer contemplated the branch for a long time. Then he turned, grabbed the chain that hung between her wrists, and hobbled up the stairs, tugging her behind him. At the top, he called over one of the Wandarobo.

"Take her away."

Before the order could be carried out, however, there was commotion and shuffling outside the throne chamber. The rich tapestries covering the carved entranceway were thrown aside, and four beast-men entered the cavern, grasping between them a man, either European or American, in well-worn khakis, jodhpurs, and dark brown boots, accompanied by a native African.

"Master," one of Wandarobo rumbled in guttural tones, "an intruder!"

"Who the Hell are you?"

The man removed his safari helmet and held it in his hands.

"Hareton Ironcastle, at your service."

The heavy iron door shut, leaving Hareton and N'desi in utter blackness.

"Don't say it, I know, it's the cursed ax." Hareton's humorless voice sounded muted in the confined space. He began tracing his hands over the rough basalt walls of their cell, thinking of how Muriel would react if he failed to return from Africa. His spirited daughter wouldn't just send her husband Phillippe and her cousin Sydney Guthrie to search for him—she would come along herself... and fall into the very trap he had.

Hareton had just about completed a circuit of their tiny prison, cursing as he tripped and overturned a half-filled, stinking chamber pot on the floor, when a dim light suffused the chamber from above. At the same time, he heard a door groan on metallic hinges, shuffling feet on the stone floor, and then the deep boom of the door slamming closed. The faint light emanating from a hole near the ceiling disappeared.

"Who's there?" Hareton shouted, hoping his voice would carry to what was obviously an adjoining cell.

For a moment, silence; and then, in haughty, feminine tones: "A queen without a throne." The words, though English, belied the speaker's native Arabic.

"Antinea!" Hareton breathed. He had thought reports of the woman and her spider-trap in the desert to be mere fiction, although his doubts had soon evaporated as he crossed the very distinctive terrain in the Hoggar which he recognized from Ferrières' famous account. And now here lay the queen spider herself, trapped by the treachery of her own web.

"What goes on here?" he asked, resolving not to judge the woman on hearsay. "Who is this man who has invaded your lair and imprisoned us?"

"A man, like any other," came the silken voice. "Except for one thing. He has no soul."

"Otherwise he would have fallen under the spell of your beauty, no doubt." He could not help himself. He had to probe her motivations, get a sense of her character.

"You have heard of me? I should not be surprised. I would have left this grotto long ago and avoided those who would seek me out, had these tunnels not housed the very thing which brings the man known as Killer. But I am patient. Soon enough will he make his home in the Hall of Red Marble."

Hareton repressed a shudder in the darkness, recalling what he had read of the woman's predilection for killing her former lovers—once she had tired with them—and embalming their bodies with orichalcum, that rare element utilized by the metallurgists of the dead civilization described by Plato in the Critias.

"Atlantis!" Hareton said aloud, feeling awed. He could hardly believe it, but had he not seen the seven dried-up canals surrounding the city, exactly as Plato had written? To think, the lost culture that so many had sought in the Atlantic lay buried here—high atop the Hoggar in the middle of the Sahara! The first thing he would do if he ever made it back to his private library in Baltimore would be to burn his copy of Donnelly's *Atlantis*–so what if it was one of Aunt Rebecca's favorite tomes.

"This land was not always desert," Antinea said, as if reading Hareton's thoughts. "Once a great water lapped the sides of my mountain home, which was then but one city in a vast and powerful empire. But if other cities survived the Reaver of Worlds, I have not heard of it. My fortress alone endures."

At hearing the phrase "the Reaver of Worlds"–the same words used by the local tribes to describe the ax he and N'desi had uncovered in the Tibesti–Hareton's entire frame buzzed as if he'd been struck by a god's hammer. But local folk tales did not matter–he could not allow his curiosity to distract him. The man who had imprisoned them meant business.

"What is this thing you say brought this Killer fellow to the Hoggar? And now that he has it, why hasn't he gone on his way?"

A low laugh purred in the darkness. "Have I said that he has it? No, only that he seeks it. And as for what it is, I know not myself, although long have I gazed into its mystery. And what I have seen–"

From the hole connecting the two cells Hareton heard the sound of metal grating against metal–the iron bolt sliding open in the door to Antinea's prison. Then metallic hinges groaned and again a dim light came from above. A moment later, the door to Hareton's cell opened. A large robed figure filled the narrow tunneled hallway outside, a white burnoose hiding the towering newcomer's face.

"I took the liberty of retrieving these," the man said in surprisingly well-modulated American English. The Reaver of Worlds appeared from beneath a robed sleeve, proffered to Hareton handle-first in a large, deeply tanned, corded hand. Then, from beneath his robes came N'desi's square-ended iron sword.

Hareton took the ax, glittering in the orange light of the tall man's torch, while N'desi's teeth gleamed like a vista of snow-peaked mountains as he grasped the hilt of his own weapon.

The giant robed man turned to Antinea. "We must move quickly. Killer has found the secret way down into to the temple."

A sickly look overcame Antinea's regal features. Her stiffened arm pointed down the tunnel and the burnoosed man whirled, heading into the darkness with Antinea following at his heels. Hareton and N'desi raced after them.

They passed through a warren of crisscrossing, rock-hewn corridors, climbing any number of winding staircases until Hareton lost all sense of the way.

"It's enough to drive one mad!" he said to N'desi.

"We trod the path into madness," the warrior replied, "when we climbed the reaches of the Tibesti. Now we only tread deeper."

Hareton did not argue with the man. The sense that fate had laid a trap for them all nearly smothered him.

Finally the nauseating twists and turns ceased and they entered a large circular chamber, in the center of which a plume of fresh water fountained from a rounded basin. The spurting water glistened redly in the light of twelve massive copper lamps that crowned the chamber's circumference, ensconced in a golden framework that disappeared into the yawning darkness of an impenetrable ceiling. Around the basin curved a number of oversized, deeply cushioned divans, which faced outward in the chamber overlooking a series of low, broad niches set in the highly polished, red marble walls. In front of one of the niches lay three unmoving bodies of the hairy half-men. It was to this alcove which Antinea's large servant led them.

"Your handiwork?" Hareton asked the man.

The fellow seemed not to hear him. Instead, he cast his torch out into the chamber, where it lay smoldering on the marble floor. Then he stepped over the bodies and, crouching on hands and knees, crawled into the niche. Antinea followed suit, sobbing angrily at the sight of a metallic statue toppled from a low-lying pedestal in the alcove. A shallow wooden case lay next to the statue on the ground.

"Ah, my poor Captain, what have they done to you!" Antinea caressed the silvery male face of rigid effigy.

The robed man turned the dark hole of his burnoose toward Antinea. "Nothing worse than what you have done to him."

"I cared for him! As I have cared for all of my lovers!"

"I am not sure the Captain's family will be so grateful when I describe to them the manner of your loving attentions." Then Antinea's defiant servant crawled onto the pedestal and dropped into a square hole in its center, disappearing from sight.

"What lies below?" Hareton asked Antinea, whose face still flushed with an anger not hidden by the room's long shadows.

"Eternity!" she hissed, and with no further explanation slipped onto the pedestal and vanished.

Hareton shrugged. Hefting the Reaver of Worlds, he looked to N'desi with a wry smile. "To eternity!" he cried, and entered the hole.

Hareton dropped two meters down to land on a stone floor. Ahead, faint light cast upward from yet another tunneled, winding staircase. He began descending, hearing N'desi's feet clap the cold stone behind as he jumped into the passage.

The stairway corkscrewed for perhaps thirty meters before passing through a nine-sided doorway, which opened upon the first of three connected antechambers. Shadows obscured the exact size and shape of the rooms, although the dim, pulsating light cast from the doorway at the end of the farthest one gave Hareton the impression that each successive antechamber was of greater size than the previous.

Seeing Antinea about to enter the room from which the light emanated, Hareton raced ahead, gripping his ax tightly. Though a relic of a bygone age, it seemed sturdy enough to do the trick in a fight. Besides, it was the only weapon he had.

He slowed as he reached the last doorway. Then, bracing himself for whatever he might find, he passed through.

Though he had prepared himself, he gasped. But it was not the strangeness of what loomed before him that surprised him–although it was indeed strange– but rather its familiarity. For the breathtaking sight that rose from the center of the enormous oval chamber he had seen before. Or at least something like it. No, it was not humanoid in form like in his dreams. But its rippling, plantlike skin did indeed glisten with the same crystalline mica deposits, which seemed to glow with an inner light. There could be no mistaking the monstrous plant-being from his *taduki*-inspired dreams.

The thick, towering trunk of the plant grew tree-like from the cracked mosaic-tiled floor in the center of the subterranean temple, rising into the darkness of the cavernous ceiling, its many green-leafed branches fanning out over the room and rustling as if blown by a wind that was not there. Great copper lamps like those in the Hall of Red Marble circled the temple, their thin red flames catching in the plant's crystal-mottled exterior. Did the plant glow with its own light? He could not say, although if he looked closely enough he thought he could make out dark forms moving beneath the translucency of the silica.

Hareton and N'desi walked forward to join Antinea and her giant servant as they stood looking up, mesmerized by the colossal tree.

Then, from behind the massive trunk of glittering cellulose, walked a man. Harry Killer. With him came a half dozen of his fierce beast-men. But this was not the same feeble man who had been carried about on a litter by his half-human entourage. No, this man did not stoop or shuffle, or need assistance of any kind to move about. He did sway as he walked forth, but certainly it was with arrogant swagger, not frailty.

"How?" Hareton whispered.

"It is the Tree of Dreams," Antinea said at his side. "I know only that it is, and the youth and vitality it brings, not by what magic it operates."

"I cannot explain it either." Killer stopped a half dozen paces before Hareton, his grin uneven and sneering. "But I do know one thing. Now that I have explained to my friends that the *ilhinen* that killed their fellows is nothing more than a robed native, they have gotten over their love affair with you, my Queen.

"Now!"

With his last word, Killer's beast-men surged forward, their large wooden-knobbed clubs raised high and swinging.

As Hareton raised his own ax, Antinea's giant servant moved like lightning. Already he was amid the howling mass, somehow jujitsuing two of the hairy half-men at once, knocking the club of one attacker to the ground, while snatching up that of the other for himself. N'desi and Hareton advanced together, the former dispatching one of their fallen opponents with a cruel slash of his sword. But Hareton felt no pity for the enemy. It was kill or be killed.

With a savage yell, he swung the Reaver of Worlds, cleaving in two the thick skull of a beast-man.

For a moment, the chaos of battle consumed Hareton. Now he was the feral beast-man, fighting as his kind had done for eons before civilization's futile attempts to weed out the strain of violence from the species.

But savage fury could blind one to danger as quickly and surely as the somnolence of civilization. And so it was that Hareton Ironcastle failed to notice that Harry Killer had slipped behind him in the furious bedlam.

Killer spun around behind Hareton and grabbed the Reaver of Worlds out of his hands.

In a last burst of energy, he had Antinea by the neck and, trembling, held the ax blade to her throat.

Antinea's servant, no longer hooded, moved toward him.

"Just stop," Killer hissed.

Antinea uttered a small cry as the ax made a thin cut at her throat. A small trickle of blood ran from her neck and down between her breasts.

"You won't make it out. You're trembling. You're at the end of your rope," Antinea's man said.

Killer saw, now that the man's burnoose was drawn back, that he was no Arab, despite the sun-bronzed skin. The man's hair was reddish-bronze and fit his head like a skull-cap. His face was expressionless, although the odd gold flecks in his eyes seemed to swirl with energy.

"Who are you?"

The man ignored his question. "Killer, you'd better look behind you."

"Haw, the oldest trick! How stupid–"

"Fairly stupid, I'd say," Hareton broke in. "He's not lying. That...'Tree of Dreams,' whatever it is, is moving toward you."

"You're mad, you're both mad." Killer pressed the ax blade deeper into Antinea's neck, and she squealed. "Any closer, any more of that, and Hoggar's going to have one headless Queen!"

"Killer–" the bronze man tried once more.

"Quiet! Not one more word. Now, the Queen and I here, we're just going to walk out, and you two are going to stand right here in this temple or whatever it is, and not move an inch. Or I'll kill her, I promise you. Understand?" The bronze man stood unmoving. Hareton shrugged in apparent acknowledgement.

"Good, then we all agree. Come on my Queen, you're my safe passage out of here."

Killer took a step forward. There was a problem, though. His feet didn't move.

Something was coiled about his ankles. It wasn't entirely smooth. Rather, it was slightly bumpy and asymmetrical, like a tree branch.

Unlike the branch Antinea had shown him under the throne room, though, this was more root-like, in that it protruded from the ground. Crystalline speckles glowed upon the root's membrane, as if powered by some eldritch source of energy within.

The root moved.

It snaked up Killer's legs, around his torso, and wound in a spiral down the length of the arm which held the ax to Antinea's pale throat. The tip of the root covered the ax and exuded an acid. Killer's eyes widened as he saw the root's digestive juices begin to melt and consume the ax. He grasped it as long as he was able, then released it with a cry.

He watched, held immobile, as the Reaver of Worlds dissolved and was absorbed into the translucent root. Then the root began to withdraw, slowly back into the Earth from which it obtruded, dragging him along with it.

Harry Killer screamed and clawed at the ground.

"Antinea, get away," Hareton called, but the Queen was already pulling herself free. She stumbled over to the explorer, while the bronze man headed in the other direction, toward Killer.

"Help me!" Killer called, and then the erstwhile Arab was next to him, one huge hand gripping Killer's arm, the other on the glowing root. Massive thews tugged and strained.

The bronze man's eyes went from gold to glassy, and his efforts ceased.

"What are you doing? Don't stop–help me!" Killer yelled.

But the colossal man, who had once posed as one of Antinea's servants, did nothing.

The bronze man's vision dimmed. All was dark around him.

Then a strange crystalline light pierced through, and within it a slender dark shape appeared. His sight cleared, and the dark shape was revealed as a massively tall building, towering over the New York skyline. A dirigible was moored to a mast atop the skyscraper. The picture shifted, and he saw Doctor Natas, from whose secret city in Asia he had recently escaped. The image blurred again, and he held a baby in his arms. The infant had his own reddish-bronze hair color. The vision snapped; he was flying an airplane over the Arctic, a beautiful, dark-haired woman beside him in the copilot's seat. Then he was in a cavern, much deeper, down toward Earth's center. He was surrounded by a circle of stone symbols lit by gas jets, and was facing a mirror. He was making hand-gestures, trying to sign, to the reflection in the mirror. Except it wasn't a reflection. It was him, but the other in the mirror moved of its own volition.

Then the bronze man was lying prone on the ground in the depths of the Mountain of Evil Spirits, still immobilized, and he saw Harry Killer's hand being sucked into the ground, along with the last bit of glittering root.

"It was a dendroid," Doc Ardan was saying, "a semi-intelligent tree being–doubtless an offshoot of the same vegetable life forms your expedition encountered a nearly decade ago in Gondokoro."

The four of them–Hareton, along with Ardan, Antinea, and N'desi–stood round the ten-meter hole in the broken mosaic tiles of the ancient Atlantean temple.

"Of course, I suspected as soon as I saw it," Hareton said, his voice rasping with astonishment, "but to think–the distance the roots must have traveled beneath the soil! And what of the Reaver of Worlds? What drew the dendroid to it and sealed Killer's fate?"

"The roots were hungry," Ardan said matter-of-factly. "I suspect there was a sort of sympathy between the two, the dendroid and the material that composed the ax-head. Perhaps even a symbiosis."

"How can that be?"

"I'm not sure. But I have seen that same composition of glittering iron once before, in a collection at my family's ancestral estate in Derbyshire. At the time, I did not have time to examine the rock fragments closely, although like the Reaver of Worlds, they had all the telltales of meteoritic origin, as well as a provenience of Africa. Zu-Vendis to be precise. And the fragments I saw in Derbyshire were laid out in the shape of a shattered ax-head, perhaps a chunk of the larger ax from which the Reaver of Worlds was reputedly crafted. While I'm hesitant to speculate on such little data, a hypothesis might be formed that a microbe fell to earth in a hollowed out cavity in the stone. Perhaps the composition of the meteorite is what attracted the microbes to it in the first place. It was food for the organism, although the latter had for some reason gone dormant while it traveled through the void of space."

Hareton shook his head, unbelieving. "And the *taduki* that gave me the vision which led to the ax?"

"The herb has peculiar properties which I am fairly certain may serve to connect it with the vegetable life forms which originated in Gondokoro. Perhaps the *taduki* somehow communicates with the dendroid, possessing its human hosts–that is, those who inhale the herb's smoke–and orders them to transport the metal food directly into the maw, so to speak, of the dendroid. Think of the *taduki* as a kind of hallucinogenic spore–a third member of a symbiotic chain: two from the plant kingdom, and another belonging to a very peculiar class of metal. Life beyond this world would likely take on much different forms than we are accustomed to, and possibly the metal is actually in some sense a life form as well. That's one hypothesis. Or..."

For a moment Ardan's gold-shot irises seemed to swirl with excitement. Then he said calmly, "Or perhaps the ax was composed of the metal of an interplanetary vessel under the direct guidance of the dendroid. The vessel might have broken up upon impact with the Earth's upper atmosphere, perhaps as it was consciously intended to do, scattering its contents in a broad swath over Africa, in order to seed our world. After all, the legends of the ax state that it was a gift of the Sky People."

N'desi shook his head. "Not a gift. No, the legends say it is *xanigew*–a curse."

Ardan broke a smile. "More data for our hypotheses, good. It will bear looking into." Then Ardan's smile vanished and he regarded Antinea.

"Is our business finished?"

Anger boiled up in Hareton. "You can't possibly mean to let her go. Haven't you seen her exhibition of death in the chamber above? She's a cold-blooded murderer! What would your father say?"

Antinea laughed coldly. "He would say let me go, wouldn't he, Docteur Ardan? Unless you think he'd like me to reveal to your enemies the source of your family's wealth?"

Now Hareton understood Antinea's pull over Ardan–the woman had somehow blackmailed him into assisting her. How she had managed to spin her web as far as the Ardans' mysterious fortune, Hareton did not know, but he resolved to suss out the details when he returned to America.

"Your punishment will come soon enough," Ardan said coolly, turning away. "And perhaps it already has."

The haughty bearing left Antinea's frame, her shoulders slouching as she gazed down into the blackness of the great opening in the floor before them. The dendroid might truly have slowed her aging as she had inferred, but now it was gone, hopefully forever.

Hareton shuddered. He would gladly forgo immortality if he never saw the dendroid again–in his dreams or in waking reality...

"I can take you in my plane as far as Tangiers," Ardan called over his shoulder as he left behind the gaping hole and headed for the staircase that led above. "Then we must part company."

Hareton and N'desi sprinted to catch up, leaving Antinea to meditate upon her mortal future in the gloom of her subterranean temple.

"You've no doubt heard of the financial crisis which has struck not only America but the very foundations of the civilized world." If Ardan's breathing grew any heavier as he began climbing the steep steps, Hareton could not discern it.

"Indeed," he said, now just behind Ardan. "That's why your father was unable to lead the search for you in the Hoggar in person." Though in excellent health for his 50-some odd years, Hareton struggled to hide his own panting.

"We spoke just a moment ago of hypotheses," Ardan said mysteriously. "I will not go into details, for I don't wish to jeopardize your safety, but I've developed a singular hypothesis about the crisis on Wall Street. And I intend to test it."

But the importance of Ardan's words faded as Hareton's mind–without the aid of that infernal herb, he hoped–transported him back to his home in Baltimore, with Muriel and Phillippe and Aunt Rebecca waiting in the parlor, anxious to hear the story of his latest adventure. Hareton Ironcastle, just this once, would sit this one out and let the younger generation step up to the plate.

He reached forward and clapped the climbing Ardan on his back.

"Go get 'em, old boy!"

Harry Killer was not dead.

He was underground, enveloped, suffocating, wrapped in solid crystal light.

He saw himself strong again, rejuvenated, gathering his criminal empire in America, from the Pacific Northwest to Denver, New York to San Francisco, commanding a secret army of mobsmen, scientists, and beast-men. He saw a figure cloaked in black, face obscured by a large slouch hat, eyes alight, laughing an eerie laugh, twin .45s blazing in the night.

The desert sands spat out Harry Killer, far from the Mountain of Evil Spirits. He lay there a while, catching his breath and orienting himself.

Xanigew. The native word throbbed in his brain.

He stood up and started walking.

One tradition of Tales of the Shadowmen *has always been to make room for humorous (but always respectful) "short-shorts" in which a writer can focus on a single aspect of a character and find something surprising and enlightening to tell about it. G.L. Gick, who penned the remarkable "Werewolf of Rutherford Grange" in* Tales of the Shadowmen 1 *and* 2, *and "Beware the Beasts" in* Tales of the Shadowmen 3, *returns with a light-hearted tale featuring Talbot Mundy's indomitable Tros of Samothrace who goes looking for help from some unexpected sources...*

G. L. Gick: *Tros Must Be Crazy!*

Gaul, 55 B.C.

The warrior had to admit he felt nervous, although he'd never say as much to his crew. It was hard enough keeping them in line on ordinary days. Let alone on a night like this...

The late autumn wind was chill, and the warrior quietly drew his cloak tighter. Above, the Moon took on a pale, leprous tinge. He was but a rank initiate into the Mysteries, but even he could deduce bad omens when he saw them.

Perhaps this was not one of my best ideas....but to defeat Caesar, I would ally myself with anyone, yea, even with the damned, twisted Wyrms of the Earth themselves! he thought.

The tiny landing craft drew up against the shore and two of his swarthy, battered crew stumbled out to pull it ashore, both reeking of stale ale and fresh urine. It was a wonder they had even gotten the craft this far without sinking it. Ignoring them, the warrior climbed out before they had finished and waded the last few feet to shore, carefully examining the surroundings as was his wont. The beach, silent and empty, stretched along for miles without obstruction. At its edge, it sloped slowly upward, its sandy waste vanishing into the midst of black, fertile forest. A few night birds cried out.

Gesturing to his men to wait, the warrior moved forward boldly across the beach, up the slope and to the very border of the thick, seemingly impenetrable trees.

"You may as well come out," he called, calmly but commandingly. "I know you are there."

For a moment, the only answer was silence. Then, the vegetation was brushed away, and slowly from the foliage stepped a bent, wizened figure, long-bearded, with every joint creaking.

The warrior grimaced in spite of himself. As a novice, he should bow before the Druid with respect, but great age had rendered the man so unattractive it was difficult to pay him proper homage. The figure grinned, showing a crooked mouth of yellow teeth, and pulled his crimson cloak closer to ward off the cold.

"You are far from Samothrace, my friend."

"That matters little. What does is whether you have what we agreed upon, Druid. Do you?"

Chuckling a bubbly, acidic laugh, the Druid reached a scrawny arm into his cloak. "I do. But what about you?"

The warrior dared turn his head enough to nod toward his men. At his signal, two reached down into the boat and then approached, lugging between them a huge chest. They dropped it at their leader's feet and backtracked, gazing apprehensively upon the white-haired Druid.

The warrior opened the chest.

"There," he said. "The treasure of the Picts. It was simple enough to take it. Over the centuries, they have descended into grotesque parodies of their former selves. Only in their aristocracy do they retain their old blood..."

The warrior's mouth twisted a moment, recalling the mighty battle he had had with their king. Surely, that man could have been a great thorn in Caesar's side. That, or his son, or his son's son... Enough. Time to get what he came for.

"I have given you what you desired, Druid. And now, it is your turn."

The ancient Druid's ugly smile drew wider. "As you wish." His arm withdrew from the cloak and a taloned, liver-spotted hand held forth a small vial. "Here. Drink this and all your troubles with Caesar will be over."

With skeptical fingers, the warrior's hand closed over the vial. He could hear a strange potion sloshing about within. "And just how do I know this sorcery you brag about so well shall truly work?"

"Do you truly doubt my–"

The admonishment was never completed. From behind the brush, a great scream was heard and, suddenly, the warrior witnessed the sight of a man, clad in Roman armor and helmet, shooting up over the trees in a wide arc, passing over the beach a good 20 feet in the air and coming to a hard splash not half a mile from shore. For a moment the calm sea foamed, then settled. The Roman soldier was gone.

"Oops! Sorry!" From the forest, a head, bearing a huge nose and scraggly yellow mustache that seemed even huger, popped out. From the warrior's viewpoint, the person owning them must have been smaller than even a Pict. "Just a spy I had to take care of! Sorry to interrupt!" It popped back into the foliage.

The white-cloaked Druid gave the warrior a sardonic look.

He sighed. "I'll take 20."

Micah Harris has regaled us with sweeping historical sagas bringing together characters as different as King Kong and Becky Sharp in Volume 3, and Solomon Kane and Fausta in Volume 4. Mindful that this fifth volume of Tales of the Shadowmen was meant to pay homage to the theme of vampires, Micah chose to feature, for this year's contribution, one of the earliest fictional vampires of all: John William Polidori's dreaded Lord Ruthven, whose adventures were also the topic of plays by other writers, including the notorious Alexandre Dumas.[2] And indeed, who better to serve as a foil for Ruthven than Dumas' notorious Count of Monte Cristo? Join us as these two literary icons duel and battle as never before in...

Micah Harris: *May The Ground Not Consume Thee...*

Naples, March, 1835
(The month before)

Above the blue cumuli of cigar smoke, the casino's gilded Cupids looked down upon the green felt plain upon which the croupier's rake, like a tide line, swept toward tiny tumuli of black and red chips–edifices raised, as often as not, only to diminish in the tide line's recession.

The Cupids, one could fancy, had observed so much for so long from their exalted position in the casino's upper reaches that they might successfully predict the odds, were a gambler below to look past their impassive faces and ask. At the floor level, amid the press and heat of so many bodies, another looked on the scene. His expression was equally impassive as those above, though his countenance was not that of a benign cherub, but rather an avenging angel.

He had been observing a threesome at the croupier's table for 20 minutes, counting, calculating. Behind this keenly watching man, the roulette wheel suddenly rattled in clicks and clacks like castanets in the hands of a dancing girl. With concentration, he blocked from his mind this distracting rhythm, as well as the discord of cheers alongside moans of abject loss. It was as though both Heaven and Hell shared the same space, its respective occupants oblivious to each other. Of the three he observed, the watcher was acutely aware of who was sinner and who was saint.

One each flanked a man who himself was in the former category. A man whose fate, though he did not suspect it, was as subject to forces as ultimately outside of his control as the die he had just sent tumbling over the table green.

---

[2] *The Return of Lord Ruthven* by Alexandre Dumas, adapted by Frank J. Morlock, Black Coat Press, 2004, ISBN 1-932983-11-2.

As the observer had foreseen, the player won yet another round. Noirtier de Villefort, the observer knew, had beaten worse odds before, having survived two unsuccessful allegiances with Napoleon. The failed bid that had been the One Hundred Days had resulted in Noirtier's exile, true, but was there ever a more lush sanctuary than this resort town on Italy's coast? Whose door swung open freely for Noirtier's friends and family, the latter represented by his daughter-in-law at his right?

"Father, please," she fondly implored him, smiling, yet her dark eyes flashing apprehension and anxiety. "Go no further. Be content with such wonderful winnings as you have already."

The young woman was lovely in her feminine chiffon ribbons and gown, yet the watcher noted what were euphemistically called "laugh lines" prematurely etched at the corners of her lush mouth. These were not mirth's passing trace, but that of the unearned sorrow which had also touched her golden hair with strands of silver here and there.

At Noirtier's left elbow stood a dark-haired, pale-faced man whose gray eyes glinted with something more than excitement... something the watcher recognized as hunger. "No, Monsieur de Villefort," the man countered the woman, "raise the stakes! Now is no time to heed feminine demureness. 'There is a tide in the affairs of men,' eh? Take this one at the full, my friend."

At this, the woman turned a frowning countenance upon their companion. "Lord Ruthven," she said. "Please! Do not encourage him!"

"Silence, Renée!" Noirtier demanded, raising his hand. Though his sphere of influence had been humbled, the old man's strong will was unabated. And Ruthven's genteel taunt that he would allow himself to be cowed by a woman stung his pride.

But the watcher had calculated the odds and his keen mind had revealed to him that Noirtier stood to lose all. And he sensed this Lord Ruthven had done the same, yet encouraged Noirtier on.

"*Garçon!*" the observer raised his voice and his gloved hand, beckoning intently with fore and middle fingers.

The servant was quick to obey. The man whispered something to him and placed a card onto his tray. "At once, Lord Wilmore," the servant said and quickly made his way to the croupier, who tucked his head as the *garçon* cupped his ear and delivered the message. The croupier read the name on the card and immediately nodded his head in agreement. The *garçon* withdrew with the card and stepped away as the croupier announced: "Ladies and gentlemen, the table is now closed for the evening..."

Moans of disappointment immediately rose in response, but a silent Lord Ruthven's eyes shone with the anger of a foiled predator. Noirtier's cheeks puffed out in frustration, but Renée sighed and squeezed the old man's shoulder.

"...Please take your winnings. In addition..." the croupier held up a stack of violet chips between thumb and forefinger "...the House wishes to give you each a free turn at the roulette wheel, or you may redeem this chip for an ice. Good evening and thank you for playing at the *Casino Monte Cristo*."

As Renée helped Noirtier gather up his chips, Ruthven's eyes swept the crowd to see if he might discern who this agent of this "House" might be. In so doing, he overlooked the *garçon* who had delivered the message to the croupier and who now stood before him. The waiter cleared his throat, and Ruthven looked down at the man who was a good two heads shorter than he. Snatching up the proffered card from the *garçon*'s tray, he quickly scanned it and smiled, revealing sharp canines which caused the *garçon* to step back.

"Tell Lord Wilmore I will join him for a late supper. Allow me to politely disengage myself from my current company, and then I am completely at his service."

Lord Ruthven arrived at the address on the card to find Wilmore at his leisure, dressed in an open oriental dressing gown, a brandy snifter in his hand.

"May I enter?" Lord Ruthven asked his fellow Englishman when he answered the door.

"Of a certainty, Milord. And while you are here, please, consider my house your own," Lord Wilmore said, stepping aside with a smile to allow the nobleman through the doorway.

"Ah," Lord Ruthven said, regarding with affected interest the mounted heads of boars and stags upon the walls and the tiger skin stretched before the cavernous fireplace. "So, is this the infamous 'House' one hears so much about at the *Casino Monte Cristo*? The one that always wins?"

"I like to think so," Wilmore said with a smile.

"The same House," Ruthven continued, "which cost Monsieur Noirtier de Villefort a victory tonight?"

"Come, come, Milord," Wilmore said, beckoning his guest be seated, "we both know it was *you* who was robbed of his moment when I shut down the table. You urged Monsieur de Villefort on hoping that he would lose."

Ruthven remained standing. "What of it? What is de Villefort to you that you should have a care?"

"One might say that I have an acquaintance with the family. It is an infamous one in his native France."

"Only old Noirtier is infamous under the current Royalist regime for being an unrepentant Bonapartist. I understand his son's reputation to be sterling," Ruthven said.

Wilmore's nostrils' flared at the mention of de Villefort *fils*, but neither his smile nor his warm countenance fell.

"So," Ruthven continued with his initial line of thought, "you admit your action was an intentional one?"

"I do not deny it."

"Why?"

"Because I wanted your attention, Lord Ruthven."

"Your card was sufficient to do that, sir."

"Very well, I wanted to stop Monsieur Noirtier from making a final play which my calculations revealed would have cost him far more than his substantial winnings. I could tell, Lord Ruthven, that you had made the same calculation."

"You are a clairvoyant, then, Milord?" Ruthven asked, his expression bemused but his tone caustic.

"Bah," Lord Wilmore withdrew to the room's bar, his silken gown billowing about him in a sudden flourish. "I do not need to be. You and I, we are of the same mind."

Ruthven all but snarled, his sharp canines flashing. "Were we of like mind, then you would have wished that puffed up toad to lose, too. Fhah! He was of a type that earned my everlasting contempt in the house of Lords–the type who took delight in my exile."

From behind his liquor cabinet, Lord Wilmore's face twisted with contempt at Ruthven's pettiness. "I am disappointed, Lord Ruthven. I had hoped your vision might be commensurate with my own. The loss of a mere game? I will not be satisfied until Noirtier de Villefort knows absolute deprivation. May I offer you a glass of claret, Milord? I believe you shall find this red Bordeaux most tasteful."

With a slight smile, which nonetheless belied that he was intrigued, Ruthven sat down on a pillowed divan and coolly crossed his legs. "Perhaps our tastes are indeed simpatico at that."

"Then we have much to discuss, Milord."

The following morning, Lord Ruthven called upon the apartments of Monsieur de Villefort and his daughter-in-law. Soon, they were established as a threesome of the Italian season. After awhile, Ruthven was as likely as not to be Renée's only escort. She thus became the envy of many eager, voluptuous young women, whose own bids for Lord Ruthven's attentions had been foiled by the fragile, saintly beauty of Renée de Saint-Méran.

When confronted with the unlikely pair at the most exclusive salons, Renée's would-be rivals chewed their sour grapes and murmured among themselves. Renée, they concluded, was too much of an ascetic to be plied by Ruthven's passion, and they consoled themselves that eventually he would tire of a fruitless hunt and turn to more willing quarry.

As for Noirtier, he was more fond of his daughter-in-law than he had ever been of his own son, whom he knew to have been ever faithless to a wife he had never loved. Ruthven was a rake; that was obvious. Still, Renée deserved to enjoy a man's attention at least once more while she was still young, and his son had taken extreme measures to insure it would never come from him.

Four weeks later, a note was delivered to the hand of Lord Wilmore as he walked the floors of the *Casino Monte Cristo*, calculating the odds of the various games, vigilant as ever that the House should win. The note read simply:

Tonight. As agreed.

R.

The Englishman returned the note to its envelope, beckoned for the *garçon* who had delivered it, then dropped the letter onto the hand held tray. He set the missive afire, quickly reducing it to ashes, and, without comment, returned to his stroll over the floor. His mind was still calculating, but not on any game currently being played under the casino roof.

April 10, 1835 – Midnight
(Tonight)

Noirtier de Villefort could not move. Only blink. And resist the inexorable urge to keep his eyes closed until the obscene violence playing out before him was done.

His helpless daughter-in-law Renée swooned in Ruthven's mad embrace, unconscious, her dressing gown ripped away over one shoulder. Blood plastered the delicate fabric to her breast. The same blood was smeared over Ruthven's mouth which was twisted in a triumphant and contemptuous sneer and turned momentarily on Noirtier before returning to Renée's neck.

The claret... the red Bordeaux... that Ruthven had brought. It was drugged. What was it he had said about it? "From the cellar of the Chateau d'If." The infamous prison to which he, Noirtier, would have been sent, except for his son's intervention. And now, after drinking from it, he was a prisoner in his own body! A Royalist agent must have found him out to render the due punishment he had unjustly escaped. But why–*why?*–unleash this monster upon poor Renée? At least her faint had spared him having to hear her piteous, imploring cries for succor while he remained frozen, helpless in his chair. For the first time in many years, tears for someone other than himself spilled from Noirtier's eyes.

Then the sound of the door opening below–was someone entering? Yes! Their footfalls sounded up the stairwell. Ruthven jerked his head up and away, his expression surprisingly similar to the one Noirtier had seen on his face a month ago, when the closing down of the table at the *Casino Monte Cristo* had pre-empted Noirtier's final bet. With a snarl, Ruthven dropped Renée to the floor and leapt across the room, out the open window and across the roof.

"Quickly! Quickly!" Noirtier's thoughts frantically urged on whoever was mounting those steps. But the pace was too leisurely... Renée would be bled to death: the poor child was hemophilic. Noirtier could only be thankful that she had not bled any more than she had already.

Yes–now! Behind him the footsteps had stopped in the doorway. Certainly the servant had seen by now. Why was he not rushing inside to Renée's aid?

Then the steps began again; once again, the pace leisurely. Now he felt hot breath on his neck as whoever the mysterious individual was bent his lips to Noirtier's ear.

"Doubtless, you wish my aid, Monsieur. You desire above all else that I should step forward to save your beloved daughter-in-law. Unfortunately, that would involve my moving into your field of vision and that cannot be. You wish to know why? Because for 14 years you had opportunity to seek my face, but you could not be troubled. By your choice, I have ever been faceless to you, so now, in your hour of distress, I choose to remain so.

"What is that? Oh, but *now* you have some use for me? I have been of use to you before. Rather, I have been *used* before in your Bonapartist schemes. I was made your unwitting courier without regard for the consequences I might suffer–that I *did* suffer. I and those whom I loved. One of them... she was torn from me while I was held helpless, unable to reach her. Much as you now find yourself, Monsieur.

"Surely, sometime during those–what was it? One Hundred Days? Certainly, during that time, you were made aware of the missive from Napoleon that did not reach you. In that moment of triumph, when your party stood in absolute power, could you not be troubled to consider what had happened to its carrier? When you might have freed him? As you watch Madame perish before your eyes, I want you to realize that if you had only cared to see my face *then*, you would not desire so much to see it *now*; if you had not used me as you did then, you would have no need of me now.

"Perhaps you hope for succor from your house servant, that he will come and find you and your daughter-in-law before it is too late. You will be surprised to learn you terminated his services earlier today. But I assure you that you, at least, shall survive tonight. In fact, I can see you living for at least 14 more years. That is my will, and I prepared the potion you unwittingly drank accordingly. Every one of those years you will spend in the prison of your body, unable to move, unable to speak.

"Of course, you would not be allowed to speak freely of the circumstances of Renée's death even if you could, since your daughter-in-law has been dead already for years. That is the fiction, at least, that her daughter believes. That her husband has determined everyone believes. The scandal of her affair could never come out. Never mind that she was driven to it by the lacerations of his many dalliances. No, your dear son made it clear he would cast doubt on little Valentine's paternity. Your issue uses his own daughter as but a pawn to obtain what he selfishly desires. I pity her. I know the feeling well.

"Now I will take charge of Madame's remains. There is something unique about the manner of her passing. Three days hence and... well, that is none of your concern.

"You know, Monsieur, I suppose I *could* tell you my name. But, what matter? It would mean absolutely nothing to you."

With that, the speaker withdrew and the room was plunged into darkness.

February 9, 1835
(Two months before)

Whenever they crossed the *Piazza dei Martiri*, those who remembered the church of *Santa Maria a Cappella Nuova* fancied that the snow visible on the distant mountain tops created cathedral-like cupolas, as though nature had moved to fill the vacuum left by that sacred edifice.

The now secular site still bore the name that dedicated it to the martyrs, and it remained holy ground that the crowd tread beneath its feet. In the jostling of the square at noontime, Lord Ruthven stood like an immobile stone, the lone figure in the piazza against which no one dare thrust himself. Rather, the flow of bodies parted about the grim, pale, gray-eyed man.

Moving in the press toward Ruthven was the proprietor of the recently established *Casino Monte Cristo*. At his side was a beautiful 16-year-old Greek girl. The plane of her breast exposed by her silken bodice shone as dazzling pale as the snow under the Sun on the visible mountain tops. Her glossy black hair was about a face so delicately formed that its subtle rendering was not to be equaled among all the Renaissance sculptures in Italy. The young woman's tiny hand held the proprietor's, which was equally pale, but large enough to completely envelop hers. He felt her tremble.

"Then, that is he? You are certain?" he asked.

"Yes," she said with a grim determination that was totally incongruous with the sweet, coral pink lips that formed the word.

"But *those* eyes are not the eyes with which you last beheld him."

"The body's sight may sometimes forget, but the soul remembers forever. Look, did I not correctly lead you to look for him here? His kind draws strength from holy ground and, after locating it, will return from time to time. It is the nature of the parasite."

Now the crowd was moving the couple faster and faster toward Ruthven. The man felt the girl slowing her pace at the realization, trying to bring her slippered feet to a halt.

"Be strong, Haydée," the man said. "Do not falter now."

"I am *Ianthe*," the girl said bitterly. "And that man is my murderer."

"Then you must do nothing to show that you fear him or recognize him if you do not wish his further attentions. Trust me and all, ultimately, will be well, even though I now give you cause to fear."

More so because of an inability to resist the rush of the crowd than confidence in he who had professed himself her protector, the young Greek girl yielded her resistance. And, indeed, as they neared Ruthven, it was not she who arrested his attention–at least, not at first.

Rather, it was the revelation of the man, her companion, that struck Ruthven. The pale skin, the intensity of the eyes, the power implicit in the body revealed in the tailored-fit of his dark clothes. The hitherto unmovable Lord Ruthven actually took a step back–and then, he saw the Greek girl.

Her presence, combined with the man's, was disconcerting enough that Ruthven began to move with the crowd flow from the opposite direction. Yet, he retained enough cunning that, imperceptible to both the Greek and her escort, he gently plucked a single ebony hair from her head in the passing.

February 28, 1834
(One year before)

Above the great marble Gate of the Sultan that leads into the first court of the Topkapi Palace, there was once a secret apartment. It had served at different times in the palace's history as pavilion, treasury, and a branch of the Sultan's harem. On a warm mid-winter morning in 1834, Abbé Busoni followed a burly, brown eunuch to this compartment. The eunuch had special charge of a slave who had once been the jewel of Sultan Mahmoud II's entourage: Haydée, the daughter of Ali Pasha, he who once held the Turks at bay.

The Sultan's own wise men had failed to release her from the grip of what held her. Somehow, Abbé Busoni had learned of her plight and volunteered his services. Desperate for relief, the Sultan had turned to this Christian priest who was not even of the Orthodox faith. Although Mahmoud himself would not deign to meet with the infidel, he had sent his servant with instructions to do within reason whatever the Abbé required to effect the girl's release from whatever force or forces had subdued her own personality.

The large Arab led Abbé Busoni up steps that apparently went nowhere until the eunuch's fingers touched certain pressure points on the wall. A section of the stone retracted enough that Busoni could slip through a passageway which led into the hidden chamber. The Abbé indicated that he wished privacy for his work, and the eunuch, after resealing the passageway, sat before it. Anyone passing by below would think he was simply enjoying the air and looking out over the palace grounds.

Inside, a teenage girl sat cross-legged on the floor near a concealed opening which was once employed by harem girls to secretly observe special events. The girl was using it to take advantage of the ventilation. She wore silken pants which bloused, tiny gilded slippers, and a bodice of the same material as the trousers. Her complexion and lips were alabaster tinged with pink, a lovely oval floating before the bluish-jet of her hair which hung loosely about her shoulders. She regarded him with calm, dark eyes, giving no hint of being driven by the *djinn* the Sultan said had taken possession of her.

She spoke first. "So, her master has resorted to summoning the enemy of his faith to release his prized possession from my grasp. Heed me, I implore you, and save yourself and me an ordeal that will only prove both exhausting and futile."

Abbé Busoni walked calmly to where she sat, and, sitting down himself, crossed his legs in the manner of the girl. He searched her dark eyes for a moment and then asked:

"And why is that?"

"Because I have a prior claim on Haydée."

"God does not recognize any other's claim on this young girl. His own takes precedence over yours, demon–and the Sultan's as well."

The girl shook her head slowly and smiled. "Already your speech betrays your Western mind's misapprehension of the situation. You have failed ere you have begun."

"I have begun already," the Abbé said calmly. "In fact, it was begun before I entered the Sultan's gate. Years before. You may be interested to know that the priest whom I succeeded trained me in the very foundation of Western thought. It is the same as yours of the Eastern schism. Your Achean forebears understood 'demon' as a driving force, not satanic in origin. One in the grip of *Eros*, for example, or the thrust of the Fates was thus driven. The word was then carried over into the English to carry the concept of an evil, invading intelligence, non-human in origin.

"Contrariwise, you claim to be a *human* spirit possessing this girl. My master, Abbé Faria, taught me that the souls of the dead were either in Heaven or Hell, and those who engaged in necromancy in actuality had contact with Satan's angels.

"But the Abbé allowed that occasionally there may be an exception, though it was extremely rare. In fact, there was only one such incident in the whole of the sacred writ: the Witch of Endor was allowed to call up the spirit of the prophet Samuel when King Saul was driven by desperation to have truck with her kind. The Witch herself seemed terror-stricken when she actually made contact with the dead. This 'calling up,' then, was not her doing, but because God allowed it in this special instance."

"Yes! Yes! It is even as you say with me!" the girl exclaimed, leaning eagerly toward Busoni despite herself.

"But what would be the exceptional circumstances of your case?" Busoni asked calmly.

"To punish a terrible injustice and he who perpetrated it upon me," the girl said austerely. "He who yet walks the Earth freely, doing as he wills, spreading more vile deeds upon the Earth. I cry out against him, but no one will hear me."

"I heed you," Abbé Busoni said, "for I also know what it is to cry out unheard for justice. Perhaps we cry out against the same man. Are you the spirit of Haydée's father, Ali Pasha, or her mother Vasiliki?"

"Neither. I am the spirit of her elder sister Ianthe whom she never knew. And I am become the nemesis of one who has escaped judgement many times, for he dies not as men do. He took my life and destroyed the happiness I might have had with an Englishman I came to know in the days after I displeased my father and lived in exile from the palace.

"My enemy destroyed my happiness only once; my love, he destroyed thrice: first, when he took me from him; second, when he married his sister, then murdered her, finally sending my lover into abiding madness and torment of the soul. For Aubrey could not expose the villain and intervene as he should on his sister's behalf, for he was in debt to his adversary for his life. This fiend's beneficence is as a canker, and his kind delights in playing the friend that he might manipulate lives and destroy them all the better."

"As a strategy," Abbé Busoni said in a reflective tone, "it has much to recommend it."

"Fie!" the girl sneered. "You sound as though you admire him! And you, a man of God! He should be anathema to you, for he is *vrykolakas*, whom they who have authority to bind in Heaven and Earth have bound to the Earth with this curse: 'May the Earth not receive thee, may the ground not consume thee, may the black Earth spew thee up, may thou remain incorrupt, may the ground reject thee.' "

"And how, then," asked Busoni, "may one release what has been bound with Heavenly authority to this natural plane, that your enemy might receive his due recompense in Hell?"

"The answer is very near, in the first courtyard of the palace," the girl said calmly. "While I still had a modicum of liberty, I learned of its location from moldering documents in the long-departed Patriarchate's abandoned archives. Will you walk with me now, Abbé?"

Hand in hand, the Abbé and the girl now calling herself Ianthe crossed the grass of the outer courtyard toward the building which served as the armory. From the angle they were approaching, it appeared to be several squat brownish-brick buildings of diverse heights ungracefully shoved against each other. From the midst of this awkward huddle, an elegant, round tower rose, its cream colored dome thrust high above the other crouching constructs, forming a basilica.

"This is the *Hagai Irene*," the girl said. "Before the *Hagai Sophia* was complete, *this* was the seat of the Patriarchate in Constantinople. It is currently a museum of weaponry, a mild desecration, I suppose. It has certainly suffered worse in its long history: burned by fire, ripped by an earthquake and used to house the booty of the conquerors of the old Christian city. But the Patriarchate knew what we seek was most likely to be safely preserved here, since this comparatively humble church would be held in contempt next to the more spectacular *Hagai Sophia*, the seat of Eastern Orthodox authority."

"This is some relic we seek, then?" Abbé Busoni asked. "Something to be spared the profaning touch of the followers of Islam?"

The girl smiled, a caustic expression so alien on her sweet features. "Mohammed's followers would have had no understanding of, nor would they have particularly cared about, the particular threat this artifact represents. They might destroy it, but they would be unable to turn its power against the Greek Church. Ah, but those Latins of the Fourth Crusade, and the Roman rulers of Constantinople who followed in the wake of that Papal siege, *they* would have understood very well indeed its lethal possibilities. They were allowed to pilfer the stone said to have sealed the Tomb of Christ, the container of the Virgin's milk, the burial shroud of our Lord... none of these took priority over that which the Patriarchate ordered concealed where we shall find it now."

"Child, what is this thing to which you lead me?"

She smiled. "Do not fear, Abbé. You are of the West. It cannot harm you. But it alone can destroy my enemy, the *vrykolakas*. Further application to *your* foes, the Byzantine church your own declares heretical, will be at your discretion. Frankly, I do not envy you the ability to bind on Earth and Heaven. It has been done before... to the undoing of many."

They passed now from the bright sunlight into the narthex of the *Hagia Irene*, currently filled with medieval weaponry of the Ottomans. But above all this, on the inside of the basilica's dome, still showed the giant cross in the Iconoclastic fashion. Light flooded the narthex from the many windows of the dome above, and the cross bedazzled the viewer.

"There," the girl said, nodding toward the large glowing roof, "was where they hung the image of the *Theotokos* when this was still a house of worship. She will help us now."

"Child, do you mean the icon of the Virgin is still here? Is that the lethal article we seek here?" Busoni asked.

"No. But when you see her image, you shall find that which we *do* seek."

"But how shall we see an icon that is not here?"

"It is said that if you stare at the cross in its glory, when the sunlight floods the *Hagia Irene*'s dome as it does now, one might still see the *Theotokos*. More, the seeking soul will gain her guidance."

Abbé Busoni stared upward into the cross's incandescing until he was compelled to blink tears from his eyes. When he looked down again, an occlusion skimmed over his vision. He felt the girl tugging impatiently at his hand. "This way," she said.

"Wait, child. Wait for the scales to fall from my eyes. Not only did I fail to see the *Theotokos* hanging there, but now I can see nothing at all."

"I did not say you would see the *Theotokos there*," she said, an impatient tone in her voice. "The atrium... the *Hagia Irene* yet retains its original atrium. It was here when the Latins of the Fourth Crusade took Constantinople. We must look there. Come!"

Busoni yielded to she who claimed to be an inhabiting spirit named Ianthe, and they moved into the church proper. And as the *Hagia Irene* began to resume its substance about him, he was startled by a third party looming out of the fastly fading darkness: a smiling woman with a child. Almost as quickly as he realized that the two were stock-still, they were gone.

"The *Theotokos*!" he gasped out, startled.

"Where?" the girl demanded. "Quickly! Where?"

The Abbé moved to the spot, and the girl dropped to her knees, her finger-tips sinking into the grooves that seamed the floor-stones together. "There!" she exclaimed after long moments. "I feel this is loose, but I have not the strength to move it. Help me!"

The Abbé joined her, and in moments the stone was pulled free. Inside was a recess, and in it a leathery parchment, rolled into a scroll and sealed with wax. He noted the impression in it: the insignia of the Patriarchate.

"Quickly!" the girl said, her eyes sweeping the interior of the church. "We dare not linger here with the *logos dynamos*. Before we are caught, replace the stone and let us return to the chamber in the gate. There I will explain all to you."

"No," said Abbé Busoni. "I will not remove this scroll until I know what is written here and the full nature of its power. How can it be both bane to vampire and Eastern church alike?"

"Why should it astound you that it is thus? Do not you Latins hold both equally within the province of the damned?"

"Demon, I need neither Pope nor Patriarchate to dictate to me whom I should hold damned and why; that is God's affair and my own. Now, tell me the truth of what is written on this parchment, or I will return it to where it has been hidden for centuries and tell the Sultan you are an incorrigible spirit, a beguiling spirit who seeks to deceive all who would help the girl you possess. I promise you that you will not soon find another ally as amenable as I to your desire for vengeance."

The young Greek maiden sighed heavily and grudgingly acquiesced. "Remember I told you that they of the Orthodox faith bind to the earthly sphere the *vrykolakas* with this curse: 'May the Earth not receive thee, may the ground not consume thee, may the black Earth spew thee up, may thou remain incorrupt, may the ground reject thee.'

"Could you not discern that in thus binding the *vrykolakas* they actually *create them*? And cause their number to multiply on the Earth to feed on the very flock their church professes to shepherd? They thus open the gate of the fold to the wolves. And they compound their guilt, for on that which you hold, written in the first Patriarchate's own hand, is the invocation which would release those souls into the Abyss and cause immediate dissolution of their bodies."

"Incorruption has always been a sign of Godly favor in the Roman Church," Abbé Busoni said.

"And of God's curse in the Orthodox faith. But is it not because they have used in self-will for cursing what God intended for blessing? The first Patriarchate sought to reverse this, so he wrote the *logos dynamos*. But his successors realized to do so would be to admit to gross fallibility and so grant a victory to their Western rival, to whom it was feared many of their flock would consequently return.

"Now do you understand its full danger? And yet why no successor to the Patriarchate could bring himself to destroy what his great precursor had done? I have done as you asked and told you all. Please, replace the stone, hide the scroll in your robe and let us away! Quickly!"

This time Abbé Busoni did as she asked. They exited the cool of the *Hagia Irene* into the sunlit courtyard, back toward the wall and its secret compartment. The eunuch still sat by its resealed entrance. The Abbé indicated with a nod that he should open it. He quickly repeated the series of esoteric pressure points which moved a portion of the backside of the wall to allow entry.

The girl calling herself Ianthe had chattered excitedly as they had crossed the courtyard. Here she had found an ally at last, someone who believed her and was now armed with the power to wreak vengeance on the creature who had destroyed her life and that of the one she loved. She passed into the compartment ahead of him, eager to discuss how they might proceed from this point.

But the Abbé stopped short of entering and motioned for the eunuch to seal the girl in. Obediently, the huge Arab repeated the sequence of touches and the wall closed again. He then looked expectantly at the Abbé.

"I am afraid I can do nothing for the girl," he said. "Nor, do I suspect anyone could. This... *djinn*, as you pagans call it, will come out of her only at high risk of life for both the possessed and the exorcist. And it is more certain that both should die than any release could be effected. I advise the Sultan that, should someone be willing to buy her in her current condition and the offer is generous, then he should accept it and have her taken off his hands."

The eunuch escorted Abbé Busoni out of the Sultan's gate. And though he could feel from its hidden window the eyes of the girl called Haydée on his back, he knew the pleading, imploring stare and the screams of betrayal were those of another young woman, long dead, named Ianthe.

April 11, 1835 – 1 a.m.
(Tonight)

Lord Wilmore approached his own home with more than his usual circumspection. He was typically wary that he might be set upon by thieves who coveted the earnings of the casino. Though he carried his sword cane, should he be attacked tonight, he planned no resistance as long as neither he nor the girl under his charge were threatened with physical harm. Let any brigands have all the money. The *Casino Monte Cristo* had served its purpose and that had never been a financial one. He had enjoyed the sport of gambling and the House winning had always been a matter of pride rather than necessity, a way of occupying his mind until he was ready for his *true* gamble. That only was played of necessity, and it occurred outside the casino walls tonight.

It was a game not yet played out.

He entered through a secret back gateway which he left grown over with the vines that covered the wall of his yard. From this vantage spot, he could see the bay windows were ajar, the curtains slightly billowing. He smiled at the intruder's arrogant disregard for secrecy. Wilmore had often turned such overconfidence in the favor of "the House."

He did not enter through those open windows but through a cellar side door which a more humble and prudent invader would have taken. Passing through this basement lined with wine bottles, he climbed the narrow steps with stealth, emerging in the kitchen's pantry. By a sleight cracking of its swinging door, which he had always kept oiled so that it moved without a whisper of noise, he could survey the dining room.

He had ordered a late repast of cold chicken and wine be placed out for him and then both the cook and butler were to return to their respective homes for the night. The plate of chicken was there with side dishes of red potatoes and French cut green beans. But as soon as the pantry had opened, a chamber pot's odor had issued from the direction of the china and sparkling cutlery.

Passing through the pantry door, and crossing the dining room, Lord Wilmore was compelled to place his handkerchief to his nose. Yet, behind it, he smiled: in the plate of chicken lay fresh excrement and the beans stank of urine.

The intruder had done this, betraying the mirror-like inverted nature of his kind, just as "Abbé Busoni" had learned during his sabbatical in Greece the previous year.

Suddenly, the chandelier began to chatter frantically with a rhythmic pounding as though a horse galloped in the room above him, and a shrill scream cut the air.

"Haydée!" he cried out as he bounded up the stairway that led upstairs. "Do not fear!"

He burst into the girl's Arabian Nights-themed boudoir, startled by what he beheld: her bed bucked like an unbroken steed, thrusting Haydée backwards and forward and into the air. Her eyes started at him imploringly, wild with fear. The bed sheets, which had managed to remain over her until now, suddenly yanked away and piled on the floor. Then the bed came to a jarring stop on its bottom end, tilting up and sending Haydée tumbling from it.

She scrambled to her feet and began to run toward Wilmore. But before her feet were off the sheets on the floor, they yanked her back. Then the sheets were tangling the struggling girl within them, teasingly. Like a cat with a mouse.

"Release her, Ruthven!" Wilmore commanded the unseen assailant. "You have already fed tonight. Do not add gluttony to the list of your sins."

A dour, mocking disembodied laughter answered, and then Wilmore could not but start at Ruthven's sudden appearance with Haydée already in his arms.

He looked at Lord Wilmore. "I stopped counting my sins long, long ago. But gluttony would not go on that tally tonight, even if I were of a mind to keep one. I have yet to sup my fill. Not only was I interrupted mid-feast, that particular cow's udder seemed intent on defrauding me. Her blood could have had the consistency of wet cement, it came so slowly."

"That is unfortunate for you, Milord, seeing that you are about to embark on a long fast in Hell."

Ruthven's expression was bemused contempt. "Wilmore, you stand like a thistle in the face of the whirlwind commanding it to turn its path. Before you can move against me, I will be across the room and at your throat."

"I have no need to approach you, monster."

Ruthven grinned crookedly. "Oh? You plan to spring some trap from where you stand, then? Do not so much as flick a wrist or bat an eye, Milord, or the wench's neck will snap and I will feast elsewhere tonight. Did you really think you have snared me unawares, Wilmore? That I would dismiss it as coincidence that this delightful Greek I marked as my own should be in your..." Ruthven's voice trailed, then his gray eyes lit. "No. *No*. Not *your* home. *His*. Your master is the man with whom I saw her in the plaza of the old church. He sought the same holy ground I did for the same reason. Was not his appearance as my own? He paraded the girl by me, knowing that I could not risk marking such luscious fruit for myself. One hair from her head was all that it took to find the rest of her. He surely knew my mind in such things, for he and I are the same!"

"More so than he would like," Lord Wilmore said soberly.

"Have I trespassed into his territory, then? Does he think to rid himself of a rival by subterfuge, the cowardly use of human intermediaries? Let him face me now!"

Then the girl in Ruthven's arms spoke, and the voice that had to this point been tremulous with fear was now so adamantine that Ruthven was taken by surprise. Yet the sound also struck a dark chord of recognition, for it was not one voice but *all* the voices of every victim who had begged and pled for a mercy he never once gave:

"Face *me*, you who would be my murderer twice over! I who embody all your sins remembered!"

Ruthven snatched away the bed clothing that swathed her face. The features no longer seemed those of the girl he had attacked moments before but of an avenging fury.

At this moment of distraction, Wilmore reached into his coat pocket and produced the leathery scroll from the *Hagia Irene*. It unfurled in his hands, and he read in the Greek handwriting of the first Patriarchate of the Eastern Orthodox Church:

"In the name of Jesus Christ, Lord of Heaven and Earth, I command you to depart into that place held for you: the Deep, the Abyss. For you, the appointed time has come and there shall be no more escape: may the Earth receive thee, may the ground consume thee, may the black Earth swallow you up; your body shall now own its corruption, and the ground shall rise up to receive thy dust until the second resurrection, that of the unjust. For dust you are, and to dust you now return and your spirit unto the God who made it, He who rightly judges every work, whether it be good or whether it be *evil*!"

As Wilmore read, a look not so much of fear as of total disbelief struck Ruthven's face. The girl slipped from his now torpid fingers and fell back on her bed, raising herself on her elbows to watch his dissolution. In a moment, he was as a sculpture of gray ash which crumbled in on itself. Then a purifying wind thrust the window open, took up the heap of corruption from the room and sifted and strew it in the finest particles over the Italian landscape.

Then, with a shout of victory and release, the Greek collapsed onto her bed. In an instant, Lord Wilmore was at her side, lifting her head up and placing it in his lap. He made quick, sharp slaps to her cheeks, shouting "Haydée! Haydée!" and for a moment he feared the grip of the spirit called Ianthe had been too strong and had dragged the young girl's own with her into the afterlife.

But Haydée's eyes were now flickering open. She looked at him quizzically, then regarded the room about her.

"Where am I? This is not the palace of Sultan Mahmoud. And who are you?"

"I am Lord Wilmore, and I serve the Count of Monte Cristo," he answered, smiling. "He purchased you at great cost from the Sultan."

"The Sultan wished to be rid of me? Did I offend him somehow? Why can I not remember?"

"You did not offend him; rather, you suffered from a malady which is the cause of your forgetfulness. The Sultan looked long and hard for a cure, but could not find it. Monte Cristo told him he was confident that he could effect your healing on condition that you become his property, so the Sultan relinquished you for your welfare. Your life now belongs to Monte Cristo, and you shall serve him and in the doing serve yourself... Do you know how you became a slave, Haydée?"

"My father was betrayed by a Frenchman in his service."

"That man's name is Fernand Mondego. He also betrayed another's trust before your father's. To steal a woman's love, he sacrificed an unwitting young man's innocence, much as he did yours. Monte Cristo is the friend of the friendless who cry out for justice, and he shall avenge you both in due course. Trust him always, though he gives you cause to fear, and all, ultimately, will be well.

"Yet three days and we depart this country, dear Haydée. By then, you should be fully recovered. And I will have had time to complete what I have set out to accomplish here."

April 13, 1835 – Night
(Three days later)

"It was tragic, Abbé," the cemetery's groundskeeper said. "That such a beautiful woman with so much life in her should die so and so pointlessly, so mundanely: pricking her throat–twice–while applying a broach. I tell you, Abbé, sometimes it seems as though the universe has turned its back upon us, all the while chuckling at the ensuing discomfiture we suffer."

"I have felt that often myself," Abbé Busoni responded. "But she knew she was extremely hemophilic. She should have taken more precaution. To prick herself once is understandable, but twice? And so near the same spot? Perhaps she died of her own vanity, thinking only of how pretty the bauble made her throat appear. And she did not even wear it in her coffin, I understand."

"There was no one to view the body, anyway," the groundskeeper said. "Her father-in-law suffered extreme paralysis upon discovering her body so that he can neither move nor speak. At least, that is the theory, for his condition makes it impossible for him to communicate exactly what happened. He was fortunate to find a friend in Lord Wilmore... Well, here is the crypt."

"Thank you, sir," Abbé Busoni said, passing a gold coin into his guide's hand. "I wish time and solitude now to pray for Renée de Saint-Méran's soul. Will you see that I have the privacy I require?"

"Indeed, Abbé," the groundskeeper said, regarding the coin he held between thumb and forefinger. "Take as much time as you need." And with that, he left Busoni alone.

The Abbé entered the crypt and went directly to the stone sarcophagus that held Renée's body. With effort, he lifted the lid, then opened the coffin.

"Awake, Renée," he said. "Rise to your new life."

Renée de Saint-Méran's eyes flickered open...

October 3, 1834
(Six months before)

From the terrace of the villa of Viscontessa Alessandro Bottero, one had a perfect view of Mount Vesuvius across the Bay of Naples. Sitting apart from the rest of the societal elite attending the Viscontessa's salon, Renée de Saint-Méran with fork and knife delicately sawed at a slice of the uniquely Neapolitan cuisine known as pizza. She enjoyed the serene landscape spread before her. The blue bay was flecked with brilliant sails under a cerulean sky. The city of Naples spread along the line of the far shore, its whitish-beige buildings compressed by distance against azure, moody Vesuvius.

The breeze off the bay was soothing as well and for a few moments, Renée allowed the burden of her heart to lift. She closed her eyes to savor the breeze coming off the bay, and thus she was unaware of how long the pale striking gentleman, a slice of pizza in hand, had stood by her table.

"Oh..." she started.

"Pardon me, Madame," he said in French. "You seemed at such peace in your meditation that I did not wish to disturb you to announce my presence. I am a stranger in this country as well. I have just opened the latest casino in Naples— which I hope will have the honor of your patronage."

Renée smiled. "I am afraid I am not one inclined to take risks."

"I have learned that the greatest gains come only at the price of great risks. I may be seated?"

"Of course," she said. "The company of a fellow countryman here is most welcome."

"Thank you."

"You eat pizza... with your hands?" she asked, nodding as he brought the slice to his mouth.

"Of course."

"Oh. Perhaps you will start a fashionable trend, eh?"

"One never knows."

Renée, however, remained intent on using fork and knife. As she again sawed at her food, the stranger continued on.

"Madame, I have sought you out, not merely as a fellow expatriate, but because we have another kinship, that of suffering. And both from the hands of the same man: your husband."

At this, Renée started, her knife slipped and she cut her hand.

"Oh!" she cried out and grabbed for her handkerchief in a frantic attempt to staunch the bleeding.

"Madame, a thousand pardons for causing you this injury. But you seem very distraught for a mere scratch."

"You do not understand! I am a hemophiliac! There are no 'mere' scratches for me! Fetch a doctor!" she exclaimed, rising.

The stranger pressed a restraining hand to her arm. "Madame, please: allow me to help." With his other hand, he pulled a small bottle from his waistcoat. "I have some skills as a chemist, and I have here a preparation which will thicken your blood so that it will staunch the wound. Trust me, be seated, and please drink this."

A panicking Renée did so, and soon her blood was clotting.

"It is a miracle!" she gasped.

The stranger smiled. "Chemistry allows for many such 'miracles.' I know of potions that can paralyze the body while allowing the mind complete activity.

Blood can be thickened, the pump of the heart slowed, the body given all appearance of being dead."

"I am in your debt, Monsieur. But whatever grudge you have against my husband, I am powerless to help you. I cannot even help myself: I suffer exile here at his will; he has seen to it that our daughter thinks me dead, and should I appear in France again, it will be the girl's ruin. My husband has promised me this."

"Your husband has been known to break his promises. But if you will do all that I request, I can promise you that one day, he will no longer stand between you and your daughter. I vow that you will live to take your child into your arms again."

"How, Monsieur? Who are you that you can promise the impossible? Are you a man of God?"

The stranger smiled. "From time to time. Names and identities are mutable things, and one soul may wear more than one."

"How, then, should I address you?"

"I am the Count of Monte Cristo. Trust me, and all, ultimately, will be well, even though I now give you cause to fear."

The encounters between Doc Ardan and The Little Prince in Tales of the Shadowmen 2, *and that between Doc Ardan and Sleeping Beauty in* Tales of the Shadowmen 4, *were arguably our most outrageous crossovers–that is, until Tom Kane, one of our newest contributors, suggested bringing together the antipodean worlds of Ian Fleming's James Bond and Pauline Réage's* Story of O, *the world-famous erotica novel, in...*

Tom Kane: *The Knave of Diamonds*

Fontainebleau, 1953

The Spaniard, the Briton, and the Belgian regarded each other hostilely across the front room of the otherwise pleasant hunting lodge in the forest of Fontainebleau. Besides hostility, the Belgian showed fear, while the Spaniard showed impatience, and the Briton showed nothing.

"Why the hesitation?" the Briton, Sir Stephen, asked. Like the Belgian, he was sitting on the floor, his hands tied behind his back with a soft silk belt from a convenient dressing gown.

"It is not hesitation," said the Spaniard, Scaramanga. He was the only one standing, and he held Sir Stephen's Browning pistol easily at his side, not even bothering to point it at his prisoners. "I have made certain arrangements for disposing of your friend..." Here, he did point the gun, but only momentarily, towards the Belgian. "...and now, I must expand upon those arrangements to accommodate you as well. As I've already told you, you weren't originally part of my plan."

Carl, the Belgian, said, "I'll give you 100,000 francs if you let me go." He was Flemish, and his guttural voice matched his ugly, florid-faced appearance perfectly.

"You've turned down a very lucrative partnership offer from my American employers," Scaramanga said, almost lecturing. "All you had to do was let them share in the wealth from your diamond mines in the Belgian Congo, and we could have avoided all this difficulty. Now, you must be made an example. Personally, I would have preferred to put a bullet in your head and be done with it, foregoing all this unpleasantness, but I've been convinced to be a bit more fancy this time..." He glanced out the window at the oak trees near the Franchard gorges, with their display of blazing October foliage. His voice betrayed his impatience. "If my friends, Mr. Wint and Mr. Kidd, should ever return with the implements I requested, we can get on with it."

"And if my 'friend' hadn't been so greedy, I wouldn't be here in the first place," Sir Stephen said quietly, but caustically.

"Greedy? Me?" said Carl. "You're the one who've turned all my investors against me behind my back, tried to steal my mines for yourself! And all by dangling your fancy whore O in front of me!"

The Belgian's red face turned even redder. That brought a bitter smile to Sir Stephen's lips.

"It wasn't difficult to lead you astray, Carl," he said. "You made a fool of yourself the first time you met O on the Blue Train. And when I sent you to Club Roissy, you were like a swine at the trough. Anne-Marie told me how O was disgusted with you every time you foisted yourself on her, but you never noticed. And you thought she would leave me to run away with you, just because you threw some diamonds her way? Ha!"

"She said she would! That's the real reason you agreed to meet me here to-day—and why you brought that gun with you." Carl nodded toward the Browning now in Scaramanga's hand. The Spaniard had seized it from Sir Stephen by surprise rather easily when he had first ambushed them in the midst of their argument. "You were so consumed by jealousy, that you thought the only way you could keep O to yourself was to kill me!"

"I instructed her to keep you happy. That's the only reason she let you think she'd leave Roissy with you. And as long as she kept you happy, you couldn't keep your mind on business, you couldn't see beyond your own desires. You *deserved* to have your mines taken from you, for you're a swine and a fool, Carl."

"You bastard! When I get free..."

"That's enough," Scaramanga interjected. He had let them go on for a while, just to pass the time, his eyes moving back and forth as if watching a tennis match. But the meager entertainment value of their little tiff had run its course. "You're both fools, squabbling over some prostitute's favors. The world is better off without you two."

"A quarter of a million francs," Carl offered. "Let me walk away, and you'll be a rich man."

"No," Scaramanga said simply.

"Then, at least tell me which of my investors betrayed me to you. You've made it clear it wasn't Sir Stephen—he's too selfish to be of any help to you. Was it the Malaysian?"

"Does it matter?"

"If you're going to kill me, it would at least satisfy me to know."

Scaramanga shrugged. "It wasn't the Malaysian, or any of your other investors, who led me to you. It was one of your own employees. Your courier, Peter Franks." Both Carl and Sir Stephen started at that. "Once he delivered those diamond bracelets and collar to you at Roissy, and saw that you were going to give them to that girl, he knew you were too soft for this business."

"How much did you pay him?" asked Carl. "Thirty pieces of silver?"

"Not even that," laughed Scaramanga. "My employers merely offered to hire him to work for their organization. He'll be doing the same thing for them that he did for you, smuggling diamonds out of Africa, and he didn't even ask for increased pay. I think the prospect of greater job security was all he really wanted."

Scaramanga let Carl fume over that while he peered out the window again.

"Where are those two bunglers? If they don't come soon, I'll just ignore my orders and dispatch you both in the more ordinary manner of my preference." He opened the front door to stick his head outside and listen for an approaching car engine.

Carl had been discreetly struggling with his bonds throughout the conversation. The satin belt around his wrists was far too strong to be broken, but the slick fabric was not ideal for holding a knot. It loosened very suddenly and unexpectedly, and the Belgian threw himself to his feet with an agility that was surprising, considering his weight. His captor was younger and much more athletic, but the Spaniard was taken completely by surprise by Carl's desperate, headlong charge at him.

Scaramanga toppled off the front stoop and into some bushes. Carl seized the opportunity to flee into the wilderness. In an instant, Scaramanga, with the reflexes of the circus performer he had once been, was up and bounding after him.

The belt around Sir Stephen's wrists showed no sign of coming loose in a similar manner, though he writhed and heaved mightily once he was alone. But presently, another figure entered through the open door.

"You!" Sir Stephen exclaimed.

"Me," replied Peter Franks. "I was wondering how to get Scaramanga out of here, but Carl did it for me." He knelt and began to untie Sir Stephen's bindings. "I knew he was a target, but I didn't find out until too late that you'd be here as well. Thought I'd come see how you three were getting along."

Sir Stephen stared into the tanned face with its strong features, which Franks fancied made him resemble that piano player who had composed his favorite song, *Stardust*.

"So you were helping that thug's people all along," Sir Stephen said, "even as you were feeding information on Carl to me. Playing both sides against the middle, eh?"

"You benefited from it, up until now. Carl may have been a simple-minded oaf, but you were always a gentleman, in your own crooked way. Paid well for my telling you the names of all of the other investors in the mines, even let me spend a very memorable day with O at Roissy, thank you very much. So when I spotted Scaramanga's boys, Winter and Kittridge, at a gas station on their way here, I sabotaged their car to delay them."

"Wint and Kidd, you mean?"

"Whatever their names are, they never even spotted me. They were going to carve you up like a Christmas goose, make a real horror show to scare all the investors into line and keep the capital coming in."

When the silk belt finally came free, Sir Stephen was helped to his feet. But he angrily pushed Franks away. "Bloody traitor!"

"Listen, this new American mob was going to take over the whole set up sooner or later, no two ways about it. Carl is a rank amateur compared to them, and no offense, but so are you. They've showed me some of their organization, the new pipeline they're arranging to get diamonds out of Africa and onto the black market. It's amazing. I had a choice between getting killed working for amateurs, or staying alive working for professionals. Excuse me if I chose to live."

At that moment, they heard a gunshot in the distance. "That'll be Carl snuffing it," said Franks. "Scaramanga never misses. We don't have much time. He'll be coming back here any minute."

"He had my gun!" Sir Stephen said. "It's registered with the French police. They'll assume I killed Carl." It was what he had intended to do anyway, but he hadn't been thinking rationally then.

"Tough luck. You'll have to dodge the mob anyway, but now you're also going to be on the run from the authorities."

"I have to go to Roissy, collect O. She and I can..."

"Forget her," said Franks, whom O had briefly known by the name Frank. "You'll have all you can do to get out of France as it is, and then you'll be a fugitive. Do you want to subject her to that kind of existence? Maybe someday you can send for her, after you've made yourself secure somewhere. Maybe. But not now."

Sir Stephen knew he was right. O had always been so pliant, so eager to please him, and he had always felt gratified, but thought he had felt no more than that. It was only when Carl had let on that he wanted to take the young woman away with him that Sir Stephen realized how much he truly loved her. And regretted having never told her so. And now he would have to abandon her.

As he collected his car keys, he said, "I hope you'll all pay someday. You, those Americans and their killers. Especially Scaramanga. I hope someone makes you all pay."

"Dream on, mate. It'll never happen."

The idea for this tale, featuring the remarkable Irma Vep, the black-clad heroine of Louis Feuillade's 1915 serial Les Vampires, *and Fascinax, a short-lived pulp hero of the 1920s, came from artist Alan Weiss; the following story was indeed developed and written by the multi-talented Lovern Kindzierski to accompany Alan's cover illustration for this volume. One will note that Irma Vep was supposed to have been killed at the end of the original serial and was mourned by her fellow criminals in Feuillade's 1918 sequel* Tih Minh, *but as we know, there is no rest for the wicked...*

Lovern Kindzierski: *Perils Over Paris*

(In which Mr. George Leicester, while aiding a friend in need,
finds that even a superman may be mistaken in the confidence
of his preternatural abilities to present him with the truth.)

Paris, 1922

Not two minutes ago, all was peaceful on the streets of Paris below. I was enjoying the stars and contemplating the sounds of the city, speculating on their significance–the stories on the winds in scent and sound. The particular tang in the air of betrayal in the offing...

My friend in the Service des Renseignements, the *Cinquième Bureau*, had requested my presence because of a threat toward some diplomatic deliberations taking place this evening. Even the ambassadors seem to have a sense for the operatic. There is something to be said about the heady indulgence that this city engenders in its inhabitants. The women swoon at the cinema over Valentino, while Anatole France captures the Nobel Prize for literature. One of so many contradictions that Paris offers. And even though the Great War has been over for more than three years now, I sit here, baby-sitting some ambassadors discussing the integrity of China's territories.

The Great Fascinax–at least that is what the press calls me. I suppose George Leicester is hardly a name for a man with the wisdom of the ages and mental powers bordering on the supernatural. Wouldn't do to have the public know that Fascinax is George Leicester, a British MD. I wonder where I'd be now if I hadn't helped Nadir Kritchna come back to life after having been put to death for a crime he did not commit. If I'd refused to follow him into the jungle and undergone those mystic rituals which gave me these powers...

It began with a moment of silence as if the streets had taken a deep breath. Then a shot and running steps pounding the cobbles, followed by more footsteps and cries of alarm. The duel had begun. Now it was feint and thrust, parry and riposte–but first it was definitely the feint. Legerdemain, but a deception none-theless. Misleading to the masses, but I am not one of those. Given the circum-stances and the construction of the meeting place, I would choose to assail from above and so as not to underestimate my foe, I am perched up here with our charlatan's audience of cats, bats and winged vermin.

And now it is time for some prestidigitation of my own. I have found the most advantageous listening post available to the task. A construction for dwelling rather than the purpose I have in mind, but possessing of all the acous-tics I shall need. Unlike the regularly assumed methods of isolating sounds, until I find the right one, my approach is to open my senses to the world. I have found a place to firmly brace my back and then I let down my normal defenses to the cacophony of the hustle and bustle of a living city. Even a city such as Paris roars to the Heavens of civilization in its slumber.

At first, the sounds are almost a physical blow, but as I open up more, they become a strong wind rushing about me, almost lifting me from my feet. Still, I am glad to have solid limestone at my back. The scents on the breeze add cur-rents and vortices to the voice of the city, and I am able to discern the rhythm and flow of its respiration. Then, as any good hunter, I seek out that which does not belong.

I find it after a moment, but I decline its probability. It is too ephemeral, like a bat flitting about its darksome slaughter. Yet it is just that sense of slaughter that draws me back to it. Then, I hear a soft clink of metal and the sen-sual rustle of leather too heavy to be the delicate wings of the bat. I lean into the wind and I am aroused at the scent of a musky sexuality.

A woman!

The assassin is a woman. But then, why not?

I have the direction now. I draw back into myself and the song of the city leaves me to be replaced by the silent reverberations of my own thoughts. This is when I key in on the rustle and clink of the assassin as she makes her way to her kill.

I scan the rooftops and calculate the best location from which a sniper might sight her target. A sniper she must surely be, as evidenced by the metallic sound of the rifle barrel lightly touching a passing feature in the local architec-ture. My course of interception charted, I start off toward my target–the hunter now becoming the prey.

As I make my way to this female executioner, I am troubled by my senses. I fear I have not shut out all of Paris' song, and so I change my breathing to en-hance my concentration. Yet, I am still plagued by the strange scent of the bat overlaid with that of the woman. Also, the amount of noise she is making does not gibe with the rate at which its volume increases. She cannot be making her way to her spot as quickly as my ears are telling me. I adjust my speed to be certain to catch her unaware, while making sure to keep my approach silent. It is then that I am struck by the most baffling occurrence. I see her! However, it is what I see her doing that gives me cause to doubt my own eyes.

She makes an impossible leap. It is not just the distance she leaps that makes it impossible, but the fact that she is leaping up an entire story as well as clearing an intervening rooftop. I suspect that I might be able to jump the same distance, but not with the obvious ease that she does it. And I doubt whether anyone but I could have heard the noise she made in her landing. She freezes in the position in which she has alighted. Yet another surprise: she sniffs the wind for the scent of hidden defenders. I too stop and check the breeze to reassure myself that my odor is being blown away from her.

The wind brings her fragrance to me and now my senses cry in protest once more. The scent of the bat *is* the scent of the woman. How can this be? I have seen things that would drive some to the brink of insanity, but this apparition tests even me! Not only is she capable of the extraordinary, but she does not present any of the signs of being human at all! Then, I realize that she is alone in this escapade. I see now that it was she who set up the distraction on the street and then rushed up here behind the lines of security to take advantage of the ambassadors' flight to safety.

I realize who she must be.

Who she can only be.

Irma Vep!

Again, I am faced with the impossible, because she is dead. Or at least, she was believed to be, but she obviously is not. Or is she? The scent of the bat, her impossible feats of strength and speed, the animalistic way she sniffed the wind... But no! They are merely nightmare creatures of legend. Another explanation is more plausible, perhaps one echoing mine. It is most probable that she has been in training somewhere to become even more unbeatable than her legends claim, especially after her near death. Whatever the story, I know that I now face a most dangerous and deadly foe.

It is somewhat ironic that, after all my supposed preparations, I did underestimate my opponent.

Very well. I must not let her find her perch, or she will achieve her goal in the blink of an eye. After a few strides, I can see that Irma will win the race and, most probably, have time to execute her task. I must rely on another stratagem. I change my path and run directly for her. I change the weight of my footfalls to alert her of my presence as I break into a full tilt attack.

Irma's speed is amazing. I am barely able to raise my cane, never mind draw out its hidden blade. Fortunately, the rapidity of our clash leaves her with no time to use her rifle. I was expecting her to use a blade, but I am still taken aback by her accuracy with throwing knives. As we close, she draws her saber out in an unusual way, as to cut her loose of the rifle slung over her shoulder. To keep her off-guard, I force the attack without drawing my own weapon.

My strategy works and Irma is forced to a defensive position. She snarls like a she-beast:

"You are a bastard, Fascinax!"

I have shaken her, and now that we are even, I push my bluff. My reply is as measured and gentlemanly as if we were on the street taking the air:

"Mademoiselle Vep. A pleasure to make your acquaintance."

"The pleasure is all yours, but I shall make it my pleasure to kill you."

"That, Mademoiselle, would be a pity, since I do so hate to disappoint."

It becomes apparent that, for all her incredible abilities, Irma reacts as an animal. She does not have the superior mental abilities that I have developed. She is not able to put together the messages of the senses and know her actions seconds before she herself performs them. I see, too, that our banter distracts her slightly, so I am able to side-step some of her more vicious attacks.

"I fear that I have ruined your plans for the evening, Mademoiselle Vep," I say.

"Hah! This distraction changes nothing now that the target has been–"

"–Flushed? Do I detect a strain in your breathing, Mademoiselle Vep?"

"Look to yourself, fool! Shouldn't you be shouting out the alarm?"

"My dear woman, it is proof positive of your inevitable defeat."

"Ha! You read too much of your own press, Fascinax!"

Irma's next slash comes close to disemboweling me. It is in that instant that I detect in her stance and her grip on the saber, thew fact that she has held back ever so slightly. However slightly, it is ample in providing an opponent such as myself an avenue of escape. I notice, too, that in her furtive sweeps of the rooftops for other defenders, she sought out a position that also leaves me an avenue of escape. I become aware of the pattern of her attacks, and now I see that she has been rejecting possible moves that might have killed me. It has only been my repeatedly thwarting her disarming blows that has forced her to attack me more forcefully.

At that moment, I feel a definite chill run up my spine. Once more, I have underestimated this woman. I make up my mind to never do so again. I should have put it all together sooner. I think she does this task under duress. I suspect she chose the rifle so she might not have to look into her victim's eyes...

"My dear Mademoiselle Vep, if your heart is not in this..." I begin.

Suddenly, an explosion bursts up out of the courtyard below. The very courtyard where I knew the ambassador would be entering his car to seek safety. The car where death lay waiting for him in a package of explosives strapped to the bottom of his seat. Both Irma and I are jarred by the force of the explosion, and she does not rejoin her attack upon me.

"Phobiarch," she whispers with her lip curled up as if to spit out the offensive taste of the word from her mouth.

"Of course. You called me a fool earlier, Mademoiselle Vep, and I fear you were correct, but I am not the only fool on this roof tonight."

"You are most correct, Fascinax. The question now is whether we are any the wiser for this experience."

"Yes. Do we continue Phobiarch's plan for himself, and perhaps destroy each other? Or do we take this knowledge and retire to return the favor to our true enemy?"

Irma salutes me as her opponent, then turns her back on me and starts to walk away. We have reached a truce, but it is not wasted on me that she has not sheathed her blade as she walks away. We may not be enemies, but neither are we friends.

Rick Lai also decided to tackle the theme of the vampirism with enormous gusto and great complexity, drawing, as usual, from a clever mixture of popular literature and cult horror films, in this case Mexican vampire movies. Rather than writing a long and convoluted introduction, we have included Rick's own Afterword to help the readers chart their course in the saga of...

Rick Lai: *All Predators Great and Small*

Mexico and England, 1892-95

Excerpt from *L'Essence du Dragon* by Charles Maurice Loridan (1866)
> *Vlad Dracula's brutality sparked his transformation into the Great Vampire. His impaling of thousands in Wallachia encumbered his soul with sins against humanity. The historical accounts of Dracula's death are false. He wasn't killed by the Turks. Resentful of his mistreatment by the King of Hungary, the Impaler betrayed his army to the Ottoman Empire at Bucharest. The Turks masked his treachery by unveiling the severed head of a double in Istanbul. Dracula actually committed ritual suicide with poison. The atrocities attached to the Impaler's soul assured his reincarnation as the Undead sovereign.*
>
> *Dracula's self-indulgence is limitless. He narcissistically pines for a Soul-Mate, a woman forged in his own image.*

Claude Gabriel Dupont-Verdier's *Journal*, October 31, 1892
> I invaded the Mexican tomb with Aguilar and his brigands. We read the inscription:
> *"Here lie Count and Countess Frankenhausen–and Frau Hildegarde, their faithful servant who would not abandon them even when they journeyed into the Great Beyond–1885."*
> My quest for the ultimate romance nears its completion.

José Alejandro Balsamo's *Diary*, November 3, 1892
> The crypt of the Frankenhausens has been looted. All three corpses were stolen. The Cult of the Undead must be the responsible. The culprits have to be attempting the resurrection of Count Frankenhausen, the last Great Vampire. The remains of the Countess and Frau Hildegarde are inconsequential. The Count's powers validated Grost's theory that "there are as many species of vampire as there are beasts of prey." All victims of Frankenhausen's bite became mindless vampires. Anyone bitten by them was similarly transfigured. The Count devoured the blood of his wife Eugenia. The resulting Undead Countess had the mentality of an idiot. Hildegarde, the Count's daytime protector, didn't

even mature into a vampire. After a spear pierced Frankenhausen's heart, she leapt from the second floor of the Haunted Hacienda. The fall didn't kill her. The injured Hildegarde became a banquet for the Count's moronic slaves. Her Undead resurgence was thwarted by my anti-vampire vaccine. The same fluid slew Eugenia and the other vampires in their graves. Even the Count's corpse was inoculated. My serum is not infallible. Its prevalence inside the bodies can be defeated with necromancy.

Count Cagliostro, my grandfather, deduced the Frankenhausen family's dominance of the Cult. Vampires of the Frankenhausen bloodline sired human offspring. Upon reaching adulthood, the firstborn of each generation evolved into the reigning Great Vampire. The Curse of the Frankenhausens was exorcised when my vaccine cured the Count's daughter. She is now happily married.

My son-in-law has a far-fetched theory. Supposedly, the Frankenhausens acted as figureheads for Vlad the Impaler, a secret Great Vampire hiding in the Carpathians. Ricardo's speculations are ludicrous. The Turks decapitated the despot in 1476. No headless husk could be afflicted with the Undead pestilence.

I pray for the safety of my daughter Anna and her children. Extra steps will be taken to protect them in our estate. A reanimated Count Frankenhausen would seek vengeance against my descendants. Even though I disowned Anna's sister decades ago, my fears extend to her. There were recent rumors of a Countess Cagliostro in Panama... Was this my Josephine, or did she have a daughter?

Claude Gabriel Dupont-Verdier's *Journal*, September 14, 1893:
The Great Vampire is in England. The horrible massacre of the *Demeter*'s crew confirmed his presence. He must have guided that derelict ship to land at Whitby. My own *Jarvee* had earlier made a far less dramatic voyage to these shores. The cargo of three Mexican coffins never disturbed Captain Thompson and his sailors. The choice to store the relics here in London rather than Paris was fortuitous.

Count Frankenhausen's remains were cremated in the cellar of my Georgian mansion. My knife slashed the throat of the young prostitute from Mrs. Blake's bordello. Her blood dripped into the ashes as I recited the incantation from Prinn's *Les Mystères du Ver*:

In the fane of Yiggurath, the Source of All Malice,
*   And his progeny Slidith, Lord of the Blood Chalice,*
I summon forth the Great Vampyre
*   By his minion's charnel pyre.*

A wave of mist erupted upward from Frankenhausen's ashes. The haze assumed the semblance of a gaunt man. His dark hair and beard were tinged with grey. I was granted an audience with Dracula.

Dr. Caber's Letter to Josephine Balsamo, September 15, 1893

Dear Josephine,

A vial of *Mediora Diphteria* was missing from the storeroom. An investigation established your sister as the culprit. I challenged Sabine about the theft. She ranted incoherently about suicide. Her offense wasn't reported to my uncle and his associates. Please hurry to London. Sabine needs you desperately.

Your friend,

Urania

Claude Gabriel Dupont-Verdier's *Journal*, September 15, 1893

Dracula returned to my cellar after dusk. I handed him the mystical ruby, Akivasha's Tear. He sliced his palm with the scimitar sacred to the Old Ones. The jewel grew brighter as the Great Vampire poured his blood on it. His lips chanted the Aklo hymn to Yiggurath, Father of Serpents.

The two stone coffins no longer contained decaying carcasses. The occupants displayed the fullness of life. Hildegarde Einem climbed out of her coffin. She wore the stern clothes of a housekeeper. Her face exhibited the ravages of age. Her blonde hair was widely streaked with grey.

"Master," she murmured, "you didn't forsake me."

"Look closely, Hildegarde," decreed .Dracula. "Who am I?"

"You're Count Franken– No; you're the nobleman whose castle the Count visited before his departure for Mexico."

"I am Dracula, the true Great Vampire. Siegfried von Frankenhausen merely masqueraded in that role. He and his ancestors belonged to the Stepsons of the Dragon, my inner circle in the Cult of the Undead. Each Stepson owns a ring identical to mine. Every Frankenhausen firstborn inherited my ring until one of José Balsamo's agents intervened."

Dracula showed his ring to Hildegarde. She recognized the thrice-coiled effigy of a winged dragon with three ruby horns. It was Slidith, the Draconic Adder first worshipped in Lemuria and Valusia.

"I don't understand" declared Hildegarde. "Why do you have Stepsons?"

"They act as my eyes and ears. While I rest in my native soil, my Stepsons are awake in diverse parts of the world. They mentally communicate their experiences to me through our rings. The Stepsons transmit glorious visions of carnage and seduction. At the very least, they relieved the oblivion of my dormancy. Vampires normally don't dream."

"Master... I'm thirsty."

"My servant Gabriel has anticipated your hunger. You may dine after I leave. Restrain any designs on Gabriel's blood. He's too valuable as a mortal to me."

Dracula pointed towards the other vampire. "Eugenia, rise from your coffin! I command it!"

A lady in a white nightgown vacated the second casket. Dark curly hair draped her shoulders. There was no intelligence in her eyes. She motioned aimlessly toward my Master. Akivasha's Tear had mutated the Frankenhausen vampire virus into the more common Transylvanian version. Eugenia now had radically different abilities than in Mexico, but her mental faculties were still damaged. Hildegarde's wits were intact because her initial Undead rebirth miscarried.

"Walk with me in the moonlight, Eugenia," ordained Dracula "The tribe of Cagliostro disrupted my supreme ambition. You shall be the instrument of my revenge." Eugenia exited with him up the stairs.

I opened a locked door with a key. "Your nightly meal," I heralded. The room harbored four female adolescents. Hildegarde immediately attacked them. Within minutes, the captives were all drained of blood. They would never be vampires. In contrast to its Mexican offshoots, the Transylvanian disease only spreads with the victim's additional drinking of the Undead's blood. Jillian Blake has been paid handsomely to deliver these maidens. The girls will not be missed by their procurer. Mrs. Blake falsely believed that her protégés were en route to Madame Delhomme's prosperous brothel in northern France.

Hildegarde advanced toward a wall mirror. "I have no reflection," she lamented.

"There is a special mirror upstairs. Permit me to escort you."

"What does the Great Vampire intend to do with Eugenia?"

"She's the subject of an audacious experiment. Who was destined to succeed Count Frankenhausen as Dracula's Stepson?"

"Frankenhausen's daughter, Brunhilde. She would have been a Stepdaughter."

"More of a Soul-Mate. For centuries, Dracula has schemed to infuse a woman with his own personality. The Soul-Mate requires superior breeding. He ordered Frankenhausen to wed Eugenia Guzman de La Selva because her maternal grandfather was the renowned soldier, Baron Kralitz. Furthermore, Kralitz's mother was a Durward and his wife was a Szandor. The Durwards were the preeminent duelists of England. Eugenia's pedigree extends directly back to Count Szandor and his Bulgarian bride, fierce rebels against King Matthias of Hungary in the 1480s. With her additional Frankenhausen heritage, Brunhilde would have been the perfect Soul-Mate. Unfortunately, she was vaccinated with José Balsamo's purifying acid. Brunhilde is totally immune to vampirism. Denied the daughter, Dracula will settle for the mother."

We finally reached the room where my "mirror" was stored. At our entry, Hildegarde was startled by a painting hanging over the mantelpiece. It was Joseph Bridau's *Hecate Reborn*. "Is this some sort of joke? I posed for that picture in 1840!" She contemplated the portrait with regret. "I was so beautiful."

"Examine your hands! They're young and firm! Blood has restored your youth!"

Hildegarde ripped off her clothes. Seeing her naked skin, she relished in her rejuvenation.

"Those garments were unsuitable, Hildegarde. These are more appropriate."

Hildegarde put on an exact copy of the white Grecian-style gown modeled for Bridau. Although her elegant legs were entirely covered, the dress closely clung to her superbly proportioned physique. A long sleeve sheathed her right arm, but her left shoulder and limb remained bare.

"It's regrettable, Gabriel, that you don't have a copy of the bracelet in the painting."

"But I have a substitute." I slipped the golden Valusian armlet on her left wrist.

"My portrait was commissioned by the Gabriel family while I was their governess in Austria. Gabriel must be your surname."

"It's my middle name. My mother was one of your charges. I've desired you since beholding Bridau's masterpiece as a boy. My adoration drove me to research your subsequent history. You left my mother's family to become young Siegfried von Frankenhausen's tutor. Accompanying the adult Count to Mexico, you ran afoul of Balsamo's vampire hunters during a decade-long battle.

"The death of my French father left me a fortune. I nearly exhausted it to bring you back to life. The *Jarvee*, my private vessel, scoured the globe in an occult crusade. In Boneport, Louisiana, I found the sole surviving edition of Loridan's *L'Essence du Dragon*. All other copies had been incinerated with the author in a warehouse fire. Besides Dracula's plans for a Soul-Mate, the book documented the rites capable of resuscitating any vampire. The Great Vampire's blood must envelop the ruby called Akivasha's Tear. It took me years to exhume the gem in an Egyptian tomb. Aided by Mexican outlaws, I violated the Frankenhausen Mausoleum. Locating Dracula in London, I offered him a singular trade. As payment for Eugenia, he would grant me my ideal woman…You."

"A fool's bargain. I only seduce with the lamia's kiss. Dracula forbids me to taste your blood."

"Your bracelet overcomes that restriction. I wear its mate. Both bear the likeness of Slidith, son of Yiggurath and half-brother of Set. The magic of this Great Old One bonds the intellects of the bracelets' bearers. My mind will penetrate yours. The Master conceded the vampire's inability to dream. I can fill your daytime slumber with carnal delights. Let me be your incubus."

"You tempt me. Gabriel is too angelic a name for a tempter. Our nuptials will be sealed with a baptism. I christen you *Satanas*."

Sabine Balsamo's *Diary*, September 20, 1893

Dr. Caber related that my sister is coming to London. When Josephine uncovers the truth about the poison, her rage will be monstrous. Death's merciful embrace attracts me. The Grim Reaper haunts my sleep, but his form isn't a hooded skeleton. He's man with a pointed beard.

The apparition of my delirium beckons me to a spectacular realm. He says it is a glorious world where the dead can savor endless evenings of narcotic bliss. The dark messenger offers me this paradise if I welcome him into my house. So far, I have refused.

Claude Gabriel Dupont-Verdier's *Journal*, September 21-22, 1893

My days were filled with wanton ecstasy. Lust consumed Hildegarde. Vampires generally arise briskly at dusk. Enthralled by our erotic fusion, my concubine reluctantly left her coffin hours after sunset. I teased Hildegarde by proclaiming her the first vampire to chronically oversleep. Purchases from Mrs. Blake satiated Hildegarde's diet. After moving Eugenia's coffin elsewhere, Dracula ignored us for days. I erred in forgetting his existence.

Soon after nightfall, our sensual refuge in the Dreamlands was interrupted by a husky female voice. "Hildegarde, you lazy slut! Attend me! I command it!"

"I obey only the Great Vampire!" replied my lover.

"Enough of your insolence! Feel my wrath!"

In the world of dreams, my darling disappeared. Waking suddenly in my bed, I rushed downstairs to the cellar. "Satanas....save me!" wailed Hildegarde. She was out of her coffin. Blood splattered her white dress. Holding her stomach, she knelt before a macabre interloper.

I beheld a woman in a black ensemble consisting of a sleeveless tunic, pants and boots. Leather bracelets adorned her wrists and her upper arms. The back of her jet hair was tied in a plaited bun. Two long braids of hair fell to her waist. She wore a dark fur cape. A gold chain clasped the cloak around her neck. A ring with Dracula's dragon crest was on the fifth finger of her left hand. The intruder's long sharp nails were stained with Hildegarde's blood.

"How appallingly domestic!" noted the cloaked brunette. "You've given Gabriel a pet name. Do not seek succor from his quarter. Your Satanas hasn't the courage to defy me."

"Countess Frankenhausen," moaned Hildegarde, "please...no more..."

"Don't address me by that name. Eugenia is dead. My progenitor, Count Szandor, was the first Stepson of the Dragon. I celebrate my lineage as Szandra, Countess Dracula."

"Forgive me, Countess Dracula."

"Effete gods grant forgiveness. I impose penance. My boots are tarnished. Clean them."

"I'll fetch a cloth, Mistress."

"No, Hildegarde. Lick off the dust with your tongue."

My dearest complied with this demand. Szandra put her fingers in her mouth. She sucked the blood off her nails as Hildegarde debased herself. The Great Vampire had altered Eugenia's appearance through sorcery. Only faint traces of Frankenhausen's wife endured. The Soul-Mate of Dracula is leaner with red eyes instead of blue. Eugenia's brain had been a blank slate. It now housed the cunning of a maniacal warrior. This female surrogate of the Great Vampire gloated over our humiliation.

"My handmaiden has been tardy due to her trysts, Satanas. I suspected a potential pregnancy. The only recourse was to dissect her belly. My suspicions were incorrect. Hildegarde, you may stop. Your odious condition merits a bath. I don't require your services any further tonight."

Countess Dracula vanished as a cloud of mist.

Vampires do not wash in water. Running water is fatal to them. They bathe in blood. I bought more specimens from Mrs. Blake to supply the cleansing fluid. Hildegarde's sanguinary immersion healed her injuries. She put on a duplicate of the torn Grecian raiment in silence. A rift developed between us. Not only had I witnessed her degradation, but I had done nothing to circumvent it.

The next day, Hildegarde's performance was …uninspired. She dismissed me from the Dreamlands long before dusk. I cursed Szandra for ruining my lecherous utopia.

Immediately upon dusk, Hildegarde emerged from her coffin. She stood patiently for hours awaiting the coming of Szandra. Finally, a swirl of smoke transmuted into Countess Dracula.

"You have learned from your mistakes, Hildegarde."

"Yes, Mistress."

"Your improvement deserves a reward. Like my consort, I mandate three Sisters of the Night to be my acolytes." Countess Dracula fondled Hildegarde's yellow locks. "As the most senior of my Sisterhood, you shall conscript another devotee of my choosing."

"Who shall be the next Sister, Mistress?"

"My consort has the ability to sense souls in torment. Do you understand this peculiar skill?"

"The Master can feel the thoughts of a person troubled by visions of death and madness. Is the candidate an asylum inmate?"

"No, merely a contemplator of suicide. Her induction into the Sisterhood shall punish the inventor of the most formidable weapon ever employed against our Cult."

"José Balsamo! Have you chosen Señora Anna Peisser, Don José's daughter?"

"No, our quarry is Anna's niece."

"I would have preferred a daughter. Anna infiltrated the Frankenhausen household posing as a servant 18 years ago. I hunger to repay that strumpet."

"My consort researched the Balsamo family. Anna and her husband Ricardo have five children. The youngest is an eight-year old girl. She's the fourth Josephine descended from Count Cagliostro. Unlike her predecessors, this Josephine has black hair."

"We could journey to Mexico and make Anna's daughter the third Sister."

"An excellent idea, Hildegarde. Her niece has a reprieve tonight because a proper invitation is lacking. Would you care to scrounge the streets for a midnight repast?"

"We can partake indoors. Thanks to Mrs. Blake, our food larder is well-stocked."

Josephine Balsamo's Letter to José Alejandro Balsamo, October 6, 1893

Dear Grandfather,

We have never met. I am the child of your prodigal daughter. Her name was the same as your mother's. It is mine as well.

I discovered your whereabouts three years ago during a visit to Panama. You may distrust the validity of this letter. Permit me to prove its veracity with information available only to our family. Joseph Balsamo, Count Cagliostro, had two wives. The tragic passing of the first, Lorenza, was publicized by the novelist Dumas. She needn't concern us. Shortly after the Affair of the Queen's Necklace in 1785, our forebear wedded Sharita, an Indian priestess. Cagliostro investigated the terrifying depredations of Kurt von Frankenhausen throughout Germany. This alleged Great Vampire retaliated by converting Sharita into a deranged lamia. The Bavarian Inquisition apprehended Sharita and burned her at the stake.

A grief-stricken Cagliostro had an assignation with Josephine de Beauharnais in Fontainebleau during 1788. Their daughter was born in the same year. She was the first of our line to be dubbed Josephine Balsamo. After her natural mother became Napoleon's Empress, my namesake posed as the goddaughter of the illustrious beauty. In the wake of Waterloo, the original Josephine Balsamo was wooed by the enigmatic Henri de Belcamp. Her lover revealed his real identity as Prince Serge Dolgoruki of Russia. Belcamp was merely his alias in Paris. Dolgoruki transported Josephine to the court of Czar Alexander II. There she adopted the title of Countess Cagliostro. Deserted by Dolgoruki in 1816, she bore his son—you, my grandfather. Born Joseph Alexander Balsamo, you utilize the Spanish variant of your name in Mexico.

The Cult of the Undead still terrorized our family. In 1818, your mother received an urgent plea from her older half-sister, Sara Balsamo. Sharita's daughter was pursued in Moldavia by Gorcha the Vourdalak and his bloodthirsty brethren. My namesake gallantly rescued her sibling by slaughtering Gorcha's band of vampires. Great-grandmother trained you to continue the war against the Undead. Your labors are devoted to combating this abomination. News of vampire outbreaks in Mexico prompted your resettlement there in the 1860's.

You married Felina de Valgeneuse in 1844. My mother's birth in 1845 was followed by that of her sister Anna two years later. In 1867, a serious schism developed between you and my mother. She rebelled against your decision to

93

move the family from Europe to Mexico. The clandestine cabal known as the Black Coats recruited her. She envisioned them as no different from the Masonic societies that your grandfather used to spread liberty, equality and fraternity. You argued that the Black Coats only promote treason, revenge and extortion. All your objections were accurate. Unfortunately, I am also entangled in the intrigues of the Black Coats. It's too late for me to escape my hateful servitude. By writing you, I risk my life. It's an offense punishable by death to disclose our organization's activities to outsiders. This rule is so stringent that no member is permitted to keep a diary.

My mother's affair with a munitions dealer led to my birth in 1868. My sister Sabine was born in the subsequent year. While I resemble our mother and great-grandmother, Sabine is slim with black hair.

My father wrongly assumed Sabine to be his child. My mother confessed Sabine's true parentage to me and Leonard, our loyal retainer. Sabine was never intended to learn her real origins.

Your daughter Josephine perished in 1880. She was lured into a fatal ambush by an ex-suitor. As my mother lay dying from her wounds, she asked me to take two oaths. The first was to protect Sabine always. The second was to destroy the family of the contemptible betrayer. Leonard buried your daughter in a purple robe befitting an Empress. Her ring bearing the golden ram insignia was bequeathed to me. Despite my current ownership, I always imagine my mother wearing this ring.

There was another legacy. You had two sliver brooches fashioned as five-pointed stars. They were presents for your daughters. My mother wanted Anna also to join the Black Coats, but my aunt sided with you. Anna's rejection infuriated my mother. She enticed a burglar to steal Anna's pentagram. My mother later regretted this sisterly feud. She cautioned me and Sabine never to repeat it. Our mother divided the brooches between us.

After the funeral, Leonard persuaded my father to provide for our upbringing. Sabine and I were sent to a wonderful Parisian school staffed by nuns. My fiery nature made me a disciplinary problem. Reports of constant infractions compelled my father to separate me from Sabine. Exiled to a strict boarding school in Provence, I took my pentagram with me. Upon graduation, I gave it as a gift to a fellow student.

I then was initiated into the Black Coats. They served as the means to fulfill my mother's dying wishes. An alliance with the Back Coats allowed me to ruthlessly avenge her. It also permitted me to provide for my sister. Sabine's enrolled at St. Swithin's Medical School in London. To avoid the onus of the Balsamo name, she was registered under the anagram of Absalom. The Black Coats agreed to pay for Sabine's education in exchange for her induction into their medical research center. The director of this group is named Urania. Although her family is a notorious criminal dynasty, she surprisingly has a trustworthy nature. Many denigrate her as scientifically brilliant but impractical. I deem her to be a real rarity–a true friend. Urania acted as a mentor to my sister. During a visit to the laboratory of the Black Coats, Sabine stole some poison. Urania immediately wrote me after covering up my sister's crime.

I own a London abode where my sister resides under the Absalom alias. Arriving there from France on September 22, I interrogated her.

"Urania is convinced you're suicidal. Why are you depressed?"

"There's no use pretending anymore, Josine. You hate me."

"How could I? We're sisters."

"No, we're only half-sisters. My father was the man who betrayed Mama."

Stunned by her words, I sought to console my sister. "You're still my flesh and blood. Mama never wanted you to know. Did Leonard say something?"

"I won't tell you."

"Then don't. The only important thing is that I love you." My voice choked with emotion. "I don't care how you learned Mama's secret. We shall always be sisters."

Sabine hugged me and wept. She still shielded her informant after our reconciliation. It must be Leonard. Because of his past fidelity, I haven't acted on my suspicions.

The next morning, my sister was much better. I expected to stay with her. An early morning edict from my superior in the Black Coats interfered. She dispatched me with a proposal for an architect in Bristol. Any funky could have performed the task, but this heartless tyrant regularly saddles me with unnecessary duties. I departed by train before noon. My return was scheduled the next afternoon.

In my absence, Sabine faced pure horror.

Sabine Balsamo's *Diary*, September 23, 1893

My endless turmoil is over. All doubts about Josine's affection for me have been eliminated. Why did Madame Koluchy send her to Bristol? I miss my sister's radiant smile.

The day was beautiful and sunny. I decided to stroll down Piccadilly Circus at noon. I met a charming woman by happenstance. She accidentally stepped on my foot. Ashamed of her *faux pas*, she insisted on treating me at the local tea shop.

My acquaintance is Countess Alucard, a fascinating aristocrat with braided raven hair. She recently arrived from Hungary with her husband and maid. The lady seemed very wealthy. She was wearing a stylish black dress and veil. A gold bracelet was on her left wrist.

The Countess was extremely loquacious in her thick Hungarian accent. Labeling tea inferior to coffee, she barely touched her cup. Amused by her ramblings, I invited the Countess to visit my home. She knows me only by my pseudonym of Absalom. The Countess asked if her maid, Fraulein Einem, could come. Of course, I assented. Countess Alucard has the most stilted way of speaking. I remember her awkward question: "Do we have permission to cross your threshold?"

As we were leaving, she noticed her husband in the crowd. He's a bearded man strangely resembling the specter of my nightmares. I am still

(*Editor's Note*: Sabine's diary terminates abruptly. There are no further entries.)

Claude Gabriel Dupont-Verdier's *Journal*, September 23, 1893

Hildegarde blocked my entry into her mind for several hours. Finally my paramour opened the door to her thoughts. I created the illusory boudoir where we always rendezvoused. Hildegarde's psychic simulacrum appeared. My astral double embraced her, but she remained cold and unresponsive. Our conversation took curious detours.

"Satanas, does Alucard signify anything?"

"It's the Master's name backwards. Some of his Stepsons use it as a nom de guerre."

"How can Dracula live in the daytime? Sunlight should be fatal to our kind."

"Years ago, the Great Vampire conducted a ritual sacred to Slidith. It was supposed to grant Dracula full immunity in daylight, but the ceremony was only a partial success. He can survive the Sun, but all his powers are rendered dormant by it. And he still needs to rest periodically to renew his strength."

"The Master imparted this ability to his Soul-Mate. She braved the daylight today."

"You're in the Dreamlands, Hildegarde. How could you possibly know?"

"Because I told her" announced Countess Dracula. I was startled by Szandra's intrusion. Her astral self wore the same barbaric garb flaunted nightly. One of her wristbands had been superseded by a Valusian bracelet. This accessory must decorate Szandra's arm in the waking world. Her clairvoyant communiqués had beguiled Hildegarde. My lover had degenerated into Sandra's daytime voyeur.

"Did you enjoy my chat with Anna's niece?"

"I did not. She's an insipid creature, Mistress."

"I detect a tone of jealousy. Don't fret; you'll always be my favorite. Sabine will merely be a thrall whose eternal suffering will amuse us."

"Thank you, Mistress. Shouldn't Satanas go elsewhere?"

"Let him stay. Some men wish to watch…such things."

I won't describe what happened next in the Dreamlands. Saturated with disgust, I fled the imaginary region to the actuality of my quarters. I went downstairs and brooded over Hildegarde's coffin. With the setting of the sun, she rose from her resting place. Icy indifference emanated from her.

"I have no time for you, Satanas. My Mistress craves my attentions."

"Don't forsake me. I yearn for your company."

"You can easily satisfy your request. Your bracelet will enable you to observe as I gratify the whims of Countess Dracula. You may even learn *something*."

"Such as?"

"How to make love to a woman." She changed into a bat and fluttered away. Regardless of her taunts, my longing overwhelmed me. Merging with Hildegarde's mind, I perceived the outside as her.

I spied a house from a high distance in the sky. Szandra abided outside the building, I took my natural form. The Countess smiled at me with fondness. "My precocious Hildegarde," she intoned.

We glimpsed a light on the second floor of the edifice. Becoming mist, we passed through the cracks of the windowsill. We materialized in a bedroom. Sabine Balsamo was seated at a desk. She was busy writing in a notebook. A diary? I will peruse it later. Finally the chronicler noticed us.

"Countess Alucard! How did you get in? Why are you wearing those clothes?"

Szandra stared into Sabine's eyes. She was plucking memories from this pathetic female. Through our bracelets, my Mistress transferred these remembrances. I projected the silhouette of a blonde in a green dress into the sight of our initiate. In her imagination, I became this other woman.

"Josine!" exclaimed Sabine. "Please tell me what is happening!"

"Countess Alucard is a gifted medium," I explained. "She can contact our mother."

"Mama..."

"Please sit down, my sister. Close you eyes and think of Mama." Sabine foolishly complied. "Remember," I resumed, "when we last saw her alive."

"Mama was on her bed. Her shoulder was mutilated from the stab wounds. She died screaming vengeance against her enemies. I can't continue, Josine."

"Open your eyes, my sister!" I dissolved the illusion and bared my fangs. "Sabine Balsamo, die like your mother!"

My scrawny prey leaped from the chair in panic. "Nosferatu!" yelled Sabine. Grabbing a star-like object from her desk, she waved it in front of me.

"A pentagram is no match for a vampire," I boasted. My right hand snatched the talisman from her and tossed it behind me. I ripped open the left side of the puny girl's blouse. My teeth sank into her shoulder. I feasted heartily.

"Don't be too greedy," Szandra whispered into my ear. "Our novice must not truly die."

I reluctantly ceased. Szandra yanked Sabine's head upward by seizing the top of her hair "Now you know, daughter of the Cagliostros, how your mother felt as life slipped away. She cried for their blood of her tormentors. Do you?"

"Blood..." muttered Sabine groggily. "Give me the blood of the woman who did this to me."

"I'm very generous with the spilling of blood" volunteered Szandra. I extended my left arm. The Mistress cut my wrist with her fingernail. She pressed my bleeding flesh over the mouth of our victim.

"Drink, Sabine," purred Szandra.

Josephine Balsamo's Letter to José Alejandro Balsamo (continued)

My train arrived in London late in the afternoon of September 24. Urania was gracious enough to meet me at the station with a carriage. Hearing of my unnecessary trip, Urania sought to expedite my reunion with Sabine. At my domicile, we made a horrendous discovery.

My sister was lying unconscious on her bedroom floor. Blood flowed profusely from two gashes in her left shoulder. Luckily, Urania always carried her medical bag. After bandaging Sabine's shoulder, Urania arranged an emergency transfusion with me as the donor. If not for Urania's ministrations, Sabine would have bled to death.

As she slept in her bed, Sabine mumbled, "Josine... Protect me... Vampires..." I knew all about the Undead from the family stories. My sister had clearly been targeted by the cultists. I didn't expound my beliefs to Urania. As a scientific rationalist, she would be unwilling to accept the reality of these supernatural predators. Presuming Sabine the victim of a demented assailant, Urania left to gather some Black Coat bodyguards.

After my friend's exit, I realized that the sun had already set. "Greatgrandmother, grant me strength," I prayed. Vampires are vulnerable to crucifixes. None were in the house. I improvised by retrieving two pokers from the downstairs fireplace. As I wandered back through the passageway to Sabine's chambers, I heard feminine giggling. My sister's persecutors had returned. Crossing the pokers, I entered the room. Two women were near my sister's bed. They had torn open the bandages on Sabine's shoulder. One was a brunette in a black leather outfit with a fur cape. Her companion was a blonde attired in the manner of a Greek goddess. The duo slowly retreated before my impromptu cross.

"You call that makeshift atrocity a crucifix" mocked the brunette.

"Our adversary's religiosity is deficient, Mistress" ridiculed the blonde.

"Of course, Hildegarde. We saw this libertine in Sabine's mind. Josephine Balsamo, Countess Cagliostro, you're merely counterfeit nobility. I am a true Countess, the Soul-Mate of the Great Vampire."

"You must be the wife of the current Count Frankenhausen."

"The Frankenhausens were merely pawns. The real Great Vampire is Dracula!"

Legends depict vampires cowering in terror at the cross. This pair merely froze as if coerced with a pistol. Are the stories false? Or was my cross diminished by its haphazard structure?

98

"The cross is only as potent as the purity of its holder" jeered Countess Dracula.

"It's strong enough to hold you here until dawn," I attested.

"The Sun will not destroy me" warned the Countess.

"But what about me?" pleaded Hildegarde.

"Do not despair. Our antagonist is flawed. I can read her soul."

The scarlet eyes of the Countess probed deeply into mine. The figure of Hildegarde blurred. She was replaced by a woman in a purple robe. Her face mirrored mine.

I gasped "Mama!"

"Please lower your cross, daughter. I must kiss you."

"You can't be Mama!"

"You always deny those who love you the most" said another speaker. There was a girl next to my mother. She was wearing a pentagram brooch. I dare not write her name. She was slender with dark hair just like Sabine. I was confronted by my former classmate from Provence.

"You were always attracted to me, Josine, but you couldn't admit your true passions."

"That's not true. I only pretended to care for you."

"Remember when the headmistress sent all the students to bed. We didn't fall asleep. You were the prefect with the keys to the residence. We crept out into the night to watch the stars together. I told you my aspirations to be an artist."

Tears filled my eyes as I recalled these excursions.

"Frequently, Josine, we went to an unused portion of the school. There I sketched you in secret. I knew every line of your face…every facet of your body."

"Please stop," I begged.

"You must relinquish the pokers, Josine. I can't come to you unless they're surrendered. Only then will you feel the caress of my lips."

Uncrossing the pokers, I gave one to my mother. She flung it on the ground. I glanced at her hands. She had the ring with the golden ram. That same circlet was on my finger. The contradiction dragged me back to reality. The mirage dissipated. My mother reverted to Hildegarde.

I plunged the remaining poker into Hildegarde's chest. As the writhing vampire fell, my classmate devolved into Countess Dracula. She gripped my throat. My hands tugged on the chain of her cape. The Countess hurled me across the room into a wall. Dazed from the impact, I collapsed.

"Mistress…" wheezed the fallen Hildegarde. "She only scraped the edge of my heart…help me…"

The Countess plucked the poker out of her lackey's torso. Hildegarde rose to her full height.

"You damaged my clasp, Cagliostro" snarled the Countess as the cloak dropped off her back. "Your sister will pay for this sacrilege."

"And so will the younger Josephine" added Hildegarde.

"All in good time" predicted the Countess. "Both Sabine and Anna's little child shall be yours. First, beat this upstart to a pulp." The Countess handed the poker to Hildegarde. The blonde raised the rod with her right hand. I chanced upon my sister's pentagram on the floor. The brooch is silver, a metal sometimes anathema to vampires. I threw the star at Hildegarde. She blocked the flying object with her left hand. The brooch's pin pierced her palm. She issued a sharp whimper. Tucking the poker under her arm, Hildegarde struggled with her right hand to remove the imbedded pentagram. The star rubbed a gold bracelet on her left wrist. She screamed "My arm is burning!" A blue flame engulfed Hildegarde. It disintegrated her and the poker. The brooch fell to the ground.

"You destroyed my servant! Now I will destroy you!" screeched Countess Dracula advancing towards my prostrate body. Her claw-like fingers slowly inched toward my stomach. "You have maternal instincts, Cagliostro. Maybe you're pregnant. Let's see!"

"Leave my sister alone!" shouted Sabine standing behind our nemesis. The lacerations on my sister's shoulder had vanished. The slaying of Hildegarde had revoked the mark of the vampire

Countess Dracula howled in agony. The tip of a metal stake burst from the front of her tunic.

Sabine had driven the other poker through the lamia's back impaling her merciless heart. The vampire dropped to her knees in front of me. I exulted over the shock and disbelief in her eyes.

"Before you roast in Hell, Dracula, learn this lesson. Never underestimate the Cagliostros."

I laughed triumphantly. Countess Dracula then smiled cryptically. Her face was filled with rapture. Then her eyelids closed as she fell back lifeless. The Countess wore a bracelet akin to Hildegarde's. I picked up the pentagram and dropped it on the gilded ornament. Blue fire blanketed the cadaver. The slain vampire faded from existence. The pentagram was unscathed.

No vampire can infest a home without being invited. My sister divulged how the Countess engineered an invitation during a contrived meeting in the street. The Countess had been with a man professing to be her husband. He must be Count Dracula. Urania arrived later with several men. I gave them Dracula's description: a tall thin man with a dark beard. The Black Coats were slowly mobilizing against the Great Vampire.

Claude Gabriel Dupont-Verdier's *Journal*, September 25, 1893

I drew Hildegarde's soul into my bracelet when her corporeality was lost. That pentagram must have been consecrated as an Elder Sign, a charm hostile to the symbols of Slidith and the Old Ones. Her right hand had held the star earlier without consequence, but the striking of the Elder Sign against the Valusian arti-fact on her left wrist ignited a devastating combustion.

Hildegarde's entrapped essence does not receive my thoughts. I can only hear her cries of despair and loneliness. Her mistreatment of me has not damp-ened my lust. I pleaded with Dracula to reconstitute her flesh with Akivasha's Tear. He would only vow to resurrect Hildegarde along with Szandra. The Great Vampire had witnessed the demise of his Soul-Mate through their enchanted rings.

As a precaution, the Master had linked Szandra's spirit to her cloak. If the mantle was extant, Szandra could live again. To ferret out the cape, Dracula em-barked on a bold strategy. He directed me to infiltrate the Black Coats. Hilde-garde stole Sabine's diary. It contained valuable data about the criminal organi-zation. The diary cited names of important members–Moriarty, Caber, Koluchy, Dorrington, Saladin and Nikola. This infamous roster included London's pur-veyor of vice, Jillian Blake.

Excerpt from *Confessions of a Black Coat* by Larry Parker (Unpublished Manu-script)

The biggest dunce in the Black Coats was Urania Caber. In the autumn of 1893, she instructed me to burn a fur cape as a favor for Countess Cagliostro. Of course, I did no such thing. Being grossly underpaid, I sold the item to Jacob Dix the pawnbroker.

Claude Gabriel Dupont-Verdier's *Journal*, October 3, 1893

Contacting the Black Coats under the auspices of Mrs. Blake, I stumbled upon a startling fact. They're searching for Dracula. When I apprised the Mas-ter, he instituted countermeasures. Already pursued by Van Helsing, he can't afford to fight the Black Coats. A retreat to Transylvania is warranted.

The Great Vampire is not content with defensive maneuvers. Dracula bids me to orchestrate new aggression. The *Jarvee* will be arriving in Mexico with a message for Aguilar. Once his desperados secure a certain prize, the ship will haul the merchandise across the Atlantic. Captain Thompson was reluctant to lug such freight. I overcame his qualms by promising him ownership of the *Jar-vee* for this final service.

Josephine Balsamo's Letter to José Alejandro Balsamo (concluded)

I'm perplexed by Countess Dracula's dying grin. My sister thinks that our opponent was at peace after her release from the vampire curse. I don't share this opinion. Her smile implied a new conspiracy against our family. The insti-gator of this offensive must be the Great Vampire. According to our inquiries, Count Dracula fled England by a ship bound for the Black Sea.

Hildegarde mentioned Anna's daughter. Anxiety over her welfare moti-vates my letter. Dracula's disciples may still seek to turn her into a vampire. Did

Anna name her child after my mother? Or was Anna thinking of your mother, the slayer of demons? Two Josephines have already disgraced the name of your esteemed parent, grandfather. My mother and I were corrupted. The youngest holder of our ancestor's name must be spared an equally cruel destiny.

As a member of the Black Coats, I am little better than a vampire. Like the Undead, the Black Coats prey on humanity. The leaders of my organization are sadistic autocrats. I never informed them about Dracula's true nature. They merely view him as a lunatic stalking my sister. My motives for this subterfuge are simple. I dread that the Black Coats might seek a partnership with the Great Vampire.

My mother during her lifetime kept a picture of Anna. I always admired my aunt's wonderful ebony curls. Is her daughter also a brunette? Does Anna call her daughter Josephine or the Spanish counterpart, Josefina?

Ever since my experience with Countess Dracula, I've been plagued by a recurring nightmare. I see a child with dark hair abused by fiends. Her persecutors are not vampires but men in black coats. Please cherish and protect Anna's daughter.

Your granddaughter,
Josephine

José Alejandro Balsamo's *Diary*, May 6, 1894
Masked bandits raided our hacienda. They kidnapped Josefina. Ricardo and the servants are out searching for her. I implore God to let no harm befall my innocent grandchild.

The Eulogy of Satanas to his Beloved, April 30, 1895
Darling Hildegarde, you can not read my words. Your disembodied purgatory persists on Walpurgis Night. One prerequisite is absent for your liberation. I require the blood of the Great Vampire, but he is no more. Van Helsing's followers exterminated him in Transylvania.

Your enemies, the heirs of Count Cagliostro, shall not flourish. I plot to avenge you by manipulating the Black Coats. Sabine Balsamo disregarded a cardinal prohibition. She kept a diary with references to the syndicate's hierarchy. Thanks to you, that book is mine. If my criminal peers study her notations, Sabine's life would be in jeopardy. At the proper time, I'll strike at Josephine's beloved sister.

You always loathed Anna Peisser. Her only daughter is enslaved. Again you're responsible, my sweet, for this development. You proposed Josefina Peisser as a Sister of the Night. Dracula dictated her abduction. Captain Thompson hired Aguilar and his pistoleros to capture the girl. The *Jarvee* smuggled her into Europe. Dracula hoped to personally turn Josefina into a vampire. His destruction caused a modification to this act of retribution. Josefina has been hidden in France. I've sold her to Madame Delhomme's brothel in Chartres. The child will be taught to be a voluptuary rivaling Szandra in depravity. The Balsamo clan rejoices in anagrams like Absalom. I mimic our foes with an anagram of "vampire." Anna's daughter has been renamed *Irma Vep*.

I excuse your flirtation with Szandra. You were attracted to the avatar of the Great Vampire within her. Szandra will no longer be a barrier to our union. I've abandoned my hunt for her cloak. There is no reason to reconstruct her anymore. The essence of the Great Vampire will never separate us. It will dwell inside my breast

Loridan has shown me the way. He described the methods that Vlad the Impaler used to become the Great Vampire. The modern equivalent of Vlad's excesses shall be my pathway to immortality. It may take decades, but I will control my own cadre in the Black Coats. My underlings will commit countless crimes of butchery to befoul my soul. The inevitable outcome will be my arrest by the police. When that calamity arrives, poison will extinguish my life. The Old Ones will reconstitute me as the Great Vampire, the successor to Dracula. My own blood will fuel Akivasha's Tear. You shall feel the fleshly pleasures as my Soul-Mate. We shall walk the Earth for all eternity.

Afterword

The Mexican films The Bloody Vampire (El Vampiro Sangriento, *1962*) *and* The Invasion of the Vampires (La Invasion de los Vampiros, *1963*) *featured a feud between vampires and the Cagliostro family. According to the first film, Cagliostro's second wife was transformed into a vampire. With the exception of the year, the inscription on the Frankenhausen Tomb is taken verbatim from the English dubbed dialogue in* The Invasion of the Vampires. *Dracula's injunction to Eugenia to walk with him in the moonlight is based on the concluding actions of Count Frankenhausen in* The Bloody Vampire. *Dracula never drank wine, but the Frankenhausens drank coffee. This is the source of Szandra's comment about coffee in her tea shop meeting with Sabine. The phrase "I command it" uttered by both Count and Countess Dracula was used frequently by Count Frankenhausen. In* The Bloody Vampire, *it was implied (but never implicitly stated) that the Balsamos in that film were descended from Cagliostro's first wife. I have made these vampire-hunting Balsamos the descendents of Cagliostro's illegitimate daughter.*

José Balsamo only appeared in The Bloody Vampire. *That film identifies him as Cagliostro's grandson, but the sequel briefly refers to him as a great-grandson. I have followed the comments of the first movie. In the second movie, José is sometimes also called Alejandro. He never fought Count Frankenhausen directly. However, he does discover a serum that destroys vampirism. The bulk of the action fell on his daughter Anna and her boyfriend in the first film. In the second film, José Balsamo is offstage as the battle is waged by his apprentice, Dr. Ulysses Alvaran. I don't make any reference to Alvaran in my tale besides a brief mention of "an agent of José Balsamo." Adding Alvaran to the mix would just be confusing the reader with another superfluous character.*

The Mexican film follows the widespread theatrical convention of vampirism being spread by the bite alone. In Bram Stoker's Dracula, *the victim also has to drink the vampire's blood for the transformation to occur. Otherwise, he or she perishes. My story glosses over the discrepancies between the depiction of vampires in Stoker's novel and the Mexican films by fostering the concept of different species of the Undead. The vampire abilities of Hildegarde and Eugenia are changed to the Transylvanian variety by magic. The idea of divergent vampirism is borrowed form the 1974 Hammer film* Captain Kronos, Vampire Hunter. *The character Grost from the film is even cited.*

I have dated the events of The Bloody Vampire *and* The Invasion of the Vampires *to respectively 1875 and 1885. An unspecified number of years separate the pair of movies. The same actress plays both Eugenia and her daughter Brunhilde in both films. Brunhilde is offstage in the first film, and approximately 20 years-old in the second. I imagine that Eugenia was about 30 in* The Bloody Vampire *and that Brunhilde was then 10 years-old. The first film ends with Eugenia's transformation into a vampire. An ageless Eugenia is stalking victims at the start of* The Invasion of the Vampires. *After injecting all the vampires with Balsamo's vaccine, Dr. Alvaran uses the same serum to prevent Brunhilde from becoming a vampire due to the curse that befalls the firstborn of each Frankenhausen generation.*

The movies don't explain what happens to the previous Frankenhausen vampire once his firstborn reaches adulthood and assumes the mantle of leadership. Neither does my story. Maybe the earlier Frankenhausens retired to their castle in Europe, like the generational vampires in Henry Kuttner's "The Secret of Kralitz," which has a similar curse falling on each firstborn? (That story combines vampirism with the Cthulhu Mythos.) Eugenia's grandfather isn't necessarily the same Baron Kralitz who appeared as the protagonist in Kuttner's story since the tale's events are undated. There were faint hints of a military background for the Kralitz family, and I made Eugenia's grandfather an accomplished soldier since Stoker's Dracula rants about warrior ancestry.

My story ties into Peter Tremayne's trilogy of prequels to Stoker's classic: Dracula Unborn *(also known as* Bloodright), The Revenge of Dracula *and* Dracula, My Love. *In all these novels, Dracula worships Draco, a dragon god. Richard Tierney's* The House of the Toad *implied that Draco was one of H. P. Lovecraft's Great Old Ones. Tremayne says vaguely that Dracula turned himself into a vampire in a ritual sacred to Draco. I have made it a ritual suicide to tie in with the old legend that suicide victims become vampires. I have conflated Draco with Slidith, the Lord of Blood worshipped by the Red Druids in Lin Carter's* Thongor of Lemuria *novels. The Red Druids were aligned with the*

Dragon Kings, a reptilian race. I have given Slidith the title of the Draconic Adder to invoke both Tremayne's Draco and Leslie H. Whitten's vampire novel, Progeny of the Adder.

Robert E. Howard had an unnamed dragon god depicted on a gold bracelet in "The Shadow Kingdom," a King Kull story. I have made Howard's nameless god synonymous with Draco (Slidith). The winged dragon in Howard's story is opposed to the Serpent-Men of Valusia, adherents of the Great Serpent. In their continuations of Howard's Conan stories, L. Sprague de Camp and Lin Carter identified the Great Serpent with Set, the snake god revered in Stygia. I made Draco and Set half-brothers to suggest a rivalry paralleling the feud between Cthulhu and Hastur in August Derleth's Mythos stories. Derleth also took Lovecraft's vague references to an Elder Sign and created a pentagram-like symbol from it.

Lovecraft ghost-wrote "The Curse of Yig" for Zealia Bishop. This story introduced Yig, the Father of Serpents. Robert Bloch mentioned someone called Yiggurath in "The Grinning Ghoul." Yiggurath is an apparent variant of Yig. I made Yiggurath the father of Set and Draco. In "The Shambler from the Stars," Bloch stated that Yig was mentioned in his fictional book, Ludvig Prinn's The Mysteries of the Worm (I translated the title into French). In "The Ivory Goddess" by de Camp and Carter from Conan the Swordsman, Lovecraft's Yig was envisioned as a separate being from Robert E. Howard's Set.

Peter Tremayne's novels are prequels to Stoker's classic. The only major discrepancy is that Stoker had Dracula able to walk in sunlight while the vampire chieftain is vulnerable to daylight in The Revenge of Dracula. *In fact, Tremayne's novel has Dracula using a magic ritual to unsuccessfully gain immunity to the Sun's rays. I have tried to reconcile this discrepancy in the text of my story. Either the ritual in Tremayne's novel was later revealed to be partially successful, or Dracula later performed another ritual. My story just mentions a ritual granting Dracula this attribute. References in Tremayne's prequels indicate the Dracula transpired in 1890. The placement o f the novel in 1893 is based on the arguments advanced by Leonard Wolff in* The Annotated Dracula.

Stoker has Dracula in telepathic communication with Renfield in Seward's asylum. How Dracula achieves this feat is never fully explained in the novel. I have rationalized it by saying that the vampire can sense souls in torment. This ability alerts Dracula to Sabine's existence in my story.

In terms of the chronology of Stoker's novel, Dracula's first meeting with Satanas happens during a gap in the novel. There is no activity for September 14 -16. Dracula then pursues Lucy Westenra. She dies on September 20. Lucy is staked as a vampire on the 29th. Dracula then flees London by ship on October 4. My idea was to have Dracula planning to create a new Sisterhood of the Night to help him against Van Helsing. However their battle is so intense from September 29 to October 3 that the Vampire Lord doesn't have time to launch such a plan. Lucy was probably originally intended to be part of Dracula's equivalence of the Sisterhood in London.

Szandra's pregnancy test is based on an actual legend of Vlad the Impaler. Vlad had a mistress who claimed to be pregnant with his child. Vlad didn't believe it and used an excessive means to prove his opinion.

Today Dracula is associated with Rumania because Transylvania (along with Vlad the Impaler's Wallachia) is part of that country. In 1893, Transylvania was part of Hungary. Therefore, Szandra as Madame Alucard posed as a Hungarian. A similar reasoning governed The Son of Dracula which was filmed after Transylvania had been briefly returned to Hungary during World War II. The Count Alucard of that movie adopted the guise of a Hungarian.

Paul Féval's The Vampire Countess [3] says that Count Szandor rebelled against two kings of Hungary, Mathias Corvinus (1458-1490) and Louis II (1516-1526). However, Szandor's grave is dated 1646. Szandor also seems to be staked more then once. Clearly, he had several resurrections (the more likely reason is that Féval was being inconsistent). Matthias Corvinus was the same Hungarian king who imprisoned Vlad the Impaler for over a decade. Although Matthias later released Vlad and equipped him with an army, it's not implausible that the Impaler secretly harbored revenge. I have Vlad betraying Matthias to the Turks. I placed Szandor's insurrection against Mathias in the 1480s in order to suggest that Dracula might have sponsored it after his transformation into the Great Vampire in 1476. It is implied that Dracula turned Szandor into a vampire.

The Durward family is from the film Captain Kronos, Vampire Hunter. The Durwards intermarried with the Karnsteins from J. Sheridan LeFanu's "Carmilla." Therefore, Eugenia is a descendant of the Karnstein family as well. Depending on when we date Kronos, Eugenia is descended from one of the two Durward family members, a brother and a sister, who survived the violent conclusion of the film. Possibly Eugenia is descended form both because director/screenwriter Brian Clemens suggests in his DVD commentary that the Durward siblings were engaged in incest.

The Golden Ram crest of the Cagliostro family is from the Lupin III 1979 animated film, The Castle of Cagliostro. The ruby called Akivasha's Tear is meant to be the jewel called Dracula's Tear in the Lupin III episode, "The Case of the Risible Dirigible." In that episode, the Gabriel family of Austria owned the jewel for generations. Akivasha is the female vampire encountered by Conan in Robert E. Howard's The Hour of the Dragon.

Claude Dupont-Verdier is the real name of Satanas in the English version of Louis Feuillade's 1915 serial Les Vampires. I made Claude a relation of the Gabriels. Presumably, his magic jewel was inherited by his Austrian cousins.

---

[3] Available in a Black Coat Press edition, 2003, ISBN 0-9740711-5-3.

Madame Koluchy is from The Brotherhood of the Seven Kings *by Meade and Eustace. Madame Sara Balsamo is meant to be the immortal Madame Sara from* The Sorceress of the Strand *by the same writers. Sara was half-Indian and half-Italian. The name Sharita suggests that Madame Sara's mother was the daughter of the Thuggee priestess in Gardner Fox's* Woman of Kali. *Like Josephine, Madame Sara had blonde hair. Sara will play an important role in a story set after "Corridors of Deceit." After the end of that story, it appeared Josephine was slated for execution by the Black Coats. She will be reprieved through the intervention of Madame Sara, who will become Josephine's new superior in the Black Coats.*

My story has a loose continuity with "The Lady of the Black Gloves." I did not want to encumber the story with the full convoluted history of the Lupin-Cagliostro feud. Therefore, Théophraste Lupin, Arsène's father is never named despite the fact that he is clearly Sabine's father. He also is the unnamed burglar who stole Anna's pentagram. The same anonymity applies to the cameo of Irene, the anti-heroine of La Residencia. Any reader unfamiliar with my earlier stories will merely conclude that the nameless girl with the pentagram was simply Josephine's lover. There are no references to the conflict between the two women.

Josephine assumed that Sabine learned she was Théophraste's daughter from Leonard. Josephine is absolutely wrong in her suspicions. A future store will reveal the source of Sabine's information.

Satanas will use Sabine's diary against her and Josephine in a future story set after the events of "Corridors of Deceit..."

Rick Lai

Jean de La Hire's Nyctalope presents us with a unique challenge in the history of pulp heroes. When France was invaded by the Nazis, La Hire–and therefore, his character, Leo Saint-Clair–opted for collaboration. After the War, the writer was arrested and briefly jailed, while the Nyctalope appeared to vanish, except for one final, heavily edited novel published by La Hire's son-in-law in 1954. La Hire passed away in 1956. That story allegedly took place in 1946, but was probably written earlier. The notion of a hero like the Nyctalope finding himself on the wrong side of History was briefly explored in the short-short "Marguerite" published in Tales of the Shadowmen 2; *it is revisited and expanded upon by Roman Leary in this tale that illustrates how no one emerged unscathed from the crucible of World War II...*

Roman Leary: *The Heart of a Man*

Buenos Aires, 1947

Giraud was enjoying a café chico at *Las Violetas* when the hectoring voice of the Belgian piped up in his mind. *How can you drink that mud, Giraud? You should have a sirop de cassis! There is a drink to delight the senses!*

Giraud cringed and set down his cup. "Why don't you leave me alone?" he muttered to himself. He quickly glanced around when he realized he had spoken aloud, but the other patrons of the elegant coffee house were lost in their own affairs and, to his relief, paid him no heed.

More and more of late, Giraud found himself thinking of the Belgian. It disturbed and annoyed him. He had spent the better part of 20 years trying to forget Hercule Poirot, and now, here, the man was, occupying his mind with all the force and vigor of a memory made only the day before. Worse, he was beginning to carry on active conversations with the little bastard, which was making him worry for his sanity.

Tut, tut, Giraud, the Belgian chided. *You should welcome my wise counsel. Perhaps some time in my presence will serve to elevate your modest intellect.*

Giraud ground his teeth. Modest intellect! He had once been called the greatest detective in France, hailed as a modern Vidocq, but then...

Ah, but then came the Renault case. You were overconfident, mon ami. If you had listened to Papa Poirot, you would not have arrested the wrong person. What a famous blunder! How fortunate I was there to save that young man from the guillotine!

Giraud closed his eyes and began to rub his temples. "That wouldn't have happened," he whispered. "I would have seen the truth in time. I would never send an innocent man to his death. Never…"

"Are you ill, Monsieur Giraud?" a man's voice asked. He was speaking English, unusual in this city…

"I'm quite all right," Giraud snapped. He was embarrassed, and was about to tell the man to leave him alone when he was silenced by a sudden chill.

The man had called him by name.

Giraud had been living in Buenos Aires under an assumed name since 1945. There were only two people in Argentina who knew his true identity, and neither of them owned the voice he had just heard.

Giraud slowly opened his eyes. Standing before him was a tall, powerfully built man in a gray double-breasted suit. He was pale, square-jawed and clean shaven, with a wiry crew-cut that gave him a military air. His black eyes, as round and cold as a shark's, regarded Giraud with analytical detachment. Giraud was a big man, but something in those eyes made him feel small and vulnerable.

Compose yourself, Giraud, Poirot said in a soothing, paternal tone. *Let us draw this fellow out, eh? Find out how much he knows.*

Giraud had to admit it was a good strategy. He smiled and chuckled, relaxing into a pose of friendly nonchalance. "I'm afraid you've mistaken me for someone else, sir," he said. "My name is…"

"I have not made a mistake," the man interrupted. He spoke in a slightly reproving tone that, despite its gentleness, hummed with an undercurrent of menace. "You are Henri Giraud, formerly of the Sûreté Nationale. During the German occupation, you worked with SIPO-SD Section Four, the Gestapo in France. When the war was over, you fled here to escape prosecution as a collaborator."

Our question is answered, Poirot said. *He knows everything.*

Giraud's heart was hammering. God, what a disaster! Perhaps he could brazen it out. "Of all the impertinence!" he sputtered. "How dare you insult me with these slanderous allegations! And in a public place, at that!" He made an expansive gesture and took the opportunity to glance at the exits. Had those men been there before? It was a warm day, but they were both wearing long coats… He reached into his own jacket and searched for the comforting heft of his only friend, a .25 Beretta. He found nothing but lint.

"Your pistol was removed earlier by one of my associates," the man said, his dark eyes boring into Giraud's skull. "I am sad to say that it was done rather easily."

Giraud felt his front of righteous indignation cracking from the pressure of his rising panic. "I don't have to tolerate this…this…" Words failed him. He started to rise, but the man held up his hand in an unmistakable warning. He then lowered the hand and Giraud, as if hypnotized, followed the motion back into his chair.

"Are you going to continue with these childish theatrics?" the man asked. "Or would you like to stop while you still have some modicum of dignity?"

Giraud opened his mouth to protest, but the words died on his tongue. He sighed heavily, gathered his nerve, and met the stranger's penetrating gaze. "I'm afraid you have the advantage of me, Monsieur...?"

"I have the advantage of most people," the man said. He sat down in the chair opposite Giraud and gestured for a waiter. He ordered water with lemon and stared silently at Giraud while he waited for it to arrive. Giraud began to feel like a naughty schoolboy who had been summoned to the headmaster: *What is this I hear about you working with the Nazis, Henri? And don't tell me everyone else was doing it because that's not an excuse!*

"Do you find something amusing?" the man asked as his water was set before him.

"Merely a random thought," Giraud said. "I would be surprised if you didn't know exactly what it was, since you seem to find me so completely transparent."

"That sounds vaguely like a gibe," the man said with a cold smile, "but it's closer to the truth than you think." He took a sip of his water. "While I may not be able to read your exact thoughts, I certainly know the spirit of them. I have always been able to see into the heart of a man, to know if he is brave or cowardly, honest or a liar."

"Dare I ask what this penetrating insight tells you about me?"

"Your immediate terror at being recognized tells me that you live in the more or less constant fear that you will be caught and punished for your misdeeds. Logically, this fear is absurd. Your contribution to the Nazi machine was fairly inconsequential and hardly merits the sort of aggressive pursuit that would follow you here. You are intelligent enough to know this, but the fear remains. Why?"

Giraud drank some of his coffee. It was beginning to get cold.

"I submit to you that your fear is merely a symptom of your guilt," the man continued. "This is unfortunate. I could use a man like you, but I have no patience for those who indulge in..."

"Stop," Giraud said. "Stop right there. What did you mean by that? That you could use a man like me?"

The man tilted his head slightly. He considered for a moment, then said: "It doesn't matter. I am afraid this interview has been a waste of your time and mine. There is no room in my organization for a man burdened with a conscience." He began to rise from his chair. "Good day, Monsieur Giraud."

"Wait," Giraud said in a firm voice. "If you really know so much, then you must know how I have made a living for the past two years."

"Of course," the man replied. He was standing now, clearly impatient to leave. "You are a private detective."

"Oh, I call myself that," Giraud said with a derisive laugh, "but I'm really just a strong-arm, a hired thug. I earn enough to keep myself fed and clothed, but that's about it."

"What is this supposed to mean to me?"

"What do you think it means? It means I am in need of money, and more than that, a challenge!"

The man looked at his watch. "So?"

Giraud wanted to grab the man's lapels and shake him, but he forced himself to be still, to speak in an even tone. "Well, Monsieur, you have gone to the trouble of seeking me out. I think you should at least let me hear your proposition. If my scruples balk at it, then dismiss me for a fool and leave me to languish in my so-called guilt."

The man looked at Giraud. Was that renewed interest lurking in his eyes, or merely contempt?

He is looking into your heart, mon ami, Poirot said softly. *What do you think he sees there?*

The man gave a small nod. "Very well," he said. "Allow me to introduce myself, Monsieur Giraud. My name is Ernst Stavro Blofeld, and I would like to hire you to solve a murder."

In dreams, they love him still...

The party is one of his wife's usual triumphs. Laure can always find the perfect balance between good taste and gross ostentation. The guests practically stand in line to lavish him with praise for the food, the wine, the extraordinary beauty of the hostess... and he cannot stop wishing he were somewhere else.

It has been several months since his confrontation with the power-mad Lucifer; months of newlywed bliss and stupefying boredom. He finds himself secretly hoping for some urgent message, some desperate summons to action that will place him at the center of an epic struggle against a deadly foe. Home and hearth and the marriage bed are all well and good, but for a man such as he, they can never be enough. Perhaps he simply was not made for this sort of domestic...

His thoughts are interrupted by an insistent tapping of silver against crystal. "Your attention, everyone," says a loud, authoritative voice. "Your attention, please." The crowd falls silent as someone steps unsteadily onto a chair. It is his old friend, Prillant. The banker's face is flushed with wine and bonhomie as he addresses the crowd. "I have just learned that our host, Monsieur Leo Saint-Clair, is a proud father-to-be!"

There is an eruption of applause and cheers. Leo waves to the gathering, twisting his grimace into a smile. Why did Laure have to start telling people so soon?

"Hear, hear!" someone in the crowd shouts. "Give us a toast, Prillant! A toast to Leo!"

Prillant grins and raises his glass. "To Leo! A young man who embodies the best of France, and therefore the best of the world! Who can match his heroism, his brilliance, his courage?"

"No one!" they respond, almost in unison.

"Who can boast of a stronger heart?" Prillant asks.

"A heart of steel!" someone shouts back, and Leo unconsciously reaches to his chest. His heart is mostly plastic, actually. But there is steel there as well. It is the only one of its kind, a life-saving gift from a medical genius, a man now long dead. Leo often closes his eyes in the night and concentrates on listening to the electric hum beneath its rhythmic pounding. He sometimes wonders if it will beat forever.

"And who, I ask, can match his extraordinary vision?"

They get the pun and reward it with laughter. His unique ability to see in complete darkness is what has earned him his alias, a name by which he is known around the world.

"To Leo Saint-Clair, better known as the Nyctalope! May he give France many fine sons!"

"To the Nyctalope!" they shout.

He raises a glass in acknowledgement and braces himself for the inevitable flood of congratulations, the endless hand-shaking and back-slapping. His eyes roam over the smiling faces, glowing with admiration, and he sees something that gives him pause.

It is the cool, sardonic gaze of a girl, one of the servers hired for the party. She is young–probably a student, most of them are–and astonishingly beautiful. She gives a small wave. Is that the glint of a wedding ring? No matter. He feels a connection, tenuous but nonetheless immediate and undeniable.

She understands, he thinks. He does not know how he knows this, but he is certain it is true. She knows he does not belong here, and she is amused by the irony of it.

Her full, red lips lift in a wry smile. He has just enough time to smile back before the first of the well-wishers come between them.

It takes a full 30 minutes to find his way to her.

And another ten to get her alone.

"It's a mistake to have your men wearing long coats in this weather," Giraud said. "The moment I saw them, I knew they belonged to you."

"Do you feel this knowledge gave you power over me?" Blofeld asked.

Giraud grunted and looked out the window. They were in the backseat of a sleek black Cadillac Sixty Special. It wasn't the most luxurious car that Giraud had ever been in, but it came close. Blofeld's minions–a pair of efficient automatons named Fitz and Carlos–were in the front.

Fitz, the driver, was handsome to point of absurdity. His blonde hair, chiseled jaw, and ice blue eyes were almost a caricature of Hitler's Aryan ideal. Giraud thought it was little wonder the man had survived the war. He had probably spent the entire time modeling for SS recruiting posters.

Carlos was younger and smaller, but Giraud thought he was infinitely more dangerous. Fitz seemed too aloof to think there could be any real danger to himself or his master, but Carlos' eyes were always moving; observing and cataloging everything and everyone around him. His long fingers compulsively clenched and unclenched, as if he were yearning to spot a potential threat so that he could have the pleasure of eliminating it. Giraud had not been surprised to discover that it was Carlos who had lifted his gun.

"You could be the best pickpocket I've ever met," Giraud had said when the little man returned it to him, empty of bullets.

Carlos' only reply was a sneer.

Tread lightly, Giraud, Poirot cautioned. *That one can barely contain his eagerness for violence. I would be wary of him if I were you.*

Well, you *are* me, Giraud silently responded. Or at least some noisome part of me, some demon of my subconscious...

Poirot a demon? Quelle idée!

Oh, for God's sake, will you just shut up!

"Did you say something?" Blofeld asked.

"No," Giraud said, with perhaps a little too much vehemence. "Tell me, where are we going?"

"Villa Soldati, one of the southwestern barrios."

"I know where it is."

"The murder was committed there, in a small apartment on Escalada Street. The victim was one of my employees, a fellow named Edouard Boucher."

"A Frenchman?"

"Yes," Blofeld affirmed, "a former collaborator, like yourself."

Giraud snorted. "Fond of that word, aren't you?"

"Does the term bother you?"

"I've been called worse."

"That doesn't answer my question."

Giraud sensed he was being tested. What the Hell did the man want him to say? "All right then, it infuriates me," he said defiantly. "I had a job to do and I did it. Crime in Paris didn't just disappear when the Nazis marched in, you know. Someone still had to investigate the robberies, the rapes, the murders."

"So your wartime activities were limited to routine police work?"

Giraud hesitated. "For the most part," he said.

Blofeld turned to him. "And the parts that weren't?"

Giraud turned back to the window.

"Fitz," Blofeld said, "stop the car at the next intersection."

"I helped them find Jews," Giraud said.

"I beg your pardon?"

Giraud turned and looked at Blofeld. "I helped the Gestapo hunt down and arrest Jews. At first, it was only a few, then more and more. Finally, it was entire families. Is that what you wanted to hear?"

"I wanted the truth. I require complete honesty from all of my subordinates."

"Well, now you have it. Do you still intend to eject me at the next intersection?"

"Eject...?" Blofeld's eyes narrowed. "No," he said. "I am curious to hear your opinion on this case. If you can give a suitable demonstration of your skills, I may take you further into my confidence."

"And if I disappoint you?"

"Then I will terminate our association."

Me, I do not like the sound of that, Poirot whispered.

Nor do I, Giraud replied.

He turned back to the window and watched the passing buildings, the bustling throngs on the sidewalks. The setting Sun cast a pulsing red radiance over it all.

The rising Sun shines through the curtains of Leo's small apartment on the rue Vavin. It warms his face as he lies on the bed, resting in a state of pleasant languor from his exertions the night before. A shadow passes over his eyes and he turns to see Nina, her exquisite form rendered in silhouette before the window.

"There are some men on the street," she says. "I think they might be Gestapo."

"So? They're everywhere in Paris these days. Come back to bed."

"What if they're looking for you?"

"Impossible. They don't know about this place, and even if they did, it wouldn't matter. They would only want me for some trivial assignment. I could put them off."

She turns to look at him, slightly amazed. "How can you be so cavalier? You speak of them as if they were harmless children, but if they ever decided you were no longer useful to them..."

He smiles at her. "They don't have the power to decide my fate."

The amazement fades into skepticism. For a moment she looks just as she did at the party, all those years ago...

She had been cheerfully cynical even then, and surprisingly unimpressed by his heroic reputation. This, of course, had only made her all the more alluring and soon he was applying the full force of his personality to seducing her. The conquest was inevitable, but no less satisfying for it. What followed was something of a surprise: He was never able to completely let her go.

In the intervening years, he had been through many wives and lovers, but she had proven to be a constant. When he wanted someone with whom he could share his moments of greatest triumph–or rare moments of failure–she always seemed to be the one he reached for. Even more than her sexual prowess, which was considerable, he was drawn to her by her fierce intelligence, and by a sense that there were passages of her soul that he could never travel, never claim.

He might even have married her, if he could have ever persuaded her to leave her lout of a husband. He was always baffled, and slightly piqued, by her stubborn refusal to divorce the man. That she felt guilt over her infidelity was perhaps understandable, but why should she punish herself by staying in a tedious union with an absolute clod? He has asked her this very question, many times, and the answer is always the same:

Because I love him, you fool. If you had ever really loved anyone yourself you would understand.

But I love you, he would sometimes protest.

Ha! You love pleasure, and excitement, and obedience. I give you these things, so you think you love me.

This last always came with a smile that lessened its sting, and was almost always followed by a touch that rendered further conversation impossible.

She is not smiling now, however. "Why do you do it?" she asks. "Why do you work with them? Do you really believe in them, in their ideals?"

"Does your husband?" He regrets the words as soon as they leave his mouth. It is a cheap evasion, and unworthy of him. He expects her to erupt with fury, but she merely sighs and sits on the bed.

"I tried to talk him out of it, you know. 'The *Milice* are nothing but lackeys for the *boche*,' I said to him. 'If you join those brutes, you will have sold your soul to the Devil.' But it was useless. 'You always think you're smarter than me,' he said. 'Even when we were children, you always thought you were smarter than me…' "

She trails off into silence, staring into some invisible distance. Then she slowly turns to him. "He is right," she says. "I have always patronized him, condescended to him. He says I treat him more like a mother than a wife. Perhaps if I had shown him more respect he would not feel that he had to…"

"Oh, he is an idiot!" Leo says, impatient with this nonsense. "He should listen to your advice. The *Milice* are the most hated *collabos* in the country. When the war is over, they'll be lucky if every one of them doesn't go to the guillotine."

"And what about you?" she asks, her voice rising. "What about the great and mighty Nyctalope? You've never really believed the Nazis could win, so why do you serve them?"

"I am a free agent! I don't *serve…*"

"Yes, you do!" she shouts. "You dare to judge my husband? You are the biggest *collabo* of them all!"

"You think I could do more good by running around in the woods with the Resistance? Don't be naïve. I despise this regime, but by working within it, I have saved hundreds of French lives!"

"Yes, and allowed yourself to become a propaganda tool for people who have slaughtered millions!"

He gawks at her stupidly. She has never spoken to him this way. No one has, in fact.

"You make me sick!" she cries, tears flowing freely down her cheeks. "You boast of your battles against men like Lucifer and Belzebuth, but what are they next to Hitler? Nothing! But do you raise a hand against the Nazis or their Vichy puppets? Oh, no. You might have to give up your fine house, and your fine car, and your..."

He slaps her. Not very hard, but hard enough. There is a moment of arctic silence, then, refusing to meet his eyes, choking with sobs, she quickly throws on her clothes. At the door, she turns to face him. "I used to worship you," she says in a quavering voice, the voice of a wounded child. "I pretended not to, but I did. I knew what we were doing was wrong, but I could never resist you, never turn you away..." She shakes her head. "I thought you were a hero."

He rises from the bed, reaching for her, but she turns her back and walks away.

He stares after her for a moment, listening to her footsteps recede down the hall. Is this the last he will ever see of her? Most likely, he decides, and the thought fills him with a sudden and profound sadness. He tells himself that this is absurd. He can easily find a replacement for her, a younger, more attractive...

He shakes his head. *Do not lie to yourself,* he thinks. *She was the only one left from the old days, the only one who hadn't fallen away. And now she's gone.*

He goes to the door and closes it. When he turns, he notices something on the nightstand, a glint of sunlight on metal. What is that? A necklace?

It is a locket. He opens it and sees two exquisite cameos; one depicting Nina, the other an image of her husband.

He smiles slightly. This is something she will want back. It will provide a face-saving pretext for her to call him, and when she does, he will do whatever it takes to make amends. They will apologize to one another, enjoy a passionate reconciliation, and things will be as they were before.

He is certain of it.

Fitz opened the door to the apartment and was unable to stop himself from gagging. The death stench that hung in the warm, stagnant air was thick, repulsive, almost tangible.

Giraud had known what to expect, and was able to maintain a mask of indifference. He noted with satisfaction that Carlos was looking green. Blofeld, however, remained a model of iron self control. *Smell something?* he might have said. *Why yes, now that you mention it. Is there a corpse around here, by any chance?*

There was. It was lying face down in the small living area, surrounded by Spartan furnishings overturned in almost artful disarray. The lean, sinewy frame was loosely clad in a cheap bathrobe, sodden and sticky with drying blood. Giraud stepped closer and his eyes widened. The man's hair had been cut away from his head, and none too gently. There were large, gory patches where the flesh had been hacked from the skull.

"Has anything been touched?" Giraud asked.

"Nothing," Blofeld replied. "Carlos discovered the body at approximately 8 a.m. He reported it to me immediately."

"Are you certain Carlos didn't kill him?"

The little man glared at Giraud, murder blazing in his eyes.

"I am positive he did not," Blofeld said blandly.

Giraud gave Carlos a benign smile. "Nothing personal, my friend. One has to explore every possibility, no?" He turned to Blofeld. "Has anyone spoken to the neighbors? I'm surprised they haven't called the authorities."

"The other tenants have been persuaded that *we* are the authorities," Blofeld assured him. "They were very cooperative with our initial inquiries. We have learned that there was a brief disturbance around midnight–some shouting, perhaps a cry of pain. The noises ended almost as quickly as they began and so no one took very much note of them."

Giraud had other questions, but he decided to delay them until after a thorough inspection of the scene. He gently turned over Boucher's corpse.

Beaten beyond recognition, Poirot observed. *The work of a hammer, perhaps?*

Could be, Giraud replied. Bruising around the neck indicates strangulation. What is that between his front teeth? Gold? Damned odd place for a filling. Oh well...

The left wrist is broken.

Yes, and the right arm is severely dislocated. His fist is clenched. I wonder if...

Giraud took out a penknife and worked at the fingers. It was a gruesome task, nearly impossible due to the rigor, but he managed to open the hand. Clutched in the palm, held so tightly that it cut into the flesh, was a locket on a broken chain. He opened it and held it up to the light.

Shell cameos, Poirot said. *Is the man our victim?*

I think so.

The woman, she is quite the beauty.

She must be a wife or sweetheart that he left behind. He must have been thinking of her as he died. Tragic, but no help to us.

Is that what you think?

I fail to see what else we can make of it. Here, let's examine the rest of the scene...

Giraud spent the next the next two hours exploring the apartment with exacting thoroughness. He picked, he crawled, he sniffed. He asked questions about Boucher's habits, his vices, his enemies. Blofeld gave polite, detailed, and uniformly unhelpful answers to all his queries. Boucher was dull and bellicose, but he had no real enemies. He drank, but not to excess. He liked women, but only prostitutes. He was a competent and reliable henchman who knew his role and performed it well.

"Did you consider him a friend?" Giraud asked as, lying prone, he inspected the fibers of a cheap rug.

Blofeld seemed genuinely nonplused. "Friend?" he said, as if he had never heard the word before.

Giraud rose to his knees. "Yes," he said. "Did you like the man? It's not such an odd question, is it?"

"He was an employee. I neither liked nor disliked him."

"Then why are you so concerned with finding his killer? Why not simply let the police handle it?"

"I see," Blofeld said with a nod. "Monsieur Boucher was a strong and capable fighter. Yet, in spite of this, someone came here last night and crushed him like an insect. I would like to meet that someone."

"For revenge?"

Carlos laughed. Blofeld silenced him with a glance. He turned back to Giraud and said: "Do not concern yourself with my motives. I would like to discuss your conclusions. Have you drawn any?"

Giraud stood up and brushed off his pants. "I do not believe this crime will ever be solved," he said.

"Why is that?" Blofeld asked, clearly displeased.

"According to you, this man had no friends, no enemies, and—outside of yourself—almost no acquaintances. There was nothing remarkable about his vices, his virtues, or even his personality. He was, in short, a dependable plodder."

"True enough, but I'm not sure I see your point."

"This man is a non-entity. Why would anyone want to mutilate him so?" Giraud pointed at the body. "What is the motive for this crime? Theft? Impossible. What little there is of value has not been touched. Passion? Excited by what, I may ask? Was someone jealous because he slept with their favorite whore?" Giraud made a face to show his opinion of the theory. "This leaves us with revenge."

Yes, it certainly does, Poirot interjected.

"Revenge for what?" Giraud continued. "The only person we can ask is lying there, and even if he could speak, I doubt he would give a satisfactory answer." Giraud shook his head. "No, my friends, this was the work of a random lunatic, a madman who, in all probability, will only be caught after he has killed many more in a similar manner."

A brilliant deduction, Giraud! You have outdone yourself!

"It is the only explanation. What else can account for this butchery? I have never seen anything…"

Go on, Giraud. This is most edifying.

Giraud was silent. He stared at Boucher, at the shorn, bloody scalp.

You were about to say you had never seen anything like it before, no?

Giraud walked over to the corpse, knelt beside it, and looked once more into the broken ruin of the mouth. He took out his penknife and worked at the shattered teeth, removing a small piece of gold. He held it close to his eyes, studied it for a long moment, then closed his hand around it with a sigh.

"Is there something you would like to tell me?" Blofeld asked with an edge of impatience.

"I was wrong," Giraud said.

"About what?"

"Everything."

Bravo! Now you are using your little gray cells!

The morgue attendant is an old man, but surprisingly wiry and athletic. His iron-gray eyes, the same shade as his thinning hair, look up from a clipboard at the sound of Leo's approach. They regard him first with curiosity, then suspicion.

" I know you," he says. "Your name is…"

Leo waves it away. "Please," he says. "I received a call. There is someone here. My address was in her things. My number."

The old man frowns. "Name?" he says, all business now.

Leo tells him, and the old man gives him a curt nod. He turns and gestures for Leo to follow. They walk between the rows of shrouded corpses. *So many,* Leo thinks. *Does this many die in Paris every day?*

They pass a pair of nuns praying over one of the bodies. Their breath condenses in the cold, their words turning to wisps of white vapor. Was the dead man a priest? Leo wonders. Did he live long enough to celebrate the defeat of the Nazis, to offer up a prayer of thanks for the Liberation?

One of the nuns, a frail young slip of a girl, glances up and notices Leo. He sees in her haunted eyes a light of recognition, which quickly darkens into smoldering ashes. There is an accusation in that gaze that confuses and angers him. He quickly looks away.

The attendant stops so abruptly that Leo almost bumps into him. "Here," the man says, pointing at a body wrapped in white.

"I want to see her," Leo says.

"I don't recommend it."

"I don't give a damn what you recommend."

"Suit yourself. Do you want the shroud removed or simply pulled back?"

"Remove it."

The man obeys and Leo feels the blood drain from his face.

Her head has been shaved. Her face–her sweet, beautiful face–is mottled and bruised. Swastikas have been tattooed on her breasts and stomach. Leo turns away, sickened by the obscenity of it.

"I warned you," the old man says, pulling up the shroud.

"So you did," Leo says, suppressing the urge to break the man's jaw. "Do you know anything about it, about this…" he gestures at the body.

"The *tonte*–the head-shaving–it's been happening a lot, you know. Now that the allies have driven out the *boche*, people want their revenge. Any woman suspected of being a *collabo* is in danger of losing her hair... and sometimes more."

"She wasn't a collaborator," Leo says.

"She was married to a *Milicien*," the man replies in a matter-of-fact tone. He is not looking at Leo. He is completely focused on re-wrapping the body. "There was a group of men. They broke into his apartment looking for him. She stalled them while he fled. They would surely have killed him if it wasn't for her."

Leo sees it play out like a film before his mind's eye. He watches the coward leaping out a window, leaving her there to defend him against the killers. He sees Nina staring at the door, watching it crack and buckle from the pounding of the vengeful mob. He imagines himself there, as if by doing so he could somehow change the outcome.

Run! he cries. *You still have time! Go to our place on the rue Vavin! You still have a key! They will never...*

No, she says sadly. *I cannot. If I don't slow them down, they will catch him.*

To Hell with him! Why should you sacrifice yourself for him?!

She gives him a wan smile. *Because I love him, you fool. If you had ever really loved anyone yourself, you would understand.*

The door collapses and they tumble clumsily into the room, shouting and snarling. They pass through him like the phantom he is, and set about their brutal work.

He is snapped out of his grim reverie by the voice of the attendant. "I'm sure they didn't intend to kill her," the old man says. He is smoothing out the white cloth, folding, tucking. "The *tonte* is more about humiliation than violence. She must have provoked them somehow. Perhaps she goaded them in order to give her husband more time to run away."

"You make it sound as if she brought this upon herself," Leo says. There is a warning in his voice, but the man doesn't seem to hear it.

"Perhaps she did," he says.

"Old man," Leo says, "you are very close to ending the day on one of these slabs."

The man does not look up from his work. "A fierce threat," he says quietly. "Was she one of your lovers? They say you have had many."

Leo is amazed at the man's gall. "What was it you said a moment ago, about goading and provocation?"

The man pauses to inspect the shroud. "You are right to be angry," he says. "I am being rude and insensitive. It is unforgivable that I should speak this way to a national hero." He chuckles softly. "You know, my son was a great admirer of yours. When he was a little boy, he used to say, 'Papa, when I grow up I will be just like the Nyctalope!' He thought you were the best man in France, even after you gave your allegiance to Vichy."

The attendant slowly lifts his head, and looks directly into Leo's eyes.

"My son," he says quietly, "was married to a Jew. At first, I didn't approve, but over time I learned to accept her, even to love her. They had two children, beautiful little girls. Would you like to know what happened to them, my son and his family?"

Leo says nothing.

"This woman had a better death than they did," the old man says. "I do not feel sorry for her. If you wish to kill me for it, then do so. If not, then leave. You have seen what you came here to see."

Leo turns on his heel and walks away into an all-consuming darkness.

Giraud stood at the door facing into the apartment. "The door was not forced," he said. "The killer was able to talk Boucher into opening it for him."

"We had surmised as much," Blofeld said.

Giraud ignored him. The scene was taking shape in his mind, almost as if he witnessed it himself. "They spoke for a moment, then the killer held this up to Boucher, held it before his eyes." Giraud lifted the locket. "Boucher grabbed it with his right hand. The links snapped, but part of the chain remained entwined in the fingers of the killer."

"What happened then?" Fitz asked, caught up in the moment. It was the first time Giraud had heard the man speak. He looked at the German with surprise, then almost laughed when he saw that Carlos and Blofeld were doing the same.

Well, do not leave him in suspense, Giraud, Poirot said.

Giraud nodded. "The killer caught Boucher's hand and gave his arm a violent twist." Giraud pantomimed the action, stepping into the role of the murderer. "Boucher's arm was dislocated. The pain was excruciating, but he tried to counter with vicious blow from his left. The killer, however, was too fast for him. He caught Boucher's fist and snapped his wrist with contemptuous ease."

Giraud could almost feel the bones crack beneath his fingers as he mimicked the deed. The sensation was uncanny, godlike. Was this how the Belgian felt when the pieces began to fall into place, when everything sharpened into almost painful clarity? If so, then he could almost forgive the man his arrogance.

"Boucher cried out in pain," he continued, "but only once. After that, things happened so quickly he barely had a moment to breathe. The killer grabbed him by the neck and sent a series of sledgehammer blows into his face. The pounding was so brutal that it actually drove a link from the chain–the chain still clinging to the killer's hand–between what was left of Boucher's front teeth. It remained lodged there until I pried it free a moment ago."

Blofeld picked at some lint on one of his lapels. "And then?" he asked, stifling a yawn.

Giraud stood over Boucher's corpse. "By now, the killer was in the grip of an uncontrollable, psychotic fury. He allowed Boucher to fall, then straddled him, pulled out a knife and..." He pointed at Boucher's head.

"Do you think the killer was a Red Indian?" Fitz asked. He was clearly impressed by Giraud's performance.

"What the Hell do you know about Indians?" Carlos asked.

"I read about them in Karl May," Fitz said defensively. "And I'll thank you not to take that tone. You have no right to..."

"Silence," Blofeld said. His voice was calm and even, but his men obeyed him as if he were Zeus bellowing from Olympus.

"The killer was a Frenchman," Giraud said.

Blofeld's eyes widened. Only a little, but they widened. "How do you know that?"

"Boucher's head was shaved in imitation of *la tonte*, a punishment meted out to women who had collaborated with Nazis during the occupation."

"That seems a bit illogical. Why would anyone do that to Boucher?"

"Because of this," Giraud said, and he held up the locket. "I thought this belonged to Boucher, but it was brought here by the killer. It was in his possession. I think the killer had an attachment to the woman represented in this cameo. I believe this woman was punished for her association with Boucher, and the killer was infuriated by it. He wanted Boucher to suffer the same way she did."

Blofeld stared at Giraud for a long, silent moment.

I don't think he is convinced, Poirot said. *Your theory is too weak. It covers all the facts, but it is ultimately just a series of melodramatic suppositions. Where is your evidence?*

"Well, are you going to answer me?" Blofeld asked.

"What?" Giraud said, blinking. "I'm sorry, could you repeat the question?"

"I said, where is your evidence?"

"I expect it to walk through that door later tonight."

Blofeld no longer looked bored or irritated. "Why do you say that?"

"I am employing an old theory," Giraud said with a thin smile, "the one which states that the killer always returns to the scene of the crime." He held up the locket. "Especially when there is something there that he wants back."

They keep him around for a while, pretending that things are the same. He is simply too useful to discard. They tell him his future is secure. *Just stay out of the public eye*, they say. *Time will pass and the people will forgive you.*

But I don't need forgiveness, he says. *I haven't done anything wrong.* The words hang flaccid in the air, sounding lame even to his own ears.

They only stare at him. A couple of them sigh and shake their heads, as if he were senile or insane. *Please, don't argue. Just do as we ask. Do that and everything will be all right.*

They are wrong. It is not all right. People have long memories and deep resentments, and one evening, some gray and faceless men in gray and colorless suits come calling.

In 48 hours you will be arrested, one of them says. *There is to be a trial, very public and very humiliating. If you would like to avoid this, leave immediately.*

Very well, he says. *If I am needed, I can be reached by my Loire Valley contact...*

The gray man holds up his hand. *We don't mean leave Paris,* he says. *Leave France. And never return.*

They walk away before he can recover himself enough to form a reply. Later, he will not even remember packing his bags, checking his guns, or setting the house on fire before driving away.

He travels far and goes through many identities and a great deal of money, and one night he finds himself in a dive bar in Buenos Aires, watching a man across the room chat up an attractive whore.

There is something very familiar about this man, something with unpleasant associations...

The man looks in his direction.

You.

The man looks back at the whore. Laughing. Drinking. Enjoying life.

I remember you.

The whore whispers something in the man's ear and he shakes his head, pulling out his pockets to show how little they contain. She shakes her head in disgust and turns away.

You son of a bitch.

The man shouts something after her, grumbles some unintelligible curses, then heads for the door.

Finishing his drink, Leo Saint-Clair, the Nyctalope, rises and follows him into the night.

Giraud stared at the door until his eyes were dry. He no longer smelled the death stench, although it certainly had not dissipated. All he could think about was Boucher's killer, and how badly he wanted the man to appear.

The watched pot, it never boils, Poirot said.

Maybe, Giraud acknowledged, but I don't care. I don't care about anything but seeing that door open.

And if it does, what then, my friend?

Then I will have been right, by God! And whatever happens after that is Blofeld's problem.

Blofeld did not seem to be in any suspense at all. He was, to all appearances, perfectly content to sit in the darkness facing the door, calmly waiting to see if Giraud's theory would bear fruit. Giraud did not know how long the man was prepared to wait, and he did not dare to ask. He and the others had not been invited to sit, and so they stood like sentries; Fitz beside the door, Giraud and Carlos flanking Blofeld. Blofeld's henchmen were both armed with automatics, but they had not seen fit to return Giraud's bullets. Under ordinary circumstances, Giraud would have felt naked and helpless, but now nothing mattered except the door.

The door...

The door to the apartment silently opened. A tall shadow stepped inside, and paused at the threshold. Giraud felt a trickle of sweat run down the side of his face. He and the others were concealed in the darkness, but the shadow acted as if it could see them.

Blofeld must have sensed it as well, for he chose that moment to speak. "Please come in," he said. "We are not your enemies."

"Then why are you pointing guns at me?" the shadow replied. "That doesn't seem very friendly."

"I think it's a sensible precaution, under the circumstances. May we talk?"

The shadow confidently walked into the room, picked up one of the overturned chairs, and sat down in front of Blofeld.

"Fitz," Blofeld said, "please close the door and turn on a light."

Fitz obeyed and Giraud was unable to prevent himself from gasping in astonishment. The man sitting before him was older than he remembered. His face was lined and careworn, and there was more than a hint of gray in the swept-back hair. The Mephistophelean goatee was a recent addition, and it leant his classical features a slightly sinister cast. The leather jacket draped over his muscular frame was, like his faded jeans, a far cry from the expensive, tailored clothes he used to be seen in. But, for all that, he was still instantly recognizable. He had once been among the most famous men in France.

"So," Blofeld said, "Monsieur Leo Saint-Clair. It is a pleasure to meet you."

"The pleasure is all yours," the Nyctalope replied. He crossed his arms and legs. He seemed completely at ease. "I see I was expected."

"We were expecting someone, not you specifically." Blofeld gestured to Giraud, who stood at his right. "The credit must go to Monsieur Giraud. He maintained that you would come here tonight."

Saint-Clair turned his eyes on Giraud. "You used to be with the Sûreté," he said.

Giraud was shocked. "You know me?"

"Only by reputation." He turned back to Blofeld. "Who are you?"

"Does the code name *Rahir* mean anything to you?"

Saint-Clair nodded. "An espionage network that operated during the war. What of it?"

"It was my creation."

"Good for you. It was very efficient, while it lasted."

"And very profitable. But my work didn't end with *Rahir*. In fact, I am currently putting together a group–a special executive, if you like–which will direct an enterprise far greater in scope and impact than any network that has ever existed."

"What does this have to do with me?"

"I would like for you to be a part of it."

Saint-Clair's mouth turned in a half-smile of amusement. "I'm not a spy," he said.

"I didn't come here looking for a spy," Blofeld said. He pointed at Boucher. "I came to find the man who did this. I wanted to meet a skilled and ruthless killer whom I could recruit for my organization; a man with an aptitude for terrorism...revenge...extortion..."

The Nyctalope's smile faded. "And you think I am that man?"

"I know that you have the instincts of a mercenary," Blofeld replied. "Anyone who has followed your career can see that."

"Is that so?"

"Oh, I am aware that you were once a well-known champion of the law," Blofeld said with a dismissive wave. "I'm sure that role that was both useful and expedient. I've played it myself, once or twice. However, I think the work you've done on Boucher is ample evidence that you're ready to dispense with that particular artifice. Why don't we move to some more congenial surroundings where we can discuss..."

"This has to be a mistake," Giraud said, shaking his head.

Blofeld looked up at him, his pale face growing red with anger. "Do not open your mouth again while I am speaking," he said. His voice was level, but only just.

"But this can't be right," Giraud said, unfazed. "This isn't... This man is no murderer! He couldn't possibly have done this!" He turned an appealing gaze on the Nyctalope. "Tell him," he said. "You're conducting your own investigation, aren't you? You're hunting a mad killer, and the trail led you here. This is the first time you've even been to this apartment, right?"

Saint-Clair's mouth opened as if he were about to speak, but nothing came out.

"Carlos," Blofeld said, "please silence this jabbering fool."

Carlos smiled and turned his pistol on Giraud. Saint-Clair leapt from his chair, but the little man moved like a cobra. He snapped the pistol around and fired a single shot into the heart of the Nyctalope. Saint-Clair dropped like a stone.

For a moment, they all stood frozen in tableau. Blofeld sighed and pinched the bridge of his nose. "Well," he said, "that was regrettable."

"I'm sorry, sir," Carlos said. "It was instinct. When I saw him move I..."

"There is no need for an apology," Blofeld said, rising to his feet. "I have serious doubts that he could have been turned to my purpose anyway. I could tell that he was still clinging to the shreds of his personal myth. I could see it in his heart." He turned to Giraud with a sneer. "As for you..."

He was interrupted by a stirring on the floor. He looked at Carlos. "Impossible," the little man said, stepping over to the Nyctalope. He leaned over the body. "That shot should have..."

He never finished his sentence. In the span of a heartbeat, Saint-Clair's hands had closed around Carlos' pistol, driving it up and back into the little man's mouth. There was a thunderclap of gunfire and the back of Carlos' head exploded.

Blofeld, with a speed that belied his hulking frame, grabbed Giraud and shoved him toward the Nyctalope, who was struggling to cast aside Carlos's body. Giraud fell over Saint-Clair, giving Blofeld a few precious seconds to get to the door. "Kill them!" he shouted to Fitz as he ran by.

Fitz fired and Giraud felt a blaze of white heat as the bullet took off the top of his right ear. He fully expected the next one to catch him between the eyes. He was raising his hands before his face in a futile gesture of defense, when he saw a small crimson hole appear on the German's forehead, and a spray of blood coat the wall behind him. Fitz, his face still set in the concentration of aiming, collapsed in a lifeless heap.

The Nyctalope rose slowly to his feet and looked down at Giraud. He pulled a handkerchief from his pocket and wiped his face, which was drenched in Carlos' blood. "It's good that you were in his line of fire," he said to Giraud, dabbing at his eyes. "That probably saved us both."

Giraud fought the urge to start laughing. He had never been so close to death, and his narrow escape had left him in a euphoric state that was close to hysteria. He jumped to his feet and grabbed the Nyctalope's hand, pumping it vigorously. "My God!" he said, grinning. "My God, but that was incredible! How did you survive that shot from Carlos? Are you wearing a bulletproof..." Giraud fell silent as he noticed the dark, spreading stain on Saint-Clair's chest.

"I will not die from that wound," the Nyctalope said. "My heart is mostly made of plastic. But there is steel there as well."

Giraud was awestruck. "We must get you to a doctor," he said. "Come, let us-"

"No," Saint-Clair said firmly. "I can take care of myself. But before I go, there is something here that belongs to me. Do you have it?"

Giraud began to feel lightheaded. "Something...? No, no, I don't know what you're talking about. Come on, you don't know what you're saying. We need to get you to a hosp..."

The Nyctalope's hand was suddenly at his throat. "That man said you knew I would be here tonight," he whispered. "If that's true, then you must know what I came for. Where is it?"

Giraud reached into his pocket and produced the locket. Saint-Clair released him and took it. He gazed at it for a moment, then dropped it into his coat. He turned and walked toward the door.

"You *did* do it," Giraud said, his voice shaking. "I didn't want to believe it, didn't want to think that you could…You beat that man to a pulp, mutilated him, and left him for dead. What kind of a man are you?"

The Nyctalope stopped. "What kind of man are *you*?" he asked without turning around. "A washed up old *collabo* working as a lackey for a terrorist. Who are you to judge me?"

Giraud's eyes were stinging, and his wounded ear felt as if it were on fire. "I'm nobody," he said. "A washed up old *collabo*, just as you say. But I thought you were better than me. I thought you were a hero."

Saint-Clair turned and looked into Giraud's eyes. His features softened for a moment, and Giraud saw him as he once was; a handsome young Charlemagne, immortal, invincible.

"I thought that too," the Nyctalope said with a sad smile. "I suppose we were both wrong."

A moment later, Giraud was alone with the dead men.

What do I do now? he wondered.

I will tell you, Giraud, Poirot said. *You thank the good God that you are alive, and you leave this place before you find yourself answering some very awkward questions.*

Giraud took his advice.

Removing the bullet is difficult and painful, but he manages. *I have survived far worse,* he tells himself, but that does not lessen the agony of each breath.

He lies on the bed in his small basement apartment, blood and sweat soaking through the bandages. There are no lights in that cool darkness, but he can see as clearly as if it were midday, so he keeps his eyes shut tight. Helped along by a generous amount of inexpensive liquor, he topples into a restless, fitful sleep.

The pain follows him into his slumber, and yet, in spite of this, there are times in the night when he smiles.

For in his sleep, he dreams.

And in dreams, they love him still.

Alain le Bussy is one of Belgium's most famous and prolific fantasy and science fiction writers. Alain contributed an Arsène Lupin story to Tales of the Shadowmen 1 *and returns with a Sherlock Holmes tale in which the Great Detective investigates some otherworldly matters...*

Alain le Bussy: *A Matter Without Gravity*

Devon, 1896

Lord Beltham was a disagreeable old man, prideful, quick-tempered, loud-voiced; in short, even more insufferable than his extraordinarily bad port. I began to regret having accompanied my friend Sherlock Holmes as soon as we had been introduced. Over the course of the following two days, the situation did not improve.

I did not understand how Holmes, usually rather proud and even a little arrogant himself, could have let himself be lured to this manor lost in the country, and then allowed Lord Beltham to treat him almost like a servant. Despite my title of doctor, I myself was considered to be merely the valet of the servant, and consequently, needed all my reserves of patience to not tell our host what I truly thought of him. It was only my loyalty to Holmes that restrained me, but I had dug deep into said reserves and I sensed that, sooner or later, I risked forgetting myself and saying something that would be completely unthinkable under ordinary circumstances.

It was perhaps for that reason that I agreed to accompany Holmes on a walk when he asked me that morning; for an hour or two at least, I knew I would be free of the company of the odious Lord Beltham.

We scarcely took the time to consume a hasty breakfast, composed of three cups of tea, a bowl of porridge, small sausages swimming in grease accompanied by two poached eggs, with some toast and decent marmalade, before we set off.

The weather was mild for the season. It had been raining and was misty; we could only see a few dozen yards ahead in the small hollow in the woods where Beltham Manor had been built. When we reached the top of the hill, we saw several neighboring hills, but the lower valleys remained concealed by the fog.

Holmes said nothing, striding along without bothering to slow down so that I could keep pace with him; with my shorter legs, I was experiencing some difficulties following him. I knew him well enough to know that, sooner or later, he was going to let me in on some new facts that he had divined, using me like a sportsman practicing the Noble Art by exercising on a punching ball. Still, no one envied the fate of that ball, struck ceaselessly, battered and bruised, never able to strike back.

It was, however, my condition, and I accepted it because Holmes had always taught me something about humanity; and the care of human beings was, after all, my profession and my vocation.

We started the descent towards the next valley. Holmes was now walking more slowly and I no longer needed to exhaust myself to follow him. I was able to review the notes I had made in my mind so far.

It had started four days earlier, when Mrs. Hudson, Holmes' landlady, had announced a visitor. As luck would have it, I was there, having taken my wife to her mother's house. The old woman was suffering from an ordinary sore throat, but mistook it for some kind of fatal affliction, which drove her to fits of anxiety. She was well cared for by her own doctor, however, and I had no wish to meddle. So I had decided to pay a visit to my friend.

The visitor was a tall, gaunt man of about 50. He told us he was Lord Beltham's butler. He gave an envelope to Holmes who then passed it to me. I unfolded the letter and read it, finding its tone and contents rather infuriating:

Mr. Holmes:

Chambers, my butler, has reserved seats for you and your servant on the express leaving Paddington at 1:23 p.m. and arriving at Exeter at 7:37 p.m. There, you will take lodgings at The Three Coats of Arms. My carriage will collect you tomorrow at 8:00 a.m. sharp and will bring you to the Manor where I shall see you. You may discuss your fee with Chambers on the way.

It was signed: *Edward, Lord Beltham.*

I nearly choked with indignation, at the way Holmes was being treated. I was expecting not an explosion of anger, for Holmes always kept a cool head, but at least some dry repartee that would leave no doubt as to the scorn he must have felt towards that outrageous missive. Yet, I was very surprised to hear him tell the butler that he would be on time at Paddington. He next made it clear that he had no servant, but that if his excellent friend Doctor Watson would be so kind as to accompany him, he would expect similar accommodation for him as well.

"Will you come with me, Watson? I might have need of your intuition."

At the time, my intuition was rather absent. However, because of the manner of Holmes' invitation, I could not refuse him. Besides, I had entrusted my practice to one of my colleagues for several days. Going with Holmes was also a way to guarantee that I would not have to see my mother-in-law. I therefore accepted.

Much later, when we were walking across the green fields of Devon, Holmes consented to enlighten me a little. I had unwittingly provided him with a vital clue when, after having read the newspaper, and just finished a cup of tea, I had remarked that Lord Beltham's butler–who would not be travelling with us, having been given only a third class ticket–seemed a little like an uneducated peasant.

"It's normal enough for a former cavalry sergeant of the Indian Army," replied Holmes.

"A former sergeant? You have spoken with him?"

"It would be unnecessary, Watson. It was enough to look at him as he stood waiting our replies: stiff, his feet together, as if he was reporting for duty before his captain."

"I see," I said. "But he might have been a private in another regiment."

"Not at all, my dear Watson. A private would have much rougher hands, from erecting palisades or digging trenches. Also, did you not notice the slight bent in Mr. Chambers' legs unmistakably pointing out to his serving in the cavalry?"

"Yes, indeed, but the Indian Army? And why couldn't he have been an officer?"

"An officer? And serve as butler to a miser like Lord Beltham, who let him go out with old boots, threadbare trousers and a summer coat when we're still in the midst of winter? Unlikely. As for the Indian Army... you only needed to take a deep breath to notice the smell of curry floating around that man. One does not often come across it in Devon and I think Mr. Chambers took advantage of his London trip to go out and eat his fill of that dish."

"All this sounds very convincing, Holmes, but the man is still uneducated, and his master's letter that I read to you was quite in keeping with the person who delivered it to us..."

"Don't think, my dear Watson, that it was Lord Beltham's letter which convinced me to come to Devon. I cannot, alas, reveal all to you, but it happened that yesterday, I was approached by a high-ranking officer, a specialist in balloons, who is pushing hard for the creation of a special military branch to be called the Royal Air Force..."

This time, I could not stop myself laughing.

"The... Royal... Air... Force! Since when have balloons been what could be called an 'air force?' Why not the Admiralty of the Air?" I suggested, jokingly.

My friend did not join in my hilarity. He looked at me very seriously for several seconds before speaking again, with the tone of a teacher lecturing a mediocre pupil:

"You must learn to read between the lines, Watson. When the next war breaks out, either with France–or more likely against the Kaiser–air combat will play an essential part in it. Last year, I traveled to Florence to retrieve a number of secret documents by Leonardo da Vinci concerning flying machines and parachutes, which would enable our troops to be dropped behind enemy lines and attack from the rear... but I have already told you too much. To return to my visitor, he informed me of the Minister's concern regarding a socialist writer whose studies intrigue him."

"A socialist writer? You don't mean that... Herbert... Herbert...?"

" Herbert George Wells, yes, Watson."

"I am familiar with his books," I said, "but I wouldn't call them proper literature."

"They're stories of machines travelling through time, animals turned into human simulacra... One will have to find a term for that kind of literature.[4] In any event, I had already decided to go to Devon, where Mr. Wells has settled, to investigate, but Lord Beltham's invitation, even if it lacks courtesy, came at the right time to present me with a more likely excuse, especially since Mr. Wells lives not far from Beltham Manor."

We were again surrounded by the thick fog of the valley. It was damp and I slipped on a round stone, which forced us to stop for a moment while I rested my ankle by sitting on a large rock.

"I can understand the Minister's interest in Mr. Wells," I said. "Especially because he is a socialist, with what's happening across Europe... but does it have anything to do with our... host?"

I had hesitated before employing the word 'host,' for if Lord Beltham was looking after us, it was in the most unwelcoming fashion. There was scarcely enough wood in our rooms to make a blaze and the meals–which he did not deign to take in our company–were composed of thin slices of roast lamb which had been cooked and re-cooked so many time that it had become as tough as the soles of my boots.

The question had been on my lips since our arrival. Holmes had had a face-to-face meeting with the Lord, to which I had not been invited, and since then, my friend had remained so discreet on the subject that I had not dared interrogate him. It was perhaps the pain running through my ankle which loosened my tongue. I briefly wondered if such a phenomenon was worth a letter to the Royal Society of Medicine.

"Beltham Manor has been the subject of some unexplained incidents. A few horses bolted in inexplicable panic. Some sheep were scattered across the moor and took hours to recapture. There have been other small incidents of the same kind. Trifles. He feels that, somehow, his new neighbor, Mr. Wells is responsible, but he has no proof. Consequently, he cannot complain to the local constable. Frankly, I would never have come down here if it hadn't been for our high-ranking friend and the mention of Mr. Wells' name."

---

[4] Thirty years later, Mr. Hugo Gernsback, originally from Luxembourg, but then living in North America, created the expression "science fiction" to describe this type of narrative. J.H.W.

I pointed out to Holmes that I, myself, did not have any "high-ranking friend." Then, we started again, except that I now limped a little. Luckily, we had hardly gone a hundred paces before we were forced to stop once again. When I say "luckily," I am of course referring to my own good luck, for our stop was not anticipated, and only caused by the fact that Holmes, who was walking in front, suddenly appeared to jump up in the air as if he had stepped on a trampoline. Then, he fell down to the ground rather heavily two paces further on. I pretended to not hear the oaths he uttered, however I promised myself to tell him later to be more careful about the type of places he chose to patronize in the East End. I rushed as quickly as I could to help him get up.

"Do not worry, Watson. No harm done, except to my pride."

"You'll need a change of clothes when we return to Beltham Manor, Holmes," I said, noticing the fresh mud soiling his good Scottish tweed coat.

"I'm pleased to see that you have taken my advice regarding developing your own powers of observation," he replied dryly.

He examined the ground and picked up a piece of bent metal, no more than a foot long and six inches wide, which he proceeded to examine carefully. He passed it over to me and I subjected it to the same examination without discovering anything special; other than that the object was out of place on the moor, there was nothing strange about it. I felt it with my hands and it was not slippery, making Holmes fall even more mysterious.

"Get rid of it, Watson. It would spoil my collection."

My friend started walking again and I followed him after throwing the piece of metal into a bush, so that no other walker should suffer the same type of fall. I thought of the closet in which Holmes kept a number of objects that had been part of his investigations: lighters, pipes, knives, fire-arms, etc. The bit of twisted metal indeed did not belong in that proud collection.

A few dozen paces further on we heard what soon became a veritable racket. Someone was hammering metal as if he were building a canon or a locomotive.

Then, we began to see flashes. The noise continued, increasingly deafening, accompanied by bright, red flames. Unpleasant smells attacked my nostrils. I wanted to turn back, for I suddenly remembered stories which my mother had told me when I was a child about the damned, Satan, and the fires of Hell.

"Come along, Watson. It's only a forge."

As Holmes spoke those words, I saw a dark mass tower above us. I could not stop from trembling. We were near to Dartmoor Prison and I imagined that we stood at the foot of its walls.

"I believe we have reached the home of Mr. Wells," said Holmes. "If anyone should ask, say merely that we became lost in the fog, Watson."

I did not say that no one would ever believe such a lie: Sherlock Holmes, lost? Impossible.

We knocked on the door and a young man, dressed in a rather disorderly fashion, came to open it. He had disheveled hair, his face was covered with soot, and so was his shirt.

"What can I do for you, gentlemen?"

"My name is Sherlock Holmes, and this is my friend Doctor Watson. We were walking in the area and became lost. Would you be kind enough, sir, to put us on the right road after–if this is not an abuse of your hospitality–we have your permission to quench our thirst?"

Our host hesitated a moment, frowning. I thought he was simply going to shut the door in our faces, when we heard a voice:

"What is it, Bedford?"

"Two lost passers-by, Mr. Wells. I am going to show them where to find the road and I shall be with you shortly."

"When it's going to rain? You're not thinking, Bedford. Let them come in."

This Bedford bade us to follow him, but the face he pulled was clearly visible; he was not pleased. The fellow walked in a strange manner, and I wondered if, despite the early hour, he had not been drinking spirits. He staggered slightly, then braced himself on a wall here and a piece of furniture there so that he could keep his balance.

We soon found ourselves in a not very impressive hall. No care had been taken of the decor when, more usually, the master of the house would establish his presence with a portrait or two, a hunting trophy or souvenirs of his university or army regiment. We were then taken into a far grander room, a drawing room, which was dominated by an intense light.

This surprised me and I instinctively looked around, sniffing a bit like a hunting-dog, without perceiving the odor which would indicate to me the method of lighting used, for there was not the least smell of oil, gas or wax. I decided that the brilliant flames that I saw above our heads must be electric.

I was not able to continue my examination much further, for the man who had commanded Bedford to let us enter was advancing toward us. He appeared to be about 30, with a balding forehead, and smiled while wiping his hands on a piece of cloth.

"Mr. Holmes! What an honor for me to receive your visit! Not forgetting that the honor is doubled since your devoted recorder, Doctor Watson, is also with us."

"And I was not expecting," lied Holmes coolly, "to encounter in this remote place an author as celebrated as yourself, Mr. Wells. I beg you to forgive our intrusion. However, we shall set out again as soon as the weather permits. We hope we have not caused you too much trouble."

"It is true that my friends and I are very busy. But lunch hour approaches and I would not be adverse to taking a small break. You will join us, of course."

The meal which was served to us was certainly not traditional, but very decent nevertheless. It consisted mainly of soft bread rolls cut in two into which was put a layer of minced meat and a slice of cheese which had melted in the cooking, plus some bits of salad and a lightly spiced red sauce. It was all accompanied by delicious thin crispy chips. Mr. Wells called them hamburgers and I supposed that this exotic dish was typical of the cuisine of this great place, but this was denied by the remarks of the table-companions without any precise origin being mentioned.

I spoke of table-companions, for apart from Wells, Bedford, Holmes and myself, someone named Cavor joined us, as well as another man whose name I did not catch. This turned out to matter not, as his friends addressed him with the nickname, "Traveler." From certain remarks Cavor made about his research and his students, I understood that he was a scholar of the science of physics, but he did not expand on this subject.

In fact, we spoke little, except to say nothing. The weather was, as always, an inexhaustible subject; foreign politics was also an area that offered little danger, since all six of us were loyal subjects of Her Majesty. However, I quickly established that Mr. Wells and his friends were not the least bit interested in recent developments in our colonial conquests or of the tensions which grew ever large with France or the Kaiser. They were a bit like those monks who live so cut off from the world that they are mostly ignorant of the great events which shape it.

I permitted myself to compliment Mr. Wells not only on the excellence of the meal but also on the almost magical use he was making of electrical energy.

"I owe this to my friend, the Traveller. And it is not just the lighting, Doctor. Do you know that the meal you enjoyed was cooked by electricity?"

I noticed that the Traveller frowned slightly, but Mr. Wells took no notice and set about explaining to us that the electricity which lighted us was produced by great propellers moved by the wind and which we had not seen on our arrival because of the fog.

After smoking an excellent cigar with our hosts, we returned to Lord Beltham's Manor, guided to the road by Bedford who continued his staggering. We knew perfectly well where we were, of course, but it was necessary to remain faithful to the lie used by Holmes to get into Mr. Wells' house.

We returned directly to Beltham Manor, making a slight detour to Two Bridges and more precisely its Post Office, from where Holmes sent several telegrams. Once at the Manor, we retired to our rooms to change, for the damp of the fog had penetrated our clothes. It was only 4 p.m. and I was wondering if I could take a short therapeutic nap when there was a knock at my door. I went to open it and found myself nose-to-nose with Holmes.

"I need you, Watson," he said in going over to sit in one of the two arm-chairs without bothering. with his customary brusqueness, to wait for my invitation.

"I am at your disposal, Holmes. What are you suffering from?"

He laughed.

"It's not in that way that I have need of you, my friend. My health is perfectly fine, I assure you. No, I am soliciting your assistance to help me think."

It was not the first time; my friend often used me thus. He had often told me that what I had neither seen nor heard was very revealing, and I was always unsure of whether this was a compliment or a jest.

"What remains in your memory of our visit to Mr. Wells, Watson?"

I spoke to him of the house, of the austere decor, of Mr. Wells himself, of Cavor–mentioning that he must be a scientist–of Bedford and his strange walk, then of the Traveler, who had not mentioned at any time any of the lands he had traveled to. I also spoke, naturally, of the electricity, and I even thought to mention the hamburgers. Holmes had his eyes closed and someone who did not know him well would have thought that my words had sent him to sleep, but I knew it was nothing of the kind. I had scarcely finished when he half-opened his eyes and started to fill his pipe. It was only after taking two or three puffs that his face became truly animated.

"That is not bad, Watson, even if there was much you did not see, and you did not understand all that you did."

"But I'm sure you're going to explain it to me, Holmes!"

"You have not mentioned the racket which guided us towards Mr. Wells' house, for example; a noise resembling that which is produced by a mechanic's workshop or a forge. Bedford was covered with soot or grease and the two others also, although they took time to wash in a perfunctory manner before joining us, which was noticeable because their skins were pink and a slightly irritated from being scrubbed."

He was perfectly right, but this detail, which had not escaped me, had not seemed worthy of mention.

Holmes took several pieces of paper from one of his pockets. Seeing there the mark of the Royal Mail, I understood that he had already received replies to the telegrams he had sent. I was burning to know about these responses, but he contented himself with putting them on the little table that separated us.

"Mr. Cavor was a professor but two or three years ago was excluded from the Oxford College where he taught. I do not know quite why, but you understand that these institutions are very discreet about what happens within them. It seems that one of the theories he upheld shocked his colleagues, and I hope to discover what subject it concerned. Mr. Bedford is a painter–as yet little known–but, it appears, of promising talent. As for the Traveler, I have learned nothing of him, except that someone bearing that same nickname mysteriously disappeared last year after an experiment which his friends regretted but about which they could not say the least word."

"We know a bit more about those who welcomed us, but it seems not to advance us very far, does it?"

"That is true, Watson, but it is often necessary to progress a bit at a time if one wishes to reach the end of the road. Are you not astonished to learn that three gentlemen–a writer and philosophical socialist, a painter, and a university professor–should indulge in manual work that others would find off-putting? And without any help, for as I verified in the village, they live alone in that house and have not engaged any of the locals, not even a cook or a charlady."

"You're right, Holmes; it is indeed astonishing. If I may, I would deduce from it that they wished to keep what they are doing completely secret."

"Do, Watson, do. And, indeed, I have come to the same conclusion. But there is another detail you have not mentioned–the color of the ceilings."

"The color of the ceilings? That had not struck me, but the electric light was so strong that I tended to keep my eyes lowered. What color were the ceilings, Holmes? White? Cream?"

"Neither, Watson. They were blue, a clear intense blue, to such an extent that I, who was not as prudent as you, and who stared at those ceilings, had the impression of finding myself in the open air, under a starry sky. For there were stars, Watson. Not many, just a small constellation, three golden stars encircling a crescent moon–all also gilded, and these were present in several of the rooms: the hall, the dining room and the drawing room."

"And do you deduce something from this, Holmes?"

At that moment, a bell chimed on the ground floor. Holmes rose with a suppleness that recalled the tigers I had hunted on occasion when I was an army-doctor not far from Rawalpindi.

"I have deduced from that sound that it is tea-time, Watson. Let us see if our host does us the honor of joining us..."

For once, His Lordship did dine with us, which did not improve the meager fare of toast, butter, marmalade, and stale, dry biscuits that almost cost me a tooth.

Holmes recounted our expedition to Mr. Wells' residence providing an abundance of details describe the inhabitants. That took long enough that Lord Beltham was wearied without my friend even touching upon the particular information that he had collected about our hosts of the morning, nor even of the electric miracles to which we had been witness.

When our host arose, Holmes excused us from the evening meal, explaining that we had need to return to Two Bridges to pursue our inquiries. I was surprised that Holmes had not spoken of it earlier, all the more so as he had told me he had already questioned several inhabitants, but I made no comment.

We set off shortly thereafter, warmly clothed, for the cold of this late winter became worse with nightfall.

"I'm hungry as a wolf, Watson," Holmes confided in me as we reached Two Bridges, "The food at the Manor is far from nourishing."

The wolf was satisfied, as was I, when three hours later we left the village's single inn. We had relished salmon caught in the local river, followed by a leg of lamb garnished with mint sauce, washed down with mead–that beer derived from honey so similar to that on which our Celtic ancestors thrived. When the meal was concluded with pudding, it was nearly worthy of the repasts provided by my wife.

Flattered at having received so celebrated a detective as Holmes, the innkeeper put his carriage at our disposal for our return to the Manor. I was going to thank him in accepting his offer, for the journey had been tiring, when Holmes forestalled me:

"Thank you, but Doctor Watson, ever the Doctor, would tell you–if I let him–that there is nothing better for good digestion than a little walk in the cool night air."

I could only make the best of it, adding my thanks to those of Holmes and following him into the night, cursing in silence, for it was beastly cold.

I was not really surprised when we pursued our way along the small, stony track instead of turning into the entrance of the Manor of Roses. And, it was the same when half a mile further on we turned off to direct ourselves towards the house of Mr. Wells.

The fog had lifted during the course of the afternoon, and the sky was perfectly clear. At the bottom of the valley, like several around Two Bridges, sprouted trees planted by the owners of the charming nearby residences, whereas the hills retained their traditional aspect of short grass sprinkled with a few bushes.

With the exception of a few pines, these were broad-leaved trees, which meant that at that moment they had no leaves at all. I must say that the sight of those skeletal trees holding their emaciated branches to the sky, while not making me afraid, somehow gave birth to a melancholy deep within me. I don't know why, but Holmes' regular pace evoked the slow march that follows a burial. From that came the thought of death, then a pace further on, of danger:; thus the inclination was easy to follow. Fortunately, before I allowed myself be led too far on that path, we saw the somber mass of Mr. Wells' residence. It was calm, the din of hammers bashing metal had ceased. Holmes stopped 20 paces from the four steps mounting to the front door.

"What silence, Watson!"

I nearly regretted that he had spoken, thus breaking the silence he celebrated, but it was too late. As if a spell had been lifted, I suddenly perceived low noises which had not been audible before, but that but now seemed to me nearly as numbing as the fracas we'd heard that morning.

There was a heavy, regular rumbling that nearly masked the other sounds, apart from the rhythms which seemed to originate from the interior of the house.

I saw that structure in its entirety for the first time, as the fog had masked it in part when we were last there. The building had a strange shape, which reminded me of a picture of Russian towns that I had admired the preceding year in the National Gallery. Indeed, above the main part of the building where we had been received at lunchtime was raised a kind of giant dome which formed at least two of the upper floors. It was surrounded by two smaller cupolas, one very visible at the front of the house, the other half-hidden by the larger one.

It was a strange sight to find 200 miles from London, right in the heart of Devon, but the fashion at this end of century was for the most unbridled fantasy, with certain people reconstructing maharajas' palaces, while others built copies of Versailles or smaller versions of the pyramids. Why, then, should some barbarian not have the right to build his own miniature Kremlin? I wondered if he had been acting for Mr. Wells, but realized that he was too young for that and must have bought the folly from another, unless he had inherited it.

Holmes did not move and stayed quite silent. Evidently I could only follow his example, contenting myself with moving in my place to struggle against the cold and the numbness which was enveloping me. I forced myself to take note of all the details which surrounded us, so that I could provide correct replies to Holmes' eventual questions and also, in all honesty, to help the time pass more quickly.

I was struck by the beauty of the sky, one of the clearest I have ever seen. In London, even well beyond the limits of the conurbation, our so typical "pea soup" obliterates the details of the sky even in clear weather. Here there was none of that and the stars were more numerous and brighter. I played the game of trying to recognize constellations to the point of forgetting for a moment where we were.

"Don't fall asleep, Watson!" Holmes chided me, "Something is happening."

I showed myself more attentive, forgetting the sky and the constellations, but I could not see any movement, nor hear any new noise. I counted slowly to two hundred before daring to address Holmes:

"I hear nothing and I see nothing, Holmes. Are you sure that something is happening?"

"But of course!" he retorted with a slightly impatient tone. "Other than the sounds from within the house, silence reigns, do you not hear?"

"I have a very sharp ear, and I hear nothing, Holmes. Not the smallest squeak of a mouse, the hoot of an owl, the babbling of a brook, the snorting of a horse, nor anything else."

"You're quite right; one hears nothing of the kind. Don't you find that strange, Watson? Silence is not natural. Nature, by contrast, is greatly furbished with noise, like that of the wind in the branches, of surf at the foot of the cliffs, of the scraping of the wing cases of millions of insects–or even the snoring of sleepers. This is almost against nature, Watson."

Listening more intently to the quiet, I was now in agreement with my friend. But could we do anything to break the increasingly heavy stillness? Should we shout or sing? That would not have been behavior worthy of two gentlemen and besides, that would not guarantee the return of normal, natural sounds.

We waited for a very long time. Holmes persisted in his belief that something was about to happen, when no perceptible indication–at least for me–let us foresee what it would be. All he allowed was that, to ward off the cold, we could walk back and forth. We even made a complete circuit of the house without learning anything, other than it was extended at the rear by an area that was totally surrounded by a high wall. Holmes approached it and struck a lighter giving birth to a flame that only burned for a few seconds.

We finished making the tour of the building and we found ourselves back where we had started, in front of the door. The walk had warmed me up a bit, but had evidently not dissipated the fatigue I was feeling. As for Holmes, he seemed as bright as a button. I did not dare complain, nor suggest that we return to Lord Beltham's. All that remained was to wait in silence until my friend decided to act.

The wait lasted until dawn. I gave way to impatience after a while and asked Holmes what we were waiting for, and he just said that we were waiting for something to happen, then intimated to me to remain silent. The second time, he whistled with impatience, proposing that I return alone to our host, which I refused in the most vehement manner, for naturally I was not going to abandon my friend alone in the night. I did not tell him that I was not much pleased by the idea of returning alone in the course of a night which I felt too charged in mystery.

When the sky became lightly tinted with grey in the direction of Mount St. Michael, the Cornish one, I started. I think I had fallen asleep on my feet, upright like a horse. Holmes was there, two paces from me, immobile, as if at attention. He must not have let himself be caught by sleep, but I did not think it good to ask him if anything had happened: it was clear that if it had been otherwise, he would have woken me.

I became aware that what had woken me were sounds coming from the house. The sounds were signs of life, and all the windows were becoming illuminated one after another.

Above our heads the sky was lightening further and the stars were dimming, winking out one by one. The birds began to sing and a light breeze stirred the branches, creating another kind of song. I had to abandon Holmes for a few moments to empty my bladder behind a nearby bush. When I turned back towards him, he had disappeared.

I forced myself not to panic, but nevertheless I was worried. I did not think I was in the least danger, but I was alone. I wondered what could have happened to my friend. Had he entered the house? Should I follow him? Had someone kidnapped him? And in that case, where could he have been taken, except into the dwelling of Mr. Wells?

I confess that I dithered for more than a quarter of an hour. I had, however, taken the decision to go and search for–and maybe help–Holmes, and I returned to the bushes, finding a dead branch that would serve as a club, and I was returning towards the steps when I was startled by a shadow; I was about to use my club when I recognized Holmes. I lowered my improvised weapon and sighed with relief.

"Now then, Watson, do you take yourself for a caveman?"

"I was afraid for you, Holmes, and I was about to go in search of you."

"I appreciate the attention, my friend, but I was running no danger greater than that of facing some nasty brambles," he replied.

Perhaps he would have elaborated if, at that moment, the surroundings had not seemed to explode. I jumped and I think that even Holmes, in spite of his self-control, did so as well. Stupidly, I brandished the improvised club I was still holding, feeling ridiculous after barely a few seconds.

Nothing happened, apart from the hammer blows which had restarted more strongly than ever, as they had when we arrived on the spot the day before. We ran to the rear of the building, and there the din moderated. Therefore, it did not come from the enclosure surrounded by the high wall.

We returned to the principal facade.

"Watson, I'm going to try and enter. You stay here, don't move under any pretext. However, I authorize you to take flight if you feel your life is threatened."

Take flight? I was hurt that my friend could think that I would retreat while he was thinking only of advancing. I wanted to tell him that I would never flee, but he was already well on the way to Mr. Wells' house and I have to admit that I had not made the first step to follow him. Then I calmed myself; after all, had he not given me a position to hold? My years in the Indian Army had taught me that the strength of armed forces lay in discipline and that a superior's orders must always be obeyed. And in a certain way, Holmes was my superior.

Keeping still did not stop me from observing. Besides, I realized that my mission was here. I saw Holmes climb the few steps and knock on the door. This opened several moments later and I saw a silhouette which must have been that of Mr. Wells. They exchanged a few words. I could not hear them, but in the increasing daylight I could see their lips move. Holmes entered, but the door remained ajar. Nothing was stopping me from joining them, except the orders I had received. I resisted the temptation, fixing my gaze on the door and mentally counting the time which was elapsing.

My countdown was approaching 20 minutes. I had not taken my eyes off the door, in spite of the ever more violent shocks which were shaking my body. Then suddenly, I was rocked by an absolutely impossible event. It was not only a mental shock, but a terrible squall knocked me over. I fell in such a brutal manner as to lose consciousness. It was only later that I thought of an article I had read in *The Lancet*. It was not really medical, and surely was almost charlatanism; it was a translation of an article published in Vienna by a doctor whose name I have forgotten. He was studying the mind's function rather than that of the body and claimed that we could be struck with blindness or amnesia when our mind refused to admit the truth of an event to which we had, however, been witness.

"I say, Watson. Are you having a nap, when it's not yet nine o'clock?"

I opened my eyes and quickly shut them again, for the light was unbearable. Some moments later, I separated my eyelids. The blue of the sky was still as painful to look at, but by good fortune, a shadow came to mask it and I recognized my friend's face which, instead of being composed as usual, seemed to me to show worry... Worry for me! That gave me the strength to react and try to stand.

"Careful, Watson! I shall help you."

Holmes put a hand on my shoulder and some moments later, I was upright. I was conscious of the presence of Mr. Wells several paces from us, then of the house, which now had a very different aspect. I turned my head. I wanted to speak, but the words would not come from my lips. Holmes was aware of my state better than I was. I think he made a sign to Mr. Wells, then took my arm and led me down the path in the direction of the track.

I lived the following hours as if in a dream, or more properly, a nightmare. I remember being returned to the Manor and of having briefly encountered Lord Beltham. Holmes gave him a succinct report of our research, assuring him that his neighbor would not trouble the peace of the moors in the future, and that, in total, this matter was without gravity.

Next, we spent some time in a carriage and its shakings sent me to sleep. There must have been other facts, but I did not succeed in remembering them. The blue sky of dawn did not cease to haunt my thoughts.

It was the lessening of the jolts and calmer rhythms of the rails that finally woke me. I stayed a while between two states, contemplating the landscape which unrolled before my eyes. The fields, the sheep looking up, the hills with the great outlines of horses traced in the chalk... We had left Devon, we were crossing Dorset, we were returning to London, and I was still alive!

"You're finally back with us, Watson! You have taken your time about it, my friend."

"I don't know what happened, Holmes."

"If it reassures you, neither do I. I invented something to pacify Lord Beltham, but it leaves me with a bitter taste of defeat."

"I mean that I remember having seen something impossible, but I don't know what it was. I have the impression of a hole in my life, as if part of my past has been stolen. A minute or an hour, I don't know even that much for certain, and I admit it bothers me strongly."

Holmes looked at me for a long moment without saying anything, drawing on his pipe until it had burnt all the tobacco it contained.

"There is perhaps a means of knowing, Watson. At least if you will allow me to try an experiment."

"Have at it, Holmes. I have confidence in you and I wish to get to the bottom of things."

"Take up something with which to write first, Watson."

I always have a notebook and pencils well sharpened for the task and I installed myself in front of the table of our compartment. I then saw Holmes take his watch from his waistcoat pocket and make it swing before my eyes while he spoke to me in a calm and soothing voice...

In my mind I saw Holmes enter into the house, in response to Mr. Wells' invitation. Then the wait had started and I set myself to count the time that elapsed. I had learnt to count off the numbers almost exactly to the rhythm of seconds during an earlier adventure. I had the impression that it had been hours, but I was scarcely at 1227 when a deep crackling resounded; its intensity was such that it far surpassed the blows that had rung out until then. I heard a cry, and then a voice shouted: "Good luck fellows!" and it was then that the impossible happened. It was so unimaginable that my eyes refused to see and my mind repressed the information.

The cupolas which covered Mr. Wells' Russian-style house began to rise into the air. I saw an arm come through an opening in the larger one and wave a handkerchief. Seen from below, it was clear that the cupolas were, in point of fact, spheres. The three small ones were linked to the larger by tubes of three or four feet in diameter. I suppose that one could, by bending or creeping, pass from one sphere into another.

The four spheres continued to mount into the more and more intensely blue sky, in a leisurely fashion, like a group of hot-air balloons linked together. The sun gave them a golden tint and with altitude caused the largest of them to resemble a crescent moon surround by three smaller ones which were no more than bright points the size of a star.

Then the distance blended all four into a single burst of light.

And that burst itself disappeared.

The waiter passed us announcing the last sitting before Paddington. I succeeded in detaching my gaze from the words I had written and of which I had just made sense in order to ask him for double brandy. Holmes did the same. He must have been particularly shaken, for, in general, he hardly drank as it harms the concentration which he always requires.

"I read the words before you, Watson. You will excuse me, I hope. For my part, I saw nothing of all that, as Mr. Wells was talking to me of a novel he has in progress, a story of a scientific genius who tries to give a human soul to animals. Then there was this crackling that you mentioned, then some cries, and Mr. Wells shouted 'Good luck, fellows!' as you yourself heard. He kept me for three or four minutes longer before I could free myself, only to find you stretched on the ground, which, I admit, strongly shook me."

"You did not see the flight of the spheres?"

"No, Watson–and even if I had, is it something I can put in a report to the Minister? Fortunately, I have something more concrete, which I shall dress up in neutral enough terms to be acceptable. Let us see what they make of that!"

Holmes then opened his travel bag and took from it an object swathed in an old copy of *The Times*. He unwrapped it and put it on the table. It was only a shapeless bit of metal. I recognized it as the one that had caused his fall and that Holmes must have gone to recover from the bush where I had thrown it. He next took his pistol and put it on the end of the metal piece. Or rather, he tried to, for the pistol persisted in floating an inch or two above the metal, then drifted slowly and it was only when it reached the limit of the small plate that it fell back onto the table.

"Holmes! This is an extraordinary discovery. I understand now how it was that you fell; when you stepped on this piece of metal, you weighed absolutely nothing. It is of great importance! And yet, you told Lord Beltham that it was a matter without gravity..."

"Calm yourself, Watson, or you shall have a stroke," Holmes replied, rewrapping the bit of metal. "Besides, think; did I do anything but tell Lord Beltham the absolute truth?"

Original title: *Une affaire sans gravité*
Translated by John Francis Haines & Randy Lofficier

This is yet another story written for the French Madame Atomos reprint series. For the most part, it is meant to explain how, after having seen her organization destroyed and being herself on the run in the "last" volume of her original series in 1970, Madame Atomos was able to effect such a flamboyant return in the final novel, belatedly published in another imprint in 1979. In it, André Caroff' deadly heroine meets with yet another archetypal Asian mastermind from French popular literature: Monsieur Ming, a.k.a. The Yellow Shadow, the archenemy of Bob Morane. But as always with Madame Atomos, not everything is what it seems...

Jean-Marc Lofficier: *Madame Atomos' Holidays*

Grand Bahama, January 1976

> *There is no rest for the wicked.*
> Isaiah, 48:22

"Your problem is that you never go on holidays," said Madame Atomos.

"I beg your pardon?" replied the Yellow Shadow.

They were both relaxing in their chaises lounges on the private beach of the magnificent Xanadu Beach Resort on Grand Bahama island. The weather was perfect ; the turquoise blue sea made a striking contrast with the immaculate white sand that was raked every morning by the *boys* of a palace which, once, had counted Frank Sinatra, the Rat Pack and Cary Grant amongst its guests.

A light breeze gently caressed the palm trees, which cast their shadows over the beach-goers and kept the temperature wonderfully cool for the season.

Madame Atomos delicately took a sip of her pineapple rum cocktail, which she had been nursing since she had come on to the beach to join her occasional associate. She had gestured to her usual companion, the hulking Isadori, to go and play in the water while she talked business with the Yellow Shadow. She wore a striking black bikini with as little fabric as the law allowed, which emphasized her splendid figure. But she entertained no illusion as to the power of her feminine charms over the stone-faced Mongol. Madame Atomos knew Monsieur Ming well enough to know that he was entirely invulnerable to her sex appeal.

They had agreed to meet at the Xanadu. In the past, her organization had lent assistance to the Yellow Shadow, in 1965 in San Francisco, when Ming had established his base in the underground city of Kowa, and later, in Africa, to help him spawn his deadly butterflies. In exchange, Ming had pretty much let Madame Atomos have a free rein in America and had given her financial support whenever he could.

"You're always working," explained Madame Atomos. "Constantly coming up with new schemes, which are then invariably crushed by that insolent Frenchman. This creates a permanent stress that must be very bad for your health."

"My health is fine, thank you," said the Yellow Shadow, rather testily, his robotic right hand clamping on his left to hide the slight shaking that had started to plague him recently.

"If you spent more time relaxing on holidays," continued Madame Atomos, "you would feel more rested when the time comes to launch your next offensive. Don't tell me that you don't occasionally feel like you're not as good as you used to be, or that you've been repeating yourself lately? Not that it doesn't happen to all of us eventually," she rushed to add, having noticed a quick, baleful look in her associate's amber eyes.

"So... What would you suggest?" asked Monsieur Ming after a pause.

Madame Atomos stretched like a big cat, boastfully displaying her perfect breasts and her long, smooth legs.

"Do as I do," she purred. "Find yourself a beautiful toy, a little corner of paradise and have some fun."

With a gesture of her manicured hand, she blew a kiss to Isadori who was still frolicking in the water.

"I don't think that's in my nature," sighed the Yellow Shadow with some finality. "I've come to tell you that I've experienced some financial reversals of late..."

"That Frenchman again?" inquired Madame Atomos, whose eyes pointedly stared at the Mongol's left hand which was trembling.

Monsieur Ming ignored her and continued :

"...Therefore I can no longer finance your organization. I know that you have suffered some major setbacks. However, because of my debt to you, I will give you the blueprints for a new type of quantum field generator that will enable you to build a new and better generation of transdimensional saucers."

"It's more than I would have dared to hope for," said Madame Atomos. "Thank you !"

Monsieur Ming got up. Even in black Bermuda shorts, he still looked like a dour clergyman.

"Are you sure you won't stay for dinner?" asked Madame Atomos.

"No. I'm expected in Macao."

The Yellow Shadow walked away.

Madame Atomos smiled. She had duped the Mongol, who was after all a potentially dangerous rival. Monsieur Ming had not suspected the real reason for her presence in the Bahamas.

She looked at the 13th floor penthouse of the Xanadu. For ten years, she had had various servants of hers surreptitiously administer a carefully prepared mixture of drugs to its occupant, who was also the Hotel's owner. Thanks to her efforts, he was now a full-blown lunatic, who barely weighed over 90 pounds, no longer cut his hair and his nails, and slowly agonized–but not without having discreetly transferred half of his vast wealth–$2 billion !–to her Swiss bank account.

Howard Hughes will be dead with three months, thought Madame Atomos, *and with his money, I will rebuild my organization and be even more powerful than before!*

As if she had the time to go on holidays!

The character of the Phantom Angel–in reality, Sleeping Beauty, awakened by Doc Ardan in the 1920s, as told in "The Reluctant Princess" in Tales of the Shadowmen 4*–returns in this story in which Randy Lofficier revisits yet another of Charles Perrault's classic fairy tales, spinning a new yarn featuring a surprising cast of characters...*

Randy Lofficier: *The English Gentleman's Ball*

Paris, The 1920s

Once upon a time, she had been called Beauty and had slept for a thousand years. But ever since being awoken, not by a handsome prince, but by a dashing scientist, she was used to being referred to as "The Phantom Angel."

This new, modern world in which she found herself pleased her most of the time. Certainly she realized that the role of women had undergone a drastic change from when she had last been awake in a time of darkness and ignorance.

As the Phantom Angel, she was free to do as she pleased. Go where she desired. Dress as the mood took her. The world was far from a paradise, but it was a vast improvement on what she had known before, even if she had been a princess in those days.

But Angel was not satisfied with her adventures of derring-do; she felt that there should be more to her life on some level, but could not quite put her finger on what that might be. Part of it was the awareness that she was still privileged in comparison to many in this brave new world. Poverty, ignorance and darkness were still out there, but the rich pretended not to see the ugliness in the corner.

Because of her own past, Angel was particularly aware that the lot of women and children still needed great improvement. She knew that she could not save them all, but hoped that she could at least aid a few individuals. Thus she kept her ears open for cases where she could intervene.

Her sources in the *Société Secrète des Aventuriers* had told her that a Gregor Mac Dhul, a wealthy man with a daughter, had lost his wife in childbirth. He had hired a housekeeper to look after the child, and in the course of time, this woman, Simone Desroches, had become his new wife. What he didn't know was that Simone was in reality the notorious masked criminal known as Belphegor. She had targeted the industrialist to gain access to his fortune.

Because Gregor Mac Dhul traveled frequently, his new wife was often left alone with his daughter, Sylvie. But Simone was not a good mother, nor even a kind woman, and treated the girl as little more than a servant.

To keep Sylvie from telling her father of her treatment, Simone told her young charge that she would kill the Professor if ever he heard a word of the truth.

The Phantom Angel decided that this would be her next "project;" to save Sylvie from her evil stepmother and allow her to step out into the sunlight once again.

Angel tracked down the mansion where Sylvie practically had to clean the cinders from the fireplace in order to earn a meal while her father was away. It was clear that Simone ruled with an iron hand.

The woman once known as Beauty decided to use her contacts to gain an introduction to the household and to see the situation first hand. Because of Simone's desire to flaunt her wealth, it proved an easy task to be invited one afternoon for tea.

Once there, it was clear that the rumors about Sylvie's treatment were accurate. The 17-year-old girl was forced to wait on Simone and Angel, and was barely introduced as "my wretched stepdaughter" before being dismissed back to the kitchens to scrub out pots and pans. Poor Sylvie dared a pleading gaze at Angel, as if begging her for help.

The Phantom Angel was quickly able to turn the conversation to the subject of a lavish ball that was soon to be held by a visiting English aristocrat who had taken up temporary residence in a *hôtel particulier* in the fashionable *Marais* district of Paris. Word had it that his family was eager for him to wed, and had sent him to France to find a suitable candidate; thus all of Paris–the part that counted, at least–had been invited.

Simone was clearly interested in this new "opportunity" to enhance her own wealth. It was obvious to Angel that the evil stepmother was suddenly aware that she had a powerful trump card in Sylvie; for although she treated the girl as a scullery maid, underneath the hand-me-down clothes and ashes was a stunning beauty.

Clearly wanting to get rid of her visitor so that she could further her plot, Simone suddenly claimed a headache and called Sylvie to show her visitor out. Taking advantage of the short time they were able to spend alone, the Phantom Angel whispered: "Don't worry, I'm here to help. Think of me as your fairy Godmother!"

Our heroine was satisfied with the turning of events and began her own plot to save her new-found friend from the clutches of the evil woman who controlled her. Indeed, she immediately went to the very same *hôtel* and knocked at the entrance, where a truly British Gentleman's Gentleman opened the door with great courtesy.

"Are you Monsieur Jeeves?" she asked.

"Indeed I am, Madam," he replied.

"Then it is you I am here to see."

The door closed behind her.

The night of the grand ball arrived, and Simone had worked hard on Sylvie to make sure that the "prize" was secured by her and no other. The young girl looked nothing like a scullery maid and could have been a fairy princess in her exquisite gown and jewels. But her eyes were still sad and she had the air of a rabbit in the snare of a hunter in her manner.

The Phantom Angel, of course, was also at the ball. She nodded towards Sylvie and received a nod of acknowledgment from that most distinguished of valets, Jeeves. What she knew from him, and what no one else present realized, was that Bertram Wilberforce Wooster, the aristocrat in question, had no intention of marrying anyone at the ball, no matter what his family desired. However, as always, he was up for a good time, and the Phantom Angel's plot as recounted to him by his "man" Jeeves sounded as if it would be the highlight of his Parisian visit.

As the evening wore on, the wheels began to turn. Belphegor tried her best to put Sylvie into Bertie's path, but each time something was contrived to interfere. The evil stepmother became more and more frustrated as she had visions of the Woosters' fortune slipping ever farther away. Each time her plot failed she reached for another glass of champagne. Soon it was clear that she was more than a little drunk and she was having trouble controlling her temper. She grabbed hold of Sylvie's arm, her scarlet claws leaving marks on the porcelain flesh and hissed, "Get over there and dance with that man or you'll be sorry!"

That was the moment for the plan to reach its climax. Standing directly behind Simone had been her husband, Gregor Mac Dhul, whom she had been told was on business far, far away. The Phantom Angel had flown her plane to fetch him and Jeeves and Wooster had sequestered him in the house, making sure that each time his wife had threatened or abused his daughter during the evening, he had been in a perfect position to observe her.

"That's enough, Simone!" Gregor cried in anger. "It's clear you're not the woman you pretended to be and it's over. You'll not get another penny from me and you will never come near me or my daughter again!"

Belphegor stared at him in drunken astonishment, then turned to see the Phantom Angel, Jeeves and Wooster watching her in triumph.

Sylvie ran into her father's arms and began to cry tears of happiness as she realized that she was at least free of the evil woman who had ruled her life so cruelly.

Angel turned to her allies, "Gentlemen, you've done a fine thing tonight. I'm afraid, Mr. Wooster, that if word of this gets out, you're reputation as a drone may be damaged forever."

"No fear of that, Madam," said Jeeves. "Mr. Wooster knows precisely how to tell a story so that he is able to continue in his life of pointless pleasure."

"What ho, Jeeves," said Bertie.

And they all lived happily ever after.

Xavier Mauméjean, one of France's most distinguished writers-editors, has come up with a story which, on the surface, challenges one of the tenets of Tales of the Shadowmen, *which is to include a connection to French popular literature. Even though Xavier's story takes place in New York and pits two remarkable adversaries against each other, its "French content" is indeed present, even more remarkably so because of its subtlety...*

Xavier Mauméjean: *The Most Exciting Game*

New York, 1930

> *No animal had a chance with me any more.*
> *That is no boast; it is a mathematical certainty.*
> Count Zaroff.

A slaughter. There was no other suitable word that one might have used to describe the horror of what had taken place aboard the S.S. *Karaboudjan*. There were torn limbs, bloodied chests clawed open, their living hearts ripped out with undreamed of savagery. The entire crew had been hunted down and slain, from the lowest holds of the ship to her top mast. There was only one survivor: the First Mate, a tall, black-bearded man, dressed in a blue turtle neck sweater, who kept muttering endlessly "Blistering Barnacles!" with his eyes wide open, but entirely unfocused, seeing no one or nothing.

"You're wasting your time," said Sergeant Purley Stebbins to the New York D.A. John F.-X. Markham, who had come aboard to inspect the horror and question the survivor.

Markham shook his head with sadness.

"I understand. You think he's suffering from some severe psychological shock..."

Stebbins laughed.

"No, I think he's drunk my entire flask of Loch Lomond! It's top-notch single malt scotch whisky. And he drank almost a month's pay's worth of it! Makes me sick to my stomach. I thought he'd only take a gulp to get his spirits back, but he downed it all."

"If the First Mate is a dipsomaniac, it might be prove important for the investigation..."

"Nah, I'm an Irishman, I can smell drunks from a mile away," replied the Sergeant, tapping his nose. "He isn't one, but after an experience like this, I wouldn't be surprised if he became one. What in the name of Heaven happened on that ship?"

"It was serious enough for the Commissioner to drag me out of bed at 1 a.m. in this rotten weather."

"You're telling me? My boys and I've been freezing our butts off for a good couple of hours already. My boss left an hour ago, ordering me to wait for you."

It was December and a piercing drizzle that would soon turn into snow fell like small daggers of ice on the wharves. The silence of the night was only broken by the occasional blaring of a foghorn, far across the dark waters. It wasn't the kind of night that Markham relished.

"Have you determined the origin of the ship?" asked Markham, lifting the collar of his coat to better guard against the wind.

"Norway," replied the Sergeant, handing him the *Karaboudjan*'s log.

"What was she carrying?"

"The usual type of goods, with maybe a little smuggling. Plus a large crate that appeared to have contained some kind of animal."

The D.A. raised an eyebrow. He was normally a rather unexpressive young man, so his reaction betrayed real interest.

"What makes you say that?"

"Because inside we found a bowl of water, some fruit, some half-rotten meat jerky–and this."

The Sergeant held up a handkerchief. It was blotted with a thick, foul-smelling clear fluid, not unlike saliva.

"Can I keep it?" asked Markham, barely able to conceal his nausea.

"By all means! The wife would only throw it away anyway. Talk about snot!"

The D.A. carefully pocketed the evidence, feeling sad that, after coming into contact with the substance, his finest camel hair coat would be ruined forever, and he would have to buy himself a new one.

"Very well, Sergeant. Try to find out more about the ship's origin from the Port Authorities. For my part, I'm going to consult a specialist."

"Don't tell me. He lives on East 38th?"

"Mr. Vance? Not this time. This is not a case for dilettante experts on Chinese ceramics. We need someone... more worldly."

Located near Times Square, the Cobalt Club was a very exclusive social club. Once reserved for men, it now welcomed women and organized very popular soirées where couples danced until dawn. It belonged to Lamont Cranston, an amazing character, even by New York's standards. Having inherited a huge fortune made in the railways, Cranston had, one day, left his family's estate of Carnegie Hill to join the Lafayette Escadrille during the Great War. Then, the flying ace had vanished; some said that he had become involved in the opium wars in Asia. No one knew for certain. He had returned seven years later, a truly transformed man, not as much marked by his adventurous life as almost a wholly different person.

Markham did not pay much attention to city gossip. Being himself the scion of a wealthy family, he knew that the rich had a tendency to exaggerate things in order to relieve their boredom. He had had to face the recriminations of his father when he had chosen to become a public servant instead of joining the powerful family law firm founded by his grandfather. After facing the harsh realities of the world, Cranston had changed; he wasn't the first one, and wouldn't be the last.

Markham stepped through the arched entrance of the Cobalt Club and was welcomed by a doorman in a shiny blue uniform who offered to take his coat. The D.A. refused. He couldn't risk losing the only hard evidence he had. Inside, the club reeked of wealth and privilege. Conversations took place in hushed whispers around square tables with small table top lamps. There was a dance floor and, behind it, a band of black musicians played jazz on a stage draped in blue and gold.

"John?"

Markham turned around and saw a divine woman dressed in a blue, skin-tight sheath dress. Her jet black hair was cut squarely. She wore rhinestone-studded bracelets and a striking diamond on her right hand. She was the woman hired by Cranston to manage the club.

"Margo Lane."

"How long has it been, John?" asked the woman in a seductive, husky voice.

"Last time I saw you, you were still taking care of your little sister."

"Lois? She isn't so little anymore. She's going to college now."

"Ah," said Markham politely.

"Yes, she is studying to become a journalist."

"She may have a rather exaggerated notion of the importance of journalists. She'll probably wind up being assigned to the classifieds, not the type of job that gets someone walking on air."

"What do you want, John?"

"I've heard it said that Mr. Cranston is a friend of the Shadow..."

Margo Lane's smile froze on her lips.

"That's absurd."

"Well, I'd like to ask him myself. Where is he?"

The young woman flashed a mocking smile.

"Oh, but you don't know Lamont. One day, he's here; the next, he may be in China, or in Tibet..."

She might as well said that he was on a retreat in the legendary Shangri-La. Markham understood that he wouldn't get any information out of the young woman and was preparing to leave when she put her hand on his arm. The D.A. stopped.

"Don't go, John," she said. "You look tired. Have a drink here, on me. I'll introduce you to someone you might want to meet."

Markham followed Margo as she made her way through the room to a table where a tall man with thick eyebrows and a pointed black military mustache sat. His eyes, too, were black and very bright. He had high cheekbones, a sharp-cut nose, and a spare, aristocratic face. He wore a white dinner jacket, a new style that had recently come into fashion. Upon seeing Margo, the man snapped his fingers.

"Ivan!"

At once, a gigantic creature, solidly made and black bearded to the waist, dressed in the black astrakhan uniform of the Cossacks, stepped forward and offered two chairs to the newcomers.

After they were seated, Margo made the introductions.

"John, this is Count Zaroff, a White Russian."

"And a former General in the Czar's army," added the man, inserting a Dimitrino into his cigarette holder.

"You fled from the Communists?" inquired Markham.

The D.A. saw a twitch in the Russian's eye, as if he had hit a nerve.

"Fled? No. I'd rather say that those damned Bolsheviks made life in Holy Mother Russia untenable."

"I see. And what have you been doing since you left?"

"Unlike many of my former peers, who have blown their fortunes at the roulette table in Monte-Carlo and ended up driving taxis in Paris, I like to travel. In fact, I came here to see my old friend Kent Allard."

"One of our members," added Margo.

"Never heard of him," said Markham.

Zaroff made a dismissive gesture.

"He uses many aliases. In Russia, I knew him as Henry Arnaud, when he was working for the Czar, spying on the mad monk Rasputin, a sorry character whose influence on the Czarina was most nefarious."

Meanwhile, Ivan served a wonderful Mouton Rothschild wine, Margo's favorite if Markham's recollection was right.

"And how do you spend your time?"

"Mostly, I hunt."

"Really?"

"God made some men poets, some kings, others beggars. He made me a hunter. I have been one since my father gave me my first gun on my fifth birthday, a little carbine made especially for me in Moscow. Today, I travel the world, taking part in safaris, looking for new game..."

"What kind of game?"

"Grizzlies in your wonderful Rockies, tigers in India, jaguars in the Amazon, crocodiles in the Ganges, rhinoceroses in East Africa, Cape buffaloes, the fiercest creatures in the world..."

"This is terribly fascinating," said Margo, with a bright smile.

"Then I have something that might be of interest to you," said Markham, pulling out the fetid handkerchief from his pocket.

"Ew," said Margo, making a face. "What is that horrible thing?"

"That's what I'd like to know," said the D.A. "It was the only clue left by some kind of wild beat that killed the entire crew of a ship that docked last night."

Count Zaroff's eyes lit up. The former Czarist General used a fork to lift the handkerchief and examine it closely, even sniffing it. Then, in a subdued tone, he whispered:

"Valusia."

Upon hearing the word, his giant bodyguard pulled out a *kindjal*, a Cossack long knife, but Zaroff sternly gestured for him to sheathe the weapon and addressed Markham.

"You are the city's District Attorney, yes?" he asked. "I have come to New York to see Kent Allard, and also Sanger Rainsford, one of the world's top hunters, whom I would have liked to meet. But as they are both away at this time, I would be honored if you allowed me to assist you in this matter."

"Well... There's an official investigation... I don't know if I can..." said Markham, feeling his eyelids growing heavier. He was exhausted and did not know when he would be able to get some sleep.

"Come on, John," Margo whispered in his ear. "Don't be such a stickler. You call on Philo Vance all the time."

The D.A. gave up.

"Where can I get in touch with you?" he asked Zaroff.

The Russian took a magnificent fountain-pen and wrote an address on one of the Cobalt Club matchbooks.

In New York, Count Zaroff was staying at the local branch of the famous Gun Club, located on Lexington. The club was proud to have, at one time or another, accommodated some of the word's greatest hunters: Allan Quatermain, Hareton Ironcastle, Lord John Roxton... Even the notorious Colonel Sebastian Moran had resided there for several months when, according to some malicious gossip, he had been wanted for questioning by Her Majesty's Police. "Baseless rubbish," had growled the valorous officer, who was the author of two of Zaroff's favorite books, *Heavy Game of the Western Himalayas* (1881) and *Three Months in the Jungle* (1884). The Russian's other favorite bedside reading was Sanger Rainsford's *Hunting Snow Leopards in Tibet*, which contained the brilliant epigram: "The world is made up of two classes–the hunters and the huntees." Zaroff

154

would have liked to meet Rainsford, whom he considered an equal, but the native New Yorker was not in town at present.

The former Russian General was in America for yet another reason. Using the services of the lawfirm of Morrison, Morrison & Dodd, whose reputation was unmatched since the matter of the Giant Rat of Sumatra, he had been looking to purchase an isolated piece of land, preferably an island, where he could retire from a world where the weak increasingly pretended to rule over the strong and enjoy his personal pursuits.

In the meantime, the intriguing case presented to him by John Markham would have to suffice to relieve his boredom. Zaroff took it as a manifest intervention of fate. The D.A.'s handkerchief was covered in a slimy substance which he had recognized at once. He had seen the very same ooze in the hands of mad Rasputin, who had owned a vial of it, which Allard (as Arnaud) had tried to steal—the same Allard who had been his host tonight under the guise of Lamont Cranston. Fate indeed. It was both a small world and a vast hunting ground.

As the Gun Club was rather devoid of guests at this time, Zaroff had been able to convert several rooms into his private, personal laboratory. If hunting was the Russian's heartfelt obsession, he did not let his passion for it obliterate the need for a methodical, scientific approach. The ability to reason was what made man superior to any beast, as he often liked to say.

During the following days, Zaroff remained in his suite, eating his usual regime of filet mignon and borsch, as only Ivan knew how to make it, drinking Chablis, analyzing the sample with a microscope and taking copious notes. No one was allowed to disturb him, not even his faithful hound, Lazarus, a massive brute of dog. His examination proved, beyond doubt, that the slime came from one of the legendary Serpent Men of Valusia who had ruled the Earth during the Paleozoic Era and had been mostly wiped out by the Atlantean King Kull. A few of the creatures had survived and used their metamorphic abilities to infiltrate the societies of Men afterward. The substance that Zaroff had recovered was protein-based and enabled the creatures' organism to withstand the prodigious stress of shapeshifting while retaining its basic cohesion, as per the Theory of Evolution. The Russian smiled, remembering some of the folk tales of his own country that also featured shapechangers: Baba Yaga the witch, the Volkodlaks, wolf-men of the steppes... These could be explained rationally by the substance he had now seen under his microscope. That understanding would give him a definite advantage over his prey.

At the Russian's request, Markham had had photos of the bodies of the victims delivered to Zaroff. From the location of the wounds and the directions of the blows, the Count had deduced that their assassin was tall and bipedal, or at least able to assume an upright position.

Having completed the scientific part of his investigation, Zaroff then opened a flat suitcase that had been especially designed for him by Dunhill. It contained a Mauser which could be turned into a rifle by mounting it onto a butt. The famous blind German gunsmith Von Herder, who had built Moran's notorious air rifle, had modified it according to Zaroff's exacting specifications. The case also contained a *kindjal*, identical to Ivan's, an ideal weapon for throwing or close combat. But Zaroff knew that his most effective weapon in this case was a millennia-old incantation which he had stolen from Rasputin's safe: *Ka nama kaa lajerama*, a *shibboleth* once uttered by throats which were almost-human or not-yet-human in order to defeat the Sons of the Great Serpent, Set.

A modern man, Zaroff found it difficult to remember it, and even more so, to pronounce it, but it would have to do.

For a mind as primitive as that of a Serpent Man, thought Zaroff, the skyscrapers of New York must evoke images of the spires of long-lost Valusia. So he thought his prey would first seek refuge in Central Park, and therefore that became his hunting ground.

Three nights later, Zaroff had Ivan drive him there. He was now dressed in a tight fitting black sweater and wore black *jodhpurs* and black leather officer's boots. Lazarus was growing agitated, next to him, on the backseat of the limousine. The hound knew that the game was afoot.

At the entrance of the park, Zaroff ordered Ivan to remain with the car. The Cossack giant grumbled, but obeyed, fearing his master's *knout*. The brute was entirely devoted to him, thought Zaroff, but it was sometimes hard to get him to obey him unquestioningly. In these troubled times, good servants were hard to come by.

Zaroff entered the night-shrouded park, his prodigious senses on alert. The thrill of the hunt was the greatest thrill of all, he thought, greater than power, greater than sex, greater than everything. Almost at once, Lazarus stopped and turned his massive head towards his master. The hound had uncovered the corpse of a vagrant, who must have been slaughtered by the snake man. Zaroff made a sign to instruct the dog to be utterly quiet and noiselessly made his way through the man-made forest. He noticed immediately that the park was devoid of any animal noises. The silence was unnatural. Every living creature knew how to be afraid of a mortal enemy, be it man or snake.

Suddenly, a shadow leaped from under a bush and attacked the Count. Zaroff felt a searing pain on his left side. He felt the wound: it wasn't deep, but one of his ribs was surely bruised. If his reflexes hadn't been lightning fast, he might have been gored.

The Russian grabbed his Mauser, but the Serpent Man whipped it away. That gave Zaroff an opportunity to stab the creature with his *kindjal*, which slowed his enemy. In the meantime, Lazarus had come to his master's rescue and was talking deep bites out of the Snake Man. However, to Zaroff's horror, if not his surprise, he saw that the shapeshifter's very substance was slowly reconstituting itself. The monster was damn near invulnerable!

It was time to use the incantation. Zaroff took in a deep breath and shouted:

"*Oungawa timba!*"

No, that was the command that Greystoke had taught him in Congo. Zaroff concentrated to remember the ancient ritual.

"*Shub ath ngaa ryla neb shoggoth!*"

Captain Marsh's prayer. Even more far-fetched. For the first time ever, Zaroff experienced fear. The Serpent Man had now thrown the hound away and was moving towards him again. He had only one more try left.

"*Ka nama kaa lajer–*" he began.

"*–rama,*" finished Lazarus in growling bark so hoarse that it unwittingly mimicked that of the prehistoric throats that had once uttered the ancient warding sign.

At once, the Snake Man from a long buried past stopped dead in his tracks. His body rippled as if it was mere clay in the grasp of some large, inhuman hand. Before Zaroff's eyes, the thing that had walked like a man began to liquefy, then to quickly resolve into a pile of fetid mire.

"So you destroyed the creature?" said Margo Lane admiringly. "But your hair turned white overnight, Count."

"That only marks me more as a White Russian," joked Zaroff. He then turned towards Markham and asked: "Did your men ever find out where the ship came from?"

"The Port Authority said it came from Franz Josef Land, an archipelago near the Arctic Circle. The only clue as to the origins of the crate itself was a label identifying as having belonged to the Ceintras/de Venasque polar expedition that disappeared 17 years ago. Who sent the thing, and to whom, is a mystery that will have to be solved by someone else. In the meantime, the City of New York is extremely grateful to you, Count. If there's ever anything I can do..."

Zaroff leaned over the table, muffling a groan of pain.

"You have already done much, Mr. Markham," said the Russian. "Thanks to your father's lawfirm, I'm now the happy owner of a Caribbean island named Baranka."

"How enticing," said Margo.

"It is perfect for my purposes–there are jungles with a maze of traits in them, hills, swamps and cliffs overlooking the ocean... It is surrounded by giant rocks with razor edges that can crush a ship like a nut. The sailors try to avoid it and call it 'Ship-Trap.' "

"Don't you think you might get bored there?" asked Markham.

"Not at all. That business with the crew hunted aboard the *Karaboudjan* made me think. I could set up lights, pointing to a channel that didn't exist which would force ships ashore; then, I could hunt the survivors, the scum of the

Earth: sailors from tramp ships–blacks, Chinese, whites, mongrels--a thorough-bred horse or hound is worth more than a score of them. Maybe someday I might even be lucky enough to have Sanger Rainsford join me for a hunting party..."

Count Zaroff seemed deadpan serious, but the other two thought it was just another eccentric musing from a bored European nobleman.

Margo Lane laughed spiritedly, ordered another round of drinks and soon forgot all about it.

If Paul Féval is the father of the criminal thriller, Emile Gaboriau invented the procedural detective novel when he created the character of the keen-eyed Sûreté agent, Monsieur Lecoq. Jess Nevins, the author of Encyclopedia of Fantastic Victoriana, *has chosen Lecoq as the hero of his latest swashbuckling yarn, which takes our fearless detective across the ocean to Mexico where he meets the strangest of opponents...*

Jess Nevins: *A Root That Beareth Gall and Worms*

May 26, 1864. Off Veracruz, Mexico

The *De Peyrac* rocked gently in the swell of the tide. Inside the ship's stern cabin, the noise of the parties in the other two ships, *La Louve* and *d'Argouges*, were easily audible. The ships were carrying Ferdinand Maximilian Joseph, Prince Royal of Hungary and Bohemia, to assume the throne of the Empire of Mexico, in accordance with the wishes of Emperor Napoleon III. Maximilian's reception–public, loud, full of bombastic pomp, and beginning with a parade through the main streets of Veracruz–was to take place the following morning. But the trip across the Atlantic had been arduous, with spring storms making the passage a two-week-long endurance test of nausea, and the festivities on *La Louve* and *d'Argouges*, celebrating the end of the voyage, were well-attended and honestly enjoyed.

But the men and women walking toward the stern cabin of the *De Peyrac* were anything but relieved. They had been anticipating the meeting they were about to attend since leaving Brest, but now that it was here, they felt tension rather than pleasure or relief. So much could come from this meeting, and none knew what it was about–or, if they did, they had refrained from telling even their closest companions. Informers were everywhere, and even the highest of position would not save a man or woman from the firing squad, should Maximilian or the Emperor so choose.

Waiting for the men and women in the cabin were six individuals: a dwarf and five Gypsies. Four of the Gypsies were guarding the two doors to the cabin while the fifth–burly, sullen, heavily scarred, and ugly, even by Gypsy standards–waited to search all those who would enter. The dwarf was no more than three feet tall, ungainly and misshapen, but his pacing was energetic, almost manic, and his vest, coat, and tails were from the finest Parisian *couturiers*. As soon as the last visitor was allowed into the cabin by the scarred Gypsy, and the door had closed behind him, the dwarf began speaking, his delivery as emphatic and excited as his movements and gestures.

"I am Dr. Miguel de Vega, and I am soon to be known as the greatest mind of either continent. Monsieur Poiret tells me that you are all intelligent men and women, and not to speak to you as if you were children. Yet, what I have discovered is in a field known to few, and so, your ignorance is childlike, especially compared to mine. Even the greatest naturalists and members of the Royal Society have scorned the humble worm, the *Annelid* and *Acanthocephala* and *Platyhelminthes* and all the rest, in favor of mammals, insects, birds, reptiles–all the so-called 'higher orders' of creatures that the world is blessed with. And yet, in diversity of size, what creature can compare with the worm? The Almighty may have an inordinate fondness for beetles, but He has clearly favored the worm.

"Consider: centuries after the Biblical 'giants in the earth' have vanished from their native countries, millennia after the death of the giant lizards, who now remain only in a few subterranean settings, or maintain an atavistic existence in isolated valleys in Texas and Mexico, or on secluded plateaus in Brazil– at a time when giants of all species are dying or extinct, we have irrefutable evidence of the existence, and even prolificity, of giant worms. Think of the albino giants whose existence in Mercia, in England, is well-documented. Consider their cousins in the American west, whose furrows and whose voraciousness is testified to by natives and farmers alike. Consider the Tibetan variety, whose appetite for iron is dismissed by some as folklore. Consider the so far unseen titan whose vast tunnels honeycomb the bedrock beneath so much of Europe..."

At the back of the room, two men stood, slightly apart from the others, and whispered to each other as the dwarf continued to speak. The younger of the two, a man in his late thirties, puffing on a pipe, wore the somber uniform of an officer of the Sûreté. His companion leaned on his cane and idly straightened his faded First Empire uniform. He said, quietly, "You see? It is as I said. He is touched."

The younger man chewed the stem of his pipe for a moment. "Yes. But insane doesn't mean murderous. And his mania seems focused on animals–worms, of all things. Such a man would butcher dogs, not women."

The older man said, "I agree with you, Lecoq. But he could have–wait, hush, listen."

The dwarf said, "Yet that is not the most remarkable aspect of the worm class. What is truly striking to the scientific mind is not the survival of the giants but the adaptability of species from the smaller phyla. And it is in this area that I have been directing my energies. With the occasional, although minor, assistance of my colleagues Moreau, Klotz, and van Ouisthoven, I have created a truly remarkable new species.

"We–I–have created–" and here De Vega paused, withdrew a matchbox from his waistcoat pocket, and opened it, "–this."

De Vega showed the room a kind of worm, or perhaps a grub, no larger than the dwarf's thumb. The worm was furry and variegated green, and one end had an oval bump with a pair of antennae protruding from it.

When De Vega was sure that everyone had seen the creature, he said, "To your eyes this is only a worm. But to the eyes of a scientist, it is an astounding achievement.

"Years ago the explorer Paturel found, in two separate meteorites, the remains of what could only be described as worm-like creatures. No naturalist had been able to classify the remains, but I, Dr. Miguel De Vega, was able to fully identify them, and to perceive that they belonged to no phyla known to man. Each represents a new phylum, each spawned on some hellish other world. I have named these phyla *Miguelithes* and *Vegamorpha*.

"Making use of these remains, and of instruments of my own design and theories of my own creation, I have bred a viable new species which I have named *Migvegaphala*. It has the attributes of both other phyla. Like *Miguelithes*, it is a parasite. It enters mammalian bodies through the ear and implants itself in the cerebral cortex. Ordinary mammals are left in a stupefied and easily handled state, while humans are rendered particularly susceptible to verbal suggestion.

"Like *Vegamorpha*, it is also a predator. Once secure in the cortex, my creation implants its young, releasing meanwhile certain chemicals. In humans, these chemicals trigger certain physical changes–remarkable changes, changes which prove that certain Scottish legends of deadly 'worm-men' may have had some remote basis in historical reality. I have managed to weaken the chemicals so that the cycle of change is interrupted, and only a human's face is affected. And with the negligible help of Morgan of Oxford, I have discovered a method for directing and manipulating this facial alteration."

De Vega began a technical discussion of how this was achieved, which Lecoq and his companion ignored. The Sûreté detective raised an eyebrow at his friend, who said, "You believe him?"

"Oh, yes. The Emperor would not have given him such support before now if he were deluded, or a confidence man."

"It is incredible. Bonaparte would have scoffed at him."

"And yet he funded de Trélern."

"The Chevalier, my dear Lecoq, produced a flying machine which anyone could see, and which the First Consul himself flew in. This dwarf, with his talk of magic and worms and–but, sssh."

Clearly reaching the climax of his speech, De Vega ranted, "Imagine the applications! The most violent of lunatics, soothed. The incurably catatonic, forcibly awakened by a command to act normally. And, of course, enemies transformed into allies, an army of them…"

De Vega paused, and the dreamy look which had crept across his face disappeared and was replaced with an alarmed awareness that he was not alone and speaking his thoughts aloud, but instead was addressing other people.

"I, uh, of course am happy to put *Migvegaphala* at the service of the Emperor."

He bowed and sat, and after a long moment the men in the room began thumping their hands on the tables or walls nearest to them. De Vega smiled awkwardly. He was approached by a short man in fashionably cut silks who had a luxuriant black mustache and cold, dark eyes. He had leaned nonchalantly against the wall of the cabin as De Vega spoke, but from the body language of the others in the room, it was clear that he was a figure of some authority. He and the dwarf began speaking, quietly, and conversations sprang up around the room.

Lecoq's companion said, "This story of magic worms is hard to believe, I know. But it would explain so much about these murders. And neither of us are strangers to the incredible. You told me of your encounter with the 'invisible vampire' in Rouen. And you know of my sighting of the Wandering Jew in Paris during the cholera epidemic. So why not believe in a worm that can change people's faces?"

"I suppose because I dislike the appearance of the fantastic in a murder case. Men kill for so many base, understandable reasons. Why drag the occult or Bavarian into it?"

"Because it explains the murders–what was done to the women, if not why. How often have I told you? The ludicrous must be believed when the inconceivable is ruled out. So much about the murders was inconceivable, but the worm, though ludicrous, is clearly not."

Lecoq scowled and shrugged.

Raphaël, the older man, smiled. The pair had met in Paris. Lecoq, a detective of the Sûreté, had been investigating a series of murders among the prostitutes of the Vaugirard *arrondissement*. All women had their throats cut, and they were all streetwalkers of the lowest sort–which would ordinarily have meant that their deaths did not matter as much as the Empress' hangnails. But the faces of the victims bore disfigurements of a disquieting and even unnerving nature, and Lecoq had been intrigued enough to pursue this most-likely-unrewarding case. His questions among the local pimps had turned up nothing–even threatened by a Parisian Sweeney Todd, the whores of Paris maintained their legendary solidarity and truculence when questioned by the police. Lecoq had finally been forced to ask for help from an old family friend. Hector Ratichon had once been a top agent of the Sûreté under Vidocq, and had been partially responsible for capturing Lecoq's father and sending him to Toulon. Lecoq had borne no grudge, however, and had struck up a friendship with Ratichon, who became like an uncle to him and had encouraged him to pursue a career in the Sûreté. He sometimes turned to him for advice on difficult cases. Ratichon did not disappoint this time. "Raphaël Carot. He was an inquiry agent in this city for many years, quite the famous man in his day, and even now, 20 years after his retirement, his advice is useful to many."

Carot was well into his eighties, and still dressed like a courtier of the Republic, but he held himself ramrod straight, and his eye was like an eagle's and was clear of confusion or rheum. Lecoq had considered himself (with reason) an experienced detective and man-hunter, but Carot had, in a short time, taught him an incredible amount, from the existence of a den of Chinamen in the heart of the city to the meaning of the different colors of mud to be found in the streets of Paris. It was Carot who had puzzled out the meaning of the peculiar tracks at the murder scenes ("a dwarf, Lecoq, and one whose pain forces him to waddle and periodically drag a foot"), it was Carot who had won the confidence of the street-walkers, and it was Carot who had led Lecoq on to the *de Peyrac*.

Carot and Lecoq watched De Vega leave the cabin, preceded by the ever-present Gypsy bodyguards, and followed by the others. One man stayed behind, a tall, handsome, middle-aged Spaniard. He carefully placed his wine glass on the nearest table and approached Lecoq and Carot.

In Spanish-accented French, he said, "You two have, forgive me, the smell of lawmen—we know it well in Mexico—and you were careful not to let Miguel see you watching him, which I know is the sign of the predator before his leap, and not during. I think we should speak, you and I."

Carot said, "And you are, Señor?"

"Don Alejandro de la Vega, Messieurs."

Lecoq said, "De la Vega? Any relation to—"

"Yes, Monsieur. Miguel is my cousin, through my father's family."

Carot and Lecoq exchanged looks.

De la Vega smiled—somewhat sadly, Lecoq thought—and said, "I know. Miguel is...not well. That the two of you were examining him so intently, and without seeming to do so, tells me that he is in, perhaps, more immediate trouble than I had feared. I should like to discuss it with you, before anything is done about it."

Carot nodded at Lecoq, reluctantly, and Lecoq said, "I am Lecoq, a detective of the Sûreté. My friend is Raphaël Carot, who is assisting me on a murder case. I'm afraid that, after what we heard here tonight, your cousin has become our primary suspect."

De la Vega sighed. "I feared it was so. He...we met in Paris, Miguel and I. The Emperor had invited me there to discuss the new regime in Mexico—I live in California, but I have some influence in Mexico City, and I may have some role to play in Maximilian's government. I had not thought to meet a relative in Paris, but there he was."

"How long ago was this?"

"A week before the *De Peyrac* left Brest."

"Did he—forgive me—did he give any indication of violence or insanity? What we heard tonight—it is a kind of madness. To take control of men's minds? Madness, without a doubt."

De la Vega nodded, reluctantly. "He has a kind of obsession with the loss of the family property. We–the de la Vegas–were given land in what is now California, early in the last century, by the King of Spain. The land was taken from us by the Americans. My side of the family survived this and have managed to prosper. Miguel's…did not. They suffered deprivations, which I fear have warped his soul. Miguel is a bitter man. He wishes nothing more than the punishment of the Americans and the restoration of the de la Vega lands. Would you tell me of this murder you think he committed?"

Lecoq said, "Murders–six in all, of whores. I believe he is responsible."

De la Vega's face showed surprise. "Whores? Miguel? That would surprise me. He has never lacked for success with women, Monsieur. Despite his deformities, they find him charming, and he has never needed to pay for their company. In Paris, rumor has it that he bedded the Empress. He even has a dwarf woman in Finland who has borne him a son."

Carot said, "Success with women hardly precludes treating them badly, Señor de la Vega. Surely you know this. And we do not think he used the women for sex. We think he chose them so he could murder them without consequence."

"But…he shows no sign of the true woman-hater. I've never heard express a cross word for woman-kind. Quite the reverse."

Carot looked at Lecoq, who said, "I would not say that the murders were done out of hatred. The bodies bore none of the marks of anger or contempt, no sign of the passion of a man who hates or fears women."

Carot said, "We think he experimented on the women, and the experiment killed them."

De la Vega sighed and nodded. "Yes, that does sound like something he might do. His affection for women is real, but is dwarfed–you will pardon the expression–by his hatred for the Americans. If his experiment would further his quest against them, he would kill every woman in France."

Lecoq said, "After what we heard tonight, we know how he did it. He used the worms on them. And from what you've said, we can guess at his reason–perhaps Maximilian will grant him lands in exchange for the worms. I'm sorry, Señor, but we're going to have to arrest him."

De la Vega reluctantly nodded. "Yes, I know. But…may I speak with him first? I will of course not mention your plans for him, but…he is family. I would not want him to think that he is alone, even in prison."

Lecoq looked at Carot, who shrugged. "He seems trustworthy. Why not?"

Lecoq nodded at De la Vega. "Yes."

Alejandro De la Vega bowed to the pair and went to his cousin's cabin. He nodded at the scarred Gypsy guarding the door.

Miguel said, "Well, cousin, what did you think?"

Alejandro said, "It was…very impressive, Miguel."

"I would hope so! I have achieved what no other man can boast of, what the scientists on the Continent scorned as *fantasias*! I have achieved scientific immortality–the man they look down upon as a provincial dwarf. Let them laugh at me now, for I have shown that I am their master!"

Alejandro looked at De Vega with a sympathetic, sad smile. In Paris, during one of the Emperor's gatherings, while being introduced to the men who would rule Mexico, Alejandro had met Miguel. A brief conversation had established that, much to their mutual surprise, they were cousins, and both from California. Although Alejandro had been born a Murieta, he had been adopted by the De la Vegas and now considered himself one of them–the only remaining one, apart from his children. So it was with no small pleasure that he had greeted a living relative, and one of obvious intelligence and sophistication. The De la Vegas, after all, were a noble line, descended from El Cid and Garcilaso de la Vega, and they should prosper, not dwindle.

But Alejandro's pleasure soon turned to trepidation, and then to sadness, and after what he had heard this evening, disquiet and even alarm. Miguel was brilliant, that much was obvious, and Alejandro had no doubt that he had achieved what he claimed. But he was also desperate for attention and for acclaim, so much so that, Alejandro thought, he would do anything to gain the respect he thought due to him. Part of it was age; Miguel was only 30, while Alejandro was a decade older, and well-remembered how rash, headstrong, and often wrong he had been at Miguel's age. Much more of it was Miguel's stature. To be a dwarf was to live with mockery and even cruelty. It was to wonder if God was playing a joke on you. But Miguel had also let slip one night, while they were both deep in their cups, that to be his kind of dwarf was to be in constant physical pain. Miguel had eyed Alejandro's wedding ring and said, "You won your wife when you were my age, and now you have a lifelong companion, someone to share your bed with, to be there when you wake up and to be there when you go to sleep. God also gave me a lifelong companion, but He did so when I was born, and it is pain."

A dwarf, unpleasant to look at, in continual pain, and with the mind of a Rappaccini... Alejandro understood that such a person would crave respect and admiration as the opium smoker needed his drug. And from what Miguel had said, he had traveled to Europe to meet with his peers, other scientists who could appreciate his achievements. Even at his young age, Miguel had done remarkable things, and had gained renown for his discoveries but, as he had had hinted, the meetings had not gone well, the scientists had not been able to see past his small stature, and Miguel had been forced to wander as an intellectual outcast, rather than being welcomed into any of the scientific societies. Eventually–Miguel was coy about how this had taken place–he had drifted into an association with Napoleon.

Alejandro had thought to use his wealth and influence to grant Miguel a chair at a college in Los Angeles or Mexico, when they returned. But now he didn't know what to do. Miguel's speech hinted at things Alejandro hadn't thought his cousin capable of... If the two Frenchmen were correct, Miguel was responsible for several murders. Alejandro felt miserable.

"It was a truly remarkable presentation, Miguel, and I salute you. But I worry that perhaps the Emperor may not put your creations to the best use."

Miguel grinned. Alejandro could not help thinking that, genuine though the smile was, it did not improve his cousin's looks. In a low voice, Miguel said, "He will not–he doesn't have the mind for it. But I do. Alejandro, listen: the Emperor and his men think me only a tool, a hammer to be thrown away once they have used me. Poiret thinks I don't know what he plans to do to me, once I have given him the secret of the worms. He thinks that I believe that the Gypsy guards he assigned to me will protect me. Like everyone else, he underestimates me."

His throat suddenly dry–*Miguel knows! How did he find out?*–Alejandro said, "What are you going to do? Miguel, if I can–"

"I mean, we can work together and take back what is ours, cousin! The De la Vega lands, all of them–and more! They owe us interest, and we can take it!"

"I...don't understand."

Miguel's grip on Alejandro's arm tightened, and his voice lowered to a hiss. "Listen: my worms, they make men think what I want them to think. I have proven this, in Paris, on some women who will not be missed. I need only put a worm in a man's ear, and he will hear and believe whatever I tell him. And I have bred the worms so that I control whatever changes they effect on their host. I can make a man look like whoever I like. But I cannot do this as long as I have these wretched arms." He grimaced, then looked up at Miguel and smiled. "You can, though. You are tall and strong and handsome, and–forgive me–unserious and not interested in much beyond women and wine, so no one will suspect you. Simply walk besides a man and slap your hand to his ear–the worm will enter the man, and then he is ours."

"Miguel... This is wrong. Even if we could take control of one man, or five, or ten..."

"No, Alejandro, you're not thinking about this the right way. Please, try to look at it through my eyes, with the vision of genius. Not one man, not five or ten, but hundreds–thousands! All under my command, all following my orders. An army–our army. We can–"

"Miguel–even if we got that many under our control, we would still face the armies of America, North and South. They would far outnumber us."

Miguel waved his hands contemptuously. "I have weapons which will re-dress the numbers gap: my Spore Cannon, my Prolapse Horn, my Inferno Gre-nade. And we will never have a problem adding more men to our army. We need merely visit a town, or come upon a lone farm, and put a worm in each person's ear, and we'll have new soldiers for our cause. And when we capture enemy soldiers–and they will be eager to be captured, rather than face the weaponry I will give our troops—we can convert them, as well, and use the worms to change their faces. Before long, we will have undetectable assassins as well as fanatical soldiers, and who can stand against both of those?" His voice lowered again, to a whisper. "Think of it, Alejandro, an ever-growing wave, sweeping east from California, across the desert and mountains and plains, all the way to Washington, and us, you and I, riding that wave."

Alejandro said, weakly, "It will be...quite something, Miguel."

"Yes, yes! And with your looks and your contacts, and my intellect, it can all come to pass!"

Alejandro sat down, suddenly feeling tired and old. He carefully removed a handkerchief from his vest and mopped his brow with it. It was even worse than the Frenchmen thought. Miguel was unbalanced, and dangerous.

"Alejandro, are you unwell? You look pale. Shall I call for a—"

Alejandro shook his head and smiled as if pained. "No, Miguel, but I thank you. I am just...tired. I think I should retire early."

Alejandro nodded a good-night to Miguel and turned to leave. Something about his gait and the set of his shoulders caused Miguel's brow to furrow and his eyes to narrow, and he quickly withdrew a small device from a vest pocket. He said, "Alejandro," walked forward, and pressed the device to Alejandro's belt while looking him in the eye and saying, "Take care of yourself, cousin—we must stick together, you and I."

Alejandro smiled weakly, rested his hand on Miguel's shoulder for a moment, bowed and left.

Lecoq and Carot had been walking to their cabin when they were stopped by a uniformed Legionnaire. He had led them to a cabin near the bow of the ship. The Legionnaires guarding the cabin door saluted and let them enter, but there had been no one inside, and the Legionnaires politely but firmly refused to let them leave, saying only, "Monsieur le Secrétaire will be with you presently."

Finally, the door opened, and two men entered. One was the short, hawk-faced man in silk who spoke with De Vega following his presentation. The other was a lanky figure, fashionably dressed in a dark tail coat, trousers, and a patterned floral tie, with an amused and superior expression. He leaned against the door, arms crossed, while the other spoke. He said, to Carot, "You, I do not know." Looking at Lecoq, he said, "You, however, I do know. You are Lecoq, one of the best agents of the Sûreté. Your presence is not welcome on this ship, and you are poking your nose into matters that do not concern you."

Lecoq said, "Murder is always my concern, Monsieur..."

"Poiret, of the Emperor's staff."

"Monsieur Poiret, I am investigating several murders which took place in Paris. It is very much my concern."

"I do not care what you think you know, Lecoq, but the dwarf is not involved in this."

"I disagree, and I look forward to explaining my reasoning to the *juge d'instruction*."

"This touches on affairs of state, Lecoq, and we do not need a cut-rate Vidocq spoiling matters or interfering with our plans."

At the mention of the disgraced Director of the Sûreté, Lecoq's face, usually genial, but always reflecting his emotions, grew cold. He waited a moment, to make sure his voice would remain smooth, and said, "I would think that the murders of His Majesty's subjects would always be a concern of the state."

Poiret's face grew red. "You would place the death of a few whores over the Emperor's wishes? Perhaps we should discuss it with him!"

Carot grinned, coldly. "It always comes to that, doesn't it? The threat of punishment from *l'Empereur*? M'sieur Poiret, I have been threatened by three Emperors, and sentenced to death by one. And yet, here I am." He let his right hand drift toward the revolver in his jacket pocket. "I should add that our numbers, in this room, are equal, and the door is closed. Are you so sure of leaving this room alive?"

At Carot's words, Poiret's companion straightened and reached for his gun. He locked eyes with Carot, grinned, and said, "Shall we match draws, you and I?"

With a visible effort, Poiret controlled himself. "I do not believe you understand the situation, either of you. Juarez is in hiding. The Legion and the Army have taken control of the major Mexican cities, but the rebels remain active, especially in the north, along the Rio Grande. They must be crushed as soon as possible so that Maximilian can begin his reign in earnest.

"We can not do so through feats of arms, however. Our sources of intelligence are simply not good enough to discover the rebels or their leaders, nor the identity of the sympathizers among the landowners. As matters stand now, we will hold Mexico, but we will be forced to release it in three or four years' time.

"Unless we have help. And, fortuitously, the dwarf and his creatures are available to us. He tells us he has a limited number of the creatures available for use, but can have more in six months. Without them, we fail, but with them…imagine it. The British have India, but we will have Mexico. Nor should we stop there. We have friends among the Quebecois *Patriotes*, and Maximilian's British advisor, the cavalry officer Flashman, knows a Confederate blockade runner, a man named Butler, who is intimate with the leaders among the American rebels. With the dwarf's creatures, in two months we can have Mexico. In six, Texas and California. In a year's time, the Confederacy. And the Empire would stretch from the North Pole to British Hidalgo. We would have surpassed what even Bonaparte dreamed of!"

His expression, which had become almost distant, abruptly turned frigid, and his voice became venomous. "And you would have us sacrifice all of this, simply because of a few dead whores?"

Lecoq said, "I never said anything about whores, Monsieur le Secrétaire."

Poiret glared at him. His companion, who had not stopped staring at Carot, said, "Jules, enough. They will not listen."

Poiret stood, and Lecoq, whose hand was resting in his jacket pocket on the butt of the small revolver he always carried with him, saw that Poiret's hand was likewise positioned.

Poiret said, "Very well. What follows is on your head, then."

Lecoq and Carot eased themselves from the room, their hands never leaving the butts of their guns, and, as casually as they could manage, walked down the hall while surreptitiously watching the Legionnaires behind them.

When they reached the nearest stair, they ran up them and nearly bowled over Alejandro, who was massaging his head.

Carot said, "No words, Señor, just follow us."

Inside their cabin, Lecoq and Carot described their encounter with Poiret, and Alejandro his with Miguel. When Alejandro finished, there was a long moment of silence. Carot finally said, "I'm afraid, Lecoq, that this murder case is destined to remain unsolved. Even if we somehow got the dwarf back to Paris, the Emperor will not allow his prosecution."

Lecoq said, "One more entry for the *Dossiers Classés*, I guess. It will deserve its own title, I think: 'The Case of the Slaughtered Streetwalkers,' or something similar. I should ask M. Parent, he's good at naming these things."

Alejandro glared at them both. "How can you be so flippant? How callous are you both? Do you not understand what will happen when Miguel and his creatures step ashore tomorrow?"

Carot said, gently, "We both know, Alejandro. To make jokes at a time like this…it is just how policemen handle tragedy."

Alejandro's face lost its anger. "My poor people. Whether it is Miguel or the French who prevail, thousands of Mexicans and Americans will die, and we will have exchanged instability for tyranny. We will still fight them, but we will lose."

The device on Alejandro's belt broadcast these words clearly to Miguel's cabin, but the device only sent messages one way, and Alejandro did not hear his cousin's anguished fury when he realized that the 'them' Alejandro meant to fight included him.

" 'We' will fight them? Who is this 'we'?"

"The Foxes."

"The Foxes?"

Alejandro raised his eyebrows, then said, "Ah–yes. You are not from here, you would not know. Zorro, the Fox, is–"

Carot stared. "Zorro? Why do I know that name…" He looked at the ceiling for a long moment, then nodded suddenly. "Yes. It was during the first of the Carlist Wars, in Madrid–I was there with Fernand, we were–well, never mind, it was a long time ago. But there was a man in a costume there, fighting the

Carlists. The Christinos called him 'Zorro.' But that was 20 years ago, and more. Not the same man, surely?"

Alejandro smiled. "Not exactly. The first Zorro, Ramon de la Torre, put on a mask and fought injustice under Philip the Third, and when he grew too old, his son donned the mask, and his son after him. It became a family tradition, to take up the sword and the mask of the Fox when innocents were threatened. The tradition has died in Spain, but in California and Mexico, it lives on, perpetuated by the descendants of the de la Torres and by others, and has even inspired imitators. You've heard of El Latigo and El Coyote? No? Well, no matter. They are part of the Zorro legacy. It is much like the Saints of Mexico City–a proud tradition of fighting for justice. I know one of the Foxes, and to know one is to be in contact with all of them."

Carot said, "How many of them are there? Enough to pose a serious challenge to Poiret or your cousin?"

"A few dozen, both men and women. They are deadly enough, with sword, whip, and gun, but they cannot fight an army. A direct clash would kill them."

Lecoq said, "I am out of ideas. Short of murdering Poiret, I–"

Carot raised a finger. "Perhaps that will not be necessary. Consider, Monsieur Lecoq: we know where the worms are now–with De Vega. If we take them from him, our problem is solved. He could make more, but not soon enough to help the French in Mexico."

Lecoq shook his head. "I thought of that, but after our encounter with Poiret, I doubt that De Vega will be left unguarded."

Carot smiled and picked up his rapier from where it lay across his traveling trunk. "I am past my prime, Lecoq, but I am still a match for Legionnaires. I will be surprised if they even know which end of a sword to thrust with."

Alejandro said, "You will excuse me for saying so, Monsieur, but I do not think that is the best idea."

Carot nodded. "Indeed. Which is why you will be with me."

"Me? But…I hardly know how to hold a sword."

"The calluses on your hands tell a different story, Señor. And while you have done a competent enough job at exaggerating your clumsiness, your reactions, to the roll of the ship, could not entirely be disguised."

Lecoq said, "The scars on your fingers and hands are typical of duelists, as well–where the guard of your rapier did not entirely block a thrust." Alejandro stared at him, and Lecoq added, "We are not entirely unfamiliar with duelists in Paris, you know."

Alejandro smiled and bowed. "Very well. I see the pretense is meaningless now. But, Carot, even the two of us may not be enough to force our way into Miguel's cabin."

Lecoq said, "Yes. Which is why I shall be in the engine room."

Carot said, "What…?"

Lecoq said, "The worms cannot be permitted to go to shore, and De Vega and Poiret must be punished for the murders they committed. If the ship sinks, both goals can be achieved, and I believe I know enough of steam engines to damage this ship's so badly that they explode and sink the ship. We may not survive, of course, but justice will be served."

Carot shrugged and nodded. "That would seem to be a fair trade."

Alejandro stared at the pair, whose nonchalance was, he thought, sincere. "I am not so eager to leave this life as you. I have a beautiful wife who will be furious with me if I do not return home. Perhaps, Monsieur, you could hold off on destroying the ship until you are sure we have failed?"

Lecoq smiled. "If you insist."

Carot and Alejandro were walking down the stairs to the deck of Miguel's cabin when they heard the sound of a detonation and felt the ship lurch briefly. They unsheathed their swords and ran the rest of the way. The Gypsies in front of Miguel's door were dead, stabbed through the heart so quickly that they had not even had time to clear their guns from their holsters, and the door to the cabin had been kicked open. Alejandro let the tip of his sword precede him and Carot into Miguel's cabin.

The cabin looked as if a horde of Cossacks had rampaged through it. Broken glass, torn curtains, and in the wall of the room, a gaping hole whose edges were large enough for Alejandro to walk through, and whose edges were still smoldering. Standing in front of the hole, staring out into the night, bloody swords in hands, were Poiret's companion and the scarred gypsy who had acted as Miguel's bodyguard.

He slipped a glass vial, which Carot could see was filled with Miguel's worms, into his vest pocket and smiled at Alejandro and Carot. Then he said, "I don't believe we've been introduced. I am Isadore Persano. You will know of me as the greatest duelist of the Continent. But I bear you no ill will, Señor, so please believe me when I tell you that this is not your concern, and you should leave immediately. What follows, you will not want to see."

Carot stepped to Alejandro's right, so that he, not Alejandro, was now facing Persano, and said, "We can't do that."

"Can't you be persuaded to step outside for, oh, five minutes? Come, name your price. I can pay it."

"And leave the worms to you? Certainly not. And there is also the issue of murders which must be atoned for."

"Forget the murders, old man. Listen to me: the Emperor's plan is foolishness–the English will never allow it to come to pass, nor the Americans, and the Emperor himself is served by fools. Poiret believes that Butler and Flashman can be relied upon, and the dwarf is sane enough to serve him well. The fool! This plan is doomed from the start. So why let the worms go to waste? I do not seek conquest, merely to help myself and my confederates. What we do, you will never hear of. So why not let me pay you to look away, while I and my friend Zee, here–" he said, indicating the gypsy, "leave the ship? I can afford to pay whatever you ask. But resist me? No, no. You cannot stop me–I was trained by de Lobo himself, while you... I say this with no malice, but you are many years past whatever prime you once had. You will not survive past the third stroke. You have spirit, but do not commit suicide out of pride. Why not enrich yourself, instead?"

Carot smiled, mildly. "Are you through?"

"So eager to die, then?"

Carot and Alejandro assumed the *en garde* position, and Persano and Zee launched their attacks. Persano feinted at Carot's head and then thrust, quickly but casually, at Carot's heart. Carot parried, feinted at Persano's face, and then lunged for his thigh, which Persano jerkily parried.

The exchange between Alejandro and Zee was less skillful and more brutal, with heavy blows rapidly exchanged and parried. As they fought Persano stepped back and coolly regarded Carot. "Not so far gone in age as I thought, then."

Carot smiled and inclined his head, and then thrust without looking, aiming for Persano's waist. Persano's parry-riposte came quickly enough to force Carot to take a rapid step back and whirl his sword in a circular defense.

Carot smiled at Persano. "So. You *do* know your steel after all, and the reputation is not just bluster and gas."

Both saluted the other with his blade, and the duel began in earnest, feints following parries and thrusts darting at eyes, throat, chest, groin and thighs with such rapidity that both men reacted on instinct alone, letting their years of training and experience take over. Carot's blows left shallow cuts on the shoulders and cheeks of Persano, and Persano's thrusts, aimed at Carot's torso and thighs, left cuts that were messy but inconsequential. Alejandro and Zee, meanwhile, were furiously hammering away at each other, as if their rapiers were longswords, and were using their fists and elbows when possible.

Carot and Persano parted momentarily, to catch their breath. Carot said, "How did the hole get in the wall, anyhow? Not your doing, I take it?"

"No–it was the dwarf. As soon as we kicked in the door, he grabbed a bag, pointed something at the wall, and then it exploded and he jumped through the hole. He may be a dwarf, but by God, can he move when he is threatened."

Another rapid exchange of blows, both men growing slightly deaf from the thumping of the feet in the cabin and the squeal of metal on metal.

They backed away a step, panting slightly and looking at each other with renewed respect.

Carot said, "Your reputation is, if anything, underrated."

"While you...how is it I do not know of you? Who trained you?"

"No one you would have heard of, and he is long dead anyhow. As for me, you would have known of me 60 years ago, when the Emperor dubbed me 'Monsieur Coupe-Tête.' "

Persano shook his head and shrugged, and Carot sighed. "No one has any memory any more."

Persano glanced at Alejandro, who carried out an intricate series of feints against his opponent, followed by a swift trio of slashes, which left the man curled up on the floor, his chest a bloody mess. Persano grimaced and said, "I believe we have also underestimated the Mexican. Not a mistake we'll make again."

Carot said, "With respect, Monsieur, I do not intend to allow you the chance to make any future mistakes. Although if you give me the worms, I will merely give you to Monsieur Lecoq."

"I'm certain you would. And in other circumstances I would gladly pursue this to its end. But I know something you do not, Coupe-Tête."

"Oh? What is that?"

"That 20 minutes have passed since I arrived here."

"And this matters because…?"

"Because the bomb which will sink this ship and cover my escape had a 20 minute fuse, and was lit 20 minutes ago."

Alejandro said to Carot, "Do you think Lecoq will have assumed we failed by now?"

"Quite possibly."

Two explosions ripped through the ship, causing it to shudder and list and throwing the three men to the floor. Persano was first to his feet, and immediately dove through the hole in the wall, ignoring Zee's pained cries for help. Carot and Alejandro stared after Persano, and then smelled smoke.

Carot said, "Go, Señor–I'll get Lecoq and meet you on the shore." The old man ran into the hall, which was filling with smoke. Alejandro watched him go, heard distant shouts and the ringing of alarm bells, and followed Persano into the waters of the Gulf. When he surfaced, he began swimming toward the lights on the shoreline.

"…And that is how I escaped the *De Peyrac*, before it sank. Most of the crew and passengers survived as well, though, like me, many had a cold and wet evening of it. I did not see any familiar faces on the lifeboats, nor have I seen them in the City since."

One of the women sitting across from Alejandro at the café said, "No one has seen your cousin, Señor. He did not arrive on shore in the boats, and none of our watchers have seen him. One of our men went south and spoke with the Hualpai–they searched as far south as Palomar and did not find him. We believe he drowned. You have our sympathies."

Alejandro sighed heavily. He knew that poor Miguel was not a sane man, and that, if he had continued on the path he had chosen, he would have been responsible for much misery and death. But Alejandro couldn't help but feel that

Miguel's death was a waste. *One more lesson about what cruelty can achieve. It is a vile weed. It was planted in Miguel, and flowered in full.* "And Persano?"

The woman shook her head emphatically. "Oh, no. We have been *especially* interested in him after your warnings, but he, too, has been unseen. He went to the bottom of the Gulf, him and his worms, and may the fish nibble his *huevos* for all eternity."

Alejandro nodded. "Good. Then, without Miguel, and without the worms, Poiret and the French will be forced to remain here and fight as ordinary men do. And we can return to California."

Elena de la Torre, great-granddaughter of Ramon de la Torre, nodded. "Yes. After so long away, there will be some who think that the Fox has died. We shall have to remind them."

On the *d'Argouges*, in the hammocks where the survivors of the *de Peyrac* were quartered, Zee glowered. Persano had left him on the ship to die, and Poiret had called him a failure and coldly dismissed him from the Bureau. After years of faithful service, from the mountains of Transylvania to the wilds of Montabania, *this* was how he was rewarded–with betrayal and insults! Worst of all, the 'z' scar that the Spaniard had left on his chest burned; it was a permanent mark of dishonor which could never be removed. *Very well, then. If dishonor, betrayal, and insults are what a faithful Romany can expect from the* gadjo*, I will show them what they can expect from an angry Romany. Let them learn why their ancestors feared the Ramogiz.* He had relatives among the Romany and Ramogiz clans of the French countryside. It would not be difficult to persuade them to come to Paris and form a gang. *And then Poiret will learn what it means to anger the Ramogiz.* As for the 'z'…the Spaniard had vanished, but the mark could be turned into an emblem, to make the *gadjo* shudder and weep and its sight, and make the mark of the 'z' a reminder of fear rather than dishonor…

North and east of *d'Argouges* Miguel de Vega was flying a few feet above the water, his personal dirigible carrying him to New Orleans and safety. He had retained several of the worms, and of course knew how to make more, but otherwise he was extremely discontented. Persano's attack had not been unanticipated, but Miguel hadn't expected how frightening being the subject of an assassination attempt would be. *Clearly my safety depends on never being seen to be the leader. Plotting from the shadows is the wisest course for me.* But much more upsetting was Alejandro's betrayal. *So Mother was right after all, and the de la Vegas not to be trusted, ever. And to think I actually thought I could depend on that smirking coward!* Miguel let himself feel a moment of deep and sincere self-pity. He was the last of the de Vegas–his genealogical researches in Bayonne and Santander had proven that–and he could not admit to being related to the de la Vegas. He would father children–he had already fathered two–but no woman would ever marry him, so there could be no more de Vegas. He was truly alone, without blood, without family, without love. *I can no longer call myself 'de Vega.' I must find a new and more appropriate name.*

A month later, at a café in Paris, Lecoq sipped his Geierslay and admired the sunset over the Seine. He smiled wryly at his friends and said to Carot, "Did I tell you of the reaction in the Rue de Jérusalem when I submitted the report about our trip to Mexico?"

Carot shook his head. "No. I haven't seen you since we returned."

"They were displeased."

"Ha. I'm surprised you retain your job."

"I am in disgrace at the moment, but I am too valuable to be gotten rid of so casually."

Hector Ratichon said, "You know too much, you mean."

Père Tabaret said, "Come, Lecoq, we know you. What did you threaten them with?"

Carot said, "A little bird I know tells me Poiret has been sent to Berlin and told to say there for the time being."

Ratichon said, "And I have heard that the entire Bureau is being over-hauled. What did you say to them, Lecoq?"

Lecoq looked at the expectant faces of his friends—older, experienced, accomplished men, the kind he had always admired and tried to emulate—and felt a warm glow at the knowledge that he was not just accepted in their company, but a welcome part of it, and that he was about to please and surprise them.

He said, "I stopped in the ship's hold before I went to the engine room. I thought a brief search of De Vega's luggage might prove fruitful." He removed a small glass bottle from his jacket pocket and held it up, for the others to see. Inside the bottle could be seen several writhing green worms. "I was right."

"What about the others?" inquired Ratichon.

"Don de la Vega is back in California," said Lecoq. "His cousin has, for all intents and purposes, vanished. As for Persano, I've made some inquiries since and found he served some particularly unforgiving masters. If his dip into the ocean didn't finish him, I have no doubt that his employers will punish him for his failure, and justice will be served."

"A third case worthy of note is that of Isadora Persano, the well-known journalist and duelist, who was found stark staring mad with a match box in front of him which contained a remarkable worm said to be unknown to science."

John H. Watson, MD.

John Peel has always delighted us in the past with clever mysteries, but this time, he has chosen to return to his literary sources, as it were, by featuring that enigmatic traveler in space and time known to some as Doctor Omega. The springboard for this story was an e-mail discussion about the significance of Professor James Moriarty's notorious oeuvre, The Dynamics of an Asteroid. *Take it away, John...*

John Peel: *The Dynamics of an Asteroid*

Outer Space, 1908

Since I had thrown my lot in with Doctor Omega, straining whatever small quantity of bravery I might by nature possess, I had faced many dangers. My name is Denis Borel, and my limited claim to fame before this was to fall heir to a medium-sized fortune and to be sufficiently gifted on the violin as to be an accepted amateur player at an occasional *soirée*. However, once I joined my rustic neighbor for dinner one evening, all manner of strange, calamitous and life-threatening events had ensued.

He had been engaged in the building and test flight of a craft capable of traversing both space and time. Together we had embarked on a perilous journey to the planet Mars at a time when it still possessed life–sentient, malevolent reptilian creatures bent on our destruction. All save one, that is, a scientist named Tiziraou. When the Doctor, his hulking assistant, Fred, and I had escaped Mars, this worthy had accompanied us back to Earth–which he found as fascinating as the Doctor's neighbors found *him*.

I mention all of this as preface to explaining why I discovered myself one day perched on the side of a waterfall, waiting for a man to fall into my lap. Nothing in my life previous to meeting the good Doctor would have ever led me to such a dangerous predicament–but since meeting him!... Well, it seemed almost perfectly natural, in a very unnerving manner.

These were the Reichenbach Falls, one of the tallest such in Europe. Near the pleasant town of Meiringen in Switzerland, they descend (perilously) some 250 meters to a large pool below. A good deal of steam is thrown up by the descent, often completely obscuring the pool if one stands at the head of the falls. The rocks, as I discovered by personal experience, are quite slippery as a result, and it seemed to me quite likely that a man could plunge to his death–in this case, myself and my own demise.

"Why must I do this?" I asked the Doctor before venturing out onto the rocks with Fred, who had already begun to affix a safety net–though not intended for us!–in place.

176

"I have already explained twice," the Doctor replied in his usual gruff manner. "I can hardly balance like a mountain goat on those rocks at my age. And Tiziraou is hardly adapted to life with this amount of moisture in the air. Besides which, anyone seeing him here might well expire from shock, and we are attempting to save a life and not destroy one. Therefore, it must be you who helps Fred. Now, off you go, and stop complaining." He made sweeping gestures with his hands and I, most reluctantly, stepped from the safety of the cabin of the *Cosmos* and onto the slippery rocks of Reichenbach Falls.

Fred held out a strong hand to help steady me, and then passed me a rope to tie off. As he and I worked, straining carefully not to lose our precarious footing, the Doctor glanced at his watch from the safety of the ship.

"Do hurry it up," he called above the roar of the falls. "It is almost time. May 4, 1891–a most momentous occasion." It was typical of the Doctor that we were risking our necks, and all that concerned him was his chronometer. He had planned this rescue down to almost the exact second. This was understandable, because as soon as anything happened, there would be only seconds in which we could act.

I strained to see anything in the mists above us, but visibility was extremely limited–no doubt a good thing, since otherwise the *Cosmos* would have been visible to the two men even now making their way along the upper falls. I hesitate to imagine what would have happened if either man had caught a glimpse of the ship. History might well have been changed had one or both men turned from their assigned fates to investigate.

Doctor Omega had explained several times, with great care, that we had to be very certain that we did not affect the natural flow of the timeline at all with our interference. The body of the man we were attempting to save had never been found, so there was no actual proof that he had died. Saving him and whisking him away, then, would alter nothing. But if the combatants were to be distracted from their fatal encounter, then history would have been altered, and there would be no way to know how this might have affected our own time.

"And I mean that quite literally!" the Doctor had snapped, emphasizing his point by wagging a bony finger under the noses of both Fred and myself. "If the past were to be changed in any way, then *our* pasts would change with it. And that change would become part of our memories, and we would believe that history had always been like that. But such changes, no matter how minor, might result in, say, one of us never being born. And I'm certain that people even with your limited intellects can see how unpleasant that might be. So–no changing of any details in the past, no matter how trifling! I trust that this is quite clear!"

It was, of course. I had no desire for my entire life to evaporate like a puff of smoke–no matter how inconsequential I might be to the history of the human race, I still feel myself to be somewhat essential, even if only to myself. As a result, I was taking great care with the placing of the safety net. Fred and I were barely finished with our chore when the Doctor announced urgently: "It is time!"

Clinging to the rocks, Fred and I stared upward, striving to see something–anything–in those wretched mists. I strained my ears in an attempt to hear some signal of the fight that was even now taking place almost 200 meters above our heads. But through the mists and over the roar of the falling waters, nothing could be discerned. We might as well have been blind and deaf.

And then, in an instant, a body came crashing down through the mists, and into our net. The lean, angular form bounced, and then almost broke free before Fred and I both managed to grasp a limb apiece and haul the badly shaken man from the net. He was stunned and incoherent, unable to stand or aid in his own rescue. Fred thrust him toward the open door of the waiting *Cosmos*, and Doctor Omega gripped the man's hands and pulled him within.

"Now," he barked, "cut free the net! We must leave no trace of this man's salvation!"

Fred pulled an axe from his ample waist-band and chopped at the ropes securing the net in place. As soon as he had severed the ropes close to him, he passed me the axe so that I might do the same to the ones on my side. Let me tell you, it is no simple matter to chop at soaked ropes on slippery rocks with one hand whilst holding on for grim life with the other.

Needless to say, I received no sympathy from the Doctor. "Hurry it up, man!" he cried. "We must be gone from here before anyone can investigate!"

As swiftly as we could, Fred and I finished the chore of disposing of all traces of the netting. We hurried back inside the ship, and the Doctor sealed the door, and then set the *Cosmos* into temporal flight. If anyone in 1891 were looking at us, the ship would simply have seemed to vanish.

Shaking from both the exertion and the strain on my nerves, I staggered to one of the chairs in the main cabin and all but collapsed into it. Fred, in his usual cheerful manner, seemed unaffected by our feat, and joined the Doctor at the controls. I glanced around and saw that the man we had rescued was sitting in another of the chairs, but he was not relaxing, or even recovering from his ordeal. He was staring fixedly at Tiziraou.

I cannot blame him, for anyone seeing the Martian for the first time would stare. He was only about two feet high, with a large head and unblinking red eyes. His skin had a greenish cast to it, betraying his reptilian ancestry. He was seated in a specially-built chair and pouring over the controls, ignoring the rescued man.

As I was the only person close to him, our guest leaned over to me, and gestured. "What manner of creature is that?" he asked. "I had believed myself cognizant of all classes and phylum of terrestrial life."

"Perhaps you are," I rejoined. "It is not reflection on your learning–our companion is a Martian."

"Ah." The lean man nodded, pressing his hands together almost as if in prayer. "That would explain matters–at least, a few. Now, of greater importance–why have you risked your lives to rescue me?"

Doctor Omega, though apparently deep in study of the ship's controls, had clearly been listening to our conversation. He turned toward up, his right hand gripping the lapel of his frock coat. "May I take it that I am addressing Professor James Moriarty?"

"You may indeed, sir–though you have the advantage of me. To the best of my recollection–and it is inevitably accurate–I have never met any of you before. I repeat then–why have you risked your lives to rescue me?"

The Doctor chuckled. "It is hardly likely that you would have either met or heard of us, Professor–though you are well known to us through the memoirs of Dr. John H. Watson."

"Watson?" Moriarty snorted. "That third-rate scribbler of the so-called deductions of Sherlock Holmes!"

"I fully understand your animosity toward both men," the Doctor said. "But please place your personal feelings aside for the moment, and I will explain our purposes here. According to the writings of Dr. Watson, you and Sherlock Holmes faced one another at the Reichenbach Falls, where you both appeared to perish."

"Appeared?" Moriarty's forehead creased. "Do you mean to say that Holmes survived also?"

"Indeed."

The Professor gave a cry of rage, and thumped his clenched fist down on the chair arm with sufficient force to crack the wood. "Damnation! I would gladly have perished if it meant the end of Holmes also."

Fred's eyebrows rose. "You'd have been happy to die if you killed him too?"

Moriarty had recovered his spirits by now, and stood up. "My pride is everything," he said, simply. "Holmes inconvenienced me, and I allow no man to do that with impunity. My death would have been a small price to pay to destroy him."

I found it difficult to understand the man. "I have long been taught," I replied, "that pride is the first and greatest of sins. It was the sin that caused Lucifer to be cast from Heaven."

"Sin?" Moriarty looked offended. "An unimaginative response from someone barely qualified to be called *homo sapiens*. A man's pride is what raises him above the animals. A man who has no pride in his achievements *has* no achievements."

"Yes, yes," the Doctor replied impatiently, "be that as it may, it has no bearing on why you are here. Allow me to continue, if you would be so kind. My friends and I are from France in the year 1905–14 years after your supposed death. This is why you could not have known us, though we know you."

179

Moriarty's eyes sparkled. "Then this... craft in which I find myself is some kind of device that travels between the ages? A chronic yacht, shall we say?"

"Yes and no, not precisely," the Doctor answered. He appeared to be pleased that our guest had worked this out for himself. "It is mainly capable of space travel–the temporal portion of our journeys are mostly a side-effect, but often a most useful one, as in this case."

"I begin to understand." The Professor bent forward, the index finger of his right hand touching the tip of his nose. "Thanks to the memoirs of Dr. Watson, you knew the date and place of my demise."

"*Supposed* demise," the Doctor corrected. "Had your body been recovered, we could never have attempted a rescue. Changing the course of even a single event known to have occurred might have disastrous effects."

Moriarty nodded. "I can see the logic in that," he agreed. "Alteration of the skein of time could lead to the unweaving of the past as you conceive it, and the future as far as I am concerned."

"Precisely." Doctor Omega beamed. "It is so pleasant to be able to confer with a man who follows my points without all sorts of silly arguing." I felt that the glance he spared me at that point was quite unwarranted.

"So, then," Moriarty continued, "we have established the *how* of my rescue. All that remains is the *why*. I find it difficult to believe that your actions were motivated by simple compassion, else you would spend eternity hopping about like a flea in time, saving all manner of unfortunate souls."

"Well, in fact," Doctor Omega replied with a chuckle, "we are engaged in a purpose something along those lines–though we hope to be able to save a considerably number of lives with only one of your hypothetical flea-jumps."

He was quite enjoying teasing the Professor, clearly hoping that Moriarty would work as much as possible out on his own. The Doctor was enjoying having another articulate man of science about the *Cosmos*. Much as he appeared to enjoy the company of Fred and myself, we were hardly in his intellectual league. And while Tiziraou was in the same intellectual stratosphere as the Doctor, his alienness made true companionship with him extremely difficult. In Moriarty, Doctor Omega had discovered a virtual intellectual equal, and he was exploiting the situation.

"The reason we rescued you is because of that scientific volume you wrote." As he spoke, he drew the book in question, *The Dynamics of an Asteroid*, from the shelf behind him.

Moriarty's eyes sparkled, and he inclined his head slight. "I am to understand that you have read it?"

The Doctor nodded, a smile on his lips.

"And comprehended it?

Again the nod and smile.

Moriarty sprang forward, his hand extended. "There cannot be three people in all of England who can say the same," he commented. "In your case, I do believe that you speak the truth in your claim, given the evidence to my senses." He waved a hand about the cabin. "So, then, the reason you rescued me has become clear. Given the evidence of my rather abstruse work in conjunction with a yacht to sail the reaches of space, I can only conclude that you have discovered an asteroid that is of some problem to you. And since you mentioned the saving of a quantity of lives, I can further only assume that the asteroid in question is on a collision path with the Earth."

"Splendid, my dear Professor, splendid!" the Doctor cried, clapping his hands in approbation, for all the world as if this were some student examination at a University, and the pupil had just managed to defend his thesis with a measure of success.

"My dear Doctor," I said, unable to restrain myself further, "you might simply have told him, instead of playing these games."

"My dear Borel," he replied, somewhat sharply, "it was necessary for me to try the Professor and ascertain that his reputation was not based on some fraud. And I find, to the contrary, that his mental abilities are almost as sharp as my own. I do therefore believe we have enlisted the aid of the right person in our quest."

Moriarty inclined his head at the praise. "I take it, then," he said, "that your aim is to somehow divert this asteroid in order that the impending collision will no longer occur?"

"Precisely," Doctor Omega agreed.

"And you require me to perform the calculations to ensure that the object will indeed miss the Earth."

"Correct again," the Doctor agreed.

"Then I have only one further question," the Professor said. "What specific force will you be utilizing in order to divert this aerial rock?"

"That," Doctor Omega replied, "you shall find out very shortly, as we are now on our way to collect the final member of our daring band of adventurers."

I had to confess that I had not taken too well to Professor Moriarty. An intellectual genius he might be, but his egotism was worse than that of Doctor Omega–and he was by no means a modest man! Also, I could not forget that Sherlock Holmes himself had called the man the "Napoleon of Crime." Trusting him appeared to me to be a very foolish mistake. I had, of course, said as much to the Doctor when he had broached his daring plan to avert catastrophe, but he had, rather typically, simply waved away my fears by stating that nobody would ever get the better of Doctor Omega.

It would have done no good to have reminded him of all the people who had, in fact, gotten the better of him–even if only on a temporary basis. And none of *them* had ever been considered a genius.

So, as you may imagine, I was not altogether sanguine about this entire enterprise. And my confidence sagged even further as Doctor Omega brought the *Cosmos* in for a stealthy landing in the Bois de Boulogne in the early evening, when there was less chance of our being observed. Moriarty elected to remain in the ship, along with Tiziraou and Fred, while I accompanied the Doctor to retrieve the final member of our band from his lodgings in the Rue Cassette.

The Widow Thibault—who owned the building following the death of her husband, and who let out rooms to one singular individual—met us at the door. "Oh," she said, in her usual surly fashion. "It's you two gentlemen again. I hope you've come to take him away. All that banging about upstairs, and me a poor widow whose nerves can't stomach all of these to-ings and fro-ings such as he indulges in, and returning with all manner of oddments and assortments."

"He has been busy, then?" Doctor Omega asked, cheerfully.

"I'll say he has!" The elderly lady looked indignant. "Can't you hear him even now?"

We listened, and heard nothing. I ventured to say as much, and in return received a ferocious scowl that would have intimidated even one of the greater cats.

"It's just stopped," she said. "I dare say it'll start up again shortly."

"I doubt that, my good woman," the Doctor replied, making for the stairs, "for we are indeed here to take him away."

"Well, mind he comes back in one piece!" Widow Thibault snapped. "I don't want to have to go looking for a new lodger at my time of life."

"We shall have him back in no time," Doctor Omega promised.

"Perhaps literally," I added, but under my breath. I did not wish to have to explain myself to the Widow. I followed the Doctor up the stairs, and waited as he hammered loudly on the lodger's door.

A moment later, it was opened by a veritable wreck of a fellow. Tall, disheveled, and remarkably ugly, Zephyrin Xirdal was always a shock to look at. He always appeared to have dressed in the dark, with one arm tied behind his back. Nothing he wore matched, and none of it was freshly pressed or worn entirely straight. His mismatched socks were twisted—one inside a boot, the other encased in a slipper. His trousers looked as if they had been slept in—and perhaps had, as Xirdal did not always remember to change clothes before retiring—and his shirt was only half-buttoned, and most of those buttons in incorrect holes.

He blinked at us both, as if struggling to recall who we were, even though (in his measurement of time) he had seen us only three days before when we had approached him with our proposal. He raised a finger, which wavered in the air uncertainly. "And you are here for...?" he asked, vaguely.

As I believe I have already mentioned, my confidence of success in our venture was rapidly approaching zero. Xirdal was another of those eccentric geniuses I seemed to be constantly stumbling across. Like both Doctor Omega and Professor Moriarty, he had a terribly high opinion of his own abilities, but, unlike them, his mind was so restless as to be unable to settle upon a single track and remain on it. The slightest, strayest thought might distract him and set his feverish imagination off in a completely unpredictable direction. Doctor Omega had required Xirdal to reconstruct a machine he had once created–a task the inventor claimed was child's play (before going off on a tangent and trying to invent a new game for the younger generation). Indeed, given his apparent intellect, it might well have been–but only if he had managed to recall just what it was that he was supposed to be building.

"Your rectilinear generator," the Doctor prompted.

Xirdal's vast expanse of brow creased as he struggled to recall. "Didn't I use that to move the golden meteor?" he asked. "I believe it was destroyed then."

"Indeed it was," the Doctor replied. "And I requested that you rebuild it, if you recall."

"You did?" Xirdal shrugged. "If you say so. I have been busy on a new invention, you know, and–"

My heart sank. It was as I feared–the pitiable fool had become distracted, and instead of building the device we needed in order to save the Earth, he had manufactured instead perhaps some device for removing the skin from rice pudding.

"We might as well give up now," I said to the Doctor. "We are defeated without his device."

"Don't be so swift to despair, my boy!" Doctor Omega replied. "True, Monsieur Xirdal is easily distracted, and apt to be a trifle forgetful–but he *did* commence the work for me, if you recall." He turned back to the puzzled inventor and smiled. "Might we just glance at what you have done?" he asked.

"By all means," Xirdal agreed, amiably. "You might find this new idea of mine most interesting. I was walking down the street this morning, and it occurred to me that we waste a great deal of our time in our daily toiletries. So I thought it would be most helpful if we had some devices that could aid us in them." He had led his way into his cluttered apartment. Did I say "cluttered?" That is too mild a word for it! There were piles of papers all over, save for a small space before the room's single window. The leaning tower of Pisa could hardly have appeared more precariously balanced that many of the stacks that lay about the room. Yet Xirdal insisted that, if the need arose, he could find any article or note at a moment's notice. The table was reasonably clear–at least of papers, as there were the remains of breakfast scattered upon it. Aside from that, and a small path to walk upon, the room was almost literally overflowing.

In the small space beneath the window stood two odd-looking constructions. One of them appeared to be all armatures, belts and small motors, and it was to this that the inventor headed. "My automatic shaving device," he explained. "I intend to mount it on the arm of a chair, you see. The head fits within this area here–" he indicated the place in the middle of what looked like an apparatus more suited to a torture chamber that a bathroom "–and then the machine will proceed to shave him while he reads the morning paper."

I examined the machine closer, and saw that there was indeed a straight razor attached to one armature. "Good Heavens!" I exclaimed. "I wouldn't trust that machine not to cut my throat! Thank you, but I prefer someone considerably more human wielding a razor near my throat!"

"Stuff and nonsense!" Xirdal replied. "My device is perfectly safe. Well, will be, once I adjust it." That did not inspire confidence.

"Excuse me," Doctor Omega broke in, indicating the second machine in the small space. "And what, pray, might this be for?"

I followed his gaze, and saw a machine even odder than the probably-lethal automatic shaver. It was a black box, surmounted by a reflective mirror on some sort of universal joint that would allow it to be positioned at any possible angle. There were a few small knobs and switches on the side, but nothing to indicate its function.

"That?" Xirdal waved a hand airily. "That's a duplicate of my helicoidal and rectilinear generator."

"The same one I was just inquiring about?" the Doctor persisted.

"Most likely," Xirdal agreed. "But to return to–"

"And is it completed?" the Doctor growled.

"Completed?" The inventor bent to examine it. "Yes, I would say so. It certainly appears to be. Why do you ask?"

Doctor Omega turned to me. "Grab one of his arms, my boy," he said, gaily. "I shall bring the generator. We must return to the *Cosmos* immediately."

I did as I was bid, and dragged the puzzled, protesting inventor along with us as we raced down the stairs. Xirdal protested weakly, but neither the Doctor nor I paid him much heed. Nor did we really listen to the Widow as she yelled: "One piece, mind you! One piece!" as we left.

We managed to secure a cab, and sent it racing toward the Bois de Boulogne and our comrades. I was now able to pause and breathe. Xirdal had completed his machine for us–and then promptly forgotten about it, lost in the plans for his later device. But we were saved–and, hopefully, the rest on Mankind along with us!

"Where are we going?" the inventor finally asked. "I do not have my coat on."

"I'll lend you one of mine," the Doctor assured him. "We are on our way to outer space."

"Outer space?" Xirdal blinked. "It's terribly cold out there–I shall require an overcoat as well."

We managed to get him back to the ship without drawing too much undue attention to ourselves, and then we were off, leaving fair Paris behind and heading into the cold darkness of outer space.

I can only leave it to your imagination to picture the wild conversations flung about the cabin as we traveled. With one alien mastermind and three human geniuses, neither Fred nor I could make out more than one word in ten, and could understand even less. Xirdal was entranced by the *Cosmos*, and immediately perceived several ways to improve upon its design. Doctor Omega vacillated between feeling insulted that anyone had the temerity to imagine they could improve upon anything he had constructed and curiosity and admiration for the suggestions that Xirdal let slip. I cannot tell how much of this Moriarty understood, but he was paying very careful attention to everything–suspiciously so in my mind, though I could get no one else to share my suspicions. Even Fred, who I felt the closest to, simply shrugged.

"If he's planning any treachery, I'm sure the Doctor has plans well in hand." How could you argue with such faith? Especially when the object of his faith wouldn't comment on the matter beyond a tetchy "Bah!" before plunging back into his animated conversations.

Thankfully, even the longest of journeys must finally come to an end, and we reached our target–the unnamed asteroid on its way to collide with our fair home planet. As we neared it, Fred and I gazed out of the observation windows at it.

It is almost impossible to successfully describe the scene we beheld–the depth of the blackness of space itself, the glimmer of billions of lights, each a pinprick of a star. Even the Sun itself, ruler of all our days on Earth, was a mere speck of light at this distance. And there, growing before us, the asteroid, our target. We seemed to be so far from the Earth that the rock surely would pose no threat. I mentioned this to the Doctor, but it was Moriarty who chose to reply.

"Bah! You cannot comprehend the beautiful intricacies of mathematical formulae! Celestial mechanics are fixed and unswerving, their elegant designs predictable to the nth degree. I have checked and rechecked the Doctor's calculations, and I concur completely–this asteroid will indeed impact upon the Earth, with catastrophic results."

"Thank you, my dear Professor," the Doctor said, with a smug glance in my direction, as if daring me to challenge his theories further. "In 12 years, humanity will face almost certain destruction."

"Shortly after 7 a.m. on June 30, 1908," Moriarty amplified. "It will strike in Russia, and the impact will be so immense that it will alter the composition of the atmosphere, and raise so much debris and dust that the face of the Earth will be completely cut off from the benevolent rays of the Sun."

"All growing plants will die as a result," Xirdal added. "And, as a consequence, any animal life that survived the initial impact will face slow starvation. In a matter of months, virtually all life on Earth will become extinct."

"Unless we prevent it," the Doctor said, completing their thoughts.

"But why here? Why now?" I objected. "Surely there is plenty of time to act, and millions of kilometers in which to pursue this would-be killer."

Xirdal sighed. "As this asteroid is pulled into the center of our Solar System," he explained, "it will speed up. By the time it reaches the Earth, it will be traveling at an immense speed. The farther from the Earth we affect its course, the easier it will be to ensure that its path avoids that of our planet entirely. A small force applied here and now will be most efficacious—were we to attempt this closer to the Earth, then a much greater force would be required." He gestured to the box and parabolic dish we had brought with us from his crowded flat. "My machine is very efficient, but even this would not be powerful enough to affect the path of the asteroid if we were to attempt to deflect it closer to the Earth."

I nodded my understanding. Xirdal had previously attempted to explain how his machine worked, but it was quite beyond my grasp. All I knew was that in some strange—yet thoroughly scientific!—manner, the machine was able to produce a force that acted upon remote objects. Once planted upon the surface of the asteroid and switched into operation, it would somehow reach out across space to Jupiter, that giant among planets. It would then latch onto the gravity of this world and using this force, create an attraction that would cause the asteroid to adjust its path slightly. Slightly, true—but sufficient to ensure that the asteroid would completely miss the Earth. And if reversed, the machine would repel other objects.

At least, that was the idea. I could only hope and pray that our small herd of geniuses knew whereof they spoke—because Fred and I were completely lost! And why, you may wonder, were we there? We whose intellect was so far below that of the Doctor, the Professor and the inventor? Why else, but to do the actual work involved.

Doctor Omega fiddled with the controls of the *Cosmos* as intently and furiously as I fingered the strings of my violin during a Caprice by Paganini. His digits flew across the controls—twisting here, turning there, tweaking everywhere—until at last he interlaced the fingers of both hands together and announced with a certain amount of self-satisfaction: "Well, gentlemen—and Tiziraou—we have arrived!"

I must confess that it was something of a disappointment. The asteroid looked like nothing so much as a rather oversized baked potato. It was covered in small craters, rather like the surface of the Moon, but there was nothing else to see. No mountains, nor rivers, or anything else. "It's rather dull," I observed.

"Perhaps now," agreed the Doctor. "But once it reaches the Earth, it will be far from such. Now, we must position the helicoidal rectilinear device on the surface and then set the timer precisely. Obviously, my dear Xirdal, you must accompany us—as will Fred and Denis."

"Me?" I objected. "I don't see what is so obvious about that!"

"Come now, my dear Borel, this is something of a unique experience—to be amongst the first humans ever to set foot on an asteroid! Surely you would not even think about passing up the chance?" He did not give me the opportunity to reply that I most certainly would, but plunged ahead. "On which point, I must caution you all. This asteroid has virtually no gravity, such as we are used to on Earth or even Mars. We shall need to fasten a safety line to enable us to move about, and you must all be careful to remain attached to it at all times. If you were to kick too hard, you would go flying off into space, and we should have to attempt to rescue you."

"What of the cold?" Xirdal asked. "I did not bring a coat, you may recall."

"Hang the cold!" Fred objected. "What about the insufficiency of air to breath? That's far more urgent."

"Actually, both items are equally important," Doctor Omega replied. "Either one would kill you in an instant."

"You're hardly making this little stroll of yours sound very appealing," I said. "It makes remaining behind more and more attractive."

"Courage, my friend, courage!" The Doctor slapped me on the arm heartily. It stung. "I have carefully considered the issue, and settled the matter. Using the *Cosmos*, I ventured forward in time a century or so and... borrowed several special sets of clothing from the future. Come along, all of you, and I shall see about getting you prepared for your perambulation."

"I shall, of course, remain with the ship," Tiziraou said. "I doubt you have protective clothing in my size."

"And I shall, if you've no objection, remain with him," Moriarty said. He glanced out of the observation window and shuddered. "Having experienced falling to my death once already today, I am not anxious to repeat the experience. I must confess it makes me a trifle nauseous simply to glance outside the ship."

"As you wish," the Doctor replied. "Then that leaves the four of us, my friends!" He seemed to have ignored my desires to remain behind. I attempted to reiterate them, but he brushed my protests aside, and I found myself swept along with the others into the store room.

Here stood four sets of the strangest clothing I had ever seen. They were a pure, almost dazzling, white, and looked a little like diving equipment, down to the helmets that rested beside each suit. They were large and cumbersome, and appeared to be very uncomfortable. Each one had a curious emblem on the arm bearing the letters NASA. I assumed that this was some sort of a ship from which the Doctor had stolen the suits.

"These are designed to protect you from the deadly environment out there," the Doctor explained. "We must each don one, and then check that there are no leaks–which would be lethal. There is no air on the asteroid at all."

"No air?" Xirdal had been examining his suit intently–no doubt thinking of a thousand and one ways in which he could improve upon it. "Then how are we to communicate with one another?"

"Each suit has a Marconi device implanted within, at a preset frequency. It enables us to converse with one another, and with a similar device I have implanted in the control room, and which Tiziraou will operate. We shall be in constant communication in case of difficulties."

"Remarkable!" the inventor exclaimed. "I'll just take a quick look at it, and–"

"First things first!" Doctor Omega replied. "After we have adjusted the trajectory of the asteroid, there will be ample time for you to indulge your whims." Xirdal wasn't happy about being derailed and set back on his original course, but he subsided and condescended to don the suits, along with the Doctor, Fred and myself.

Yes, myself! Despite all of my protests, I somehow found myself inside one of those infernal contraptions!

We moved through the ship to the exit. Here Doctor Omega handed Fred a harpoon, to which was attached a long, coiled rope. He then opened the outer door. There was a hiss as all of the air within the small room was sucked outside. "The natural force of a vacuum," the Doctor explained. He then pointed a gloved hand at a small hillock. "Fred, if you would be so kind as to throw that harpoon and embed it in that mound, we shall have an anchor point."

Fred eyed the distance dubiously. "That's some throw, sir," he finally said.

"There is very little gravity, my boy," was the reply. "You'll discover that it is a comparatively simply toss when you try it."

Fred looked by no means as certain of this claim as was his employer, but he hefted the harpoon and threw. I watched with interest; I have always known that Fred was strong, but that throw was astounding–the harpoon slipped through the air as if fired from a cannon. In moments, it was indeed deeply embedded in the stony side of the hillock. Fred gave the rope an experimental tug and pronounced it safe to use. The near end was tied to a stanchion on the ship just outside the exit door, and we all attached cords from the belts of our extra-vehicular suits to it.

"Now, remember," The Doctor cautioned, "there is minimal gravity, so there is no need to press down hard with your feet. If you do so, you will literally step off this world and float away. Take very small steps to begin with until you are comfortable moving about. Xirdal, you have your device? Good. Now, then, gentlemen–let us be the first to step upon the surface of this strange world."

Despite my trepidation, and a mild feeling of claustrophobia from being encased in my mechanical suit, I found the experience novel and even stimulating. As Doctor Omega had said, even a tiny step was akin to a stride wearing the legendary seven-league boots. It was extremely difficult staying close to the surface of the asteroid, and without the restraining ropes, we should all have certainly floated off into space, perhaps to be lost forever. Or, at least, until our air supply was depleted. However, there was a certain exhilaration in being able to leap about unfettered by the ties of gravity that bind us to our Earth, and after a short while I began to actually feel glad I had agreed–however reluctantly–to go along on this strange excursion.

After a short while, Doctor Omega recalled to us that there was a purpose to our expedition, and we set off, more or less together, to find a good place to plant Xirdal's strange device. The inventor and the Doctor conferred and eventually selected a small depression about 30 meters from the ship. The two of them set about playing with the controls, until they were happy with the settings.

Fred and I, meanwhile, simply looked around. I cannot convey the absolute desolation of the asteroid. There was nothing living, and nothing of any color save a slate gray that varied only slightly from place to place. The horizon was astonishing close, and even a few steps in any direction would bring fresh vistas to be seen. Of course, these vistas looked entirely the same as the one we already could see, so there was no variety at all. The sky was uniformly black, punctuated by the brilliant lights that were stars. It was not a place one could love.

Suddenly, Fred gave a warning cry: "Doctor!" I turned to see what had startled him, and found myself rising from the surface. A quick grab by Fred located my foot, and he pulled me gently back to–well, not Earth, but Asteroid, I suppose I should say. But I did see what had startled him.

The farther end of our safety rope, the one attached to the *Cosmos*, had come unfastened. It was floating in the sky. If it had not been for the other end, anchored in the hillock, we should also have been floating in the sky.

"Professor," Doctor Omega called. "The safety line appears to have come detached from the ship."

"I know that," came the Professor's voice. "For I am the one who detached it."

"What is the meaning of this?" the Doctor cried.

"Mutiny, my dear Doctor," Moriarty answered. "This ship of yours is far too valuable and intriguing a device for me to allow it to remain in your hands. I therefore propose to take it for myself and utilize its capabilities to aid my life of crime."

"And what is to happen to us?" the Doctor asked, his voice gravely quiet.

"You will perish, I am afraid," Moriarty replied. "But you may go to your Maker in the knowledge that you have died saving the Earth. Not many people can claim so much."

The staggering enormity of what Moriarty was saying was not lost on me. "He aims to kill us!" I cried.

"Not I," the Professor said, emphatically. "It is merely circumstance that dictates you must perish. I had to seize my opportunity while so many of you were missing that taking over the ship was simple."

"And Tiziraou?" the Doctor asked, anxiously.

"He is safe, but incapacitated," Moriarty replied. "I look forward to immensely entertaining discussions with the Martian."

"Good," the Doctor said. He did not sound at all bothered by what was going on.

I could not be as calm. "I warned you that he was treacherous!" I cried. "And you ignored me! As a result, we are going to die."

"On the contrary," the Doctor said. "I agreed with your estimation of the Professor's character from the start–that he could not be trusted."

I was confused. "Then why did you allow him to take over the ship and strand us here?" I asked, bewildered.

"Because I cannot condemn a man for what he *might* do, only for what he *does* do. I was certain Moriarty would betray us, but I might have been wrong. He deserved the chance, and he has used it to show his true colors."

"I don't understand," I had to confess. "You *wanted* him to seize the ship?"

"Wanted? No. Expected? Yes. And I was certain he would not harm Tizi-raou–but I could not say the same about you, my boy. That was why I insisted, against all of your wishes, that you accompany us on this expedition. I wanted you safe outside the ship if the Professor betrayed us."

"Safe? Outside?" I felt like screaming. "Doctor, we will *perish* out here. Our only safety lies inside the ship."

"The young man is correct," Moriarty said. "And, I am sorry to say, that safety is now about to leave you. Farewell, my friends, and my sincere thanks for this gift to aid me in my future career."

"I only *appeared* to dismiss your warnings, my boy," Doctor Omega continued, as if we were not about to be abandoned to die in the cold depths of space. "I am afraid I slightly misled you. I knew that Moriarty might expect that Zephyrin and I, as men of science, might be somewhat unrealistic in accounting for human nature, and Fred he would dismiss as some simpleton employed only for his strength. But you – you, my boy, he would have been very suspicious if *you* had not suspected him of malicious intent. So we had to keep our plans from you in order that your most natural outcries against the Professor were not stifled."

I was commencing to understand what the Doctor was saying. "You *planned* all of this? And left me unknowing?"

"Precisely, my boy." He sounded smug and unrepentant.

"Then I have been worrying all of this time for nothing?" I cried.

"There was no other option. My dear Denis, you have many talents, but play-acting is not one of them. If we had told you of our plans, then you would never have been able to convince Moriarty that he was safe in his machinations."

"But he has the *Cosmos*!" I pointed out. "And we are to die here."

"No. To both points."

At that instant, there was a cry of frustrated rage from over the Marconi connection. "What have you done?" Moriarty cried. "Why will the ship not move?"

Xirdal cleared his throat. "That would be my doing," he replied. "I have used the helicoidal forces to anchor the *Cosmos* to this asteroid. It will not be able to depart until I adjust my machine–and that will not be until you return control of the ship to the Doctor." He turned to me. "My machine can either repel or attract matter," he explained. "At the moment, it is set to attract–but only specifically the ship. That is why we are not affected by its forces."

There was a moment's silence, and then, of a sudden, the asteroid beneath our feet began to shake. "What is happening?" I cried.

"It's the ship," the Doctor said. "Moriarty is boosting the power, hoping to shake free of the holding force. Grab a hold of the rope, everyone!" We all did so as the asteroid trembled beneath our feet. I glimpsed the Doctor's face within his helmet, and for the first time he appeared to be showing concern. "I confess, I had not anticipated this exact eventuality."

He hadn't expected the Professor to attempt to break free? How foolish!

Like a dog shaking itself to attempt to free himself of fleas, the rock beneath our feet quivered and cracked. I could see fissures commencing to open, all in a terrible silence. The foundations of the asteroid were being torn apart by the two opposing forces of Xirdal's machine and the mighty engines of the *Cosmos*. I could see that it scarcely mattered which won–all of us on the surface of the asteroid would be the losers. The anchor rope we depended upon for our lives would be of little use if the rock broke apart. We would be attached to the rope, but the rope would be attached to nothing.

"Cease this foolishness!" the Doctor cried. "You cannot break free of the machine, and if you cause our deaths, yours will shortly follow. Even now, the engines must be overheating. Turn them off, and allow us to return to the ship if you wish to live."

For long moments, it appeared that his appeal to reason was unavailing. Portions of the asteroid continued to shudder and break free, floating apart from the main body of the rock. In moments it looked as if we might have a strange experience of rain–instead of water falling downwards, that of rocks, pebbles and dust falling upwards. Then, of a sudden, the shaking stopped.

"Very well," came Moriarty's voice. "I am in your hands."

As we recovered our equilibrium, Doctor Omega called out: "Tiziraou–is he telling the truth?"

"Yes," came the Martian's flat reply. He sounded as if nothing that had happened was of any consequence–and possibly, to him, it was not. It was always difficult to discern his emotions–if he possessed them at all.

"Then we are returning to the ship. Kindly open the outer door."

I cannot convey the tremendous relief I felt when we re-entered the ship. I, who had been certain I was on the brink of death, was alive again! Relief flooded through me as we all–save for Xirdal–divested ourselves of the cumbersome suits and then returned to the control room. The inventor remained behind. Our Martian companion was seated at the controls, and Moriarty was standing, hunched, head bowed, to one side.

"Fred," Doctor Omega said with grim satisfaction, "perhaps you would be good enough to lock the Professor within the store-room?"

"Fine," Fred agreed, with a wide grin. "Come on, you." He gripped the Professor's arm and led him off to be imprisoned.

Doctor Omega turned to the Marconi device on the main panel. "Zephyrin, my friend," he said, "you may now go outside and turn your splendid machine off. It is of no further use." Xirdal acknowledged the order, and he left the ship again on his quest.

"No further use?" I asked. As usual with the Doctor, I was at a loss again. "I thought it was needed to steer the asteroid away from the Earth?"

"That was merely what I wished the Professor to believe," the Doctor answered. "I desperately needed Moriarty to confirm all of my calculations concerning the asteroid–which was the reason for this whole charade. Normally, I would have trusted my reasoning implicitly–but with the fate of the human race at stake, I could not take such a chance. Moriarty, for all of his faults, is indeed a mathematical genius, and I knew I could rely on his calculations. The Earth was never in any peril all along."

I suppose I shall one day get accustomed to the feelings of confusion and futility I inevitably feel around the Doctor, but I have not yet risen to such heights. "Then all of this was for nothing?"

"Far from it!" Doctor Omega answered, clapping me on the shoulder. "If we had not intervened, then the Earth would certainly have experienced the catastrophe I described. But I knew that we *must* have intervened, since history shows that humanity faced no such disaster. Remember, I have stressed that we cannot alter history in any way! Since the human race was not to perish, then, clearly, my scheme to save is must have worked."

"But the asteroid is still on a collision course with the Earth," I protested. "And it will still strike Russia in 1908."

"As indeed history said it did," he replied. "It will cause great devastation– but only over a small area in Siberia. Our activities have shaken the rock apart, so that most of it will no longer impact on the Earth, and much of the rest will be small enough to burn up from friction. Only the central core of the asteroid will survive entry into Earth's atmosphere, and it will cause the explosion known to historians of the future as the Tunguska Event. So you see, my boy, our actions were both absolutely critical and absolutely inevitable. We did what we had to do, what we *must* have done, and the Earth is saved and history is conserved. We do, however, have one small matter to resolve."

"And that is?" I asked.

"What we are to do with the Professor."

I smiled. "I would suggest we do to him as he would have done to us–leave him on the surface of the asteroid as we depart."

Fred shook his head. "Why don't we take him back to when we found him and toss him out, so that he can complete his interrupted journey down the Falls?"

"Gentlemen, I am surprised at you," the Doctor answered–though there was a twinkle in his eye. "Both suggestions would make murderers of us."

"He was doomed to die anyway," Fred objected. "We would only be allowing history to run its natural course."

"And you have said that there is no future record of him," I argued. "So he cannot be set free."

"On the contrary, I think that we must indeed allow him to go free," the Doctor answered. "It is simply a matter of finding a suitable prison for him where he can no longer affect events. And I have the perfect solution–Pitcairn Island."

"Pitcairn Island?" I asked.

"A small island in the Pacific far from any shipping lanes. The mutineers from the *HMS Bounty* ended up there in 1790, and the island was uninhabited at the time. So I suggest we drop the Professor off there in 1750–he is an elderly man already, and he can live out the rest of his natural life there without being able to cause any trouble for anyone else again."

Fred and I glanced at one another. Despite our blood-thirsty suggestions, neither of us really wished to be the cause of death for even such as Moriarty. "Very well," I agreed. "Pitcairn Island it is."

"Splendid." Doctor Omega rubbed his hands together in glee. "As soon as Xirdal is back aboard, we'll head there directly. And after that, my friends–who knows? Who indeed?"

For more than 50 years, Henri-René "Jimmy" Guieu (1926-2000) was one of the most popular writers of French science-fiction. Starting in 1952, Guieu became a pillar of publisher Fleuve Noir's legendary "Anticipation" imprint, contributing over 100 genre novels, often dealing with UFOs, "X-Files" and "Ancient Astronaut" themes, and becoming a leading French authority on the subject, predating Erich Von Däniken by several years. One of Guieu's earliest recurring characters was archeologist Jean Kariven, a dashing hero patterned after Clark Gable, who, like TV's Fox Mulder, investigated signs of hidden extra-terrestrial activities amongst Earth's long-lost civilizations, before finally becoming involved in a secret war à la This Island Earth between the good Polarians and the evil Denebians. The following story was written by our new contributor Frank Schildiner for a French anthology honoring Jimmy Guieu, scheduled to be published at the end of this year...

Frank Schildiner: *The Smoking Mirror*

New York, 1955

"We appreciate you giving us your time, Dr. Kraven," the New York Police Inspector said. His name was Cramer and he was tall and powerfully built, with broad shoulders and a round face. An unlit cigar was held clenched in his teeth and he was far more intelligent than he demonstrated.

"Kariven," Jean Kariven corrected. He wasn't fooled by Cramer's rough exterior, recognizing the detective possessed a keen mind that missed few details. The mispronounced last name was a tactic, a feint that caused some to underestimate him.

"My apologies. I'm not good with foreign names," Cramer said, his eyes locked on the French archaeologist. "You staying in the City long?"

"Just long enough to complete my research at Columbia University. May I ask why you brought me here, Inspector?" Kariven asked. He had been about to leave his hotel room when his presence was summonsed to a small tenement apartment in Manhattan's lower east side. The large, solid police Sergeant named Stebbins assigned to drive him there had offered no information beyond an immediate need for his presence.

"We needed an expert, one that wasn't from the area. If you hadn't been in town, the next closest was in Mexico," Cramer said, leading Kariven into the basement apartment.

"Am I suspected of something?" Kariven asked, intrigued.

"Doc," Cramer said, "the only people I don't suspect is me and the mayor... and I ain't too sure about him. But you're on the low end of my list, somewhere between the Pope and my wife."

"How very reassuring," Kariven said, smiling despite himself. He ran a hand through his dark brown hair and was about to ask again why he was brought to this location, when the reason became apparent.

The statue of a man stood in the middle of the bare apartment and appeared to radiate an ancient power that caused everything nearby to recede into shadows. Three feet high and made of a golden brown stone, its ancient eyes seemed to pierce straight to your very soul.

"Xipe Totec," Kariven said. His voice was hushed and reverential, respectful of the majesty of this ancient idol.

"Who?" Cramer asked, pulling out a pristine black notebook and pencil.

"Xipe Totec," Kariven repeated and spelled the words out to the detective while approaching the statue and examining the hieroglyphs at the base.

"I guess we got the right person here for once. Who is this Zippy?"

"Xipe Totec was the Aztec God of agriculture," Kariven explained, standing and looking at Costello. Pointing to the ridge-like bumps on the skin, he added, "The identity is easy to determine, even if I couldn't read the inscription in the base. His skin is pebbled because Xipe Totec is also called the Flayed God."

Cramer visibly flinched, but regained his composure a few seconds later. "Flayed? Like removing the skin?"

"Exactly," Kariven said. "The priests of this God would perform this ritual every year to one of their prisoners. The act was supposed to represent rebirth and renewal of the land."

"And here I thought learning Hail Mary's was rough. Any chance one of these Aztecs might be mad at their little God being here instead of...where is they from?"

"Mexico, and no. Hernando Cortez destroyed the Aztec culture in the 16th century. Some followers may exist, but I have my doubts. Did you find a flayed body?"

"What makes you ask that?" Cramer said, his eyes narrowing.

"Your reaction and questions about Aztecs," Kariven said with a shrug.

Cramer frowned and stared at the French scientist for a moment. Finally he seemed to decide something and said, "Yes, that's why we was called in. A neighbor complained of a smell and found the victim in the bathtub. No skin left on the corpse."

"Interesting," Kariven said, remembering that the high priest of Xipe Totec would wear the skin of their victim to symbolize the god's presence.

"Does the name Joseph Brown mean anything to you?" Cramer asked.

"No, should it?" Kariven replied.

"That's the name on the wallet we found here, Joseph Brown. Worked for the transit authority."

"He's not an academic. There are few that study Aztec culture, I would know if a Joseph Brown was an authority on the subject."

"That's why I brought you here," Cramer said.

He then led Kariven out of the building. After a brief word of thanks and no offer of a ride back, the Inspect and his solid assistant stepped into a waiting police car and were gone.

Kariven was about to raise his hand to hail a passing taxi, when a heavy hand landed on his shoulder. Turning, he found himself standing before a short gray-haired man in a blue coverall. The man's eyes were pure black and his skin was a pale, bloodless white. The man moved his hand quickly to Kariven's neck and lifted the archaeologist from his feet with no visible exertion.

Choking from the vice-like grip, Kariven grabbed the hand, pulling the pinky and palm and breaking free. Landing on his feet, he fired a hard Savate kick to his attacker's midsection. Kariven's shin hit his foe's liver, a vicious blow that his teacher Jerrod used to end most matches.

The kick was perfect, but the man didn't move an inch. He backhanded Kariven, a clumsy but fast blow that knocked the Frenchman stumbling backwards. It was then that Kariven could see the nametag across the front of the coverall: *J. Brown*. His attacker was the man whose apartment held the Xipe Totec statue!

Joseph Brown swung his arm again, knocking Kariven to the pavement. Sliding back while remaining on the ground, the scientist pressed his back against a wall and kicked out with both feet against his enemy's knees. It was a desperate attack, a crippling move meant to end the fight for good, because when the knees were kicked in this fashion, the hard bones would shatter and the pain was excruciating.

Under any other circumstances, the kick would have been perfect and the opponent would have shrieked in agony as he fell. But Joseph Brown merely stepped forward and picked Kariven up from the pavement by his throat. Once again, he began choking the archeologist, this time with both hands.

Kariven, unable to break the grip of his attacker, immediately began to claw at his enemy's face. The skin was dry to the touch and punctured easily, without any blood appearing. A silvery metal was visible beneath the skin, which began to turn black and smoke the minute sunlight hit the open wounds Kariven had just created.

Emitting a high-pitch shriek, Joseph Brown dropped the archeologist, covered his face with his hands and stepped backwards. Moving to a nearby patch of shade, he reached down and pulled up a manhole cover, diving into the depths of the New York sewers.

Kariven's lungs were on fire and his neck felt swollen. He took great gulping breaths, attempting to regain some measure of control. But his mind was immediately jumping ahead. He had just discovered that Xipe Totec, the Flayed God of the Aztecs, was a construct of either the Denebians or the Polarians. He knew that their ancient space war had spilled onto Earth and, long ago, it had become a part of the Aztec culture.

He was about to walk back to the apartment that contained the Xipe Totec statue, when a pair of men stepped into view. They were dressed in blue suits and ties, with dark hats pulled down low over their eyes. The guns in their hands weren't human manufacture, larger and seemingly made of a blue-green glass.

"Do not move," the first said, raising a coin. Kariven recognized it as the Aztec sun calendar, a series of hieroglyphic images with the face of the Aztec God Quetzalcoatl in the center.

The sun coin glowed and a beam of golden light covered Kariven from head-to-toe. He felt a slight but not unpleasant heat across his skin; the beam vanished a few seconds later.

"Uninfected," the first man said. "We apologize for the inconvenience."

"I've experienced Polarian probes in the past," Kariven said. "That one was rather different. And the Xipe Totec has fled into the sewers. It could not stand the sunlight."

"A human that knows of our existence, interesting," the second man said, tucking his pistol out of sight. "Then tell us where we can find Tezcatlioca?"

"I'm not sure of the location at this time. But I have some ideas," Kariven replied, needing a moment to think. Tezcatlioca was the Aztec God of Night and Temptation and he was known as the God of the Smoking Mirror. It was said that he carried an obsidian mirror that enabled him to see all men and tempt them into evil acts. The beneficent divinity, Quetzalcoatl, who was known as a lord of the sky, had defeated him.

It was simplicity for Kariven to put most of this puzzle together. Tezcatlioca, obviously a Denebian, had subjugated the Aztecs for a time, until he had been defeated by Quetzalcoatl, a Polarian. Tezcatlioca's obsidian mirror was obviously some advanced technology lost in time. The Aztec history of human sacrifice fit the Denebians' philosophy of conquest. Kariven remembered that Quetzalcoatl had rejected human sacrifice, protecting life and peace, which was in accordance with the Polarians' own beliefs.

"So, Tezcatlioca was a Denebian and Quetzalcoatl a Polarian who opposed him. And you believe that the former's smoking mirror is somehow present in New York City today?"

"Correct," said the first Polarian. "When the mirror is charged with life energies, it enables the viewer to access any location in the universe. It is the ultimate intelligence-gathering device."

"What was it doing on Earth?" Kariven asked, finding the idea rather puzzling. The Polarians might be benevolent aliens who respected life, but neither they, nor the Denebians, ever thought of Earth as anything more than a backwater zone.

"Tezcatlioca was the Denebians' chief scientist; he was exiled for making enemies of their Bloodlord," the Polarian replied.

"I see. And the creature that attacked me?"

"A shock troop called the Xipe Totec. It was an infiltration construct Tezcatlioca created to destroy planets from within," the Polarian said. "Where is the mirror?"

"As I said earlier, I'm not sure. But there may be a way to determine its location quickly. Are the Denebians also searching for this item?" Kariven asked.

"Our reports suggest they are unaware of it as of this time. But the Xipe Totec's activation might change that situation," the Polarian replied.

Kariven nodded. "Then I must find a telephone. If I can determine where the victim of the Xipe Totec was employed, the location of the mirror should follow."

"I see the connection," the Polarian said. He stared at the French scientist for several seconds. Pulling a small box from his jacket's inside pocket, the alien handed the item to Kariven. "We will assist you. State the location you wish and the communicator will connect you through the human telephonic line."

"A portable telephone? Useful item. I imagine we humans will invent one shortly," Kariven said and added, "New York Transit Authority."

"Working," the box said in an electronic voice, which was quickly replaced by the ringing sound of a telephone. "Transit Authority, how may I direct your call?"

"This is Inspector Kramden," Kariven said in a passable imitation of and American police officer's voice. The French scientist couldn't remember Cramer's name so he used the name of a popular sitcom character in replacement. "I need to find out where a Mister Joseph Brown was employed and who was his boss."

"One moment, I'll connect you to personnel," the operator said in a bored voice. A buzzing sound could be heard through the communicator and another female voice answered. Kariven repeated his request and was forwarded onto a third person. Finally after several more transfers, he spoke to a man named Beeman who may or may not have been Joseph Brown's direct superior.

"Joey got killed? Well, I don't like to speak ill of the dead but he was lazy and a pain in my huge rump. Spent most of his time wandering around, trying to find abandoned stuff he could sell," Beeman said, his voice a harsh smoker's rasp.

"Where was he working last?" Kariven asked.

"Waldorf-Astoria station. It's an unused station under the hotel, exclusive for important types who stay in the hotel. We got word the President may be entertaining some foreigners there so we cleaned it up in case."

With a quick word of thanks, Kariven handed back the communicator to the Polarian. "I have an idea where the mirror is."

The Polarian looked skeptical. "If the mirror or any other of Tezcatlioca's devices were in a subway station, they would have been discovered by this time."

Kariven indicated they should follow him and started walking. "Your people may be more advanced than mine, but you know little of our history. Does the name John D. Rockefeller mean anything to you?"

"He was a wealthy man, owner of an American oil fortune."

"Rockefeller was one of the wealthiest men in history, a billionaire whose power was closer to an ancient potentate than a businessman. He resided in a special suite in the Waldorf-Astoria and had a private elevator to his personal subway station beneath the hotel," Kariven explained.

"I fail to see…" the Polarian said, but was cut off by an impatient gesture from Kariven.

"Rockefeller was a great philanthropist and patron of the arts, though none truly knew where he kept many of his purchases. Where better to create a private vault than beneath his own subway station? We can suppose that something about this items disturbed him and he shut them away for good."

"How do you know this information?" the Polarian asked, as he led Kariven over to a shiny, new black sedan.

"An archaeologist who does not examine all of history is as blind as a one-eyed man," Kariven answered. "You see some, but not the full picture. I study past and present and I am better equipped than many in my field of study."

"Brace yourself." The second Polarian said, speaking for the first time. The car pulled out without a sound and was speeding through the streets at a pace that reduced the whole world to a blur. Kariven was not surprised by the velocity, having experienced Polarian technology many times in the past. Still, the distance they covered in mere seconds was quite impressive.

They pulled up in front of the Waldorf-Astoria, a towering grand hotel built in the 1920s and still one of New York's crown jewels. There was a quiet majesty to the hotel that was apparent, even to the Polarians who turned and looked at Kariven, looking for further information.

"We must go upstairs to the Royal Suite. That was once Rockefeller's dwelling. He had a private elevator there to the station."

Kariven led the Polarians inside the hotel. The interior was as magnificent as the exterior, and the atmosphere of quiet elegance was rather similar to famed European hotels such as London's Savoy or Paris's George V.

"May I help you, sir?" a tall thin man in a black suit and black tie glided to their side. His accent was vaguely English, a façade meant to impress the guests; in fact, he was just a man from Brooklyn who had started as a busboy. As the concierge of the Waldorf-Astoria, he was snootier than a penniless English Lord and twice as self-important.

"Yes, you may," Kariven said, thickening his French accent so that it was practically incomprehensible. "I am his Royal Highness's personal secretary and

I was told we would be allowed to examine the Royal Suite! But I have been in your hotel for many minutes and I have yet to be accommodated with any speed!"

The concierge frowned, barely able to follow the flow of words but figuring out just enough to realize that this loud Frenchman was the representative of someone Royal. Nothing impressed him more than the suggestion of important persons with titles, so he immediately changed from the self-important protector of the hotel to a groveling worm.

"My dear Monsieur, I do apologize on behalf of the Waldorf-Astoria! Please accept some refreshments of champagne and caviar as I lead you up to the finest suite in America!" The concierge bowed and took Kariven and the two Polarians towards the elevators that led to the exclusive tower containing the hotel's best suites.

The suite itself was, if possible, more impressive than the hotel itself. A huge series of rooms decorated in the French style, antiques and new furnishings majestically awaiting the next occupant.

The concierge was apparently still speaking, though Kariven had been ignoring him until then. "...of Windsor stay here every time they are in town. No doubt that is where his Highness..."

"I have heard there was a private elevator in this suite," Kariven said, interrupting the flow of useless babble.

"Yes, sir," the concierge said, smiling apologetically. "But it is no longer in use. It led to a personal subway station that has long been closed."

"And it is located where?" Kariven asked.

He followed the concierge into a sitting room and watched as the man opened a closet door. The elevator door was wire mesh, obviously made many years ago, but appeared well maintained.

"This will get us to Tezcatlioca?" the first Polarian inquired.

"I believe so," Kariven stated, as he watched the second Polarian pull out his glasslike pistol.

Before the archeologist could speak, the Polarian fired the gun at the concierge. A blue beam of light struck the man, who stiffened and toppled over, falling to the soft carpet like a marionette with its strings cut.

"He is merely stunned," the second Polarian said. "He will awake, not remembering the last hour of his life."

"Impressive," Kariven said.

The first Polarian pulled out a metal disk and pressed it against the elevator lock. The disk glowed green and, a few seconds later, they heard a click and the elevator door swung open.

The beauty of the simple cage immediately struck Kariven as he stepped into the elevator. It was a rectangular box, slightly larger than most elevators, with white and black stones covering the walls and floor. Despite himself, he was impressed and took a moment to examine the large black stone that covered the area above the buttons.

The Polarians appeared unimpressed; the first pressed the down button after the second closed the cage door. "How will we find this so-called vault? he asked.

"Rather easily I should think," Kariven replied. "Joseph Brown was not a professional thief, merely an opportunist. He discovered the Rockefeller vault by accident, I believe. I doubt he would have fully locked it for fear he could not get it open a second time."

The elevator lurched to a stop. The Polarians opened the door. The metallic clank echoed in the dark subway station before them. A light switch was visible near the elevator and the second Polarian flipped it on. After a moment of blindness, Kariven saw the secret station and was not surprised by its lack of amenities. Subway stations were rarely interesting visually or architecturally; this one, despite its impressive history, was merely a white tiled room with a concrete floor. There was a door at the far end of the station, leading to a maintenance room containing the wiring for the station.

Kariven examined it with the eye of an archaeologist. The door was twenty to thirty years old and the hinges were rusted with disuse. But on the floor beneath it were several flakes of rust and no dust lay upon them. This was the door Joseph Brown had used.

The archeologist tried it and the door opened with a mild squeak. The room within contained several electrical panels covered in a thin layer of dust and a set of footprints leading to the far wall.

Kariven crossed to the wall and spotted a small panel box uncovered by the layer of dust that filled the room. Opening it, he found a combination lock. That was the best technology available at the time, and the caretaker had probably been careless enough to leave the tumblers open out of convenience.

Kariven turned the lock slowly to the left, listening for the final tumbler to open. He had learned this trick from a cousin; a reformed professional thief turned antique storeowner. He smiled as a loud click filled the room. The far wall of the room slowly dropped downward, revealing an unlit chamber. The Polarians pulled a pair of small red balls from their pockets and tossed them within the room. The balls did not bounce, but dropped to the ground and began to emit a soft glow.

The room was long and narrow, filled with statues, paintings and other *objets d'art* that Kariven unconsciously began classifying. He stepped inside and was about to begin a search when he heard voices coming from the subway station.

"Destroy them, find the mirror," said a voice, in a low whisper filled with malice.

Kariven turned and felt his stomach drop, unable to miss the green skin and red eyes with yellow streaks. It was a Denebian, a race of evil warriors who seem determined to conquer all life in the universe, starting with the Polarians.

The Denebian was joined by another; both were carrying shining metallic rifles and began firing beams of red light at the Polarians. The latter dove for cover behind the collected artwork, which burst into flames upon contact.

Kariven moved further back into the room, horrified by the loss of ancient treasures. He stooped to study a mirror that he immediately identified to come from 18th century Germany, when a heavy hand landed on his shoulder. With a sinking feeling, the French archeologist spun around and jumped back, barely avoiding the grabbing clutches of the Xipe Totec.

The Denebian construct swung its arm out, hitting the Frenchman in the face and sending him reeling backwards. The blow was like getting hit by a lead pipe and Kariven immediately felt the coppery taste of blood in his mouth.

But falling backwards into the room had an unexpected benefit: the archeologist noticed the statue of the Aztec God Tezcatlioca, standing in the far corner of vault. Kariven quickly pushed through the artifacts, the Xipe Totec a short distance behind him. Unfortunately, the construct was faster and the French scientist was sent stumbling forward from another backhanded blow. He crashed to the ground next to the statue and several other Aztec artifacts.

One, in particular, caught his eye: a sun disk with Quetzalcoatl's face in its center. Kariven remembered that the Polarians had identified the so-called sky god as one of their people, and had used similar disks to ensure that he wasn't a Xipe Totec. This disk was larger, approximately the size of a dinner plate, and appeared made of solid gold. Kariven thought it had been made at approximately the same time as the Xipe Totec statue that was in Brown's apartment.

Another Polarian device? I hope so! Kariven thought as he reached for the disk. Raising it up, he attempted to place his fingers in the same position that he had seen the Polarians use to hold the smaller one before him in the streets.

The Xipe Totec stopped in its tracks, its mouth moving but no sound emerging. It stepped backwards and seemed about to flee when the disk blazed with light. A heavy ray that resembled sunlight struck the Denebian construct, causing the stolen flesh to crumble and vanish. Kariven got a brief glimpse of a metal skeleton beneath, but was forced to look away as the light intensified and caused the creature to incinerate in a ball of flame.

Placing the sun disk down, Kariven turned back to the statue of Tezcatlioca, immediately spotting a small mirror in its extended right hand. Smiling, he pried it from the statue's fingers and turned back to the warring aliens.

"Here is what you seek," the archeologist said, tossing it in their direction.

The mirror crashed to the ground and shattered into tiny shards, which flew about the vault and vanished from sight.

"Pull back. Target has been destroyed and the construct is gone," the Denebian leader intoned, firing his rifle, destroying more artifacts.

202

Without looking back, the Polarians followed, their glasslike guns firing as they chased their enemies down the sewer tunnels.

Kariven walked out of the vault, deciding to contact the authorities and allow them to rescue the remaining *objets d'art*. Turning off the light, he entered the elevator and closed the cage, but did not press the button to return the surface. Instead, he once again studied the stone above the buttons–a smooth black stone.

It was not a stone, but obsidian, a type of glass found in nature that was pure back. In other words, a smoking mirror. Rockefeller had probably found the obsidian to be so beautiful that he had included it in this elevator.

There was only one way to find out. Putting a finger to his bleeding mouth, Kariven collected a drop of blood and pressed it against the glassy black surface. A small curl of smoke rose from the surface of the obsidian mirror, causing the archeologist to chuckle. Tezcatlioca's infamous mirror was lost forever to both Polarians and Denebians–but not to Humanity! Despite all their advanced science and intelligence, the two alien races had never learned to think like humans, who searched for double meanings in everything.

Stepping over the fallen concierge, Kariven checked his watch. Just enough time to get to Columbia University and complete his work...

Tevye the milkman is the hero of several of Sholem Aleichem's stories, origi-nally written in Yiddish and first published in 1894. The story of this pious Jew-ish milkman in Tsarist Russia, and his six daughters (Tzeitel, Hodel, Chava, Shprintze, Bielke, and Teibel) was popularized by the musical Fiddler on the Roof. As was the case with Tom Kane earlier in this volume, Stuart Shiffman penned an unusual crossover in which the Milkman crosses path with several of our favorite Shadowmen...

Stuart Shiffman: *The Milkman Cometh*

Russia, 1905

The hotel room was well appointed, decorated in a French style that was only five years old. It was attractive, in an overstuffed Belle Epoque manner, with lots of heavy red velvet and brocade. Personally, Rouletabille preferred a sim-pler style. The young man stepped out onto the balcony and shook out his check sack suit jacket, which still stunk of gunpowder. He had ordered a pot of coffee from the front desk, the thought of samovar-brewed tea not being attractive to him right now, and yearned to sit and relax over it. However, he first had to exe-cute his responsibilities to his employers, as well as reassure them that he was well and on the job. He rumpled his hair and took the telegram form and his Montblanc pen in hand and began to write:

To: Editor, L'Epoque, Paris, France.
From: Joseph Rouletabille, Hôtel Anglais, Yehupetz, Kievska Oblast, Russia.
Spoken with envoys of the Tsar about bomb murder of King of Bohemia. Things very tense here. Followed when attempted to interview witnesses. Multiple se-cret police agencies active. Intense fear of international action. Tension between Russia and Austrians over Serbia. En route St. Petersburg to meet with Tsar over murder threat against General Feodor Trebassof. Advise.
Rouletabille

Rouletabille wondered if the secret police would find their man, who was said to know the mean streets of Yehupetz as well as he knew those of Paris, Berlin or St. Petersburg. The prime suspect, Ivan Dragomiloff, carried a passport of the French Republic and would continue to be newsworthy because of that. They couldn't just make him disappear into a prison cell while the Western press followed the case. Personally, Rouletabille had a list of more likely sus-pects. It could be the work of the Socialist-Revolutionary Party, perhaps of Vladimir Bourtzeff, the so-called "Sherlock Holmes of the Revolution," at least according to his sources in that organization. Another possibility was Yevno Azef, better as Eugene Azeff the Anarchist, who had succeeded Gershuni as the head of the Socialist-Revolutionaries' Combat Unit.

The reporter put it all out of his mind. The Tsar wanted him to save Feodor Feodorovitch.

He poured himself his first cup of coffee. It was execrable.

Boiberik, Ukraine

The lean man was exhausted. He had fled Yehupetz by the narrowest of margins, with the Okhrana, the Tsarist secret police, on his heels; he was now a fugitive, with the arm of law behind him. It had been the perfect frame.

He ran through the underbrush outside the town of Boiberik, a summer colony that served as a retreat for the wealthy, full of dachas and small estates. It was the closest to civilization that he had passed since fleeing Yehupetz. He had no luggage, no disguises or weapons; all his belongings had remained at his hotel in that city. His suit was torn by nettles and spattered with mud; his shoes looked like a scientific experiment. His spats were long gone too. Somehow, he had to find a refuge until his work could be completed and the truth revealed. Why else was he striving? What was that piece by Andrew Marvell?

"Could by industrious valour climb
To ruin the great work of Time,
And cast the kingdoms old
Into another mould."

He fell before he realized it, and never even felt himself drop into the weeds and the mud on the side of the road.

"Hello, Mister Sholom Aleichem. So you are back from the great and evil city to rest in Boiberik?

"I would love a glass of tea. I have minutes enough to sit and talk with you. Fire up the samovar.

"So, how is Tevye, you ask? Tevye is how the good Lord, *baruch hashem*, made him and ordered his days. If strange and unusual matters occur, it is not for him to berate the Lord God of Hosts for what He has decreed.

"Oh, yes. Strange and unusual matters, and stranger and more unusual people, have come into Tevye's life than you might reasonably expect in such a small and insignificant town. You know about the outrages reported to have happened in the capital? Those revolutionaries—only God in his wisdom can distinguish their separate ideologies!—and their infernal devices! They do this, I have been told by my son-in-law Pertchik, one who knows as he is still in prison in Siberia and may be forever, to confront the government that it might reveal its evil and repressive power. As if the Tsar ever needed an excuse! Madness it was that would just feed the anger and paranoia since the assassination of Alexander II by the Nihilists and the succession of Alexander III. These revolutionaries all just seem to make things worse.

"As ever, this can't be good for the Jews. The peasants are just tools in the hands of the secret police. But then, when has it ever been easy to be a Jew?

"Yes, you do well to shake your head, Mister Sholom Aleichem, over the folly of mankind. I know that I can trust you, so I will tell you about the man I found on the side of the forest road from Boiberik, where the rich Jews from Yehupetz have their summer dachas. My milk deliveries had taken longer than expected that day. It was getting on to dusk, and I stopped to say the evening prayers. My horse, you remember my horse, is a properly Jewish horse and always stands with his head bowed in quiet respect at such a time.

"Well, almost always. There was that time that he got a bit feisty, and I had to chase him down while reciting the *shimenesre*, the 18 benedictions.

"I heard a groan from the brush at the road's edge. Such a groan as the Torah says, 'They shall cry out!'

"There was a man concealed there, rather the worse for wear, but obviously a man from the city, dressed in such a suit of clothes as you would imagine an English milord or a princeling might wear. It was the worse for recent wear, but we don't often see such in our little village. I helped him up.

" 'Mister,' I said, 'how did you get in such a state, noble sir?' For you see that I showed respect, to his tailoring if nothing else. There was a great deal of blood on his face from a scalp wound, and those always bleed copiously out of proportion to their severity. He was lean and had the look of an exhausted whippet with eyes glazed from fatigue.

" 'Drag...draaakh...' He coughed and vomited into the grass. It all seemed too much for him. A head wound then, and a recent one, or so it seemed to Tevye, who you know is a practical man. I could not leave Mister Drakh, for as the rebbes tell us, 'If you save one person, it is as if you save the world entire.'

" 'Don't despair, noble Drakh," I said. 'Tevye the milkman will take care of you.'

" 'Tevye–are you a Jew?'

"I nodded since there was nothing to deny that was not written in my face. The poor man did speak Yiddish, although it was quite Germanized, very *daytshmerish*. He was obviously an educated man from the West. Drakh said, 'Where... doctor?'

" 'No doctor here, my lord,' I said. 'There are some midwives, but I doubt that you need their ministrations. And it's too early for you and the priest.' I could tell that he was not of our people.

" 'My friend... the doctor... we were traveling together. Badenov must have captured him.' Drakh seemed to be speaking to himself. 'My name... is Ivan... Dragomiloff... and I must find the doctor, Reb Tevye... before Badenov questions him... or passes him along to the senior Okhrana officers.'

"I almost dropped the man then, for who wants to attract the attention of the Tsar's secret police. The village constable, Sipowicz, is a good man, albeit with a peasant's innate prejudices. But the secret police? Even if he was lucky, a man could find himself on a slow train to Siberia, from whence few if any return. Man is but dust, as we say. But Tevye is a brave man, as any man with a wife and so many daughters must be.

" 'You must hide me, until I'm strong enough to evade them. They've blown up the King of Bohemia, to the tune of the Radetzky March, during a stop in Yehupetz en route to a State Visit in St. Petersburg, and the government is blaming it on the Anarchists. I was lured from Paris to Yehupetz to meet with a fictional client just to give them a suitable scapegoat.'

"You can imagine my further dismay at this. More bombs. Dragomiloff later worked out, as nimbly as any Talmudic scholar, that the same secret police must have conspired to blow up Tsar Alexander II so many years ago with a ready scapegoat in the person of some messianic revolutionary *schlemiel*.

" 'So, from now on,' I told him, 'you are my cousin Yankl Drakhman from Chelm. No one expects a Chelmer *chochem* to understand anything. Let us go before anyone else comes. 'If there is no flour, there is no Torah,' as the sages say. My Golde will help me clothe and feed you. So, don't be such a golem: say something at least.'

" 'Thank you, Reb Tevye, for your kindness.'

" 'Good. We'll take the road through the cherry orchard. My home is not far.' "

Kasrilevke, Ukraine

An elegant man with silky hair the color of butter descended from the railway coach at Kasrilevke station.

Konstantin Vassily Illyavitch Couriakine, a lieutenant in the Imperial Military Intelligence, scanned the crude railway platform. The lineaments of a Scottish grandmother could be seen in his face. He was well-dressed with just the touch of the dandy in his cravat. His ebony walking stick flicked away a bit of smut that threatened to attach itself to him.

The usual sort of crowd was on the platform: there were commercial travelers, mostly Jews from third class, a couple of *babushkas* with lunches wrapped in kerchiefs, and several peasants in infantry uniform. The village looked the usual assortment of unpainted ramshackle buildings, except the painted onion dome of the Orthodox church, and the streets were rivers of muddy gumbo. Nowhere was the man that he hoped to see, the French agent with whom he had worked innumerable times. If his enemies in the Okhrana, or his superior, General Strogoff, only knew that he had shared information with a foreign officer!

One of the peasant soldiers approached Couriakine. Now he seemed taller, and a matinee idol's face peeked out from below his service cap. He had a papirosa, a Russian cigarette, in one hand.

"Noble sir," said the man, "do you have a Lucifer to spare?"

It was Solitaire, the French agent of the Deuxième Bureau de l'Etat-Major Général, whose real name–which Couriakine was not supposed to know–was Charlemagne Solon. As always, his accent in Russian was perfect for the persona that he inhabited.

"Of course, Sergeant," said Couriakine. Sotto voce, he added, "Good to see you, Solitaire. I must admit that this is a relief. I was worried not to have spotted you before."

"Thank you, noble sir." He saluted. Then, pianissimo, "I'm usually where I need to be, my friend. Badenov is here, on the track of Dragomiloff. He may already have the doctor. He is working with a female Okhrana informer; that *babushka* there with the plaid shawl is much younger than her disguise would indicate. This is all part of their plan, to blame the bombing on the Anarchists and the Nihilists, and on the supposed laxity of the government caused by the liberalization program. They want an excuse to come down hard on the liberals, the foreign businesses and the Jews. You know how much they love the knout."

Couriakine nodded. It was as he and General Strogoff had thought: The secret police had its own agenda, and those of the army and state ministry be damned. The question was, of course, how high did this go? Was it simply an internal conspiracy, or was some terrorist mastermind such as Natas or Leonid Zattan at work behind the scenes? Surely, they could have achieved these aims without including the spectacular death of an Austro-Hungarian King in their program? The picric bomb had reduced the King of Bohemia and his escort to their essential atoms; it had been so much more efficient than the anarchist Armand Denis's attempt on Prince Otto in Nice. What was next? Emperor Franz Josef was old, but not yet dead to the world. His decrepit honor and that of his ramshackle empire might need to be satisfied. It was quite amazing the number of things and inflammatory confrontations that might trigger a general war among the European Powers. It was why he and Solitaire collaborated in this fashion.

"You go on to Kishinev now, Sergeant?" And nearly unhearable, "There are other agents here, Solitaire."

"No, noble sir, our unit goes to Bialystok, and then to Berditchev." There was a pause. "Yes, I have identified the Englishman spy Waverly and the German Siegfried slinking about. The King of Bohemia was related to both their royal houses. The American Nat Pinkerton has already been engaged by the Bohemian royal house to investigate."

"Fandorin is on the way here from St. Petersburg, Solitaire."

Solitaire grunted at that. Ordinarily, they would welcome the presence of the famous investigator, the so-called "Sherlock Holmes of Russia," but this was not a time for him. The fewer outsiders and incorruptible civilians involved, then the happier he and his master would be. If he and Solitaire could neutralize Badenov and his associate as well as the bomb artificer, it would be quite satisfactory enough.

Boiberik, Ukraine

"So, I, Tevye the milkman took in the wounded man and gave him of his hospitality, for as the Torah says, 'Take the stranger within thy lintels.' Golde and I made a good kosher Jew of him, with a cast-off set of my clothes altered for his frame and the fringes of a small prayer shawl hanging out, and with a workers cap and yarmulke on his head. It was a regular Purim carnival. It is written in Leviticus, 'Every raven after its kind.'

"He took readily to it, revealing what seemed to me a strong affinity for play-acting and disguise. Even his stance and manner of walking changed. The rebbe himself would have accepted him for a *minyan* for prayers. And brains, you never saw such a mind among the *goyim*. He could both see and observe, and you know the difference, Mr. Sholom Aleichem, and deduce all manner of things just by looking at me.

"Golde's table of good beet *borscht* and *blintzes*, chicken soup with dumplings, milk and cheese helped build back his strength. We would talk by the barn, while I milked the cow and otherwise tended to the lady. Reb Yankl would smile and tell me that I reminded him of a friend in England, the noble Milord Emsvort with his beloved pig, the Tzarina of Blandinks.

" 'You are very sweet with our poor dumb chum, Reb Tevye.' he said.

" 'My friend, she is another of God's creatures and the financial foundation of our family. How could I not give her full attention?'

" 'You are a man with a true heart, Reb Tevye.' Our guest smiled slowly at me and our cow.

" 'No, no, I'm just a *shtarker*, a man with strong and willing back and cowshit on my boots.' I told him about the legendary Lamed-Vav. 'Note the number, 36," I said, 'which is twice 18. Since our Hebrew letters are used for numbers, 18 in Hebrew spells out the word *chai* or *life*.'

" 'I suspect that this is simplified for my sake, Reb Tevye. I'm sure that the full exegesis of Jewish numerology would make my head spin,' he said. I laughed at that.

" 'The lamed *vavniks* are usually poor, and obscure, and no one guesses that they are the ones who bear all the sorrows and sins of the world. It is for their sake that God does not destroy the world, even when sin overwhelms mankind. They may also contribute to *tikkun olam*, a Hebrew phrase which is usually rendered as *repairing the world*.'

" 'And it needs a lot of repair, my friend,' he said. This time we both laughed.

" 'God is great and good, but we still have to shovel out our own cowshit, my friend,' I replied.

" 'What would you do if you had the comfort of a fortune, Reb Tevye?'

" 'There are innumerable things that I'd want for my family, including fine marriages for the last of my daughters. I'd want to make a contribution to charity and perhaps open a free school for poor children. I'd have a proper tin roof made for the synagogue instead of the wretched old wooden roof it has now, and build a shelter for all the homeless people who have to sleep there at night, the kind any decent town should have.'

"It was a laudable dream, replied my guest. Yes, it was a fine wisp of a dream, while my own family members had some times when they were starving to death three times a day, not counting supper."

Kasrilevke, Ukraine

Most of my business is with customers in Boiberik, but now I visited Kasrilevke, the town of the little people, to deliver some cheese and sour cream and run a few errands. Confidentially, I wanted to get a sense of things there. There is something very charming about the clamor and bustle of the marketplace after the peace of the farm, forest and fields, the flax-spinners and embroiderers diligently laboring, housewives bustling about the marketplace in their checkered shawls and evaluating the chickens, with children in the street playing hopscotch. There were few peasants about, as it was not a proper market day.

I tried to imagine what my guest would make of a *shtetl* like Kasrilevke. Would he find it wretched and ugly in comparison to the great capitals that he had seen and that I could never imagine? Spring and fall were seasons when the rains turned the unpaved streets into seas of mud, as it was now. The wooden houses suddenly seemed more neglected and crowded together now that I thought about it, another reason that I liked the open countryside around my farm near Boiberik for the fresh air and greenery.

Two old men, clad in ragged clothing, were leaning on the back of a cart and stared expectantly into the distance. A passing teacher, Reb Yosifl, conducting the dignified solemnity of a Talmud class in disputation is broken up by the chuckles of a pair of young scholars, the bedbugs. I visited with Reb Mendel and his strangely intellectual daughter Yentl. She always astounds me with her skill in Talmudic disputation. When do girls do such things?

There were more soldiers lazing about the marketplace than are usually seen about the town. What business do Cossacks have in a quiet, Jewish town, 2000 miles away from Manchuria? There seemed to be more ferment in Kasrilevke than had been seen with the noise that erupted when the news about Captain Dreyfus had turned the place upside down. Then they nonetheless stubbornly had refused to give up their faith in the eventual triumph of *yoysher*, justice. Did this mean a pogrom was in the offing, or were they just part of the force hunting my guest?

Then I saw my son-in-law, the tailor Motl Komzoyl in his shop. He told me that Golde's cousin, Menakhem-Mendl, had reported the presence of many strangers in town beyond the soldiers. Could I trust Menakhem-Mendl, a *luft-mentsh*, a man who lived on air? His investment advice had misled me before; he chased pipe dreams of instant wealth and squandered his earnings with greed; always sure that the next fortune is around the corner and ready to drop on his foolish head.

This time, the schoolboy Motl, Peysi the cantor's son, that little bedbug, and the innkeeper Moisei Moiseyevich all supported Menakhem-Mendl's stories. Some of these strangers must be the men hunting my guest, Ivan Drago-miloff.

Why had I accepted his version of the facts so quickly? There was something special that struck me about him, something shining. He had a quality of honor and truth. Could he have been just a confidence trickster and thief? I suppose that he might have been such. As the morning prayers say, "All are beloved, all are elect, all are intrepid, all are holy, all perform the will of their Maker in awe." It was a matter of recognition–he was *unzer gibor*, our hero, a man who was there to do good and deal justice.

Maybe I'm secretly one of the *Lamed-Vav-Tsaddikim*, the 36 Hidden Saints who prop up the world according to Jewish legend, known also as the *Tzaddikim Nistarim*, or the Hidden Just Men. Ah, Reb Tevye, imagine yourself a lamed *vavnik*! A creature out of legend would have come in very handily right then. We could use the Golem of Chelm, much less the better known and flashier Golem of Prague. The Chelmer goylem was created by the kabbalist rabbi Elijah Ba'al Shem of blessed memory to defend the Jews of that town, while that of Prague was created by the even more renowned and learned Rabbi Yehuda Loew, the Maharal, and supposedly still lies quiescent in the attic of the Altneuschul. Rabbi Elijah of Chelm used a figure of clay given life by the use of the Shem-Haforesh or Ineffable Name of God on a paper in the Golem's forehead. When he was finished with it, he just removed the paper and, pfft!, a pile of inanimate clay.

Badenov was a squat little bald man with a measly mustache inadequate to give his face personality. Born of a failed merchant family in Moscow, he had determined that his destiny was a sparkling seat on the right hand of the powerful. The way of the spy and secret policeman was his vehicle to that goal. He did not lack for a deluded sense of himself and over weaning pride. He brooded in his dark corner of the Kasrilevke hostelry room, still in his black trilby and woolen overcoat.

His companion, the woman Natasha, was an interesting contrast. She had shed the grey wig and grease paint of her *babushka* persona, and had lit one of the *papirosen* from her reticule. She had long and very dark hair against an aristocrat's pale skin, with almond-shaped eyes a shocking emerald green. She had a husky voice with overtones of warm syrup. When Natasha told Badenov not to worry, he stopped worrying. He stared at her a lot when he thought that she wasn't watching him. A tall, spectacular and elegant figure no matter her costume or disguise; she had claimed to be the daughter of an aristocratic army officer's wife and her Romany lover. In fact, unbeknownst to her companion, Natasha was really Sylvia di Murska, the daughter of Israel di Murska who ruled the Terror as "Natas." Natasha was the "Angel of the Revolution" to the Brotherhood of Freedom. She was a dark one, in more ways than one.

Natasha made him want to work hard for her–which he did.

"You are being a fool, darling," she said. She blew a smoke cloud that suggested a ribald sheep.

"No!" spat Badenov, "I am not the fool here. I am the master of strategy, the spider at the center of my own web of intrigue–and I feel the tug on every strand. Dragomiloff will fall into my hands very soon." He sprang from his chair, a Napoleonic figure beneath the chin of the lounging woman. "We have his traveling companion, the good doctor. Why should the master slip through my traps so far?"

"Perhaps he is simply smarter than you, darling?"

"Inconceivable! The planning was precise and elegant on my part. Dragomiloff should have been taken at his hotel, with the incendiary materials that we had already planted in his room. I would have stridden in with the officers and collared them. Bang goes Dragomiloff. Badenov is showered with honors. His mother at last acknowledges his worthiness. Instead, the Assassin and his cohort escape while a smoke bomb is set off in the suite. I am left to look like a bumbler before our Leader."

"You must not disappoint General Trepoff, Boris," Natasha advised. *He really was a horrible little man*, she thought. "He has ways of making subordinates very regretful of failures. I do not wish to share that fate with you."

"Raskolnikov! He will make me pay! Our fearless leader and the Double Eagle Cabal do not allow failure to stay unpunished."

Badenov had Dragomiloff and his local *zhid* associate in his hands now. The village policemen Wojciehowicz and Sipowicz had brought them in on his command once they were located near Boiberik. The blond special constable, Couriakine, recruited to Badenov's service, held Tevye's arms fast. There was nothing that the milkman could do now.

The special constable dragged Dragomiloff forward, pulling off his cap and the false side-curls.

"What a fine *zhid* you made! Ha! You won't enjoy the firing squad, Playactor." The middle-aged Jewish prisoner, a burly bearded fellow called Tobias or Tevye Milkhiker according to his file, said something in his jargon. Part of it sounded like a curse, while the rest seemed to be a recitation to the Heavens. Badenov didn't understand *zhid*-speech, although he noticed that Natasha's head came up at the man's words.

"Ah," replied the prisoner in Russian, "some things never change. A kind friend has written that the stage lost a great one when I gave it up for my chosen profession. Therefore, the melodrama must be served. This is it, Gospodin Badenov. Journeys end in lovers meeting, as they say, and villains are sure to be foiled by the pure of heart." The prisoner sighed and smoothed his hair. He gave Tevye a smile. "As for you, my dear Badenov, it is a singular error to form a theory in advance of data. One irresistibly begins to massage the data to fit the rigid bounds of one's theory."

"What are you talking about, Dragomiloff?" Badenov spat. His associate, Natasha, sat in the dark corner and smoked a vile cigarette. She shook her head.

"You still think that I am Ivan Dragomiloff. That is an elementary error on your part, but one that you were intended to make. Your Paris office, the Zagranichnaia okhranka, was very efficient in many ways in monitoring the revolutionaries, terrorists, and nationalists driven out of Russia. The Okhrana's initial assumption had been that exile in Europe rather than Siberia or some other remote place would act as a safety valve for such groups had proved erroneous. These movements have an international element and the Parisian agents, double agents, and agents provocateurs never got as close to Dragomiloff's Assassination Bureau as they would have liked. That is how I was able to substitute for him."

"Of course you're Dragomiloff. Who else could you be? Nat Pinkerton?"

"My name is Sherlock Holmes," he said quietly, "and I don't think that my associate Doctor Watson has enjoyed his accommodations here." The sergeant with the matinee idol face smiled, and nodded across the room to the blond special officer, Couriakine. They relaxed their holds on the prisoners. Natasha gasped and leaned forward, as if mesmerized by the spectacle.

"Where is the head of the Assassination Bureau?" she asked.

"Mr. Dragomiloff is still back in Paris where he belongs and attending to his personal business." Holmes paused, as if weighing his next words. "I regret that I was unable to prevent the death of the King of Bohemia. However, I rejoice that I have been in a position to give you your comeuppance. This also gave me a salutary opportunity to pay back Mr. Dragomiloff for his timely assistance during the cases of Huret, the Boulevard Assassin and of Klopman the Nihilist. I received a letter of thanks from the French President and was inducted into the Legion of Honor for the former." Holmes smiled slowly. "My blushes, sir."

"Oh, god," whispered Badenov.

"I'm sure, Gospodin Badenov, that you've been under the illusion that you are the smartest and most dangerous man in the Russian Empire, but I assure you that this is not so. You've long been under the cold and calculating stare of beings far above you in the evolutionary scale. I had been engaged by members of the Russian royal family as well as your Imperial Military Intelligence service in the person of General Strogoff. Your fearless leader, General Trepoff, is already under arrest." His hands free, he removed and unfolded a heavy rectangle of paper. "I am filled with perplexity in regard to a secret government conspiracy which would connive at the violent death of a faithful official and that of a member of a foreign royal for the sake of bringing opprobrium and punishment to the revolutionists and credit to the secret police." Holmes caught his breath again. "This is the Imperial Warrant from the hand of the Little Father himself. The Double Eagle Cabal is finished."

Badenov fell to his knees with his hands over his face. Natasha wept. Her father Natas's plan to eliminate the Anarchist ring-leader was dashed, as well as the effort she had expended in deep cover with Trepoff and Badenov.

"It is never as simple as that," muttered the chastened Badenov.

As for Tevye, he was well aware that you never know where and when the Angel of Death will schedule a meeting.

Lower East Side, New York City, 1915

"Mr. Sholom Aleichem–how strange to find you here in the Golden Land–New-York, Amerike–and sit with you and visit over Wissotsky tea in a café. We never know what is written in the Lord's book and how he will order our paths.

"So, Mister Sholom Aleichem, I was the same man then that I am now, only not at all like me; that is, I was Tevye then too, but not the Tevye you're looking at now. When my son-in-law, Motl Komsoyl, died, and the order came for the Jews of our area to move, your old friend Tevye knew that it was time to try some place else. How can it be, I thought, how is it possible that such a thing can happen in times like these, in such an intelligent world full of smart people? Why doesn't the Lord our God do something? Why hadn't the Messiah come yet? Ai, I thought, wouldn't it be clever of him, the Messiah, to come riding down to us on his white horse right this minute! Why doesn't He say something, do something? 'But there shall be a sign in the Heavens... a pillar of smoke by day and of fire by night...' Perhaps the rich men like Brodsky in Yehupetz or Rothschild in Paris don't need the attention, but we poor Jews of Kasrilevke, and of Mazapevke, and of Anatevka, and even of Yehupetz, and yes, Odessa too, can't wait for him any longer–no, we absolutely can't wait another day!

"So Tevye brought himself and the remnants of his family across the sea from Hamburg and through Ellis Island. Here we are in New York's Lower East Side, where my daughter Tsaytl, or Sadie as she is now, runs a neat-as-a-pin candy store and soda fountain. Chava can run a sewing machine like a dream and makes a living. Bielke was left behind with her rich husband, the obnoxious and soulless Padhatzur, who paid to send me to Palestine in order to be rid of an embarrassment.

"Poor man. I never got there by the time my son-in-law Motl died.

"The grandchildren go to the public school like free people. This Amerike is a pretty tough town, however. It was not like cultivating your olive tree and sitting in your grape bower in Eretz Yisroel, but the danger of pogroms was much lower in the brick and stone ghetto of Manhattan than in the Pale of Settlement. And Tevye is not so old that he can't sell from a push-cart in the street and be useful.

"Sherlock Holmes? I saw him again in 1912, when he was in disguise here as an Irish-American. I don't know who was fooled by his strange attempt at an Irisher Yankee dialect. After all, we see enough Irishers here, policemen and politicians particularly. Somehow, he found out where we were and wanted to wish me well. He just walked into Tsaytl's candy store and ordered a two cents plain in his Germanized Yiddish.

"He was one of the best and wisest men that I ever knew."

A Tales of the Shadowmen *volume wouldn't be complete without an Arsène Lu-pin yarn. According to Maurice Leblanc, in November 1904, after challenging Sherlock Holmes in the case of "The Blonde Phantom" (included in our epony-mous collection of* Arsène Lupin vs. Sherlock Holmes *tales), Lupin left France and, in a series of heretofore untold adventures, traveled successively to Uru-guay, where he failed to save the life of the Duke of Charmerace, whose identity he then borrowed, Antarctica, and Saigon, where he came across an obscure civil servant named Lenormand, whose identity he would also appropriate, and finally Armenia and Turkey, where he fought the Red Sultan. Lupin finally re-turned to France, landing in Marseilles in April 1905. (The tale of his belated return is the subject of "Arsène Lupin Arrives too Late," also included in our* Blonde Phantom *collection.) Our latest contributor, David L. Vineyard, decided to tell the story of what really happened to Lupin during his stay in Saigon...*

David L. Vineyard: *The Jade Buddha*

Saigon, 1905

Heat. Oppressive heat. And in January at that.

Mon Dieu! What a country. Saigon might be the Paris of the East, but on a January evening, at least Paris had the good sense to be cold. Why, it almost made a man long for the extremes of the Antarctic!

Almost.

The Duke de Charmerace smiled. To be homesick was the perpetual state of the traveler. At least, he wasn't one of those Englishmen traipsing around the desolate ends of the Earth, forever rhapsodizing over the green fields of Eng-land. He had undertaken this journey as a necessary evil in light of the eventful year and a half behind him. He was a reluctant, if enthusiastic, traveler. He must tell old Passepartout about these revelations, when next he saw him, and his master, that bizarre elderly English madman Fogg.

He was seated at an outside table in the early evening waiting for his com-panion for dinner, a Major of the *Légion Etrangère* by the name of de Beaujo-lais, a charming fellow whose perpetual seven league boots and work in Intelli-gence had carried him to the four corners of the French Colonial Empire. Such fellows were good company and, more importantly, a source of vital informa-tion.

As he waited, nursing a gin and tonic–an impossible drink, yet one of the few tolerable in this ridiculous heat–wine lay on the belly like lead–he watched the people. He was an inveterate observer, an occupational necessity, and the study of mankind both hobby and vocation.

And Saigon was a veritable theater of the *Grand-Guignol* variety, busily crowded streets full of rickshaw boys, noisy quarrelsome merchants of everything, from jade trinkets to pickled snake and tiger powders for one's virility, swaggering legionnaires, ladies of assailable virtue–what a sensation they would be in Montmartre or Marseille!–and gawking tourists taking it all in while surrounded by barefoot beggars and aggressive vendors. But for the last half hour, his attention had been focused on a less chaotic sight. Across from the café was a small shop dealing in Oriental antiquities, and in front of that shop sat a large and shiny Rolls-Royce guarded by the largest and ugliest character one could imagine, a Dacoit by his look, liveried like a chauffeur, glowering at any one reckless enough to approach the great car.

After a while, a remarkable Chinese exited from the little shop, followed by the anxious owner who bowed and nodded and fawned at the skirts of the other man's long traditional robes. And little wonder, there was something almost princely about the man, an aesthetic aristocratic face, a high brow, a haughty manner, and something else, something almost–what?–reptilian. Yes, reptilian. The man seemed to glide across the pavement like some huge cobra raised on its tail and sliding toward its prey. The Duke would not have been surprised if a forked tongue had slicked forth from his thin lipped features.

Nor did the Duke fail to notice another figure: a brown man who appeared to be an Arab and who kept a watchful, if discreet, eye on the serpentine Chinese. Indeed, there was something as unusual about the Arab as the Chinese. For one, why did the fellow work so hard to disguise his height, bearing, and virility, and for another, why did an Arab darken his hair with boot black and how did he come to have such penetrating gray eyes–A policeman's eyes...

"I see you have discovered the mysterious Hanoi Shan, Monsieur le Duc."

It was the handsome Major de Beaujolais. Not many men could approach the Duke de Charmerace without his knowing it. He warned himself not to underestimate the seemingly simple soldier. There were depths to the man.

Charmerace began to rise and the Major waved him down. They shook hands as the soldier took a proffered seat and signaled a waiter. When he had ordered a brandy and soda–another English drink–and been served, Charmerace again spoke as the Dacoit assisted the curious Chinese into the Rolls. The Arab had faded into the crowd as if he had never been there. How odd.

"Hanoi Shan," repeated the Duke. "A remarkable looking fellow. Some Chinese Prince, perhaps?"

"No, not a Prince, though he comes from a wealthy and quite well-placed family. He used to be the Governor of some province in Tonkin–before my time. You no doubt noticed that strange gait of his–like some great worm. It's the result of an accident during his years as a civil servant. They were rounding up elephants for clearing forest to make new farmland when one of the beasts panicked. Poor devil's spine was crushed..." the Major shook his head. "Since then, he's lived in constant, excruciating pain, alleviated only by opium and other less wholesome and rarer drugs. He came here seeking a surgeon to help him, but found no one. Now they say he plans to move to Paris. He makes his way dealing in antiquities–not always of the most honest kind."

"How exotic," Charmerace said, trying to disguise his obvious interest. "But if he is suspected of criminal association, surely the police..."

The Major smiled and sipped his drink. "Even in Saigon, rumor isn't enough for the police to act on. My own office hears all kinds of rumors, but nothing concrete we can act upon. Not every criminal ends up behind prison bars, you know."

How true, Charmerace thought. "Still, one would like to know more about such a colorful character," he said aloud.

The Rolls had moved forward into the narrow street and parted the busy thoroughfare as it did so. Seeing his companion's interest so aroused, the Major made a proposal:

"If you feel up to a little adventure tonight, there's a fellow who might know more about our friend than I. He's an old Legionnaire, colorful fellow by name of Corday, Thibaut Corday. I know a bar where he's likely to be around midnight, and if Monsieur le Duc..."

"Splendid," Charmerace said. "Just splendid. The sort of adventure one hopes for when one undertakes such a journey. Exactly the sort of oriental tale one hopes to bring home to one's friends."

True to his word, after they had dined while discussing the Major's adventures in North Africa–he told a story that particularly interested the Duke, about three brothers, a stolen jewel, and a fort in the desert exotically named Zinderhuff, or Zinderneuf–the Major escorted the Duke through the colorful back alleys of the city, until they found a small dive off a narrow street, identified only by pale yellow light and the sing song music of a tinny Asian band.

There, the Major found them a table in a private room–as private as a beaded curtain could make it, and disappeared on his mission. Fifteen minutes later, the curtains parted and the Major ushered in a grizzled Legion Corporal carrying a bottle of wine, his kepi tucked under his arm.

"Monsieur le Duc, may I introduce Corporal Corday of the Legion? Corporal Corday, the Duke de Charmerace..."

Charmerace extended his hand and was met with a strong, firm shake. He gestured and Corday took a seat. He was clearly out of his element in this company, yet had enough of that swagger that was part and parcel of the Legion to overcome his nerves. After offering to share his bottle of Algerian Red, and being met with a polite decline, he launched into his story:

"The Major tells me that you're interested in old Hanoi Shan? I can't say that I'm surprised. He's quite a odd fellow. I can't claim to know all the facts, but I know the gossip as well as any foreigner can hope to. There are secrets in the East that are better kept in the East, and it doesn't do to dwell on them too much. Those who do are likely to find themselves lost–or worse. I've known many a Westerner drawn too deeply into the mysteries of this part of the world who never found his way back. Still, if it's Hanoi Shan you wish to know about...

"As the Major has probably told you, he was once the Governor of a province in Tonkin. The son of a wealthy family, well connected at the Imperial Court, though from what I've heard, there were questions of loyalty. Something about the old Manchu line and the Empress–rumors that the family was too well acquainted with the Brotherhood of the Celestial Fists–the Boxers. Just rumors and gossip, mind you, but in this part of the world, such things take on a life of their own. Old Shan–that's not his real name, of course, just one he took after the–the accident. It's a strange tale, and I'll try to keep it as simple as I can...

"A dozen years ago, Shan was the wealthy and happy Governor of a prosperous province. He had a beautiful wife and two lovely children–a young heir, and a daughter he doted upon. A young French diplomat was assigned to the province as Consul, a handsome and self-assured man, with a romantic western turn of mind. He was introduced to the Governor and his family, and as sometimes happens, there was an immediate attraction between Shan's young wife– the marriage had been arranged by the families as is their wont–and the dashing young Frenchman. No doubt both resisted the temptation, but eventually nature took its course. The affair lasted for some time before Shan's spies informed him–and that was the beginning of his problems."

Corday took a swig of wine and continued: "Now as you might imagine, that was not a situation likely to have a happy conclusion. A Frenchman–even an Englishman–might have lost his temper and thrashed the young fool, but not our Shan. He was of a more diabolical turn of mind and wanted to see the lad suffer. He made certain contacts–questionable friends of his family–and in due course, his revenge was taken. The young Frenchman was diagnosed with leprosy..."

"But surely," Charmerace interrupted, "even a man like Shan wouldn't... Besides, how would he have spread the disease?"

"Ah," Corday said after another swig of wine, "this is the East and they don't think as we do. There are ways, *magics*, if you will, and science too I suppose... However it was done, the boy was infected, and as any man might, rather than suffer a lifetime of exile and horror, he took the easy way out and put a bullet in his brain... That might well have been the end of it had Shan's wife not suspected her husband's part in her lover's death. She took poison and gave it to their two children as well. They say he found them in their beds, as if they were sleeping...

"Well, after that, Shan changed. He had been a stern, but fair man before. Now, he became bitter and cruel. His people, who had respected, even loved him, now came to hate him. Letters reached the Imperial Palace and scandal threatened. Of course, no one can say... Perhaps it was only an accident–elephants have been known to stampede–but there have been stories that his wife's family wanted revenge, that the government in Peking wanted him out...

"He lay near death for nigh six months. When he finally began to live again, it was in a fog of pain and drugs. It was then that he took the name of 'Hanoi Shan' and began to operate in the business of antiquities–an old passion of his. They say he turned to those shady friends who helped him avenge the insult to his manhood, and now nothing moves through this part of the world–legal or not–without Hanoi Shan getting his cut."

Corday took another swig of wine. "That's all I can really say with anything like authority, gentlemen. But if Monsieur le Duc is interested, I know a fellow who works in the local police–not a policeman mind you, a civil servant, name of Lenormand... If anyone knows the details of Shan's alleged crimes, it would be him. He'd be able to tell you more about the Jade Buddha too..."

"The Jade Buddha?" Charmerace asked

The Major smiled. "A legend, Monsieur le Duc. One as unusual as Shan's own. Don't tell me you believe in it, Corporal?"

"Well, I can't say, sir. I've seen some strange things in my years in the Legion. The Jade Buddha may or may not be real, but the tales..."

"Please, gentlemen," the Duke interrupted. "This Jade Buddha, what do we know about it."

The Major smiled. "The story, Monsieur le Duc, is simple enough. At the time of the Han dynasty, the first great empire of China–some 5000 years ago–an artisan–I suppose we'd call him an alchemist in the West–was asked to create a figure to be placed in the tomb of the Emperor, a Buddha. The figure was made of the purest jade that could be found. It was set with emerald eyes and gold and diamond necklaces, and in its navel rests one large, perfect diamond of legendary value. Its base was a piece of unmarred ivory, inlaid with gold and jewels and fit into a teak base."

"It sounds beautiful, but..."

"Oh, I know what Monsieur le Duc must be thinking, but there's more to it than just its value," Corday said, his tongue somewhat loosened by the wine. "The artist–the wizard, if you ask me–claimed to have done something strange to the statue. He claimed to have trapped part of the Emperor's soul in the jade–you know how such things go in the East. That makes it a sort of holy relic–not just priceless, but worth dying for."

"There are rumors," the Major continued, "that the Boxers had the thing and used it to recruit followers–stories that Genghis Khan used it to consolidate his power... Some say Tamerlane carried it with him and tried to have it buried with him in Samarkand, but thieves–funny, but every story about the Jade Buddha seems to get around to thieves sooner of later..."

"Thieves," the Duke said. "How droll. And this Hanoi Shan would have the Jade Buddha?"

"Well," Corday said, "that's the word on the street, Monsieur le Duc. The Buddha is supposed to have surfaced a dozen years ago in the Gobi desert somewhere, and since then, it's been in the hands of one sect or another... Some chap named Nicholas, or was it Nikola... There's even talk that the Si Fan and the Shin Tan..."

"What?"

"Two rival tongs," the Major said. "More complex than that, two criminal conspiracies with their fingers in everything. Supposedly, Shan acquires and handles *objets d'art* for them. I believe the word is fence. Gossip has that the Jade Buddha is with him, here, in Saigon."

"He must live in fear of those thieves you were talking about," Charmerace said.

Corday snorted. "There's not a thief in Saigon–Hell, in the whole of Indochina–that would dare touch Shan and that Buddha. Even if there was, his villa is a veritable walled fortress, built by a crazy Frenchman who feared a natives' revolt. Aside from that, he has an army of murderous Dacoits, and his grounds are patrolled at night by a matched pair of black panthers who are underfed and have acquired a taste for human meat. Of course, those are all stories, but what thief would risk his life if there was a core of truth in them? I doubt even that rogue Arsène Lupin would dare try!"

"Arsène Lupin?" the Duke asked.

"Arsène Lupin," the Major replied. "Surely Monsieur le Duc must have read of his exploits in the Paris newspapers?"

Charmerace made a dismissive gesture. "Oh, but I'm afraid I never read the cheap press. So tawdry, don't you think? Arsène Lupin, you say. Well, I shall remember the name..."

The next day Charmerace rose uncharacteristically early, only to be disappointed when he called on the police and learned that Monsieur Lenormand was on an extended leave. But rather than waste the day, he visited an acquaintance at the Saigon office of one of the large Paris papers and garnered more gossip about Hanoi Shan, though nothing solid.

That afternoon, he ventured into the vaults of the bureau of public works and spent some tiresome hours among the blueprints of some of the city's more obscure structures. After that, he made some curious purchases, which he had delivered to his hotel, and then, did some touring around the edges of Saigon. That evening, he begged off his engagements–a bit too much exotic food–and was served a meager meal of thin soup and Vichy water.

It was close to 1 a.m. when a figure slipped unnoticed from the kitchens of the hotel. Had one possessed keen enough eyesight and a discerning eye, one might have noticed that the figure, dressed in the loose, black pajamas of a rickshaw boy, and wearing the same broad hat and soft slippers, possessed a certain breadth to its shoulders and was perhaps too well fed and virile for the role assumed. Not that even the keenest eye would have made these observations, for the figure was able to transform himself in such a way that few saw through his disguises. Only one man, an Englishman, had ever seen the truth behind his disguises, and it was no shame to be recognized by an eye such as his. Indeed, one of the very few defeats in his career had been recently at the Englishman's hand–rectified soon enough, but still a sore point.

Keeping to the shadows, the man made his way across Saigon, and quickly arrived in the vicinity of the fortress-like estate of Hanoi Shan. For perhaps an hour, the figure remained still, only watching and observing. Then, as if on some unseen cue, he began to circle the walls, studying them and listening intently.

Ah. There it was. Only a whisper through the thick walls, but still perceptible. The soft chuffing, growls, and light pad of the big cats on the far side.

When he was sure of their location, he drew a package wrapped in paper from his shirt and took out two lean cuts of meat filched from the hotel's kitchen, laced with opiates purchased earlier in the day. These, he tossed over the high wall, only to be rewarded by the sounds of the two cats yowling and chewing. Another fifteen minutes and he detected soft snores like the purr of some huge kitten.

It was no trick to find a vine trailing down the wall sturdy enough to hold him and scramble up it nimbly like a monkey. Once on top of the wall, he allowed his eyes to adjust to the darkness until the could make out the two sleeping brutes below. Then, satisfied that their sleep was sound, he dropped to the ground.

The garden was a small jungle, but with the cats drugged, he had no fear. The army of Dacoits would likely keep in close with the cats on the loose and even their handler would be a fool to venture into the darkness with his two half-starved charges. The trouble with such elaborate security was that one became too dependent upon it. Like avoiding the Dugrivals' diabolical trap, or arranging Gilbert's escape from the island prison of Re... But this was no time to rest on past laurels. Carefully, the man moved forward past the sleeping cats, their great maws open, their terrible yellow fangs exposed, their mouths red with the fresh blood from the uncooked meat.

The beast nearest him stirred.

Stirred, stretched, extended its great paw, brushed his leg.

The huge paw curved around his leg the way a kitten grips a finger to draw it close.

This was no kitten.

He froze.

He held his breath.

The beast sighed deeply and snuggled on its side with a grunt of expelled air through its nostrils, freeing its captive.

He suppressed a sigh of relief. *Next time, use more opium*, he thought.

He made his way to the house without any more incidents. As he expected, he met with no Dacoits or other sentries, and it was no real difficulty to find a high window in a darkened room and force a paneled shutter. A moment on the sill and he was inside, his slippered feet on the delicate Persian carpet.

The afternoon studying the blue prints of the house registered at the public works' office now paid off. Though much had been concealed, his keen eye had quickly picked out the telling details–a room which appeared too small for the schematics must surely mean a hidden compartment, and that large cellar, what might it conceal?

But where was the army of Dacoits?

He quickly detected a number of crates–some packed and closed, some open and in the process of being packed. Hadn't the old Legionnaire said something about Shan moving to France? But the Jade Buddha would no doubt travel in the Chinese's personal luggage–certainly the last object to be removed from the house. As for the Dacoits, they too would have gone ahead to prepare for their master's arrival, leaving behind only a small loyal guard. He smiled imagining the reactions of the estate agent in Paris encountering an army of Dacoits. How amusing.

Trusting in his senses, keen as those of the big cats sleeping outside, and in his knowledge of the schematics imprinted on his mind, he made his way to the too small room he had marked as his first target. It proved to be devoted to a private collection of art and antiquities–any of which would normally have been worth the effort expended until then. Many were already packed, the shelves that held them standing empty. Still, his mind was focused on something grander, and he unerringly made for the wall where he had detected the anomaly in construction.

He carefully examined the shelves set in the wall where he had detected the extra space. They held an array of delicate pieces of jade and ivory of magnificent workmanship. There was a little jade elephant that was exquisite. But as he admired the delicate artworks, he also noted that none of the objects had yet been packed. They represented an elite guard, a tempting treasure to distract the untrained eye from the true treasure hidden behind the...

Yes. There. A hidden spring!

A finger's pressure–no more.

The shelf of delicate artworks slid open. And there it sat. The Jade Buddha of Hanoi Shan!

It was then that he heard the scream. The all too human scream.

It came from the depths–the elaborate cellars he had noted in the schematics. His nerves were steel, but the sound of that scream played on them like a fiddler's bow on catgut. He felt a chill along his spine.

Some poor devil. None of his business... He lifted the Buddha–surprisingly heavy...

A second scream, this one lifted from the very soul.

Damn and blast... It was none of his...

He found the entrance to the cellars quickly enough. Shan was so reliant on his fearsome reputation that he had let his security grow lax. The stone stairs into the depth were dank and the smell of death was entrenched in the walls themselves. Cellars be damned, this was a dungeon.

It was no trick to follow the sounds of human pain and the growing light into the depths.

In a room poorly lighted by torches, like some Oriental version of the Spanish Inquisition's torture chambers, he saw a native, stretched on a low table and covered in blood, whose limp form proved that rescue had come too late. Across from him stood Hanoi Shan, serpentine and magnificent, delicately cleaning his hands on a small towel as if he were wiping away some minor bit of dirt, and not a man's life. Two Dacoits stood on either side of him–one the muscular chauffeur–both stripped to loin cloths, their skin shiny with sweat, oblivious to the blood on their own hands which their master so delicately wiped from his.

But it was the fourth figure in the room that captured his attention. It was the Arab whom he had observed watching Hanoi Shan.

Save that this was no Arab.

The man was lean and fit. Stripped of his shirt, it was now obvious that his face and arms had been dyed darker. The streaks of black on his face that had run from his hair showed that this, too, was the work of a dye. Even in the flickering unreal light of the torches, the thief could see the man's thickly curled iron gray hair showing under the remaining boot black, and above all those keen gray eyes–eerilie reminiscent of the eyes of a troublesome Englishman he knew.

"Your servant died badly, Monsieur Lenormand," Hanoi Shan said in French to the man chained to the wall. His accent was perfect, but his voice was as cold as a serpent's blood. "If Lenormand is your true name. No doubt you will last longer and give my servants a greater challenge, but in the end you *will* talk. The fate of your servant was only a demonstration, to acquaint you with what is to come..."

The man called Lenormand showed no sign that the threat had moved him. *What magnificent nerve*, thought the thief.

"My master–yes, I, Hanoi Shan, acknowledge one man as master–warns me that you are a clever enemy–one to be respected and feared. I confess I cannot share in that. Still, if he respects your intellect, then I will give you some benefit of the doubt. You have a few hours in which to think about what you have seen tonight–and to choose whether your death will be swift, or lingering."

Of course, hadn't Corday mentioned the Si Fan? And wasn't there talk in the gossipy hen's cackle of the underworld's pipeline of an English policeman–Jones or–no, Smith–something Smith–one of those curious English names with the hyphen–some big wig with Scotland Yard who had served in–was it Burma? Didn't the fellow have some sort of bug in his ear about that secret Chinese criminal society and its mysterious leader–the master Hanoi Shan had spoken of? No, this was no Lenormand. But then, didn't the gossip also say that this English policeman was a master of disguise and spoke a dozen obscure dialects...

Would it be unreasonable, then, to assume that such a man might pretend to be an obscure colonial civil servant so that he might surreptitiously investigate one branch of the Si Fan's vast organization–in particular Hanoi Shan's...

Hanoi Shan and the two Dacoits turned to leave.

The thief pressed himself into the shadows and held his breath as they passed. For an instant, he could have touched one of the Dacoits if he so much as expelled his breath.

Once the three Asians were gone, he slid into the room. The English policeman spotted him immediately and the thief was certain that the man had seen through his disguise. He raised his finger to his lips to keep the policeman silent.

He opened the chains and the Englishman slumped into his arms. He supported the man and whispered in English:

"We haven't long, Mr. Smith. We have to get out of here before they come back."

"You must be one of de Beaujolais' agents," the Englishman answered. "You just get out and tell the Major. Leave me, the two of us will never get past Shan's guards, or those two cats of his..."

"Just lean on me... I've taken care of both."

As if on cue, a cry erupted from above.

"Fire!"

"Actually–mostly smoke," the thief said, helping the Englishman toward the door. "All that straw for packing plus a little match, and–*voilà!*"

The Englishman actually chuckled. "Good man. I'll have a promotion for you if we both get out of here alive. A promotion for you and a rope for that devil Hanoi Shan."

The household was busy with the fire, well away from the exit from the cellar, and as they moved, the Englishman quickly regained his natural strength, so that by the time they had passed the two cats, only now showing any signs of coming around, it only took a slight boost to help him over the wall. Then, a leap, a drop, and a brief sprint...

They remained in the darkness outside for near half an hour, but when the Englishman turned to thank his rescuer, the thief was gone. The policeman was alone.

It should be noted that, on the following morning, the Englishman, Denis Nayland Smith, who had heretofore been known as Monsieur Lenormand, joined Major de Beaujolais and the local constabulary in a raid on the home of Hanoi Shan, only to find that their intended target had already fled. The two great cats had been slain in their cages and with them, they found the two Dacoits who had failed in their duty, dead by their own hand.

It was deemed odd, too, that Hanoi Shan's home showed signs of a desperate search before it had been deserted, as if Shan had misplaced something of importance. Nor could Smith persuade de Beaujolais to reveal the name of the agent who had saved his life the night before. Indeed, the Major behaved as if he had no idea what the Englishman was talking about. Curious fellows, the French...

Nor did anyone—not even the sharp-eyed Smith—notice that, during the raid, they were joined by one more policeman than had been sent for, or that, once in the deserted house, this policeman made his way to a certain spot and then slipped out again carrying a heavy object wrapped in cloth that had been carefully if quickly secreted the night before...

And still later that day, when Major de Beaujolais called on his friend the Duke de Charmerace, he was surprised to find that that worthy visitor had been called away suddenly. More curiously yet, when he checked the records of the vessels sailing from Saigon that day, there was no Duke de Charmerace listed amongst the passengers. All very odd, but what with this business of Hanoi Shan and the Englishman Smith, there was no time to follow a mere whim. Too bad, for he was sure Charmerace would have enjoyed this little coda to the other night's excursion.

It will also be noted that, had Major de Beaujolais looked farther among those listed as sailing out of Saigon that day, he would have found a familiar name—one Monsieur Lenormand, listed as a civil servant—and had he asked around, he would have been told that this Monsieur Lenormand traveled lightly, with only one bag and a rather heavy object which he kept quite close at all times.

One of the most eagerly anticipated features of the Tales of the Shadowmen *series is always the latest installment in Brian Stableford's continuing homage to Paul Féval,* The Empire of the Necromancers. *Drawing characters and themes from* John Devil, The Vampire Countess, Revenants, *and now* The Black Coats, *the plot thickens in this fourth chapter in which we meet...*

Brian Stableford: *The Vampire in Paris*
(Being the fourth part of
The Empire of the Necromancers)

The Story So Far

In Paul Féval's John Devil *(Black Coat Press, 2005), that legendary pseudonym is adopted by Comte Henri de Belcamp in support of his mother's career as a notorious member of London's underworld, where she is known by her maiden name, Helen Brown. After attempting to rescue her from an Australian prison camp, Henri takes news of his mother's death to his long-estranged father, the Marquis de Belcamp, in the small town of Miremont, and is reconciled with him. Meanwhile, Henri is secretly engaged in financing the construction of an unprecedentedly powerful steamship with which he intends to rescue Napoleon from St. Helena and conquer India; in pursuit of this plan, he takes over a secret Bonapartist organization, the Knights of the Deliverance. Henri is assisted in this project by his long-term companion Sarah O'Brien, the daughter of a murdered Irish general.*

When a potential traitor to the Deliverance, the opera singer Constance Bartolozzi, is murdered in London, the case is investigated by Gregory Temple, the senior detective at Scotland Yard, assisted by his junior, James Davy. John Devil is identified as the murderer. Temple strongly suspects that the person behind that name is Helen Brown's son, known to him as Tom Brown, but the evidence seems to point to Temple's former assistant, Richard Thompson (who is secretly married to Temple's daughter, Suzanne). Actually, James Davy–who is another of Henri de Belcamp's many aliases–has framed his predecessor, exploiting the account of his methods Temple has published in a book on the art of detection. Henri de Belcamp/James Davy persuades Thompson to flee to France, where Suzanne is a guest at the Château Belcamp, but he is captured and convicted of the Bartolozzi murder.

When Henri is reconciled with his father, Sarah rents the so-called "new château" on the Belcamp estate under the name of Lady Frances Elphinstone. Henri commissions the murders of his dead mother's wealthy brothers, but there is one further obstacle to the fortune Henri intends to collect by this means, in the name of Tom Brown: Constance Bartolozzi's daughter, Jeanne Herbet, who also lives in Miremont. Jeanne is the designated heir of both brothers, neither of whom knows which of them is her father. Henri falls in love with Jeanne after impulsively saving her life, and decides to marry her fortune rather than murdering her.

Henri eventually marries Jeanne under the alias of an English entrepreneur, Percy Balcomb, in which guise he slips out of the jail where he is supposedly confined. Henri is in prison because the obsessive Temple, having failed to prove that he murdered General O'Brien or Constance Bartolozzi, found out where the bodies of his hired killers were buried. Temple has obtained this information from the drunken mistress of the vertically-challenged petty criminal Ned Knob, who was a witness to the murders and disposed of the bodies. Ned had also schooled the false witnesses at Richard Thompson's trial, using members of a troupe of vagabond actors.

On the eve of Thompson's execution, Henri inveigles his way into Newgate Prison, helping him to escape by taking his place. When Temple tries the same trick, Henri confronts his nemesis in the condemned cell, almost driving him insane by telling him that Tom Brown is not, after all, one of his pseudonyms but an actual half-brother, sired by Temple. After escaping in Temple's place, however, Henri finds that everything is going awry. The Deliverance is betrayed, his new steamship is destroyed, and his mother has returned from Australia, accusing him of having abandoned her. He finds it politic to commit suicide–or, at least, to appear to do so.

Part One of The Empire of the Necromancers, *"The Grey Men"* (in Tales of the Shadowmen 2, *Black Coat Press 2006*) picks up the story four years later, in November 1821. Ned Knob, now directing the acting troupe, is unexpectedly confronted with his predecessor in that role, *"Sawney"* Ross, who has been hanged, but now appears to be alive again, though somewhat slow-witted. When the reanimated Ross is collected by a diminutive French physician, Germain Patou, Ned follows them a boat where they are met by a man in a Quaker hat like the one Henri wore in his guise as John Devil.

After being knocked unconscious, Ned wakes up in Newgate and is interrogated by Gregory Temple, now working for the secret police. Temple is supposed to be investigating a series of body-snatching incidents, but his attention has been caught by a report of the Quaker hat. Following his release, Ned tracks Patou to a house in Purfleet. There he renews his acquaintance with Henri and witnesses the resurrection of a man from the dead using an elaborate electrical technique recently discovered by a Swiss scientist.

The demonstration is interrupted when Henri's ship is attacked by a rival group under the command of the only one of the reanimated Grey Men to have recovered all his faculties: a person who styles himself General Mortdieu. Mortdieu's hirelings seize the electrical apparatus from the house, taking it to their own ship, the Outremort. Ned is arrested again, but makes a deal with

Temple. As the Outremort *is about to depart from her berth in Greenhithe, a three-cornered battle develops between Mortdieu's hirelings, Henri's followers and Temple's men. The fight eventually arrives at an impasse, but a hastily-contrived treaty permits Mortdieu to sail away, taking Patou with him.*

In Part Two of The Empire of the Necromancers, *"The Child-Stealers" (in* Tales of the Shadowmen 3, *Black Coat Press 2007) Gregory Temple is woken one night by Henri, who tells him that they must join forces, at least temporarily. Temple's grandson has been kidnapped from the Château Belcamp, where Thompson and Suzanne are now resident, along with two younger children of much richer parents; one is the son of Henri and Jeanne, the other the son of the former Sarah O'Brien, now the widow of a German Count.*

Temple and Henri set out to make their separate ways to Miremont, where Temple has to break the news to Jeanne that she is not a widow. Henri is de-layed and Temple has to respond to the first ransom note with no one to help him but Ned Knob. He is taken prisoner in his turn. Temple's captors are mem-bers of a long-dormant society of heretic monks known as Civitas Solis, *who are even more interested in securing the secret of resurrection than in the ransom money that will help finance their exploitation of it.*

Henri's delay has been caused by his traveling under the name George Palmer, in which guise he was involved with a vehm *(a secret society of vigi-lantes) at the time of General O'Brien's murder, and in whose eyes he is still a wanted man. Having made his peace with the* vehmgerichte, *however, Henri is able to attack* Civitas Solis *and liberate Temple and the captive children before disappearing again, intent on joining forces with* Civitas Solis *in the expectation of using them as he had formerly used the Deliverance.*

In Part Three of The Empire of the Necromancers, *"The Return of Frank-enstein" (*Tales of the Shadowmen 4, *Black Coat Press, 2008), set in the vicinity of Spezia in Northern Italy in the summer of 1822, Ned Knob has been commis-sioned by Gregory Temple to keep watch on a villa rented by Victor Franken-stein, the original inventor of the technology of resurrection carried forward by Germain Patou, and his friend Robert Walton. Frankenstein is about to resume his own experiments, aided by a group of Englishmen headed by Lord Byron and Percy Shelley. Ned is also reporting his findings to Henri de Belcamp.*

Ned is by no means the only spy interested in Frankenstein's work. He is approached with an offer of cooperation by a man who calls himself Guido, who eventually turns out to be a Magyar working for a reputed vampire–one of "nature's Grey Men" rather than a legendary bloodsucker. He also meets a burly but uncommonly articulate Grey Man who is somewhat resentful of being portrayed as a murderous "daemon" in the sensationalized version of Franken-stein's story that Robert Walton issued by way of Mary Shelley; Frankenstein's first creation prefers to think of himself as an authentic Lazarus, or the Adam of a new race and is attempting to negotiate a reconciliation with his creator. Ned also has a less amicable encounter with a fanatical warrior monk named Malo

*de Treguern, who appears to be working for a more orthodox and more inqui-
sitorially-inclined arm of the Roman Church than Civitas Solis.*

*Owing to the interaction of these various interested parties and Percy
Shelley's collapse as a result of a wound inflicted by a member of the local mili-
tia, Frankenstein's villa is besieged and his attempts to renew his experiments
are thwarted. Frankenstein and most of his associates escape, but will have to
find a more hospitable spot to resume work. Ned hears of Shelley's death by
drowning a few days later, but does not believe the rumor.*

Now read on...

Paris, 1822

Chapter One
Fog in Paris

As Gregory Temple was about to turn the corner of the Rue de la Lanterne, he
heard a curious sound, something between a hiss and a whistle, which was evidently intended to attract his attention. He turned to look at the dark doorway
from which it had come, but the combination of shadow and fog made it impossible to discern the face of the man who was lurking there. He cursed the bad
weather; fog was the curse of London, but he appeared to have brought this one
with him to the streets of Paris, where it seemed to him to be just as foreign as
he was.

"Monsieur Temple!" The man in the door way was evidently impatient.

Temple did not move, although he had stopped dead. If the other man
wanted to talk to him, then he would have to step out into the street, where he
face would be lit, vaguely at least, by a street-light.

Eventually, the other accepted the necessity. He was a small man, but a
wiry one, dressed with unusual flamboyance for someone who maintained vigils
in dark doorways, although he did not seem to have acquired sophisticated
tastes, any more than he was blessed with natural elegance. He might have
passed for a dandy in the worst kind of *licherie*, but he would have been a
clownish caricature in the Bois de Boulogne.

"We'd do better to step into the shadows, Monsieur Temple," the caricature said, speaking in vulgar French but obviously expecting to be understood.
"You're being followed, and you're not the only visitor that Monsieur Sévérin is
expecting tonight. Monsieur Vidocq suggested that I should look out for you,
and make contact if I could. Don't worry–we're on the same side."

Temple scowled in dire annoyance. He had not been in the best of tempers
for some time, ever since discovering that Ned Knob had held back a consider-

able fraction of the story of what had happened in the Spezia. It was bad enough to be betrayed by one's own petty low-life spies without having their French equivalents greet him as if he were a brother-in-arms. He had heard rumors at the Prefecture regarding the gang of ex-convicts who had set up as an arm of the detective police in the Petite Rue de Sainte-Anne, with the reluctant blessing of the Prefect, and was not at all pleased to learn that they had apparently heard rumors of his business—rumors that had evidently been updated as a result of his findings in the Prefecture files, which he had assumed to be known to no one else but himself. "Is that hulking brute dogging my footsteps another of Vidocq's damned *bagne*-sweepings?" he demanded, angrily.

The agent did not seem at all alarmed by his attitude. "Monsieur Vidocq is a great admirer of your work, Monsieur Temple," he said, earnestly. "He considers your book on the art of detection to be a masterpiece. My name is Coco-Lacour. I'm Monsieur Vidocq's most trusted associate—and I can assure you that the person following you is not one of our men. If you will agree to work with Monsieur Vidocq in this matter, we can easily relieve you of the inconvenience of being followed."

Temple suspected that there was probably little competition for the title of "Vidocq's most trusted associate," but he struggled to remove the cutting edge in his voice. Coco-Lacour might be the worst kind of police agent, but he was a policeman nevertheless. "That's very kind of you, Monsieur Lacour," he said, warily. "I shall be pleased to call on Monsieur Vidocq at the Petite Rue de Sainte-Anne when I have the time—perhaps tomorrow."

"*Coco*-Lacour," the other corrected him, understandably anxious that no one should think that Coco was his forename rather than part of a nickname he had doubtless been given in the *bagne* from which Vidocq had plucked him. "Would you like me to have your follower arrested tonight? I would have to summon several of my colleagues in order to make the arrest, but I could do that if you wish. He'll doubtless linger nearby while you're talking to Monsieur Sévérin."

"Please don't go to any trouble," Temple replied. "If he's not one of your men, he must belong to another branch of the Prefecture, and I wouldn't like to cause Monsieur le Préfet any inconvenience."

"I'm sorry to have to correct you, Monsieur Temple" said Coco-Lacour, who did not sound in the least sorry, "but he has no connection whatsoever with the forces of law and order. I dare say that your presence in Paris is not without interest to the political police, but the *hulking brute*, as you call him, is in the employ of an Englishman. Would you like to know his name?"

"If you've got something to say," Temple retorted, "spit it out."

The *licherie* dandy sighed. "Lord Byron," he said, briefly, immediately adding: "But you probably knew that already."

Temple had not known it already, but he did not find the news surprising. The fact that Byron was in Paris—although there was no suggestion in the reports received in London that Victor Frankenstein was with him–had been one of the factors that had drawn Temple here, although his principal motive had been a desire to consult the Prefecture files with respect to the infamous *vampire affair* of 1804. Thanks to Ned Knob's disloyalty, he was apparently late on the scene, at least one step behind the other players in the game–including, it now seemed, the vampire himself. It was even possible, Temple thought, that Henri de Belcamp, *alias* John Devil–to whom the perfidious Knob had presumably made a fuller report of his discoveries in Spezia–might be among the people taking a sudden interest in the vampire of Paris, but he was not about to ask one of Vidocq's gang of poachers-turned-gamekeepers about the one man in the world they undoubtedly admired more enthusiastically than himself. "Why are you watching Jean-Pierre Sévérin's house?" he growled, instead.

"Monsieur Sévérin is a very popular man nowadays," Coco-Lacour replied, still seemingly confident that he had the advantage of knowing more than his interlocutor. "If I were to tell you the names of some of those…but I have my duty to the Prefecture to consider, and you're a foreign spy. Our countries are no longer at war, but still…"

"Monsieur Sévérin has always been a much-respected man," Temple said, stiffly. "When he was in charge of the morgue at the Marché-Neuf, he had occasion to meet many influential people. It's remarkable is it not, what a generous cross-section of Parisian society the…what do you call it in France?…the *salle d'exposition* brings out. You and Monsieur Vidocq must be regular visitors yourselves, in search of old friends and adversaries."

"Monsieur Sévérin is not as well-respected as he used to be," Coco-Lacour told him. "The political wind is a little chilly nowadays for old Bonapartists. A little unfair, perhaps, since he was never associated with the Deliverance, and his son-in-law is a *chouan*–but he did know the Emperor personally, and that counts as a black mark nowadays. You visited the *salle* more than once yourself in the old days, I believe, war or no war–breakdowns in diplomatic relations are God's gift to the criminal classes, are they not? You were not one to let petty international disputes keep you from maintaining contact with *old friends and adversaries*."

The point was a fair one but Temple was not about to call *touché*. "Goodnight, Monsieur Lacour," he said.

Coco-Lacour frowned "There is no need to be impolite, Monsieur Temple," he said, in a wounded tone. "We are colleagues, after all. Our little band of heroic crime-fighters might well be able to render you invaluable assistance–if you were to get into difficulties."

Temple did not bother to ask whether that was a veiled threat. He was, after all, the man on foreign soil; it was inevitable that the Prefecture should be enthusiastic to maintain a monopoly on detective work conducted in the capital, even of the crazy kind in which he was presently engaged. He could not help wondering, though, why Vidocq's agents–who were supposedly affiliated to the criminal police, although they were rumored to be nothing more than organized criminals themselves–were taking such an interest in a representative of His Majesty's Secret Service.

"I do not anticipate getting into difficulties, Monsieur Lacour," Temple retorted, "and we are not colleagues. I'm no longer employed by Scotland Yard; I have retired from police work and am here in Paris simply to look up a few old friends, of whom Monsieur Sévérin is one."

"Oh, have it your own way," Coco-Lacour replied, probably more put out by the continued deliberate mangling of his name than by any disappointed expectations. "Monsieur Vidocq will be disappointed, but he's come to expect such ingratitude." He stepped back into the shadowed doorway so abruptly, that Temple turn round, expecting to see that a third person had come into view further along the street–but if Coco-Lacour had seen someone, the other had been very quick to take evasive action.

Again, Temple cursed the fog. Then, he swiftly rounded the corner of the Rue de la Lanterne and sounded the bell of the first house whose door he encountered.

It was not a concierge who answered but a young woman, perhaps 17 years of age. She had beautiful blonde hair.

Temple told her his name, and asked, in French, to see Jean-Pierre Sévérin."

"I'm afraid that Monsieur Sévérin is very old, Monsieur," The young woman replied. "He hardly receives visitors at all, and never at this advanced hour."

"He'll see me," Temple said. "I knew him long ago, when he was in charge of…the establishment at the Marché-Neuf. I was a detective at Scotland Yard at the time, but I'm retired now, just as he is."

The blonde girl's dark blue eyes looked him up and down, as if estimating his own antiquity, and any worth he might have acquired in consequence. She was not about to be convinced, through.

"I'm afraid…" She began–but was then interrupted.

"It's all right, Angela," said a male voice from the stairway behind her. "This isn't the one we were expecting. I'll handle it."

"Yes, father," the young woman said, meekly. She stepped back, and was replaced in the doorway by a melancholy man with dark hair, who must have been in his late 30s.

"Monsieur de Kervoz, I presume?" Temple was quick to say. The corridor inside the door was too dark to allow him to judge the extent of the other's surprise at hearing his name spoken.

"I don't believe I've had the privilege," René de Kervoz said, in English–with almost as much stiffness as a genuine Briton might have contrived.

"I need to speak to Monsieur Sévérin," Temple said, not wanting to stand on the foggy street any longer than necessary. "I'm sorry to call at such a late

233

hour, but I've been busy since my arrival. You will both be interested in what I have to say. It concerns Countess Marcian Gregoryi."

This time, the young man's start of surprise was very clearly visible. "What do you mean?" he demanded.

"I need to see Monsieur Sévérin," Temple repeated.

René de Kervoz hesitated, then nodded. "Please go to your room, Angela," he said. "I'll take Monsieur Temple up to see your grandfather. If the other one comes, tell him that Monsieur Sévérin is engaged, and cannot possibly see anyone else tonight."

"I'm glad that my unannounced call has provided you with a potentially-useful excuse," Temple murmured, as they mounted the staircase to the first floor. "I shall feel a little less embarrassed by my inability to warn you that I was coming."

Kervoz made no reply, but stood aside politely as he ushered his visitor through the doorway of a bedroom. Jean-Pierre Sévérin evidently had no reception-room or study, although he belonged to the respectable ranks of the poor and was the proud possessor of two large bookcases as well as a capacious writing-desk. The bed-curtains were closed, and the retired morgue-keeper was sitting in an armchair by the fireside. He was, as his great-granddaughter had said, very old–but he was not frail, and he stood up to greet Temple with a polite bow, followed by an English handshake.

"Gregory Temple," Sévérin said, immediately. "Why, it must be at least five years since I saw you last. How are you?"

"Quite well," Temple lied. "I wanted to come to see you when I was last in Paris, but I was exceedingly busy."

"The affair of the two assassins buried at the Trocadero," Sévérin said, as he resumed his own seat and indicated that Temple should take the one opposite the hearth. René de Kervoz fetched a less comfortable chair from the bedside for himself. "The trial at Versailles caused quite a sensation–we followed its course eagerly in the newspapers. Should the young man have been convicted? He came from a very good family, did he not? But he committed suicide immediately after his release, so I suppose he must have had some cause for shame."

"His father's family is a very good one," Temple admitted, not bothering to tell his host that he had been in Paris far more recently than the trial at Versailles, in order to visit the Château de Belcamp and contend with a gang of kidnappers, "but his mother…well, that was another story. Henri de Belcamp was something of a chimera, his dark and light selves seemingly in continual conflict. Yes, he should have been convicted, but no, he did not commit suicide. That was yet another of his seemingly-miraculous evasions."

"Mr. Temple says that he wants to talk about Countess Marcian Gregoryi," René de Kervoz put in, apparently eager to blight the old man's gladness at seeing an old friend.

Jean-Pierre Séverin did not react with alarm, though, or even with undue astonishment. "I did not know that you were party to that affair," he said, in a voice that was low but perfectly even. "Our countries were not on the best of terms at the time–although such petty disputes did not always prevent you from visiting us, of course."

"I've only read the reports filed at the Prefecture," Temple admitted. "I don't know how accurate the information contained therein might be, given the extreme unreliability of its sources, but I have some reason to suspect that it is not as fanciful as it must have seemed at the time to Monsieur le Préfet."

"Do you, indeed?" murmured Séverin, cocking an eyebrow. "I have not seen the files myself, of course, but I remember that old villain Ezekiel, who must have supplied much of their content. I wish I could say that the Prefecture no longer hires men of that stripe, but I fear that it would not be true."

"There's one watching your house as we speak," Temple told him. "He seems to have been posted to look out for someone else who was intending to pay you a visit tonight–the one you asked your granddaughter to put off."

"I seem to have become somewhat sought-after lately," Séverin admitted. "Everyone is hungry for information about my old friend Germain Patou. I seem to have convinced people that I have no news of his whereabouts, but I cannot seem to persuade them that I know nothing about his experiments, or that I do not know where he hid any records he might have kept. Even some of my old friends from the morgue can find no other topic to discuss."

"I'm interested in Patou too," Temple admitted. "Obviously, I take your word for the fact that you have no knowledge of any records he kept–but I'm a little concerned to hear that you've attracted the attention of people who might not. Would you mind telling me who you are expecting to call tonight?"

"Not at all," the old man replied. He took up a visiting-card from the occasional table beside his armchair and held it out to Temple. "He did not request an appointment," Séverin said, with a slight sigh. "He simply asked the Dominican lackey who brought the card to say that he would call on me this evening, if he could. The Church takes the Restoration very seriously, and seems to regard the King's resumption of his throne merely as a symbol of its own renewal."

The name on the card was *Malo de Treguern*. There was no address, but there was a design beneath the name: a red Cross of Calvary, entwined with a thorny briar that might–or might not–have symbolized Christ's crown of thorns.

Temple was considerably intrigued, not so much by the fact that Malo de Treguern wanted to consult Jean-Pierre Séverin as by the odd circumstance that Monsieur Vidocq had posted one of his men at the corner to watch out for a Churchman operating on the direct authority of a Papal warrant. "Do you know this Treguern?" he asked.

"Only by reputation," René de Kervoz put in. "He's a legend in my native province. He was a Knight of Malta before the Emperor disbanded the Order, and then spent many years on a quest to find a fragment lost from the tomb of one of his ancestors. He was thought to be mad, but the object of the quest–the restoration of his family's fortune–was eventually fulfilled, with or without the stone in question. After that, he disappeared from Brittany. It was rumored that he had gone to Rome."

"He did," Temple supplied, feeling that he ought to offer as much of a *quid pro quo* as his duty permitted. "He's working for the Holy Office now."

"As a heresy hunter?" Kervoz said. "What has that to do with us?"

"I don't imagine for a moment that you're under suspicion of heresy," Temple hastened to reassure him. "He has a different quarry in view–the same one, I suspect, that I am pursuing. All my rivals are ahead of me, it seems, and I must count myself fortunate that I seem to have overtaken him, at least."

"What quarry do you have in view?" Jean-Pierre Sévérin asked. "And by what authority are you hunting on French soil?"

"Monsieur le Préfet knows that I am here," Temple said, taking the easier question first. "I have his permission, if not his blessing. I came to Paris to investigate the vampire that terrorized the city 18 years ago–and was both astonished and alarmed to learn that he seems to have returned."

"She, not he," René de Kervoz put in.

"Countess Marcian Gregoryi," Sévérin said, pensively. "Has she returned?" Temple was glad that the old soldier wasted no time with any futile protest that the Countess was dead. The old man had seen René de Kervoz shoot her in the head, but he knew now, if he had not then, that the eyes of men were subject to gross deception in the presence of that remarkable woman.

"A woman of that name is now in Paris," Temple told him. "I am not certain that it is the same woman that was here in 1804, since she is said to be in her early 20s, but I have learned to expect the seemingly impossible in this affair. That is one reason for my presence here–I was hoping that you might be able to identify her for me if your memory is good enough. Monsieur de Kervoz's attempted correction might be mistaken, though; if my information is trustworthy–which is, I admit, dubious–the Countess you encountered in 1804 was not the actual vampire, properly speaking, but merely his instrument."

"That was not my impression," René de Kervoz murmured, doubtless recalling the fateful day on which the Countess had seduced him, while pretending to be her own dark-haired sister, seemingly in order to obtain the secret of his uncle's whereabouts. "But you need have no fear that my memory has faded. If Countess Marcian Gregoryi is indeed in Paris, whether she had aged a full 18 years or not a day, I will know her as soon as I set eyes on her."

"Is it possible, do you think, Mr. Temple," Jean-Pierre Sévérin asked, "that the woman now using the name might be the same one, even though she looks no older?"

"I think it is," Temple said. "It is possible that she is a different person altogether–an innocent instrument, completely in her master's power–and that even if she seems to be the same, that appearance is merely a clever illusion. I

236

really do not know what to expect of this vampire–but I do not think that he is the bloodsucking monster of superstition. He appears to know secrets that science has not yet discovered, which might perhaps have been known to mages of old and then lost–but it is equally possible that he made them himself, if he is as old as the facts suggest."

"There was no rumor of bloodsucking in 1804," the white-haired ex-morgue-keeper said, softly. "The manner of predation attribute to the Countess was even more bizarre–but people died nevertheless. Who does the Countess intend to marry and murder this time?"

"I doubt that she intends to marry anyone," Temple said. "Her master is in search of the same thing as everyone else: the records of Germain Patou's experiments, and those of Victor Frankenstein, if any exist. I suspect, though, that the so-called vampire, like Malo de Treguern, is more intent on destroying such secrets than making use of them. Like the Church, albeit in a very different fashion, he is probably a would-be monopolist in matters of resurrection."

"You said that asking for our help in deciding whether the present Countess Marcian Gregoryi is the same one that was in Paris before was one reason why you came," Sévérin asked. "It seems a trivial one–what are the others?"

"I thought that you would like to know," Temple said, simply. "I thought that you ought to be warned–and…"

René de Kervoz cut him off. "Warned?" the Breton said. "She is the one that ought to be frightened of us. We have a score to settle. I tried to shoot her once, and believed that I had done so; I'll be delighted to have another chance. She killed my beloved Angela–the mother of the girl who answered the door to you just now."

"It would be unwise to shoot her again," Temple said. "It would be reckoned as murder if you succeeded this time, no matter what crimes she might or might not have committed in the past."

"Might or might not?" Kervoz echoed. "Are you saying that she did not kill Angela?"

"I have no reliable information as to that, one way or the other," Temple told him. "Neither, I think, do you."

Kervoz was about to protest, but Sévérin silenced him with a gesture. "René was deluded when he was seduced and drugged by the Countess, and was in no fit condition to form reliable judgments," the old man said, addressing himself to the Englishman. "What I saw on the river that night–all of which must be neatly recorded in the Prefecture's files–was admittedly impossible, and I have every reason to doubt that my own eyes were telling me the truth. I have had abundant cause to wonder whether I collaborated wholeheartedly in an illusion, because I could not bear the thought that my daughter had committed suicide. She was my step-daughter, as you probably know, but I loved her no less for that. The fact remains, though, that she did die–and that Countess Marcian Gregoryi *was* responsible, directly or indirectly, for her death."

"If you really did catch a glimpse of a supernatural creature in the river that night," Temple told him, "it might have been the actual vampire rather than his glamorous instrument–I can draw no firm conclusion on the matter until I find out more."

"You were about to give us another reason for your visit when René interrupted you," Sévérin said. "Is it that you want our help in trying to find out?"

"Yes," Temple said. "I am alone in this business, mistrusted by my superiors and unable to place the slightest faith in my hirelings. I need assistance if I am to get to the bottom of it. All the other interested parties are ahead of me–including, it seems, the infamous Monsieur Vidocq. I hoped that you might give me the help I need, given that you have your own very powerful reasons for wanting to understand what really happened in 1804. I must warn you both, though, that it may not be possible for you to take your vengeance. If, as I suspect, the vampire has already died at least once, and has powerful means at his disposal to create illusions, he might be more difficult to destroy than you or I can imagine."

"I thought I saw the Countess reduced to ashes once, and was then convinced that I had blasted her brains out," René de Kervoz muttered. "Was all that really no more than illusion?"

"I suspect so," Temple said, "but I cannot be entirely sure. There are more things in Heaven and Earth than I once dreamed of–but I need to find out, and I need help that I can rely on."

"I'm glad that you consider us trustworthy," Sévérin replied, courteously, "but my granddaughter is always assuring me that I'm far too old for adventuring nowadays. It's a long time since I took my little skiff out on the river. René, on the other hand…"

"René can speak for himself," Kervoz interrupted, sharply. The Breton did not seem enraptured by the prospect of working for an English policeman, even though the prospect of hunting down the vampire that had killed his young wife-to-be was obviously tempting, even after all these years.

"Might I ask you an exceedingly delicate question, Monsieur Sévérin?" Temple said, hastening to interrupt any possible dispute between the two men.

"Of course," Sévérin replied, suggesting by his tone that he was not promising an answer.

"You spent the whole of your working life in the Paris morgue," Temple said, his own tone one of deadly earnest, "and you succeeded your father, who held the same position before the Revolution. There is no one in the world more qualified to give an expert judgment on this matter. Tell me, Monsieur Sévérin: *do the dead ever return to life?*"

"You are the second person to ask me that, in so many words, within a week," Sévérin said, pensively. "Like you, the other was an old acquaintance from my days at the Morgue–a genuinely good man, though, not a polite ghoul like some of those who haunted the *salle*. I told him that I could not be sure, and

I will give you the same answer. You must know, of course, that the morgue was first established in consequence of a panic regarding the possibility of premature burials, rather than for its ostensible purpose of allowing the dead to be formally identified. I do not know how much truth there is in the many gruesome tales of men awakening in their coffins and tearing off their fingernails scrabbling hopelessly at the wooden lid, but it must have happened on occasion. It is certainly true that a small number of those brought into the morgue as dead eventually began to move again, and to sit up on their slabs demanding to know where they were.

"The official attitude to such cases has always been that they could not have been truly dead, but only cataleptic, and I have always agreed with that judgment in public...but *I cannot be sure*. Some of the *revenants* did not seem to their relatives to be the same person they had been before. Again, the official attitude to such cases has always been that their brains must have suffered some damage as a result of their catalepsy, which affected their minds, and its is certainly true that most of those undergoing such transformations were damaged beyond repair, having been rendered stupid or mad...but again, *I cannot be sure*. I am not at all certain what a man who really had returned from the dead, or a spirit that had possessed the body of a dead man, would be able to do to persuade an unprejudiced observer that he really had been resurrected, or that he really was a different person from the one who had died.

"If you were to ask me whether I believe in vampires, Mr. Temple I would have to say that I really do not know whether I believe in them or not, simply because I hardly know what I might mean by the word when I pronounce it. Germain did believe in the evidence of his own eyes, wholeheartedly–and, having convinced himself that Countess Marcian Gregoryi really had returned from the dead, he immediately set out to discover a means of restoring *all* the dead to life. He was equally convinced that he had found the road to success, and I was present at some of his earliest demonstrations...but at the end of the day, all that I can truthfully say on my own behalf is that *I cannot be sure*."

"Thank you for your honesty, old friend," said Temple, sincerely. "I appreciate it. I, too, cannot be sure, but I have grown so familiar of late with the notion that the dead can return, with the proper assistance–and sometimes without any assistance whatsoever– that I am no longer certain even of my own uncertainty. Who, by the way, was the other old friend who asked you the question?"

"Colonel Bozzo-Corona–you might have heard of him. He's said to be very rich, and a great philanthropist, although he lives quite modestly in the Rue Thérèse."

It was Temple's turn to be astonished, and slightly alarmed, although he was unable to tell his host why that was the case, and was not entirely certain himself. "Colonel Bozzo-Corona is interested in this affair?" he repeated, playing for time.

"Not in this business with the vampire, or even the matter of Germain's supposed secret–but he did ask the question about the dead returning to life. He has known me for a long time, as I said. He was always interested in the morgue–fearful, I think, of his own mortality. You do know him, then?"

"Yes, I do," Temple replied. "He has visited London several times, and had more than one occasion to make himself helpful to the police. He was directly or indirectly responsible for more than one of Scotland Yard's early arrests."

"He does not travel as much nowadays," the old man told him.

Temple had to remind himself to get back to the immediate point of his visit. "I have not yet found out where Countess Marcian Gregoryi is staying in Paris, but I believe that I know where she will be tonight. I shall try to follow her myself, but I am not as young as I once was, and she will doubtless have at least one man with her on her carriage. Monsieur de Kervoz has followed her successfully before, I believe. If we were three instead of one, I think we would stand a greater chance of tracking her to her lair, despite the fact that two of us are no longer well-fitted for such work–and we shall certainly be able to learn more about her."

"Where will she be?" Séverin asked.

"I discovered, quite by chance, that she has made an appointment to see a lawyer named Robert Surrisy at his office, not far from the Tuileries. I do not know, as yet, what she wants him to do for her, and it might not be easy to find out once she has told him–he is another old acquaintance of mine, who has occasionally acted on my behalf in French legal matters, but he takes his duty of confidentiality very seriously, and would not have let it slip that she was about to become his client had he imagined that the fact could be of any professional interest to me."

"And how do you propose we get to the Tuileries?" René de Kervoz demanded. "Have you a carriage?"

"No," said Temple, evenly. "We shall have to take a fiacre. We will be followed, but that does not matter. If we split up thereafter, the follower will probably stick with me."

"While I…" Kervoz began–but again he was interrupted by the old man's peremptory gesture.

"We will both go with you," Séverin promised, standing up and reaching for a slender cane that was leaning on the arm of his chair. "If this woman really is Countess Marcian Gregoryi, René will run after her carriage when she leaves the lawyer's office, and he will report back to us here when he has found out where she goes thereafter. But I must ask you one question first, Mr. Temple, since you have not asked it of me: Do you know where Germain Patou is?"

"I have information on that score that I believe to be reliable," Temple replied, without hesitation, "and I have dispatched agents to find out whether it is accurate or not. I wish that I could reassure you that he is safe and well, but I cannot. He left London in very bad company: a small army of Grey Men, led by a veritable demon who calls himself Mortdieu. Did you witness his resurrection, by any chance?"

"No," said Séverin, who was already in the corridor, retrieving his coat from a stand. "That was not one of his early experiments. Germain left Paris in order to carry out a particular mission, but I do not know what it was–except that, now you mention..." he trailed off, as if struggling hard to recover a memory that had surfaced momentarily and then sunk back into oblivion.

"Except what?" Temple prompted.

"There was a lawyer involved in that negotiation too," Jean-Pierre Séverin said, as he set off down the stairs with an expected spring in his step, twirling his cane like a dandy in anticipation of some amorous adventure. "Now that I come to think about it, I believe that his name, too, was Surrisy..."

Chapter Two
Three Ladies of Quality

When the hired fiacre set the three men down at the southern end of the Avenue de l'Opéra, Gregory Temple's first action was to look back carefully along the thoroughfare, searching for evidence of their likely followers. Coco-Lacour, he presumed, would not have bothered to remain at the corner of the Rue de la Lanterne when he saw the three men come out together, figuring that there was nothing to be learned from watching Malo de Treguern turned away from an empty house. Temple could not see any evidence, however, that any other cab had followed theirs, and there was no sign of the burly man who was reputedly working for Lord Byron. Then, he checked his watch, to make sure that they were still in advance of the time that Countess Marcian Gregoryi had fixed for her appointment with Robert Surrisy.

While the three men walked to the side-street in which Surrisy's apartment and business office were located, Temple mulled over the possible consequences of what Jean-Pierre Séverin had told him immediately before they had set out. He had certainly mentioned Germain Patou's name to Robert more than once without obtaining any response whatsoever–which implied that Robert was deliberately hiding something from him, presumably something that the lawyer considered to be protected by his duty of confidentiality. Temple already knew that Patou had entered into some sort of compact with Henri de Belcamp, and if that compact had been negotiated by a lawyer, Henri might well have asked Robert to act for him–though probably not directly, given that Robert was supposed to believe, like everyone else in Paris, that Henri really had shot himself. It would undoubtedly have amused Henri to do that, given the past that he and Robert shared. Robert had been in love with Jeanne Herbet before Henri came home to Miremont, and had even tried to win her back after Henri's disappearance–but she had been determined to remain true to the memory of the father of her son.

The three watchers had no difficulty, in a street almost as badly lit as the Rue de la Lanterne, in finding a covert where they could watch Robert Surrisy's door without the slightest danger of being seen. They had not been waiting a quarter of an hour when a sumptuous carriage pulled up outside the door in question.

"She always did believe in traveling in style," muttered René de Kervoz.

"She's ten minutes early," was Temple's only comment–but then he drew in his breath sharply.

"What's the matter?" Séverin asked.

"That's not the same…" Kervoz began, the disappointment in his voice very obvious as he stared at the woman who had just got down from the carriage while her footman went to knock on the door.

"Shh!" said Temple. In order to forestall questions, he added, in a whisper: "That's Countess Boehm–the former Sarah O'Brien. She's Robert Surrisy's half-sister. She bought the so-called new château in Miremont not so long ago, intending to make a home there, but there was an unfortunate incident some little while ago that gave her pause for thought. I was under the impression that she was intent on returning to her husband's estates in Germany." He did not bother to explain that his source for these items of information was his own daughter, now resident at the Château de Belcamp.

"There's another carriage coming," Kervoz observed, almost as soon as Countess Boehm had disappeared into the house. "This one has a French coat-of-arms."

Temple could not quite suppress a curse, which escaped as a half-strangled gasp.

"It's another Comtesse, though," the Breton went on, his own voice gaining inconvenient volume as his excitement revived.

"It's the Comtesse de Belcamp," Temple was quick to supply, hardly able to believe his eyes. "Of all the nights to come calling…"

This time, a full quarter of an hour ticked by.

Neither of the two women who had gone into Robert Surrisy's house had come out again, despite the fact that he must have told them that he was expecting a client imminently. For a moment, Temple wondered whether Countess Marcian Gregoryi might have cancelled her appointment–but then a third carriage turned the corner, coming from the direction of the *quai*. Far from being early, the vampire's minion was actually five minutes late. Her coachman had to draw to a halt a good 30 meters from Robert Surrisy's door, but the Countess did not seem to mind. She walked along the pavement behind her footman, resplendent in her flowing blonde locks, unrestrained by any hat.

"Mon Dieu!" said René de Kervoz. "She *is* the same! She had dark hair when she seduced me, and claimed the blonde was her twin, but there's no doubt–she's the same, and not a day older!"

"That is the woman I saw in 1804," Jean-Pierre Sévérin confirmed, in a whisper, his tone perfectly sober and rather pensive, "and she has not aged a day in 18 years. What does it mean, Mr. Temple?"

Temple made no answer, having none to give; he was holding his breath.

When the footman knocked, the door was immediately opened, and the third countess vanished into the interior.

Gregory Temple let out his breath. "She must have summoned them to meet her here!" he said, wonderingly. "Perhaps she *is* after money! But how does she propose to persuade Jeanne and Sarah to hand it over, if that's her objective? The old château is almost as well-protected now as it was in the days when every fine house had to be a fortress, and Jeanne is not in a trustful frame of mind nowadays." Even as he spoke, however, he had a sinking feeling in the pit of his stomach. If Countess Marcian Gregoryi were to persuade Jeanne that she had reliable news of Henri, Jeanne might well be willing to pay for the information–and if the Countess really did have such information..."

"Perhaps it's as well, after all, that there are three of us," Sévérin suggested, cutting off Temple's train of thought.

"I already know where the other two live, and I have eyes and ears in that camp" Temple told him. "I wish I were a fly on the wall of Robert's office, though. Jeanne and Sarah have not the slightest idea who this woman is, because I never thought for a minute that I ought to warn them. I can only hope that Robert has had time–and has taken the trouble–to warn them that she is a person of interest to me. That will put them on their guard, if they are not sufficiently suspicious already."

The waiting soon became painful for the detective, who was now in a state of high tension. "You must not lose her, Monsieur de Kervoz," he said to his new acquaintance. "We must know where she is staying, if we are to frustrate her master's plan. We must know everything we can discover, as soon as possible–I might have to go to Vidocq after all."

"You can depend on me," the Breton assured him, grimly.

"Do you know that man, Mr. Temple?" Sévérin suddenly asked, using the tip of his slender cane to indicate a passer-by who was walking purposefully along the pavement, as if he were late for an appointment, but who darted sideways glances at all three of the parked carriages as he passed them by.

Temple cursed again. "I met him for the first time tonight," he said. "His name is Coco-Lacour, and he's one of Vidocq's gang–wolves in sheep's clothing, like your old friend Ezekiel. He's good, though–I never caught a glimpse of him following us. I wonder whether my other stalker is also here?"

Having passed the third carriage, Coco-Lacour paused and looked around attentively. Temple groaned. He and his two companions were quite invisible, but a man like Coco-Lacour, once convinced that they were nearby, would have no difficulty at all in identifying their hiding-place. Astonishingly, having picked the spot out, the police agent proceeded to saunter insouciantly across the street to join the three watchers.

"Bonsoir, Monsieur Temple," he said. "Monsieur Sévérin, Monsieur de Kervoz, you may be interested to know that Malo de Treguern did eventually arrive at your house, but that he went away disappointed. He'll be back, mind– he's a man who knows how to stick to a task, when matters of duty are at stake. It's said that he's far cleverer at appealing to the conscience of the devout in the course of his interrogations than Monsieur Vidocq has ever contrived to be."

"How do you know that Treguern arrived, if you followed us?" Temple demanded, suspiciously.

"I didn't follow you," Coco-Lacour said, with a broad smile. "I already had one of my colleagues close by, in a fiacre–just in case. He drove you here, then reported back to me. You *were* followed, of course–but you already know all about His Lordship's man. Would you care to tell me why the Comtesses Jeanne de Belcamp and Sarah von Boehm are visiting Monsieur Surrisy, and who the third party is who seems to have an assignation with them?"

"No," Temple said, through gritted teeth, "I wouldn't."

"So much for professional courtesy," observed Coco-Lacour. "Do you mind if I wait with you? Professional curiosity will now oblige me to follow the third carriage."

"I'd rather you didn't," was all that Temple could think of to say.

"But this is Paris," Coco-Lacour pointed out, "where I have full authority to act and you merely have permission from the Prefect to go about your business unhindered. It really would be better if you were to accept our co-operation."

"This does not concern you," Temple told him, frostily. "It's not a criminal matter."

"Now there, I must correct you," the agent said. "This is most definitely a criminal matter." He leaned forward, as if to impart of confidence, and said, in a carefully-contrived whisper: "It concerns the *Gentlemen of the Night*," He pronounced the final phrase in English, his atrocious accent only serving to emphasize the mockery in his tone.

The remark took Temple by surprise, but he controlled his irritation. "Is *that* who you're hunting?" he asked, contemptuously. "I wish you the best of luck, then–I've chased them myself, and only caught smoke."

"Who are the *Gentlemen of the Night*?" Jean-Pierre Sévérin inquired.

"The name originated as a myth," Temple told him, "invented by the crooked magistrate Jonathan Wild–but it's a myth that continually intrudes upon reality, as one gang of more-or-less organized criminals after another lays claim to the name and its associated reputation, in order to intimidate their recruits and victims alike. Tom Brown, *alias* John Devil, was the head of one such gang.

That's dispersed now, but I dare say that someone else is taking over the legend even as we speak–perhaps more than one someone. I thought the equivalent title in Paris was the *Habits Noirs*–although we've had Blackcoats in London too, so I suppose Paris is entitled to its own *Gentilhommes de la Nuit*."

"*Will it be light tomorrow?*" Coco-Lacour quipped, cheerily. "Yes, I believe that it will, fog or no fog. But there were *Ladies of the Night* too, were there not? Tom's mother, Helen, was the real gang-leader, and the operation fell apart when you shipped her off to Australia."

There was nothing surprising in the fact that Vidocq's right-hand man had these items of information on the tip of his tongue, but the fact that he had bothered to repeat them here and now caused Temple some anxiety. Was Vidocq's motley crew of notionally-reformed villains now in the pay of Henri de Belcamp, alias Tom Brown, alias John Devil? Was that why they were keeping an eye on Malo de Treguern? Were they, perhaps, working–knowingly or unknowingly–for *Civitas Solis*?

"If you are intending to slander the Comtesse de Belcamp or Countess Boehm," Temple said, darkly, "you had best be careful."

"I wouldn't dream of it," Coco-Lacour replied. "They are most certainly not Ladies of the Night–but I do not know who the proprietor of that third carriage is, and I do know something of Monsieur Surrisy's reputation. He's a Bonapartist too, Monsieur Séverin, of a more dangerous type than yourself."

"Bonaparte's dead and buried," Temple said, shortly.

"Dead, yes," Coco-Lacour agreed. "Buried–I'm not so sure. There are rumors."

"There are always rumors," Temple retorted. "Go away, please, and leave us in peace."

"To lurk in the shadows watching over the houses of honest Frenchmen?" Coco-Lacour queried. "I'm a member of the Sûreté, Monsieur Temple–I'm duty bound to prevent such things from happening. I could have you all arrested and thrown into the Conciergerie. Can you give me one good reason why I should not?"

"Because the Prefect would love to have an excuse to throw you out on your ear," Temple retorted, although he was by no means sure of that, "and nine Parisian policemen out of ten would cheer your departure. Now…"

He had no chance to go on. The door of the house he was supposed to be watching had just opened, and three women emerged: three extraordinarily beautiful young women, each one guaranteed to turn heads and attract admiring glances. Of the three, though, Countess Marcian Gregoryi–the only one, presumably, never to have borne a child–probably had the edge. Had Paris of Troy been judging this contest, and judging it fairly, the golden apple would doubtless have gone to her.

The three women seemed to be on very friendly terms. They exchanged kisses on the cheeks as they separated and went to their respective carriages. As each of the three prepared to mount the steps unfolded by their faithful footmen, Countess Marcian Gregoryi called out to the other two: "Remember, I can be contacted at the Hôtel Trianon in the Rue Caumartin."

"That's lucky!" Coco-Lacour observed, in a whisper.

Gregory Temple, who thought the remark far too apposite to have been made by chance, knew that René de Kervoz could not see his face well enough to read his expression, so he had to take it on trust that the younger man would follow the prearranged plan.

When the carriages drew off, René immediately set off to follow the vampire's minion—and so did Coco-Lacour, who was evidently not a trusting man. Gregory Temple stayed where he was, and Jean-Pierre Sévérin stayed with him.

"I'm sorry about that," Temple said to his companion, once the three carriages had all disappeared and Vidocq's agent was safely out of earshot. "It's an inconvenience, but not a fatal one. The agent won't do René any harm. This is unfamiliar territory for him—he's more used to picking up petty thieves—and he's improvising as he goes along. I dare say that Vidocq's put him on to this out of simple curiosity—all that stuff about Gentlemen of the Night was probably just bluster."

"You don't need to convince me of anything," Sévérin reminded him. "What do we do now?"

"Now," Temple said, "we go to see Monsieur Surrisy—and hope that he's prepared to give us the information we need. Now that Jeanne and his sister are involved, I should be able to persuade him that there are more important loyalties at stake than his duty of confidentiality."

The two men crossed the road and Temple knocked on the lawyer's door. The concierge who admitted them seemed heartily sick and tired of the continual stream of visitors, but let them in without too much ill grace, and led them to Surrisy's study. Surrisy did not seem pleased to see them, but he greeted Temple courteously enough.

"Robert," said Gregory Temple, as the lawyer came to shake his hand, "may I introduce Jean-Pierre Sévérin. He's had dealings with Countess Marcian Gregoryi before. If I can't convince you that there's anything uncanny about her, he might be able to do so."

"I've heard your name, Monsieur Sévérin," Robert Surrisy said, bowing and waving his guests to leather-clad armchairs who seats were still slightly warm. "It has a fine reputation in the circles in which I once moved—but I must confess to both of you that the Countess seems to me to be perfectly delightful. Jeanne and Sarah evidently like her too—although I confess, too, that I was surprised to see them here. I had no idea that they had been invited to the consultation."

Temple gritted his teeth slightly. Robert Surrisy's attitude made it all too obvious that he had been charmed by his beautiful client, even in the presence of

246

two women he had loved very dearly indeed. It was not going to be easy, now, to persuade the lawyer to co-operate.

"And what was the consultation about?" Temple asked.

"I can't tell you that," Surrisy parried. "I have a duty of confidentiality to my client."

"And I have an offer of collaboration and support from Monsieur Vidocq," Temple told him. "Their interest ought to inform you that something is amiss here. Is Countess Marcian Gregoryi's business such a closely-guarded secret? Did she forbid you to mention it to anyone? You know full well that I can simply ask Jeanne–why not save me a little time?"

Surrisy sighed, but he obviously had no powerful reason to be stubborn. "Countess Marcian Gregoryi merely wants to buy the new château at Miremont," he said. "Even though Sarah has only recently acquired it, she wants to sell up and return to Germany, because of the kidnapping. She has promised that she would not sell it to anyone who might compromise Jeanne's security at the old château, so she invited her to be party to the negotiation as a matter of courtesy. I don't think Jeanne will raise any objection to the new owner now that she's met her, though. Everyone seems perfectly satisfied, and there's nothing in this that could possibly concern you, Mr. Temple, as a detective."

"You may be perfectly certain that Jeanne will raise an objection," Temple said, flatly, "once I have talked to her."

"Once you have told her that the Countess is a vampire's minion?" Surrisy's tone had suddenly become firmer, if not exactly hostile. "She might not believe that, Mr. Temple, even from you. You were the one, after all, who once told the old Marquis that Henri was not guilty of General O'Brien's murder. I have not yet forgiven you that lie–and probably never will, given what it did to my mother."

"I apologize for that," Temple said. "My intention was to alleviate a friend's misery, not exacerbate misery in anyone else. You must believe me, though, when I tell you that Countess Marcian Gregoryi is a highly deceptive and thoroughly dishonest person. Monsieur Séverin can confirm that she is the same individual who visited Paris in 1804, during the vampire panic, and was implicated in several murders–and that she does not seem to have aged a day in the interim."

Surrisy did not even glance at Séverin in search of that confirmation. "She explained about her mother," he said, shortly.

"Her *mother?*" The incredulous interpolation came from Séverin.

"Yes–surely you cannot really believe that the Countess Marcian Gregoryi with whom you had dealings some 18 years ago was the same one as this, who is only a few years older than that? It was to secure the present Countess's future that the original Countess committed her crimes–which, her daughter assures me, were greatly exaggerated at the time. She was not a multiple murderer, as rumor now claims, or even a serial bigamist."

"Marcian Gregoryi is the name of the supposed Hungarian Count to whom the mysterious lady claimed to have been married," Jean-Pierre Sévérin pointed out. "Her daughter would not–could not–have the same name."

"She could," Surrisy countered, "if she were the one and only true Countess Marcian Gregoryi, fully entitled to a name that her mother was not really entitled to wear. She is, in fact, legitimately married to the son of the man whose mistress the first so-called Countess was."

"She is the same woman," Jean-Pierre Sévérin stated, flatly. "I would know her anywhere."

"There is no need to press the point further, Monsieur Sévérin," Temple said, calmly. "There will be no sale–I can guarantee that. Now, Robert–what else did you find out? Did she tell you that she is staying in the Hôtel de Trianon, on the Rue Caumartin?"

"If you already know that," Surrisy countered, "why ask?"

"Because I do not think it is true, and I do not understand why she should take so much trouble to advertise the address," Temple retorted. "Monsieur Sévérin's friend is following her carriage, and so is one of Vidocq's agents. Hopefully, they will discover where she is really staying. Did you, perchance contrive to notice anything that was not a mere show put on for your benefit?"

Temple realized immediately that he had made a mistake in phrasing the question in that mildly insulting manner; his fraught nerves had got the better of him. Robert Surrisy took offense, and became even less ready to help than he had been before. "No," the lawyer said, coldly, "I did not. I repeat that the Countess seemed to me to be entirely honest and perfectly charming–and I really ought not to have told you anything that passed between us."

"In fact," Temple said, "you ought to be extremely enthusiastic to give me all the help you can. You should also have told me what dealings you had with Germain Patou before he left Paris some three or four years ago. You mentioned at Miremont that you knew him, but you did not say that you had acted on his behalf."

For a moment, Surrisy seemed genuinely puzzled. Then his face cleared. "But I didn't act on his behalf," he said. "I drew up a contract of partnership for someone else, to which he was a signatory. I only met him once, and everything I know about him is based on hearsay rather than acquaintance. I had no idea at the time that the contract in question had to do with this business of attempting to bring the dead back to life, to which you introduced me a few months ago–and I certainly did not connect it in my mind to this new nonsense about vampires!"

"Was the other signatory to the contract Henri de Belcamp?" Temple asked.

"Good Lord, no!" Surrisy replied, his shock seeming quite genuine. "I was still under the impression at that time that Henri was dead. No, I can be absolutely certain that he had nothing to do with it. I was acting for quite a famous man, as it happens–but I really should not tell you who he was, for that would certainly be a breach of trust that could land me in hot water."

Temple knew that he would only have one chance to surprise a reaction from the lawyer; if he guessed wrong the first time, it would put Surrisy on his guard. He only hesitated a moment, though, before saying: "Lord Byron."

Robert Surrisy was too honest for his own good; he could not maintain a blank face. "If you already know the answers to all the questions you're firing at me," he said, resentfully, "why are you even here? And why are you dangling other names before me, when you know they have nothing to do with it?"

"I'm trying to complete an enormously complex jigsaw, Robert," Temple told him. "It's very difficult to see where each piece fits, until it is actually in place. Henri de Belcamp has everything to do with this, no matter how determined he is to keep a low profile–but Lord Byron has already been mentioned to me tonight, by someone else fishing for pieces of the jigsaw. I already knew that Byron and Shelley were associated with Victor Frankenstein, and that Patou must also have had some communication, however indirect, with Frankenstein, although I had not imagined previously that there was a formal contract involved. What you need to know now, Robert, is that Germain Patou also encountered Countess Marcian Gregoryi in her first incarnation; that was what first set him off on the hunt for the secret of resurrection. Whether he found Frankenstein's associates or they found him, his inquiries evidently led to an alliance of some sort. Lord Byron is in Paris now, and it seems that he is interested in the Countess too; he has apparently set someone to follow me, so he is also aware of my interest. If he comes to call on you again, you might end up more deeply embroiled in this business than you want to be. I suppose Lord Byron must be just as enthusiastic to meet the vampire as I am..."

"Perhaps more so, if the rumors that have been circulating of late are true," Surrisy observed, cutting in on Temple's train of thought. "He's reputed to be something of a vampire himself–not that I'm sure, any more, as to what the word is supposed to mean. Are we really talking about reanimated corpses with a thirst for human blood?"

"Reanimated corpses, certainly," Temple said, soberly. "Bloodthirsty, perhaps not literally. Lord Byron is alive, though, and he's no bloodsucker, literal or metaphorical, no matter what Lady Caroline Lamb and John Polidori might allege. If he's trying to track down the vampire, it's not to meet his kin but to find out what the creature knows–and that's a dangerous game, even if he does have Frankenstein's daemon to assist him."

Temple shut up of his own accord then, realizing that he had let his mouth run away with him while thinking aloud. Surrisy did not seem to have taken what he said at all seriously, though; he was still under Countess Marcian Gregoryi's spell.

"I know that you got Sarah's son back from the kidnappers," the lawyer said, "and Jeanne's too, at some risk to your own life. I'm grateful to you on both counts. I feel obliged to warn you, though, that the reputation for madness you gained while pursuing Henri so obsessively still holds firm in Paris, and you will not find many men here willing to entertain this new insanity." As he finished speaking, Surrisy's gaze went to Jean-Pierre Sévérin's face, questioningly. Sévérin did not rise to the bait, though.

"Henri de Belcamp did his level best to drive me mad," Temple stated, flatly, "but he did not succeed. That did not prevent him asking for my help when he needed it, or trusting me when I gave it. Please be careful, Robert–you cannot get mixed up in this affair without exposing yourself to danger. If Countess Marcian Gregoryi asks anything else of you–and she will, if I cannot stop her–you really ought to refuse, until I have found out what is really going on. Until then you ought, at the very least, to tread exceedingly carefully."

"Thank you for your advice, Mr. Temple–and yours, Monsieur Sévérin," Surrisy said, obviously eager to put an end to a conversation that had become distasteful to him. "Now, gentlemen, it is rather later, and if you will forgive me…"

Chapter Three
A Brief Skirmish

"What now?" asked Jean-Pierre Sévérin, as he and Temple paused at the end of the street, where they had the choice of turning towards the Pont Royal or heading back towards the Avenue de l'Opéra. "Shall we return to the Rue de la Lanterne to wait for René?"

"Not yet," said Temple, searching the street for a fiacre, in vain. "It will only take a few minutes to get to the Rue Caumartin. It's probably worth going down to the *quai* to pick up a cab."

"But you don't believe that the Countess is staying there."

"No, I don't–but she did go to some trouble to give the address to anyone watching Surrisy's office. I doubt that she knew that you or I would be there, but she might well have expected Vidocq's man, and perhaps someone else."

"Lord Byron's agent–the one you referred to just now as Frankenstein's *daemon*?"

"Perhaps–but a different agent. If it really was Byron who put the Grey Man on my tail–and I'm not prepared simply to take Coco-Lacour's word for that–he's likely to have delegated someone else to follow the Countess: Robert Walton, perhaps. The vampire's primary objective, I now suspect, is to make contact with Henri de Belcamp, which might or might not mean making contact with *Civitas Solis*. Countess Marcian Gregoryi has probably made the acquaintance of Sarah and Jeanne with that in view–but he'll certainly be interested in Victor Frankenstein too, so Byron's interest will likely be welcome, however cautious Milord is inclined to be. I didn't see anyone else set off after the carriage, so the other watcher, if there was one, probably waited until we went inside to slip away."

By this time, they had reached the corner of the *quai*; there was a fiacre waiting–but it was empty, and Temple had to look around for he missing driver. He spotted the man outside the door of a quayside drinking-den, standing at a small table at which a card-sharp was offering passers by the chance to *cherchez la femme*. The cab driver had just placed a bet and lost it.

Temple strode over to the table, enthusiastic to vent a little of his accumulated bad temper.

"Does Monsieur Vidocq know that you are plying your vile trade within shouting distance of the Tuileries?" Temple inquired of the sharper. He had seen the trick worked in a dozen locations, from Drury Lane to Ascot racecourse, and had long since taken a hearty dislike to its practitioners.

"I should think so," the sharper replied, morosely. "He sends that popinjay Coco-Lacour round once a week to collect his rake-off."

"And does he know that you mention that fact to every English detective you meet?" Temple demanded, stretching the truth a little for the sake of effect. "Now, return this fellow's money immediately–I need him to drive me to the Rue Caumartin."

"No, sir," said the cabman, mournfully. "He won the money fair and square. I was certain that I could find the lady this time, but I couldn't."

"Do you mean that you've fallen for the trick before?" Temple asked, incredulously.

"A dozen times and more," supplied the sharper. "He's one of my regulars. I'm an honest man, sir–I tell them over and over again that the hand is quicker than the eye, but they never will believe me. They insist on believing that if they only look hard enough, they can follow the lady. They just won't accept that it's impossible."

Temple released a strangled impression of disgust, and dragged the cabman back to his vehicle. There did not seem to be any need to waste a moment's anxiety on the question of whether this man too might be one of Vidocq's agents in disguise–although, he reflected, as the cab set off, it might have been as well if he *had* managed to find another policeman in disguise, just in case some kind of trap had been set in the Rue Caumartin to catch anyone showing too much curiosity about Countess Marcian Gregoryi's whereabouts.

The Rue Caumartin was a reasonably respectable street, and the Hôtel Trianon a moderately respectable hotel, much patronized by English visitors. When Temple asked the night-clerk whether Countess Marcian Gregoryi was in residence, the man simply replied, in English: "The Countess is not here at present, sir. If you would care to leave a message, I'll make sure that she gets it when she returns."

Temple hesitated for a moment, then said: "Thank you, no," in his own language. "I really need to see her in person. Tell me, is Lord Byron in his room, by any chance?" The second question was a stab in the dark, but he felt so completely at sea that any amount of guesswork seemed justified.

"I believe that he is, sir," the clerk replied, somewhat to Temple's surprise. "If you would care to give me your card, sir, I'll have it sent up to him."

Temple handed over the card, and then took a seat in the lobby.

"That was a good guess," Jean-Pierre Sévérin observed, sitting down beside him, although he did not seem capable of relaxing. "But what does it signify that Byron and the Countess have both retained rooms here? Have they already made some sort of alliance, do you think?"

"If they have," Temple replied, "then we're further behind the game than I thought–and the Countess's suggestion could not have been addressed to Lord Byron's man. I might have been wrong to think that her remark could not be aimed at me."

"Is his Lordship in danger?" Sévérin asked.

"I really don't know," Temple had to confess.

A few minutes passed before the clerk reappeared. "His Lordship will see you, Mr. Temple. He's waiting for you in the garden behind the hotel."

"The garden?" Temple queried. "At this time of night?"

"It's a private garden," the clerk told him, as if that somehow explained everything.

Temple shrugged, and allowed the clerk to lead him through the corridors of the ground floor to a rear door that let out into a small, high-walled garden. There was someone sitting on a bench at the far side of the lawn; he was directly beneath a lantern, but the fog made it impossible to make out his face or his costume. The clerk closed the door behind Temple and Sévérin as they set out across the lawn.

Temple had only taken half a dozen paces before becoming certain that the man waiting for them was not, in fact, Lord Byron. As soon as he stopped, though, two other men appeared out of the bushes behind the bench, both armed with thick cudgels. As the man on the bench stood up, he lifted up a sword that had been laid horizontally on the bench beside him.

"Monsieur Temple," said the unknown man, in English that was severely tortured by a thick Parisian accent. "We've been expecting you. Who's your friend?"

Jean-Pierre Sévérin had not stopped when Temple did, and was now two paces ahead of him. He was already lifting his cane; it was a perfectly ordinary cane, not a sword-stick, but he was holding it now as if it were an *épée*. "Jean-Pierre Sévérin, at your service, sir," he said, in perfectly-enunciated English. The excitement in his voice was palpable, and Temple realized that the old man must have been starved of this sort of stimulation for far too long.

To his amazement, Temple saw that all three of the waiting men reacted nervously to the name, with which they were obviously familiar. The ringleader switched back to his own language to say: "It's all right, you fools–he must be 70, at least, probably nearer 80. Feet of lead and a wrist like a dry stick." So saying, and without standing on the least ceremony, he lunged forward with his blade, obviously expecting to take Séverin by surprise.

The tactic did not work. Séverin deflected the blow with ease–and then he moved forwards.

Temple presumed that the old man must, in fact, be somewhat slower in his paces than he would have been in his heyday, and his thrusts considerably less elegant than they had been at their finest. Even so, the tip of the cane became a mere blur, which would surely have been impossible to follow even in broad daylight. Temple, who had the advantage of watching from a distance, had to presume that its effects must have seemed like pure magic to the clumsy street-brawlers who were facing the flickering stick head on.

It took Jean-Pierre Séverin less than three full seconds to disarm his three opponents and leave them sprawling on the ground. One of the cudgel-wielders was clutching at his throat in agony and another was shielding his right eye, which must have been badly bruised if not actually punctured. The swordsman was holding himself rigid, hardly daring to lift himself on his elbow, with the point of his own sword poised an inch from his breast, directed at his heart.

"My God!" Temple said. "I heard that you were once the best swordsman in France, but I had no idea…"

"I was never quite the best," Séverin corrected him, although the denial somehow seemed prouder than any boastful admission could have been, "and am now so poor that I could not stop these poor fellows without doing two of them severe damage. I thought for a moment that I would actually have to run this one through–which would have been a great pity, as you presumably need him in a fit condition to talk. Shall I cut off an ear by way of encouragement, do you think? It will be an untidy job, I fear, for this blade is in a terrible condition. People do not take as much pride in their instruments as they used to."

"No!" the bravo protested. "No one told me that Temple had a protector, let alone one such as you! I was simply hired to do a job–I feel no loyalty to an employer who gave me a mere pittance to do the impossible!"

"What employer?" Temple demanded, harshly.

"Countess Marcian Gregoryi–or her lackey, at any rate. Calls himself Guido, but I doubt that he's Italian. Dirty Magyar, if you ask me."

"And where can I find this Guido?"

"Damned if I know–he came to me. All I know is that that he isn't here himself, curse him. Called away on urgent business, he said–and that certainly seemed to be the way of it. You're not the only one who has to be requested to stay clear, it seems. We never intended to kill you, I swear–our orders were to pink you in the leg, to make sure that you couldn't walk straight for a week or so. That's true, on my mother's life!"

"I believe you," Temple told him, "although I can't say I'm sorry that your friends got worse than they were supposed to give. You know, I suppose, that Monsieur Vidocq's men are also in search of the Countess and her lackey?"

The man on the ground groaned; evidently, he had not been warned about that, either. "Don't turn me over, sir," he begged. "Guido told us that you were an Englishman, with far more enemies in Paris than friends. How was I supposed to know that you had such allies?"

"What's your name?" Temple demanded.

"Eugène Fantin. Vidocq knows me well enough–he'll testify that I'm an honest villain, if you care to ask. I've had dealings with the *fera-t-il jour demain?* brigade–who hasn't?–but I'm just a common arm for hire, nothing more."

"What's all this nonsense about daylight?" Séverin asked, evidently remembering Coco-Lacour's flippant remark.

"I'll explain at another time," Temple told him. "The rumor of this affair has obviously run through the whole of Paris. No one knows the truth of it, but everyone knows that Germain Patou's hypothetical records have now become a precious object of desire. I dare say that there'd be half a dozen forgeries on the market already, if anyone had the slightest idea what to put in them. In the meantime, the vampire is in a hurry to make deals with anyone who has hard information on techniques of resurrection, and seems to be enthusiastic to hobble the competition by any hasty means that comes to hand. If his minions are stooping to this kind of farce, he must be genuinely anxious. Let him up, Monsieur Séverin–I think he's lost his appetite for his appointed role."

Séverin not only allowed Fantin to get to his feet but returned his sword to him. The bravo carefully put it down on the bench, to make it clear that he had no intention of attempting to make further use of it.

"Do you have any idea where Guido went?" Temple demanded, harshly.

"No," Fantin replied. "I only know that it must have been important, else he'd have been here with us, lying in wait for you."

"Damn!" said Temple. "This is worse than I imagined. Come on, Monsieur Séverin–we've been doubly tricked. Perhaps I should have made a deal with Coco-Lacour after all. Better the Devil you know..." While he was speaking, Temple had already set off back to the door through which they had come. It was not locked, and they made their way through the hotel without difficulty. The night-clerk was no longer at his post. The fiacre was still waiting on the Rue Caumartin, although Temple had not retained it.

"Are you one of Vidocq's men, perchance?" Temple demanded of the luckless gambler, although he had little hope of receiving an affirmative answer.

The coachman's surprise seemed perfectly genuine. "Me, sir?" he said "No, sir–I'm an honest man, sir."

"More's the pity," Temple murmured, as he hauled himself into the carriage. "Rue de la Lanterne–and hurry, if your nags are capable of anything more than the gentlest trot."

The driver swore that his horses were a fine pair, thus demonstrating the limits of his supposed honesty, but they did prove capable of a slightly faster pace than many of their sort.

"What is it?" Jean-Pierre Sévérin asked, a hint of anxiety creeping into his tone.

"Evidently, it *was* me they were expecting," Temple told him. "When the Countess took care to give the address in such a clear voice, she knew that I would be watching. She must, in consequence, know that Byron's having me followed, and that I came to see you tonight. I fear that she might have taken advantage of the fact that I took you and Monsieur de Kervoz away from home to send Guido in search of German Patou's records–or some leverage that might enable her to demand them as a ransom."

"But I don't have any such records!" Sévérin protested.

"The vampire doesn't know that–and he'll probably stop at nothing to make sure."

The lamp inside the fiacre cast enough light to allow Temple to see that his companion's face had gone pale. "You think they'll take Angela!" he exclaimed. "And demand a price for her return that I can't meet!"

"I fear so," Temple said. "Let's hope that I'm wrong."

They said nothing more while the cab completed the journey, but Temple could see that Jean-Pierre Sévérin's hand was tightly wound around his seemingly-inoffensive cane, his fingernails digging into the palm of his hand. He had been excited before, glad of the opportunity to bring back the old days of adventure one last time, but now he was afraid–afraid that history might repeat itself, and that he might lose a second Angela to the dreaded Vampire of Paris.

When they reached the Rue de la Lanterne, however, everything seemed perfectly calm. When Jean-Pierre Sévérin knocked at the door, it was immediately opened, without the necessity of withdrawing the bar or the bolt, by his blonde grand-daughter, who flung herself upon his neck. She, apparently, had been afraid for *his* safety. Temple understood why when he perceived that she was not alone.

He moved past the hugging relatives to confront the man who was lurking in the corridor. "I believe that you answer to the name of Lazarus," Temple said to the creature to whom Frankenstein's sensationalized memoirs referred as a *daemon*. "You have met my employee, Ned Knob."

The Grey Man drew himself up to his full height, which was impressive, in order to be able to look down on Gregory Temple. He also pushed back the hood he was wearing to conceal his face; evidently, he had been reluctant to frighten Angela de Kervoz, but had fewer reservations about alarming the man he had been following for most of the day. "I will answer to that name if you wish, sir," was all that he said.

"Where's Guido?" Temple demanded, not standing on ceremony. "You haven't killed him, I hope?"

"I have not," the giant replied. "I could not prevent his companions from running off–I have only one pair of hands, after all–but I made certain of securing the vampire's chief minion. He is probably the only one who knows where the vampire is. Even Countess Marcian Gregoryi may not be party to that secret, at present."

"She's made contact with Lord Byron, I presume."

"She has attempted to employ her wiles against his Lordship," the Grey Man said. "Thus far, he has been very wary. He is certainly intrigued, and vulnerable to temptation–but he does not know what he is dealing with, and he has heard too many terrible tales of vampiric predation to rush in where angels would undoubtedly fear to tread. He is cautious, and feels rather isolated in a city in which he does not know who he can trust."

"His caution must have annoyed her ladyship," Temple observed. "Why, might I ask, is Lord Byron having *me* followed?"

"The principal reason is that he thought your detective skills might locate the vampire before he did," replied the creature who answered to the name of Lazarus.

"And the secondary reason?"

"As I said, his Lordship feels rather isolated, and does not know who he can trust. He has reason enough to be wary of Lord Liverpool's government, and its hirelings. He suspected that you might have been sent to Paris to investigate him."

Temple shrugged his shoulders. "I cannot hold his suspicion against him," he admitted, "but my one and only concern, at this moment, is the vampire. Assure Lord Byron, when you see him, that I am not his enemy."

"And what would you do, Mr. Temple, if you found the vampire?" Lazarus asked, mildly.

Temple scowled at that, because he had no good answer ready. The real question, he knew, was what *could* he do?

Jean-Pierre Séverin released himself from his granddaughter's embrace in order to step into the breach. "If Mr. Temple were able to confirm that this vampire or his minion is guilty of any of the crimes laid against them in 1804," he said, sternly, "then he would be fully justified in taking justice into his own hands–and I, Jean-Pierre Séverin, shall be more than ready to stand by his side."

"Ah!" said the Grey Man. "In that case, Mr. Temple, I'm afraid that you and I might be somewhat at odds in this matter–and I regret that I waited for you."

"You're in search of enlightenment regarding your own genesis and nature," Temple deduced, easily enough. "You believe that the vampire might be able to instruct you as to what you are–and what you might become."

"There are textbooks of anatomy that provide some slight clarification of the conventional human reproductive process," the giant observed, with a hint of sarcasm, "but the only books that speak of the risen dead–even those produced by supposed scholars–are far more superstitious in their character. They cannot assist me any more than they console me. Count Szandor is reputedly the most ancient and wisest of nature's grey men–and you should not chide me for hunting for him, any more than you should chide me for seeking enlightenment from Lord Byron and my creator. Remember that I was the one who gave the information to Ned Knob that must have brought you here."

"As it happens," Temple retorted, "Master Knob was a trifle economical with the information he gave me regarding his discoveries in Spezia. I had to find out by another route, and still have not found out what everyone else already seems to know–but I will not be shut out of this affair, by anyone."

Séverin, meanwhile, had been staring at the giant, albeit more in curiosity than amazement–as had Angela, who had obviously not seen him clearly before. Lazarus made as if to raise his hood again and step back into the shadows.

"There is no need to be afraid, Mademoiselle," Temple told the young woman. "This is not the first Grey Man I have seen, and I can assure you that he is a phenomenon of nature, not some supernatural monster. The dead *can* return, Monsieur Séverin, and here is the living proof. Thanks to Victor Frankenstein and Germain Patou, the world is on the brink of a new era–one of unprecedented triumph, if the new knowledge is used responsibly, or horrific chaos, if it is not. Malo de Treguern would have told you that the old era must be protected at all costs–and probably still will–but he is the least of our adversaries at present. The vampire is evidently the worst–and our friend here has contrived to turn the tables on that one, by capturing one of his principal agents." He used the word "friend" hopefully, having taken due note of what Lazarus had said about their being at odds.

"I am honored to make your acquaintance, sir," the giant said to Séverin, respectfully.

"I'm delighted to welcome you as my guest," the old man replied, "in view of the service that you have rendered my granddaughter. I lost her mother to the vampire once... I could never have forgiven myself had it happened again."

"I'm glad that I decided to remain here rather than following Mr. Temple," the Grey Man said. "When I saw that the police agent was not following you, I knew that something else must be about to happen here, and when I saw Malo de Treguern, I feared that others might be hot on his heels–as, indeed, they were."

"We need to interrogate this Guido," Temple said. "Where is he?"

257

"In the cellar," the Grey Man replied. "I have every faith in my knots, but I thought it best to put him in a room with only one issue. I should have taken him away, but..." Without finishing his sentence, the giant led the others to the door leading down to the cellar, unhooking a lantern from the wall as he went.

Jean-Pierre Sévérin told Angela to go to her room, but she refused, and he did not press the point. She was involved now, and there was no virtue in trying to pretend otherwise.

The giant's faith in his knots was fully justified. Guido was lying on the stone floor, trussed up so tightly that he could hardly move a muscle, and obviously in considerable distress. When he saw Gregory Temple's face in the light of the Grey Man's lantern, he groaned. "That fool Fantin," he murmured. "I'd have hired someone better if I could, but the *Habits Noirs* have mobilized the mob tonight, and only left the dregs."

"You recognize me, then?" Temple said, curiously. "I do not believe that we have ever been introduced."

"No," said Guido, with a sigh, "but I was hoping to see someone else–hoping for a rescue, in fact. I never meant to do the young lady any harm. That is not my way."

"Your master is not so scrupulous, by all accounts," Temple replied. "Once you had delivered her into his hands...but that's irrelevant now. What we need to know is where your master is, and we shall brook no delay in obtaining an answer."

"I should have taken the Grey Man to him, when I had the chance," Guido lamented. "I beg your pardon, Monsieur Lazarus, but you cannot blame me for my little stratagem. In fact, the last thing I wanted was to wait until Temple returned before taking you to my master, for I never expected him to return–I was expecting my associates to arrive in his stead. The sensible thing to do now, for both of us, is to come to a private arrangement. Temple is an unnecessary inconvenience that we can both do without."

Temple deduced from this speech that Guido had played for time by promising Lazarus that he would take him to his master when Temple came back–while hoping that his friends might regroup and counter-attack, with or without Fantin's help. Now that Temple and Sévérin had returned, and with Fantin out of the game, the men who had been put to flight were highly unlikely to risk another assault.

"That would be rather impolite, don't you think?" said Lazarus to Guido, somewhat to Temple's surprise. "He has surely earned the right to an interview with your master."

He's afraid too! Temple thought, although he kept his face very straight. *Whether we're at odds or not, he wants me with him when he confronts the vampire! He does not want to go alone. I can hardly blame him, though, for I sought out help myself, and was very glad to have it when danger actually threatened.*

258

"Suit yourself," was Guido's grudging reply. "Perhaps I'll take my chances and remain silent. You'll have to let me go eventually, even if no help comes."

"He seems to think that we won't apply pressure to get him to talk," Temple said to Lazarus. "Are you really that scrupulous? If so, we could always turn him over to Vidocq, who seems to be itching to take a hand in this affair. He has a free hand in dealing with enemy aliens."

That threat worked better than Temple had anticipated. "There's no need to involve Vidocq!" Guido was quick to say. "That's the last thing any of us needs. I'll take you both to see my master, if that's what you really want–but it's a long way to Miremont, and you really ought to let me go if you expect me to be in any fit state to lead you."

"Miremont!" Temple exclaimed. "Your master is in Miremont?"

"He should be, by now," Guido replied. "Don't worry, Mr. Temple–he's not so unsubtle in his methods as the pious brutes of *Civitas Solis*. He'll do no harm to your daughter or your grandchild, or to any of the other innocents of Miremont, but he does need to flush Henri de Belcamp out of hiding–urgently, if possible. Belcamp is the one man who's privy to *all* of Germain Patou's secrets, despite the fact that Lord Byron contracted a partnership with the physician. I beg you, please, to let me continue this discussion in less uncomfortable circumstances–I'll give you my word not to try to escape, but I fear that I might lose a limb if the circulation of my blood is interrupted much longer."

"Shall I?" asked the giant. Temple gestured his consent, and the Grey Man plucked Guido from the floor, stood him upright and then set about undoing the knots he had tied. His thick fingers were surprisingly nimble.

By the time that the Magyar was able to start rubbing his wrists and stamping his feet in order to restore normal blood-flow, Temple had collected himself. "Countess Marcian Gregoryi's offer to buy the new château was a means of getting access to Jeanne de Belcamp, was it not?" he said.

"Of course not," Guido replied, his voice dripping with sarcasm. "She fell in love with the mock-classical architecture and the beautiful location."

It occurred to Temple, a trifle belatedly, that he had no idea where Sarah Boehm had been going when her carriage had left the vicinity of the Tuileries. If she were staying in Paris, leaving the new château open for inspection by potential purchasers…

"I'll take you to my master, since I have little alternative," Guido continued, "but I won't guide an army to his hiding-place. I'll take you, Monsieur Lazarus, provided that we leave now. If you want to bring Temple with you, that's up to you, but not Sévérin. If I were you, I'd leave Temple behind too–but you'd best prick his leg to make sure he doesn't follow us or run squealing to Vidocq."

Temple bit his lip to forestall the protest that rose instinctively to his lips– but he need not have worried. "I think I'd prefer it if Mr. Temple were with us," Lazarus replied. "That way, I can keep an eye on him." He too was speaking sarcastically, evidently having realized that Guido was trying to provoke a quarrel between him and Temple.

Guido shrugged his shoulders–rather painfully, it seemed. "Very well," he said. "It's your decision. We must go immediately, though."

"What about René?" asked Jean-Pierre Séverin. Evidently, the old man was not disposed to argue with Guido's demand that he be left behind, presumably feeling that his first responsibility was to protect Angela–although Temple assumed that he had taken very careful note of the mention of Miremont.

Temple took his old acquaintance aside and whispered in his ear: "This is another trap, I suspect, although I'm not entirely sure who's setting it for whom. You must decide what to do when René returns–if he does return. Vidocq's men might be inclined to delay him, in order to play their own hand freely, and they have the authority to do it. If I don't come back, you might eventually have to go to Vidocq and tell him everything–you won't get any action out of anyone else at the Prefecture. Byron's party might be more trustworthy allies, but they have no more authority here than I do. The best thing of all would be to play your own hand, if you can."

"That's always been my way," Séverin observed. "I wish I had a better understanding of all this, though."

"So do I," Temple assured him. "There seem to be more pieces in the jigsaw than I could have anticipated–but you and René must concentrate on Countess Marcian Gregoryi, for the time being. At the very least, keep track of her movements, and find out everything you can about her intentions."

In the meantime, Guido and the giant had started climbing the stairs towards the cellar door.

"I had not anticipated that we would have to go as far as Miremont," Lazarus observed. "I have no carriage, and we can hardly hire a fiacre. We'll have to hire horses, if we can find a livery stable that's open at this hour."

Temple looked at Séverin again. "I know where you can obtain horses," the old man said, "Although I'm not sure there's a horse in all Paris capable of carrying the giant more than a kilometer–you might need a Percheron for that."

"We'll hire six and ride them in relay," Temple assured him. "Your part will be the hardest, old friend, for there's nothing you can do for now but wait."

"I'm a patient man," Jean-Pierre Séverin assured him. "I've lived with the dead all my life, and I know how to wait."

Chapter Four
The Ghosts of the Deliverance

The giant tied Guido's hands behind him and secured his ankles to the stirrups of his horse, which Temple kept on a leading-rein along with the three spare mounts. They rode through the *barrière* not long after midnight, but could not make too much haste thereafter, for the road was very dark. The Moon was only half-full and the stars were barely visible through the fog. Once they were in the forest Temple lit a lantern and hung it on a pole which he extended before the lead horse, but it was a poor guide. Fortunately, there had been relatively little autumn rain thus far, and the road was not too badly muddied.

When the time seemed ripe, Temple maneuvered his horse into step with the giant's. "You must have suspected that Guido was merely playing for time," he said. "Why did you wait?"

"I could not be sure," the Grey Man said. "To tell the truth, though, I was uncertain what to do for the best." Temple remembered what he had said about Lord Byron feeling isolated in Paris, and not knowing who to trust–how much worse must his own predicament seem?

"Are you any more certain now?" Temple asked.

"No," the new Adam admitted. "Are you?"

"I have no alternative," Temple told him. "I'm involved now, and cannot let it alone. I must keep going forward, however blindly."

"I know how you feel," the giant said. "My commitment is greater than yours, I believe."

Temple had to concede that point. In spite of what he had just said, he did have the alternative of letting the matter alone; the Grey Man did not. "Ned Knob told me that you and your creator were estranged," he said. "If you're now in Lord Byron's service, I assume that your differences have been reconciled."

"I doubt that Frankenstein will ever be reconciled to my independence of his will," the other replied, dourly, "And I am not in Lord Byron's *service*. Our interests happen to coincide, for the moment. I agreed to follow you because I agreed with his Lordship that you might succeed in tracking down the vampire– you do have the reputation of being a great detective as well as a madman."

Temple was disposed to take exception to the last word, but swallowed his pride, knowing that he had a golden opportunity to fish for information. "My detective work has uncovered far more questions than answers, alas," he said, "and the scientists that I have tried to interest in the possibility of resurrection have mostly thrown up their hands in horror, accusing me of ludicrous superstition."

"I have had similar experiences," the Grey Man admitted, "although I did have one fascinating conversation with the Chevalier de Lamarck, who seems glad to have an audience of any sort nowadays."

"But you have the invaluable advantage of experience," Temple said. "What are you, really? Is your condition a matter of a temporarily-dislodged soul repossessing its body? Did it require the reignition of some kind of vital spirit? Or was it some anomalous kind of spontaneous generation–a flaw in the natural pattern of life's origin and development?"

"I wish I knew," the giant said. "What are *you*, Mr. Temple? Are you a soul in a body, a vital spark or a mere routine product of spontaneous generation? Does merely being alive make you an unimpeachable savant in matters of biology?"

"No," Temple admitted.

"We have too poor an understanding, as yet, of what death really means," the giant said, "and how it differs from such states of suspended animation as catalepsy. I hope that the vampire might be able to tell me more, if he is inclined to be generous."

"I fear that he must be alarmed by the reaction that his arrival in Paris has provoked," Temple observed, "and might be regretting his decision to return. You realize, of course, that we are putting our heads into a lion's mouth?"

"Of course–but we have already agreed that we have no alternative but to go forwards. Having stirred up a hornets' nest, the vampire will probably beat a hasty retreat–but he came here in search of knowledge, and might count us precious because of that."

Temple could not help wondering whether the giant's use of the word "us" might be over-generous. He could easily imagine that the vampire might be glad to forge an alliance with the scientific Lazarus–and also that he might have a very different attitude to an aging English spy.

"Do you know why Vidocq is interested in this business," Temple asked. "He must surely be doing someone else's bidding–but whose?"

"I don't know. Lord Byron has made reference to the *Habits Noirs*–in London, he says, they're more likely to term themselves *Gentlemen of the Night*–but I'm not sure that he even believes in them."

"Coco-Lacour attempted to tantalize me with that very phrase, when he took pleasure in telling me that Byron had set you to follow me," Temple said, reflectively. "He was probably just playing games–but there's always a real villain behind such attempts to capitalize on myth and legend: a would-be John Devil or *Jean Diable*. The Prefect suspects Vidocq himself of being the current Parisian Napoleon of crime, but I can't believe that he's the spider at the center of the web. Tom Brown might be better qualified, but he's been too long away from London and Paris to retain a firm grip on the Underworld of either capital. Someone else must have stepped forward to take on the role, because someone always does–but I don't know who it might be. Are Vidocq's men making things difficult for Byron, too?"

"Very difficult," the giant admitted. "He did not want to come back here at all, but the fiasco in Spezia was an awkward setback. When he heard the rumor that the vampire was coming here…we knew no more than that, alas. If only we had as many spies at our disposal as you must have at yours…."

Temple suppressed an ironic laugh, knowing that there was not a single spy in Europe on whom he could truly rely, and that his own commanders were heartily sick of his escapades. "What contract did Byron make with Germain Patou?" he asked, curiously.

"I'm not free to tell you that, Mr. Temple," Lazarus replied, conscientiously. "I've made a contract with him myself, and am bound by it. I can't tell you my master's secrets, so there's no point in your asking me where Frankenstein is, any more than there is in my asking you where Germain Patou is. What I will offer to do, though, when our present business is concluded, is to arrange a meeting between you and my master. You have common ground enough to make an agreement, I think–he is English, after all, although his homeland has not been very generous in its treatment of him."

"You have information of your own that you might give me, were you so disposed," Temple pointed out. "You must have found out a great many things while you were estranged from Byron's party. It was you who found out about vampires, if Ned Knob can be trusted–and about the particular vampire we are about to meet."

"I have not been idle," the Grey Man agreed, "but I have only been a Grey Man for a few meager years–not much longer than the infamous Mortdieu. There is a sense in which he and I are both mere infants, however adult we seem. I have been unrelentingly curious–but I cannot lay claim to any settled wisdom. Rumor has it, though, that the vampire who calls himself Szandor has been a Grey Man for centuries, and is certainly not as stupid as the vast majority of his kind. If anyone has learned to refine the process of resurrection–or is able to refine it–he is the most likely candidate. Ned Knob must agree with that judgment."

"I dare say that he does," Temple said, bitterly. "Alas, he was not inclined to share the judgment with me. I think he planned to track the vampire down himself, or in collaboration with Henri de Belcamp–but I put a stop to that, albeit at the cost of putting him on Patou's trail. Sometimes, I cannot help hoping that his ship will sink in mid-Atlantic, and free me of the little imp forever."

"I rather liked him," the giant admitted.

"Nearly everyone does," Temple admitted, gloomily. "It's the child in him, I think. It's almost impossible to hate him, no matter how one tries. He even charmed Tom Brown once, who was very nearly caught in consequence. I have to keep reminding myself that he is all the more useful to me because he also in the pay of my arch-enemy, and will one day lead me to him."

"Not for a while, though, if he's embarked on a sea voyage," Lazarus observed.

Temple wondered briefly whether he ought to have kept that fact to himself, but he could not believe that Byron did not know it already. The conversation was dying now, because they had reached that hour of the early morning when all energy drains away, even for those who do not give way to sleep "How powerful is the vampire, do you think?" Temple asked, in a desultory tone. "Are you confident that we can stand up to him, if it comes to a contest?"

"If he were powerful in body," the giant replied, after an expansive yawn, "he would not need to hide away so cleverly, or equip his favorite minion with so much glamour and trickery. That he is deceptive, I do not doubt, but I do not fear any sort of physical attack." After a pause, he added: "I wish I had brought some food and water from Paris, though, for I shall not be inclined to trust anything that he offers me to eat or drink."

Temple was thirsty too, although he had long since disciplined himself to pay no attention to hunger pangs while he was about his business. Lack of sleep was, however, a more troublesome attrition. "Agreed," he said, and lapsed into silence.

The silence weighed upon him more heavily than the conversation had, and he soon became frustrated with the slowness of their progress–which was not much ameliorated by the fact that the giant switched horses twice as frequently as his companions.

When dawn broke, they were still on the road, having not yet reached the turning that led to Pierre Louchet's former residence–a turning they did not take. They went all the way to Miremont itself, but then deviated from the expected route. Instead of heading for the "new château," they turned on to another path, which led to an isolated cottage by the Oise.

Of course, Temple thought, when he realized what the cottage was. *I should have guessed. Robert's mother lived here, and he retains it as a perverse shrine to her memory. The Knights of the Deliverance once met here, if I remember right, on the night when Henri de Belcamp assumed command of the conspiracy. If only I had known that at the time!*

Temple was somewhat dismayed to find that there were four burly men in the grounds of the cottage, all of them tougher customers than the hirelings that Jean-Pierre Sévérin had put to flight. Guido greeted them cheerily and instructed, in Italian, one of them to come and untie his bonds–an instruction to which Temple and the giant raised no objection. Temple's Italian was far from perfect, but he understood when Guido asked the same man how long it had been since the company arrived. The answer he received was that they had only been there for little more than two hours.

"Is the master asleep?" Guido asked. The reply he received was in the negative; the man who gave it indicated by his attitude that he would have preferred it if the master *had* been asleep.

"You're in luck, gentlemen," Guido said to Temple and the giant, in English. "My master does not like to be woken up when he's asleep, no matter how urgent the reason might be. May I go in before you, to warn him that I've brought him unexpected guests?"

"No," said Temple, shortly, and did not wait for anyone else to go to the cottage door ahead of him. He marched forwards recklessly and opened the door himself, without knocking, leaving Guido and the Grey Men to jostle for position behind him–a contest that the giant inevitably won.

The interior of the cottage was dark. No lamp was lit therein, and the windows were shuttered. The thin beams of wan grey light that filtered through the cracks in the ancient shutters provided some illumination, but Temple's eyes had adapted to the silver glare of the morning mist, and some seconds elapsed before he was able to make out the figure seated at Madeleine Surrisy's old dining-table. In the meantime, he knew, the other would have been able to make a much more efficient assessment of him.

As his slowly-reacting sight gained sensitivity, Temple became aware that the atmosphere within the cottage seemed to be filed with dust, and that the dust was stirring in numerous draughts introduced through breaches in the wood-work, in a rather eerie fashion. For a moment or two, it was not just the grey figure seated at the table that seemed more like a ghost than a solid entity. That central figure seemed, in fact, to be surrounded by a host of other ghosts–almost as if the Knights of the Deliverance had been compelled to return to the scene of their last meeting, following the ultimate failure of their mission and their purpose. It was, however, the central figure that was studying Gregory Temple and Frankenstein's *daemon*, with a stare that seemed inhumanly penetrating.

Temple had to make a positive effort of will to ignore the imaginary ghosts and focus his attention on the one that was real: a surprisingly thin creature, no more than skin and bone, whose skull was so entirely bald, save for a few wisps of white hair, that it did indeed resemble a skull cleansed of all flesh…except for the eyes. The eyes were still there, and their dilated pupils were jet black, although the thin irises surrounding them were so palely grey as to be hardly distinguishable from the whites. The eyes were exceedingly disconcerting, their stare impossible to meet, for the moment–although Temple had a dire suspicion that it might also be impossible to avoid, if the other were that way inclined.

The vampire must have been astonished to see him, but the ghostly head remained quite motionless, as if the creature were literally imperturbable. Temple had come in with considerable impetus, and a determination not to be intimated, but all that vanished like smoke and he too was rendered motionless. He knew, within an instant, that he had overestimated his own capacity to deal with this confrontation–but he was committed, and had to follow through with it.

"My name is Gregory Temple," he contrived to say. "Are you the vampire who calls himself Szandor?"

The vampire's elbows were leaning on the table, while his hands were joined, as if in prayer, in front of his shriveled nose. His fingers were almost all bone, with the articulations clearly visible, but they were still flexible, and they moved so as to grip more tightly as the newcomers took up position side by side, with only the width of the table separating them from the creature. The vampire made no reply to Temple's question, but simply stared at his unexpected guests. It was impossible to tell whether the skeletal creature was smiling, or whether his face was permanently set in a *rictus sardonicus*.

265

"My lord..." Guido began, attempting unsuccessfully to elbow his way between Temple and the giant.

"Explanations are unnecessary, Guido," said a soft and serpentine voice that might have come from anywhere in the room, speaking in Italian. "You may leave."

Guido seemed glad to have permission to give up his futile struggle and step back. He wasted no time in backing up out of the doorway, closing the door behind him to make the interior of the cottage even gloomier than before.

Temple opened his mouth to speak again, but no words came out. The giant seemed similarly dumbstruck. Temple could no longer believe that he had ever imagined himself equal to this situation, and suspected that he could be struck dead on the spot, if the vampire so wished.

Apparently, the vampire did not wish it–yet. "I see that you have not come equipped with wooden stakes and firebrands," the voice resumed, disturbing the dust as its sibilant sound moved through the unnaturally thick atmosphere, "so I assume that you have come in peace. I confess that I was not expecting you so soon. I congratulate you on your persistence, Mr. Temple, although I really do not think that this business has anything to do with you. You, on the other hand, Monsieur Lazarus, I am glad to welcome to my temporary abode, given that events have moved too quickly for me to contrive a meeting on my own terms. Would you like to sit down, or would you prefer to stand? Many people do prefer to stand in my company, even though I was never the aristocrat that I sometimes claimed to be when I...or the person I once was...was alive."

Temple took no offence at the insulting dismissal of his relevance. His hands, acting without any instruction from his conscious mind, had already pulled out one of the crude dining-chairs, and he sat down, as awkwardly as a puppet in a marionette theatre. The giant followed his example, lowering himself on to a second chair rather gingerly, perhaps because he feared the rickety object might break and perhaps because he was saddle-sore.

"I understand that you have both been searching for me, at least since Guido got into difficulties in Spezia," the vampire continued. "I did not expect you to find me quite so easily, but Paris has changed a great deal since I was last here. Whatever else the Terror achieved, it certainly encouraged men to mind their own business and not inquire too closely into other people's. Nowadays, it seems, the population is a veritable hydra, every head of which has a thousand avid eyes. It is a pity that you have by-passed my most trusted aide, who would have managed everything much more diplomatically, but her first priority was to deal with Lord Byron and Lady de Belcamp. As you can probably imagine, I have poured my heart and soul into her creation. Sometimes, I think that she is now more *me* than I am–but that might be wishful thinking. I am not quite as handsome, I fear. Once your eyes have become accustomed to me, though, you will not find me as fearful."

Temple's eyes were still adjusting, unhurriedly, to the meager light, and the skeletal figure had not yet emerged as fully from the darkness as it ultimately might–but he could not imagine that the sight would be any more pleasing when it did become distinct.

"If it will comfort you to know it, I have no wish to harm anyone in Miremont, or in Paris, on this occasion," the vampire went on. "I have often found it convenient to make superstitious people live in fear of me, and I have killed without compunction for more reasons than you might credit or imagine, but I am not the ravening monster that legend considers vampires to be. We are supposed to be in the heart of civilization, after all, and I ought to behave in a civilized manner, even if my enemies are less inclined to do so. The trap that I set for you at the Hôtel Trianon, Mr. Temple, was a crude and hasty contrivance–but one must sometimes cause a small injury in order not to cause a greater one. You have placed yourself in grave danger by avoiding that trap, not only from me, but from others. You are a brave man, though, and that is your way. I, on the other hand, am a consummate coward. The living have no conception of how fearful of annihilation those who have already died can be. Monsieur Lazarus may not have had time, as yet, to come fully to terms with his condition, but he will learn, with or without my help–always provided that he can survive the fear and loathing of the living."

The voice paused, and Temple felt his chest constrict as his breathing seemed almost to stop. The dust in the air was worse now than the fog outside, and it seemed to him that all the ghosts within that dust were avidly attentive, eager to see him die.

"Sometimes," the voice resumed. "I wish that all the silly tales about a vampire's bite creating more vampires were true. If they were, I'd have raised an army of the dead long ago, to establish an impregnable stronghold, if not to conquer the world. If rumor can be trusted, your friend Monsieur Patou has had more success in a few brief years than I ever had in centuries of practical experimentation, although he has inevitably run into the same difficulty that eventually disheartened me. I have known more than a few of the reanimated dead in my time, but never one with whom I could have a decent conversation. I am interested to meet you, Monsieur Lazarus, for that very specific reason–but I ought to warn you that I no longer crave company as much as I once did, and I might be inclining more to jealousy in my second old age. I am a coward, as I say, and I confess that the prospects of this new revolution are alarming. The Church and I might have more in common than I ever suspected, despite our diehard enmity. Still, I pride myself on being a rational...individual. I had hoped to create an opportunity to have a few friendly words with Victor Frankenstein. Patou and General Mortdieu are, it seems, out of reach for the time being."

Again the vampire paused. Even in the extremity of his discomfort, Temple found it possible to wonder whether the motionless death's-head might be exactly what it seemed: a mere scarecrow, an inert marionette. Might the real vampire, he wondered, somehow be incarnate in the strangely swirling dust? No sooner had he formed the thought, however, than the skeletal form *did* move, as if to prove him wrong and mock his folly. The chin moved free of the supportive hands, and the terrible stare grew even more intense and menacing. The timbre of the voice remained as soft and sibilant as ever, though.

"I had also hoped to find a way to make contact with Henri de Belcamp," the vampire went on. "Not in the hope that Patou left him some sort of written legacy, for I am far too wise and jaded to believe in convenient treasures of that sort, but simply because he was a witness to so much of Patou's work. I suppose, all things considered, that it might work to my advantage that you have both come to see me, since one of you can probably tell me how to contact Frankenstein and the other has at least one means of getting a message to Henri de Belcamp. For that assistance, I might be prepared to trade a little information, as well as a measure of mercy–but you must not think, if I am disposed to be merciful, and prepared to adopt a mercantile approach, that you are my equals in this matter. If…"

The monster was interrupted then–and the mere fact that he could be interrupted, and that his control of the situation could thus be shown to be less than absolute, seemed to Gregory Temple to be a very welcome revelation. The door to the cottage was hurled back, and a man–not Guido–rushed in, babbling in a language that Temple could not understand. He rushed out again as soon as he had made his seemingly panic-stricken report.

The skeleton remained sitting, though not as languidly as before.

When he claimed to be a coward, Temple thought, *he was not being ironic. And if he is a coward, he must have good cause to be afraid. There are things that can hurt him, things he is obliged to flee, no matter how powerful his mesmeric authority might be when he confronts his adversaries one or two at a time.*

He was breathing more easily now, and knew that the vampire's power over him was already weakening.

I can survive this, he thought, *whether I am his equal or not, I am not helpless in his grip. I might even be able to speak, if I exert myself.*

And when he exerted himself, Temple found that he could, indeed, speak. "Guido ought to have taken better precautions to ensure that we were not followed," he said to the vampire. "No one can make a move in Paris just now without attracting unwelcome attention."

"That's true," Lazarus added. "The *Gentlemen of the Night* are hot on your heels, it seems, and my guess is that the weight of numbers is one thing with which you cannot cope–like your minion, you only have one pair of eyes. Paris has no shortage of rabble for assembly into unruly mobs, and that rabble has been roused."

Temple joined in again to say: "Monsieur Vidocq will not show his own hand, but he will have given strict orders, in which the words *dead or alive* might well have figured prominently."

For a moment, he thought that he might be struck dead for his temerity, but the vampire was not a hot-tempered creature.

"There's no need to be afraid for me, Mr. Temple," the voice whispered, with more than a hint of mockery. "Your anger is greater than mine!"

Temple tried to stand up then, although he did not know exactly what he intended to do—but as he stood up, he felt an appalling pain his right thigh, as if he had been stabbed.

He collapsed back into the chair, unable to prevent his eyes from closing reflexively in response to the agony. His closed eyes could not, however, shut out the sight of the ghosts that had been drifting in the air, dully resentful of having a vile Englishman in the midst of their Bonapartist company—ghosts that suddenly seemed to gain new authority and new opportunity.

It was not that the superabundant dust-motes gained real substance, but they did gain *impetus*, and they rushed upon him in vengeful millions, blinding him and choking him. Temple flapped his arms madly, although he was aware of the absurdity of the action, which only served to intensify the pain in his leg. A swarm of flies might have been disturbed by his flailing, but the cloud of dust was immune to it.

This is not real! Temple shouted at himself, silently. *This is a trick of magnetic suggestion—and I am not some hysteric young woman, vulnerable to such flummery!*

Hysteric or not, though, he could not fight the dusty ghosts any more than he could fight the psychosomatic pain. Imaginary they might be, but he could not fight the ghosts of the Deliverance or the wound inflicted by an invisible blade. Utterly helpless, in the grip of forces far beyond his control, Temple fell back as his chair tilted and spilled him on the cottage floor.

The dust piled up on his face like a death-mask, consigning him to Hellish darkness and preventing him from—conclusively, this time—from drawing breath.

The detective would have called for help if he could have done so, but his lips were sealed—and he had no reason to expect, in any case, that Frankenstein's new Adam had any interest at all in helping him, even if he were in any condition to help himself.

Chapter Five
On the Sidelines

Gregory Temple awoke as if from a drug-induced sleep, conscious of a dull but nagging pain in his right thigh. He moved to touch the afflicted limb under the blankets that weighed him down—discovering as his hand moved that someone had taken off his clothes and dressed him in a nightshirt—but his probing fingers could find no trace of any cut or contusion. The pain was deep within the flesh;

or, more accurately, deep within his treasonous consciousness. He tried to flex the leg, and then made as if to get out of bed, but was left in no doubt that he would be unable to walk, for the time being, even if he could stand up.

He opened his eyes, and tried to figure out where he might be. There was a night-light burning on his bedside table, and the bed-curtains were not drawn, so it was possible to make out the walls of the room and its furniture, but the only thing of which he was sure, to begin with, was that he was not in Madeleine Surrisy's cottage. He was in a much finer house than that, furnished with good taste and a certain effortless luxury.

He had never been in that particular room before, so there was nothing he could actually recognize–but he guessed readily enough where he must be once his head was clear. He seized the little hand-bell set beside the nightlight and agitated it madly. He was not unduly surprised when the person who eventually came in response to the summons was his daughter Suzanne.

He was in the Château de Belcamp–and even though his leg had not been "pinked" by Eugène Fantin's ill-kept sword, he was sure that he would not be able to walk without a limp for some time to come. The vampire had not put him out of the game entirely, but had relegated him to its sidelines. Temple knew that that had been an exercise of mercy, but he could not bring himself to be grateful.

"Daddy!" Suzanne said, as a dutiful daughter was bound to do. "Thank God you're awake, at last! Do you need a doctor? I wanted to call one, but Jeanne said that we ought to wait."

"I need a glass of water," Temple growled. "My mouth feels as if it were full of dust. And I need my clothes." The latter remark brought forth a pang from his leg, as if to remind him, dutifully, that he would not find it easy to dress himself.

There was a pitcher on the dressing-table, and a crystal goblet. Suzanne filled the goblet and brought it to him. He did not empty it at a single draught, in spite of the temptation, but eked it out, using a gradual flow to clear the lingering impression of the ghostly dust. When his mouth felt sufficiently normal again, he said: "Who brought me here?"

"A policeman," she replied.

"The local *garde champêtre?*" he asked, hopefully.

"No–an inspector from Paris. His name is Coco-Lacour."

"*Is?*" Temple repeated. "You don't mean that you *let him in?*"

"We could hardly refuse him entry. You were laid out unconscious in the back of a cart that he was driving. He apologized profusely for the untidy state of his clothing, but said that his men had been involved in what he called a *razzia*. Some bandits had taken possession of Madeleine Surrisy's old cottage, apparently, and a company of police agents had to be summoned from Paris to capture them–but you must know that, since you were their prisoner. Did the policemen not save your life?"

270

"The policemen might well be under that impression," Temple admitted, grudgingly. "Where is Coco-Lacour now?"

"Sleeping peacefully in another bedroom," Suzanne told him. "Jeanne could hardly send him packing, in the circumstances–and he's very polite, despite his unorthodox style of dress. He says that he needs to question you with regard to your abduction, but that will surely wait until morning–unless you want me to wake him right away."

"No, don't do that," Temple said. "I'm sorry–I never seem to have an opportunity to see you in placid circumstances. How are you? How's Richard, and little Richard?"

"Very well," she assured him, sitting down on the bed. "Which is more than can be said for you, it seems. What on Earth are you doing getting mixed up with bandits in Miremont? I thought that you had done with all that and had become more of a diplomat than a thief-taker?"

"They weren't bandits," Temple grunted. "Well, actually, they probably were–except for their master. Did Coco-Lacour tell you whether his *razzia* was a success?"

"Two villains were killed, he said," Suzanne reported, "and the rest taken prisoner. He seems very pleased with himself."

Temple could not believe that the raiders had actually managed to capture or kill the vampire–and was no longer certain as to whether he ought to wish that they had. If Coco-Lacour was pleased with himself, though, they must at least have managed to deprive the vampire of his remaining human hirelings.

"He's insistent that he needs to see you in order to complete his report," Suzanne continued. "I gather that you're not enthusiastic to talk to him."

"He may carry papers affiliating him to the Prefecture," Temple said, "but he's no better than the thieves he chases, and perhaps worse. His superior has a dark reputation, and my guess is that it's not undeserved. They pretend to be combating organized crime, but I suspect that they're the most organized criminals in Paris, for the time being–or part of some such organization, at least. They've infiltrated the Prefecture, and now they've infiltrated the Château–but I can't believe that they've actually succeeded in killing the adversary they went after. I have to talk to Jeanne, to warn her against...well, against things it might be better for you to know nothing about."

Suzanne slapped him, and did not make any attempt to soften the blow. Fortunately, his astonishment blotted out the stinging pain. She leapt to her feet and placed her hands on her hips, although there were tears in her eyes. "How many times must we go through this?" she complained. "I will not let you do this, Father! I will not let you decide for me what I ought and ought not to know!"

Temple stared at her for a full ten seconds, then shrugged his shoulders. "Against Countess Marcian Gregoryi," he said, simply. "The vampire's minion." He watched the expressions that crossed his daughter's face, more fearfully than inquisitively–and then his heart sank. "Oh my God," he said. "Please don't tell me that she's here too!"

"Not yet," was the slightly discomfited reply. "She's supposed to be coming to Miremont this afternoon, with Sarah. She's buying the new château. Jeanne has been invited to dinner there tonight."

"That plan has probably been abandoned," Temple murmured. "In which case, she won't come. On the other hand…"

"What do you mean, *the vampire's minion?*" Suzanne demanded, before he had time to follow the thought through.

"There is a creature," Temple began, a little uncertainly. "A monster, some might say….but probably only a man, of an admittedly unusual sort. A man returned from the dead–not by any intervention of chemistry and electricity, like others of more recent provenance, but by some accident of nature, long ago. Such accidents are apparently less rare than we have recently supposed. In the distant past, they were credited to miracles or black magic; more recently, they have been dismissed as products of superstition, or cases of catalepsy. The simple fact is, it seems, that death is not always the end–but what succeeds it, when some kind of new life does succeed it, remains something of a mystery, even to its beneficiaries."

"A *vampire?*" Suzanne repeated, her incredulity mingling with fear as she realized that her father was perfectly serious.

"Not the kind that sucks blood," Temple told her, offering what scant reassurance he could. "Dangerous, certainly, but…well, he did not kill me when he had the chance." He thought it best to return to safer ground, and continued: "The point is that Countess Marcian Gregoryi is the vampire's instrument. Their plan has gone badly awry, thanks to the involvement of the *Habits Noirs* and their agents in the Prefecture, but they might not be finished yet. Was there another man with me in Coco-Lacour's cart–another victim of the so-called bandits? Is he here too, perchance?"

Suzanne stared at him, obviously wondering whether he was mad. She had had reason enough to suspect him of that in the past, and he could not blame her for it. Eventually, she shook her head and said: "You were alone. No mention was made of any other victim."

Temple was not surprised. Whether the new Adam was still with the vampire, or had returned to Lord Byron–or even if he was in Vidocq's custody–Coco-Lacour would not have been disposed to mention him to the residents of the Château de Belcamp. Temple was quite ready to consider the Gray Man an ally now, although he knew full well that the only person in whom he could place any real trust was Jean-Pierre Séverin.

He made a mental note to send a message to Séverin, at least to reassure the old man that he was alive, and as well as could be expected.

Temple's gaze strayed to the bedroom window, and he saw through the crack in the curtains that the sky was turning silver. There was evidently still some mist in the air, but the quality of the light suggested that today would be much brighter than the last day to which he had actually been witness. The Vampire's magnetic powers had obviously put him out of contention for almost twenty-four hours, causing him to miss a whole cycle of daylight. He shifted his leg tentatively, but the movement caused the pain in his right thigh to flare up again.

"It's all in my mind," Temple muttered, addressing himself rather than Suzanne. "The leg itself is perfectly healthy. All I need is the will-power to defy the vampire's suggestive command."

"I'll have the cook make you a good breakfast," Suzanne told him, making no response to what he had said. "You need to get your strength back. You're far too old for this sort of nonsense–but I'll get you some clothes anyway. The ones you were wearing when you were brought in will need extensive mending once they've been washed."

"I'm not as old as Jean-Pierre Séverin," Temple observed, a trifle resentfully. "He can still take on three bravos, armed with nothing but a light cane, and put them all *hors de combat* in a matter of seconds. It's not just the dead who can sometimes renew life, Suzanne–the living can sometimes do it too. That's the real holy grail for which Frankenstein and Patou are searching. If they can understand how the dead return, they might be able to understand how death can be prevented in the first place. That's a goal worth fighting for, even for an old fool like me–and I won't let the vampire toss me casually aside, while I still have the strength to stay in contention. Make sure it's a very hearty breakfast, my darling–I haven't had a bite in almost two full days, and I really do need to get my strength back. Tell Jeanne, as soon as she wakes up, that I need to see her urgently."

Suzanne's temper had calmed, and she left the room quite meekly. It was neither her nor Jeanne who came to see him next, however, but Coco-Lacour.

"Good morning, Mr. Temple," the agent said, cheerfully. "Did I not tell you that you ought to join forces with us? Still, we contrived to rescue you from the vampire's clutches, did we not? We've beaten him out of that particular lair, and eliminated all his minions save one. Paris has a thousand eyes alert for the slightest glimpse of him, and he's quite helpless. Everything is for the best in the best of all possible worlds!"

"You make an unconvincing Dr. Pangloss," Temple observed, dryly.

"So did Dr. Pangloss, in Voltaire's estimation," Coco-Lacour retorted. "I am a literate man you see–never let it be said that no one ever learns anything in the *bagne*. There really is scope for a man to reform there. One day, I might perhaps rise through the ranks to be Prefect of Police!"

"Have you just come to gloat," Temple asked, "or is there some purpose to your visit?"

"You must forgive me if my natural good spirits give me the appearance of gloating," the agent replied. "I'm here on police business, for the mutual benefit of the Prefecture of Paris and Scotland Yard–a fine example of co-operation for our many untrustful colleagues. Do you know, by any chance, where the vampire and Frankenstein's monster might have gone?"

"They didn't take me into their confidence," Temple said, wishing that it were a lie.

"I suspected as much–but you did meet the vampire, did you not? You can give me a reliable description of him."

"I can tell you what I saw," Temple said, "but I cannot vouch for its reliability. Like you, I have always been a trifle cocksure, and I was always perfectly certain that no Mesmerist charlatan could ever cast a spell on me–but Count Szandor has evidently learned a trick or two in centuries of unnatural life, and he's no charlatan in matters of suggestion. I saw him as an ambulant skeleton, with very little flesh on his ancient bones–but his eye-sockets are by no means blank, and if you ever meet him yourself, you'll find his stare extremely disconcerting."

"That does seem to be a problem," Coco-Lacour admitted. "I had 100 men at my disposal last night–not all official deputies, I confess–but they couldn't lay hands on him, or even give me any sort of description of him. Lord Byron's pet giant, on the other hand, was all too visible and tangible. He put a dozen men in the hospital, although he seems to have made an effort to be gentle, just as your friend Jean-Pierre did when he gave Fantin a fencing-lesson. Since René de Kervoz will doubtless bring you up to date when he has the chance, I might as well tell you that he and I followed your mystery lady–Countesss Marcian Gregoryi, as I now know her to be–to the Faubourg Saint-Germain, where she attended a very select dinner-party at the house of the Duchesse de Broglie. She stayed overnight, and apparently has a fistful of similar invitations at her disposal. According to the Duchesse's butler, she is very popular, and is sure to be introduced at court within the week–which puts her far beyond my reach, alas. And yours, of course."

"Except that you also know that she is supposed to be coming to Miremont today, with Sarah Boehm," Temple said, "and you presumably have 50 or 60 hirelings of the *Habits Noirs* available to set in ambush."

"The *Habits Noirs* are a myth, Mr. Temple, as you well know," said Coco-Lacour, serenely, "and I am an agent of the Sûreté, sworn to combat any such evil, were it ever to spring up in reality. Arresting Gentlemen of the Night is my duty and vocation, just as it is yours. There will be no ambush–as I said, the Countess is out of our jurisdiction, and must be left to our friends in high places. In the final analysis, you and I are birds of similar plumage, unable to fly into the rarefied heights of the aristocratic atmosphere."

"We are birds of very different plumage, Monsieur Lacour," Temple retorted. "At the very least, I am determined to persuade the Comtesse de Belcamp not to accept Countess Marcian Gregoryi's dinner invitation–but I might go myself, if I can. I always carry a long spoon with me, in case I'm required to sup with the Devil."

"Monsieur Vidocq told me that you were a very stubborn man," Coco-Lacour observed. "I can see why he admires you. You need not worry about the horses you hired last night, by the way. I sent them back to their owner in Paris–although one is lame, doubtless in consequence of having to carry a giant. Please don't worry about the dinner party either; even if you were to be invited, it would be better for everyone concerned if you were unable to attend. You can easily offer your excuses–say that you sustained some injury in this morning's scuffle." The agent smiled broadly.

Temple scowled. "I can still walk," he said, although he was not at all sure that he could. "I sustained no physical injury, although the vampire was very enthusiastic to score an argumentative point. He simply used his magnetic powers to plant a suggestion in my mind, as much by way of a challenge as a simple disabling move."

"Paris is full of Mesmerists," Coco-Lacour observed, laconically. "Would you like me to summon one to put you in a trance and attempt to overrule the vampire's suggestion?"

"Thank you, no," Temple said. "Since I've been challenged, I feel obliged to accept. Jean-Pierre Séverin would expect no less. Incidentally, since René de Kervoz will tell me anyway, was Lord Byron present at the Duchesse de Broglie's dinner-party?"

"He was," Coco-Lacour admitted. "But he left in his own carriage, under no evident compulsion. He seems to be more resilient than most men to magnetic charms–even more resilient than you, perhaps. He has no difficulty at all in walking, so he will certainly be able to accept his invitation to dine at the new château, if any such gathering actually takes place. Our men will be in the neighborhood, of course, to make sure that the party is not disturbed by...undesirables."

"You still hope to catch the vampire, then?"

"We are agents of the law, Mr. Temple" said Coco-Lacour, stressing the word *we*. "It is our duty to preserve the order of things." He turned towards the door as he spoke; it had opened again.

This time, it really was Temple's breakfast-tray–but the person holding it was neither Suzanne nor a servant. Jeanne de Belcamp had brought it herself. The stare she directed at Coco-Lacour had no magnetic power in it, but was sufficiently intimidating to send him on his way without further ado.

When the door had closed behind the agent, the Comtesse set the tray down on the bed. As responsive as ever to his request, Suzanne had indeed prepared a good breakfast, even by English standards. Gregory Temple wasted no time in getting to work on the bacon and eggs; he was extremely hungry.

Several minutes passed while the Comtesse was content to watch him eat, but in the end she could restrain herself no longer. "Have you seen Henri since you were last here, Mr. Temple?" she asked.

"No," Temple said. "Have you?"

"No. Have you any news of him?"

Temple knew that he was bound by a duty of confidentiality even more powerful than Robert Surrisy's, but he prided himself on knowing a higher duty when he encountered it. "Reliable news, no," he said. "But I do have reason to believe that it was on Henri's instructions that Ned Knob set his conscience aside and agreed to work for Lord Liverpool's secret police. Ned is reporting to him regularly, and believes that I do not know. I have no firm proof, but I believe that Henri is presently in Spain, educating himself in the secrets of *Civitas Solis*, whose agent he has consented to become–at least until he can stage a *coup* and take over the organization. I've packed Ned off to the Caribbean to ascertain the truth of a report that Germain Patou and Mortdieu are there; I presume that *Civitas Solis* will send agents of their own, but I doubt that they'll entrust Henri with the mission. They're undoubtedly monitoring the situation in Paris, but they certainly don't need Henri for that–they have better access to the Faubourg Saint-Germain than any of us, now that the Restoration has revived the Church's fortunes, and they surely have their own means of getting close to Lord Byron. In brief, my lady, we can't rely on Henri's help this time. We must contend with Countess Marcian Gregoryi ourselves."

The Comtesse glanced towards the door through which Coco-Lacour had recently made his exit. "I could not turn him away," she said, simply.

"Of course not," Temple said. "Have you heard from Robert? Has he warned you against the Countess?"

"He sent me a note to say that you had warned *him* against the Countess," Jeanne admitted. "He did not seem convinced that your warning was appropriate. She is a very charming woman, and I confess that I would not have dreamed that there was anything suspect about her until I received the note. Robert was even more taken by her, I think."

"There's more to her glamour than mere beauty," Temple told her. "She is an extremely accomplished Mesmerist–more accomplished, I believe, than Mesmer ever was. She is probably much older than she seems. I confess that I do not know exactly what she is, or what to make of her master–but I know that they are both direly dangerous to anyone who gets in the way of their plans."

"And what are their plans–besides acquiring the new château?" Jeanne asked, mildly.

"They must have hoped to do that quietly, without attracting any attention," Temple said, trying to draw inferences as he spoke, "but Paris has changed a great deal since they were last here, 18 years ago. The rumor has spread like wildfire, faster than even I could have anticipated. In two days, they have been exposed to more danger of detection and destruction than in the pre-

276

vious two decades–perhaps centuries. Szandor, the so-called vampire, has evidently had time to cultivate a good deal of occult wisdom, but he is even further behind the times than *Civitas Solis* or the new arm of the Holy Office. He has been caught off-guard by the scum of the Parisian Underworld–as, I confess, have I. I have no idea what he will do in response, or even whether he can get a message relaying new orders to Countess Marcian Gregoryi, but if she keeps her appointment with Sarah Boehm, there might be trouble."

"I've taken your advice, Mr. Temple," the Comtesse replied, calmly. "I have 40 strong men on my staff now, and a series of sturdy fences around my property. The house is very secure, especially the nursery. I can make sure that the children are safe, and I can protect my guests as well."

"That's good," Temple said, "but I'm not in need of protection. The vampire could have killed me, but he wants me alive, probably in the hope that I might eventually lead him to Henri. You must not go to the new château tonight, Jeanne, for he and the Countess will certainly use you in that same cause, if they can."

"I'm not afraid," Jeanne replied.

"I know," Temple told her. "On this occasion, though, fear would not be out of place. This creature does not live on human blood, but he probably has no more compunction about killing the living than the living have about swatting flies or slaughtering livestock. You must not go."

"Very well," she said. "I shall remain in my fortress. What about you?"

"I have no invitation–and I'm not sure that I'd be able to accept if I had– but Coco-Lacour will keep his ruffians close at hand, ready to act if any order comes, and I ought at least to hold myself in readiness too. It is quite possible, by the way, that a man named Jean-Pierre Sévérin will make his way to Miremont, having heard that the vampire is here. If he comes here asking for me, let him in–he can be trusted."

She nodded to signify that she would broadcast the instruction. "If I am to stay meekly at home, though," she said, soberly, "you must keep me fully informed, Mr. Temple. I have been involved in this strange business since the moment when Henri plunged into the mill-stream, with my burning body clutched in his hands. I have cheated death myself, and am well aware of it. Had he let me die that day, he would have become rich, but he could not do it. The angel in him was stronger than the devil then, and it will win in the end."

"Yes, my lady," Temple said, meekly, as the Comtesse turned to leave the room. He was not about to point out that the only way that Henri de Belcamp could have claimed the fortune left by Helen Brown's murdered brothers was to assume the identity of Tom Brown publicly–something that he was, by then, extremely reluctant to do. To marry that fortune, whether as Henri de Belcamp or Percy Balcomb, must have seemed the preferable option on purely rational grounds. Even so, Temple did not doubt for an instant that Henri de Belcamp really had fallen in love with Jeanne Herbet, whatever his *alter ego* Tom Brown might have thought of the match.

As soon as he had finished his breakfast and set aside the tray, Temple threw back the blankets and attempted to ease himself from the bed. He contrived to stand up, but it was agony. He even forced himself to walk a few steps; his legs, as he had anticipated, worked perfectly well–but still, it was agony. He cursed the vampire, although he could not help feeling that he was being somewhat unfair in doing so. If the so-called Count Szandor had merely wished to injure him, he could have done so–and could, of course, have snuffed out his life like a candle-flame–but that was not the point of what he had done to Temple. This really was a challenge as well as a lesson, and it was a challenge that Temple needed to meet.

One way or another, Temple thought as he took a rest, slumped in an armchair, before trying again, *what my deceptive acquaintance Giuseppe Balsamo called the* Empire of the Necromancers *is about to dawn. The dead will return in ever-greater numbers, no matter what the likes of Malo de Treguern might do to prevent them. They will bring a new enlightenment, as well as a force to be reckoned with, and there is no question in the world more important than the question of who will guide that Empire as it grows and bears fruit. Count Szandor knows that now as well as I do, if he did not know it before. Fate has given him a chance to take a hand in that decision, as it has given a chance to me, and I cannot blame him for wanting to take it. Powerful as he is, though, I must still do my utmost to use my own opportunity well, not on behalf of Lord Liverpool, or King George, or even God Almighty, but on behalf of humankind.*

Chapter Six
An Unexpected Invitation

Had Gregory Temple had full mastery of his legs there were a great many things he might have done that morning. He might well have returned to Paris, in order to go in search of Countess Marcian Gregoryi before she set out for the new château–if that was still her intention–or to seek an interview with Lord Byron, or to confer with Jean-Pierre Sévérin. As things were, however, he could not conquer his psychosomatic pain to the extent that would permit such an excursion. The vampire had got the better of him, at least for a matter of hours. He was, however, able to refuse his hostess's offer to supply him with a wheelchair and a lackey to push it around the grounds of the château; he contrived to walk short distances, albeit with some difficulty, with the aid of a cane like the one that Sévérin used.

The time was not entirely wasted though; there were bridges to be built and fences to mend within the family, and Temple–unable, for once, to offer an excuse for hurrying away–had no alternative but to take a holiday from his obsession and begin that work of domestic repair. Thus, for the first time ever, he conversed for more than an hour with his little grandson. For the first time in five years, he conversed for more than an hour with his former assistant. For the first time in more than ten years, he conversed for more than an hour with his daughter.

It was, as he had anticipated when he saw the early light of dawn filtering through the curtains, a fine day, with not a hint of fog about it, or any of the stink of the city. The valley of the Oise was green and tranquil, as the whole world always seemed to be in his rare dreams of childhood.

"If you were ever to retire, Father," Suzanne told him, as they sat on the mound that offered the best view of the valley available in the château's grounds, while the sun eventually began to sink again into the west, "you would be very welcome in Miremont–perhaps in the village, if you would prefer that to the château."

"I cannot," Temple told her. "Mine is not the kind of vocation that permits retirement. I shall die in harness, if I do not find a way to go on forever–and even if I die..." He left the sentence unfinished.

"Would you really want to come back from the dead?" she asked him. "The rumors I have head about the Grey Men do not make that sort of resurrection seem an attractive prospect."

Temple thought about Szandor and what it must be like to live among men as a horrid caricature of human form, loathed and feared in equal measure. "The process must be capable of refinement," he said. "There will doubtless be many failures along the way–but a man might be proud even to be one such failure, I think, provided that he could offer a valuable stepping-stone to eventual success. Germain Patou is a long way away, but Victor Frankenstein is still in Europe, and Lord Byron knows where he is. If and when I have the privilege of meeting his lordship, I shall be glad to volunteer myself as a future test-subject, just as Keats and Shelley were."

Suzanne was beside him, but her hand was resting on his shoulder and he felt her shudder. "Don't be afraid," he said.

"I can't help it," she confessed.

A carriage came in sight then, still very distant, on the hunting-path that led from the woods surrounding the crossroads on the road between Paris and l'Isle Adam to the two châteaux. Temple immediately plucked the Marquis de Belcamp's old field-telescope from his pocket, having purloined it for this very purpose.

"That's Sarah's carriage," Suzanne said, immediately.

Temple trained his instrument upon the vehicle. It was, at first, impossible to guess how many passengers that body of the carriage might contain, especially as the blinds were drawn over its windows, but it seemed obvious enough from its seemingly-perfect condition that the vehicle had not been the focal point of any pitched battle such as might have followed any sort of ambush. It had obviously not been stopped on the road from Paris.

"She's aboard," he murmured. "I feel it in my bones. The vampire is not easily put off, it seems. He must be assuming that the influential friends the Countess has gathered with such remarkable rapidity will shield her from any potential harm. I cannot believe that he will actually buy the château, though; he is accustomed to discretion, and surely will not try to establish himself in a known location of that sort. He must be hoping that the Countess will be able to make a compact with Byron tonight, before they all disappear. If Frankenstein's Grey Man has returned to his master as a messenger, his Lordship might be amenable to that possibility–but he will surely still be wary of the Countess's magnetic powers. The last thing he would want is to be reduced to the status of a mere instrument himself."

In the meantime, his right eye remained glued to the telescope's lens, studying the carriage as it made its patient way to the courtyard of the new château; he was eager to see who might descend when it pulled up in front of the perron.

When the suspense was finally ended, three people got down from the carriage: two women and a man. The man seemed to be very old; he had to be helped down by the others.

"Is the lady in the red dress Countess Marcian Gregoryi?" Suzanne asked. Temple was surprised that she was able to see the blood-red evening-gown at all, with the naked eye, given that the Countess was wearing a white fur coat over the top of it, leaving only half a meter visible beneath the coat's hem.

"I've only seen the woman at a much closer distance," Temple told her, scrupulously, "but I have not the slightest doubt that it is."

"And who is the man? It's not Robert Surrisy–is it Lord Byron?"

"No, it's not," Temple said. "I can't be absolutely certain, because I haven't seen him for many years, but I believe that it's Colonel Bozzo-Corona. If *he*'s fallen under the Countess's spell, then she really does have a firm foothold in the cream of Parisian society, and not just the *haut ton...*"

"There's another carriage," Suzanne interrupted. "And a third, further away–but the third isn't coming up the hill. It's stopped by the old mill."

Temple stood up, wincing as he did so, and swiveled the telescope back and forth. Supporting himself on his cane he watched the second carriage–the one that was climbing the hill. "*That*'s Byron," he said, positively, although he could not quite make out the coat-of-arms on the carriage door. "So she has succeeded in arranging a meeting–I wonder if the Colonel helped her to negotiate that.

"Who is Colonel Bozzo-Corona?" Suzanne asked. "I don't know the name."

"He's a much-respected man," Temple told her, "but he lives a somewhat reclusive existence, it seems. I met him in London before the war–he took a keen interest in the founding of Scotland Yard, and said that Paris really ought to have something similar, to protect the interests of honest men. He's met Séverin recently, it seems–to consult him about the possibility that the dead might return. If he's taking an interest in the business, Frankenstein will have no lack of funds available to him…"

He trailed off as the second carriage reached the perron, and three men got out. All three were of ordinary stature, but all three were wearing hats that made identification difficult.

"Is it Byron?" Suzanne was avid to know.

"I believe so," said Temple, altering the focus of the telescope slightly. "He's the one bringing up the rear, I think. The other two must be his guests, or his bodyguards–but I can't tell who they might be."

Two of the newcomers, including Lord Byron, went into the house; the third, after a brief consultation with the other two, set off in the direction of the Château de Belcamp.

"Is he coming here?" Suzanne asked.

"Apparently," Temple confirmed. In the meantime, he switched his instrument to the third carriage, which had stopped by the mill, on the near side of the bridge over the Oise. This one was the largest of the three, and seemed to be somewhat loaded down with passengers; it disgorged no less than eight men, who must have been very cramped inside. Temple had no difficulty in recognizing their leader by the slightly bizarre manner of his dress.

"Coco-Lacour," Temple said, shortly. "He must have received new orders from Vidocq. Still hunting for the vampire, no doubt–he probably has at least another dozen men lurking in the vicinity. It's sheer optimism, though; he might as well hope to catch a shadow."

After a brief inspection, the group broke up, and the eight men dispersed. They vanished into the woods soon enough, but Temple guessed that they intended to form a picket around the new château's park, so that they could monitor any traffic in or out.

Temple returned his attention to the lone man making his way toward the gate of the Château de Belcamp. He collapsed the telescope and put it away. "Go back into the house," he said. "I'll go down to the gate to find out what the fellow wants. It's a good opportunity to tell him that the Comtesse is indisposed, and won't be able to come to dinner."

"No," Suzanne said. "I'm coming with you. What if your leg gives out?"

Temple pursed his lips, but made no objection. As he set off, there certainly seemed to be a possibility that his leg *would* give out, but he gathered all his strength and did his utmost to ignore the taunting pain.

Pierre Louchet was already waiting at the gate, with the attitude of a faithful bulldog. Temple joined him and took up a position by his side as the messenger approached. He was well-dressed, in an unmistakably English style

"Bonjour," he said, and continued in French: "My name is Robert Walton. I should like to see the Comtesse de Belcamp, if that's possible."

"I'm afraid it isn't," Temple replied, in English. "The Comtesse has been taken ill. She will not be able to see anyone until tomorrow, at the earliest. Pierre was just about to set out for the new château to express her regrets to Countess Boehm, but you have saved him the trouble. Please ask Countess Boehm to accept her apologies."

Walton looked him in the eyes, with perfect frankness. "Gregory Temple, I presume," he said, "late of Scotland Yard."

"Indeed," said Temple. "This is my daughter Suzanne, who lives here with her husband, Richard Thompson. I was in Paris, and took the opportunity to visit."

"Lord Byron mentioned that you might be here," Walton said, equably. "He also anticipated that the Comtesse might not be able to join us, although I have no idea how he came by the suspicion. We have a doctor in our party—would you like me to ask him to come over to attend to the Comtesse?"

Temple heart skipped a beat. "A doctor?" he said. "You don't, by any chance, mean Victor Frankenstein?"

Walton smiled. "No, Mr. Temple," he said. "Dr. Frankenstein is not in Paris just now. The doctor who is with us tonight is an Italian gentleman by the name of Giuseppe Balsamo. I believe you know him, slightly."

Temple did not know whether that was good news or not. "I believe I do," he said. "I admire his courage in coming here."

"Why so?" Walton asked. "It's a harmless social call, after all." His voice had now taken on a slight hint of irony.

The reason why Temple esteemed it an act of courage for "Giuseppe Balsamo" to visit the new château was that all of Sarah Boehm's staff were affiliated to a *vehm* that had lately been involved in a dispute with the organization to which the man now employing that pseudonym belonged–and they were the kind of men who bore grudges for a long time. Balsamo doubtless thought himself safe in his present company, though.

"Of course it is," was what Temple said aloud. "I hope you have a good dinner, and a pleasant conversation."

"Actually," Walton said, "Lord Byron wondered if *you* might care to join us. I think he would be glad to have another fellow-countryman present."

Temple felt Suzanne jab him in the ribs with her elbow, as if to tell him to follow the advice he had given to Jeanne and refuse–but she knew him well enough to know that there was no chance of that.

"I should be delighted," he said. "Please thank Lord Byron for me–it's a great honor."

"Should we send a carriage to collect you?" Walton asked. "You seem to have injured your leg."

"That won't be necessary," Temple assured him.

"Milord also mentioned another person who might be here, who would also be welcome to join us: a Monsieur Jean-Pierre Sévérin."

So Frankenstein's new Adam did get back to his Lordship, Temple thought, *and has told him that if he came to this meeting–as his curiosity was bound to drive him to do–then he ought to recruit trustworthy reinforcements. I'm flattered.* Aloud, he said: "I was hoping that Monsieur Sévérin would contact me today, but he has not done so as yet. If he does arrive, I shall be glad to bring him with me. What time shall I come?"

"As soon as you like," was the reply. "We shall be dining at seven, but I dare say that the conversation will be well advanced by then." Walton took off his hat, bowed politely to Suzanne, and turned to leave.

"Will you go down to the village for me, Pierre?" Temple asked Louchet. "Look for Sévérin–I'm sure he's there somewhere, probably keeping his ear to the ground in the inn. You'll know him easily enough by his white hair and cane–he has one just like this."

"I know Monsieur Sévérin." Pierre Louchet replied. "I had, alas, had more than one occasion to visit the morgue in the days when he was its keeper. He knew the Emperor, you know."

"I know," Temple said. "Bring him back, if you can, in a hurry. I'll have to borrow some better clothes–and so will he, I'd guess–but this is an opportunity not to be missed. History might be made tonight. I never thought I'd ever volunteer to serve as Lord Byron's bodyguard, but life is full of surprises, thank God!"

Chapter Seven
A Masquerade with Invisible Masks

Pierre Louchet came back with Jean-Pierre Sévérin before Temple had finished dressing. The old man seemed slightly out of breath after climbing the hill, and he leaned on his cane for support when he paused, but there was a flame of naked excitement in his eye. "Thank you, my friend," he said to Temple, with evident sincerity. "René wanted to come with me, but I would not permit it. Someone has to guard Angela. In any case, he is a trifle hot-headed at times. He does not have our cool maturity–but you're hurt! What happened?"

"The vampire pinked me in the leg after all," Temple told him, "but I think I have the better of the injury now. I can't wield my cane as you wield yours, but it will get me to this diabolical conference. You'll find another old friend of yours there, by the way: Colonel Bozzo-Corona. I suspect that he acted as a broker between Countess Marcian Gregoryi and Lord Byron–we must make certain, if we can, to protect him as well as Lord Byron."

"Is that our mission now–to protect Lord Byron?" the old warrior asked, uncertainly. "I thought we were here to slay the vampire."

"That may not be possible–but we might hope, at least, to prevent his taking control of this entire business. Here–put this suit on. Like mine, it's more than a trifle old-fashioned, having belonged to the old Marquis, but it's respectable."

Sévérin put on the Marquis' old evening suit, and the two men set off for the new château immediately afterwards. Temple had already given stern instructions to Richard Thompson to keep the house sealed at all costs.

The walk from one residence to the other was not easy, but Temple negotiated it without overmuch discomfort, with the aid of his stick.

As they approached the main gate of the new château two corpulent ruffians armed with naked blades moved out of the bushes to either side of the path, blocking their way. Jean-Pierre Sévérin immediately placed himself *en garde*, but the situation was immediately defused when Coco-Lacour came running out of a covert, making hasty signals to his men to stand easy.

"Mr. Temple is a colleague, lads!" he scolded them. "He's one of those we're here to protect, not one of those we're here to arrest–and this is Monsieur Sévérin, who was the finest swordsman in France before the Revolution, so you must count yourselves lucky that you did not fee the blunt end of his walking-stick in your overstuffed guts."

Having arrived in front of the two visitors he bowed ostentatiously. "Out of bed already, Mr. Temple!" he said. "I hope I have your powers of perseverance when I reach your age."

"But you'll be the Prefect of Police by then, Monsieur Lacour!" Temple retorted, matching the other's mocking tone. "You'll never have to quit your desk, with fine fellows like these to do your bidding."

"You're too kind, Mr. Temple," Coco-Lacour assured him. Looking Temple and Sévérin up and down, he was quick to add: "I had not realized that Countess Sarah's party was a masquerade–but I have to admit that the mothballs have kept the Marquis' old clothes in good condition." He obviously knew that the insult would carry an extra edge, coming from him.

"A masquerade without masks," Temple replied as lightly as he could. "Or perhaps, more accurately, with invisible masks. Be careful, won't you, not to let any shadows slip past you. There will be vampires abroad, once dusk falls."

That reminder struck home, but Coco-Lacour did not cry *touché*. He simply shoved his men aside to let the Countess's guests pass.

In fact, the pause did Temple good, allowing him to vent a little of his bile and permitting his aching leg a useful truce. He felt quite well again when the door of the new château was opened by a German footman. Temple was not displeased to see that the domestic was a strong man with a military bearing–the presence of the *vehm* would, at least, guarantee that Sarah Boehm would be well defended, and her protection would presumably extend to her guests.

The two newcomers were shown into a reception-room where the assembled company was relaxing in a circle of armchairs. Sarah got up to greet them, and introduced them formally to the circle, beginning with Countess Marcian Gregoryi, whose blood-red dress was now displayed in all its considerable glory, emphasizing the contours of her figure with a skill that only the best Parisian couturiers could achieve.

The vampire's minion met Temple's eyes with a smile that seemed to radiate innocence and purity. Her eyes were bright blue, and her complexion was wondrously clear. "Lord Byron has just been telling us all about you, Mr. Temple," she said, in English. "You were once quite famous in England, it seems, for your expertise in bringing villains to justice. I'm delighted to meet you."

Temple acknowledged the compliment as gracefully as he could.

"And the Colonel has told us about you, too, Monsieur Séverin," she said, turning to his companion. "You are, in his estimation, the last of the great swordsmen of the Revolutionary era."

Jean-Pierre Séverin glanced sideways at Colonel Bozzo-Corona, perhaps puzzled as to why the old gentleman should describe him in those terms rather than as the one-time keeper of the morgue. Her eyes and her smile did throw him into confusion though. "I met a Countess Marcian Gregoryi once before, in 1804," he said, with a marked edge in his voice, although his tone was perfectly polite.

"That was my mother!" exclaimed the lovely blonde, apparently delighted with the news. "She's dead now, I fear—but she lived to see me earn the right to the name that she coveted so dearly. Poor Marcian is dead too, alas—like our charming hostess, I was unfortunate enough to be widowed young." And with that the lady relaxed back into her seat.

Sarah Boehm continued the round of introductions.

Giuseppe Balsamo nodded in recognition of the fact that he had met Temple before, while Lord Byron, whose impeccable jet black costume made a sharp contrast with Balsamo's slightly rumpled blue one, assured him that he had long wanted to meet the famous detective. Walton's acknowledgement was very brief, but Colonel Bozzo-Corona looked at Temple long and hard, in a slightly quizzical manner, and stood up as if to study him more carefully. "You were a young man when we last met," the Colonel said, as if he were surprised to see the extent to which Temple had aged—and Temple had to admit, although he did not want to say so aloud, that the Colonel hardly seemed to have aged at all, having already been old before the war began.

"I know, I know," the Colonel said, apparently reading Temple's mind. "I am far too old for this kind of diplomatic mission—but I tell myself perpetually that whatever business I am involved in must be my last affair, and never seem able to take my own advice. It is hard to reconcile oneself to growing old, is it not, Monsieur Séverin? Mentally, we might remain young forever, if only our bodies did not let us down—but I fear that the cure for which Lord Byron's associates are hunting is unlikely to materialize in time to help us."

Jean-Pierre Sévérin had followed Temple around the circle, bowing respectfully to everyone. The old warrior was not at all put out by the prestigious company; indeed, he seemed to make a point of looking everyone straight in the eye, as if he had every right to be as proud of his own heritage as they had of theirs. No one, so far as Temple could see, objected to that; none of them was too proud to meet the gaze of a morgue-keeper's son who had followed in his father's footsteps. Indeed, it seemed that they all warmed to the old man immediately.

The German footman had poured glasses of *kir* for Temple and Sévérin; after serving them, he retired. When Temple and his companion had taken their seats, the Colonel and Sarah Boehm sat down again too. The conversation immediately became fragmented, individuals chatting with their immediate neighbors—as they had presumably been doing before the two new arrivals had been shown in.

Colonel Bozzo-Corona was, however, still looking at Temple, and Temple looked back at him, still puzzled by the old man's astonishing state of preservation. "The company is almost complete," the Colonel remarked, placidly.

Temple glanced around, and saw that there was, indeed, one seat in the circle that had no occupant. Sévérin leaned over to whisper in his ear: "Will the vampire come in person, then?"

Temple was almost willing to believe that—although another alternative did occur to him. "Who else are we expecting?" he said to the Colonel, unable to contain his impatience.

"Countess Boehm's brother and lawyer, Robert Surrisy," the old man said. "There is a little business to be transacted after dinner it seems—I don't know the exact details."

Temple looked at Countess Marcian Gregoryi, who was talking to Robert Walton, while Byron and Balsamo were involved in some hushed exchange. She seemed quite oblivious to his suspicion and hostility—and Walton seemed to be as entranced by her as Robert Surrisy had been. Temple could not help experiencing a pang of regret at the discovery that Henri de Belcamp was not, after all, due to spring one of his surprises.

They did not have long to wait for the company to be completed; less than five minutes had passed before the footman opened the door again and ushered Surrisy in. Sarah moved to greet him, but the young lawyer seemed slightly flustered, and did not greet her as gallantly as might have been expected, and was certainly her due. "Did you know that there's some kind of manhunt going on in the vicinity, Sarah?" he said. "My carriage was actually stopped by some buffoon in a clownish costume, who wanted to search it."

"That is Monsieur Coco-Lacour," Temple supplied. "You might be seeing a lot more of him in future—he is ambitious to rise through the ranks, and might well be chief of the Sûreté one day, even if he never becomes Prefect. Tonight, he's hunting for a vampire."

The pronunciation of the last word would probably have imposed an instant silence on any other social gathering of that size, but there was no reaction in this one. Robert looked at Temple, unable to hide his amazement. "Thank you for your advice, Mr. Temple," he said, insincerely. "I must admit that I did not expect to find you here–and Monsieur Séverin is here too, I see."

"Lord Byron took the liberty of inviting us," Temple explained, taking some relish in the other's evident confusion. "Much to my delight–I've always wanted to meet him."

Byron raised his glass in acknowledgement of that remark, and met Temple's eyes with a gaze that was full of significance. Temple nodded, hoping to convey the reassurance that he and the rebel aristocrat were on the same side, at least for tonight. Byron got up then–which provided a signal to everyone else that it was permissible to move around, and came to take Temple's arm in order to draw him aside.

"A mutual friend told me that you had been hurt," he said, glancing down at the stick. "I was very glad when Walton told me that you were able to come tonight. I might need your counsel–and Monsieur Séverin's too. Weight of numbers, I'm assured, is the best defense against mesmeric wiles."

"The Countess has only one pair of eyes," Temple quoted. "Her spell-casting powers are limited–but she might well be prepared to deal honestly with you, if she cannot secure an advantage. Her master seems genuinely curious–but if you do intend to sup with her, in the broader sense…"

"I must use a long spoon," Byron completed. "I had gathered that. You and I should have come to an understanding some time ago, I suppose, but I was reluctant to trust you, despite your reputation for honest dealing. You're an agent of Parliament, after all–although you seem to have enthusiastic radicals in your employ, and your employers are rumored to disapprove of your recent exploits."

"My superiors have almost reached the end of their tether," Temple admitted. "I might be kicked out of the King's employ at any moment–but that does not mean that I would be content to be anyone else's agent."

"Understood. We both have agents on the *Belleville*, though, and I think they might find common cause before they reach the Carib Sea."

"Master Knob thinks that he is his own man," Temple said, with a sigh. "He makes common cause with all and sundry, when he thinks it suits him. One day, he'll forget what he's doing and stab himself in the back."

Byron nodded to acknowledge the quip, and murmured: "We'll talk again, before we get down to business." Then he allowed himself to be drawn aside by Sarah Boehm, who sat him down on a sofa and then arranged herself beside him, presumably because she was genuinely delighted to meet the greatest poet of the age rather than being motivated by any conspiratorial fervor.

Temple took a quick look around, Jean-Pierre Séverin was standing on his own, his penetrating gaze roaming from one face to another–although his eyes never lingered long on Countess Mercian Gregoryi, who was still flirting with

Robert Walton. Perhaps, Temple thought, he was afraid that they might be captured and entranced–which might turn out to be a wise precaution.

Giuseppe Balsamo had taken Robert Surrisy aside, to sit on a window-seat, but they did not appear to be talking business. Colonel Bozzo-Corona was sitting very quietly, seemingly studying the assembled guests with as much attention and intelligence as Temple. Temple stepped back to join Sévérin.

"Lord Byron's head is clear," Temple said, speaking out of the corner of his mouth. "He has plenty of supporters here to distract her hypnotic gaze, if and when she turns her attention to him. So has Sarah Boehm, although she has not the same suspicion of the danger she's in. I think we can negotiate our way through the pass, when the danger materializes–but we'd best be careful not to drink too much during dinner."

Sévérin did not reply immediately, and Temple turned sideways to look him in the face. The old man's eyes seemed remarkably dark, and Temple was suddenly aware of a sinking feeling in his stomach. He opened his mouth to speak, but was interrupted before he could say a single word.

"Does it not seem to you, Mr. Temple," Sévérin said, very mildly, "that the atmosphere in this room is surprisingly dusty, for such a fine and modern house?"

As soon as those words had been voiced, Temple became aware that he was drawing breath with difficulty. It was as if the air had become gradually heavier, by such imperceptible degrees that he had not noticed it until it was pointed out, and was now so thick that it weighed down upon him.

There were three chandeliers in the room and a dozen wall-brackets holding candelabra–at least 60 candles, in all, of pure white wax. The light should have been bright, but he realized now that it had been dimming for some time, by similarly imperceptible degrees. Moreover, as Jean-Pierre Sévérin had calmly observed, the air was thick with dust…or something that resembled dust.

"Damn it!" muttered Temple, finding it oddly difficult to pronounce the words. "He's here! Despite Coco-Lacour's ragged legion and all the German guards, he's here!" His first thought, then, was to warn Sara Boehm–but as he took a step in her direction, he saw her lie back languidly against the back of her sofa, as if in a coquettish gesture aimed at the pillar of English Romanticism, and he saw her eyes drift shut.

Temple attempted another curse, but could not get it out. He saw that Byron's eyes were closed too, although the poet was sitting up straight. Having observed that, Temple thought it best to raise the alarm himself, and tried to turn towards the door–but his legs, although there was no longer the least twinge of pain therein, simply refused to obey him. He darted a glance at Balsamo and Surrisy, and saw that they had both slumped against the window, apparently having passed out. Even Colonel Bozzo-Corona had relaxed his patient vigilance, and had closed his eyes as if to rest them.

But this is impossible! Temple thought. *Even if he were here, he only has one pair of eyes! Even if he and Countess Marcian Gregoryi have two pairs, that...*

As he formed the thought, he redirected his glance towards the Countess in the blood-red dress. She was not looking at him, though; she was still staring into Robert Walton's eyes. The seafarer's eyes were still open, but they seemed to Temple to be blind to everything but his immediate companion.

Temple turned back to his own companion, Jean-Pierre Séverin, hoping that he, at least, was still alert and capable of action. He was—but Temple saw, far too late, that his companion was not Jean-Pierre Séverin at all.

Where Séverin had been standing only a moment before there was now a walking skeleton, with hardly an ounce of flesh on his bones, on whom the Marquis de Belcamp's old suit hung like a bizarre shroud.

"Have no fear, Mr. Temple." whispered a sibilant, serpentine voice that might have come from anywhere. "The real Monsieur Séverin is safe in Paris, where I visited him this morning and found him under clandestine house arrest. It will take a more powerful friend than you or Lord Byron to release him, although Monsieur Coco-Lacour did not seem to know that, if Monsieur Vidocq took the trouble to inform him of that part of his scheme. Don't worry—no one in or near suspected that I was there. I was particularly careful not to trouble the lovely Angela—this time. All that I stole was a mere appearance, for the sake of a little masquerade. I have, as you so dutifully repeated on my behalf, only one pair of eyes—but I think you and Monsieur Lazarus might have underestimated what one pair of eyes might do, if given leave to roam for a while."

I am the Trojan Horse! Temple thought, despairingly. *I brought the enemy here myself, without suspecting it for a moment! What a fool I have been!* "What do you intend to do?" he whispered, hardly able to force the words through his lips.

The room was full of dust now, much thicker than the fog that had afflicted Paris two nights before—and the dust seemed, once again, to be full of hungry ghosts. Temple remembered that the Deliverance had met here, too, on the night when the organization had met its Waterloo, despite the warning delivered by Ned Knob, which had allowed the ringleaders to scatter and save their lives. That was the night that Henri de Belcamp had committed suicide, at least in the deluded eyes of his poor distraught father, while Helen Brown lay dead in an alcove at the other château. Was her ghost here in this insistent crowd, he wondered, hungrier for revenge than all the rest combined?

"You know what I intend to do, Mr. Temple," whispered Count Szandor the vampire, as his lovely alter ego glided across the floor to join him, leaving the hapless Robert Walton behind, slumped unconscious in his chair. "I intend to make contracts and discover secrets—but I intend to make and discover them on my own terms, and no one shall bargain with me, let alone prevent me. Certainly not you, my unwitting friend."

Gregory Temple saw, in that horrible instant, that all was lost: that the vampire had won, despite everything that had been done by way of defense. Now, it only remained for him to seize the opportunity he had created, not only to captivate Lord Byron and Robert Walton, but also Sarah Boehm and Robert Surrisy, and Giuseppe Balsamo of *Civitas Solis*–and also, by way of a bonus, Colonel Bozzo-Corona, one of the most highly esteemed men in Paris. All that might take time–in fact, it certainly would take time–for he would have to work on them one by one to obtain that kind of control over them and make them speak, but he *had* time, now, and one pair of eyes would suffice, even if he and his minion only had one effective pair between them.

They obviously intended to start on the very least of their captives, by way of *hors d'oeuvres*. They intended to start by enslaving Gregory Temple, formerly of Scotland Yard.

It was the woman's eyes–the eyes of Countess Marcian Gregoryi–that suddenly filled Temple's with their magical blueness, as infinite as the sky, while the avid ghosts clustered round, gloating. Temple tried with all his might to struggle, but he knew that he could not do it. He was utterly helpless. One pair of eyes was all it took...

He tried to cry for help, but he could not. He prayed, instead, for one of Sarah's servants to come in–but he knew that dinner would not be served for an hour, and that no one would appear if no summoning bell was rung.

Unlike her master, Countess Marcian Gregoryi was extremely beautiful: as beautiful as love itself, if his memory served him right...

Then, astonishingly, both battens of the reception room were hurled back– and from the utmost corners of his not-yet-bewildered eyes, Temple glimpsed two figures stride in, insistently claiming the attention of the blue eyes that had been about to consume his sight.

The one thing with which a Mesmerist could not deal, Temple reflected, as time seemed to stop, was *weight of numbers*–but that was no mere matter of simple arithmetic. It did not require a host, or even a crowd; it only required weight enough to divide his attention, and throw him momentarily into a quandary, provided that advantage could then be taken of the moment of confusion. Two men would be enough, and a mere split second, provided that the two were sufficiently surprising in their appearance, and sufficiently fast-moving in their action.

The two men who had burst in were not *just* two, in fact–there was a whole company of German guardsmen behind them, alerted and armed and ready to fight–but it was the two who led the charge that broke the vampire's spell.

The two men were both grizzled, having the appearance of men who had outlived their natural span, and ought to have had no natural vitality left–but they were very much alive, and they were ablaze with vitality. They wasted no time in challenges or questions, but hurled themselves forwards into the furious dust-storm that formed around them–and the blades they carried seemed to move like streaks of lightning, cutting through the forms that were trying to take shape there.

This time, Jean-Pierre Sévérin–the *authentic* Jean-Pierre Sévérin–had a real épée, not a cane, and his companion–who must, Temple realized, be none other than Malo de Treguern–had a blade like the Breton knights of the age of chivalry, more broadsword than saber.

Count Szandor reacted immediately, and might still have had the power and presence of mind to turn the tables back if he had only been facing Treguern, or two men like the warrior monk–but Jean-Pierre Sévérin's blade was momentarily unstoppable, and his hand had already demonstrated that it was *much* quicker than any mortal eye. The old man was young again, just for that instant, and he knew exactly what to do. This time, it was not clumsiness that compelled him to seek out his opponent's eye.

Count Szandor had no sooner squared up to his unexpected opponents than he staggered back, wounded: sorely wounded, it seemed, in the right eye. Now, he no longer had even one complete pair of eyes.

Countess Marcian Gregoryi still had two eyes intact, but they were not independent of her master's. Those blue orbs, distracted by the commotion, were no longer staring into Gregory Temple's eyes, and no longer holding him prisoner. Even as he reached out to seize her, though, never taking his own eyes off her incredible lovely face, that face began to crumble, aging 100 or 1000 years within a fraction of a second–and then she disintegrated into dust, seemingly no different from the hundreds of other ghosts that had been clustering around, but which were fleeing now, panicked by the mighty sweeps of Malo de Treguern's shining blade and the darting thrusts of Jean-Pierre Sévérin's épée.

Gradually, the dark and cloying air was clearing and becoming bright again–and when Temple looked down, to where Count Szandor's stricken body should have been, that too appeared to be melting into dust. That ghost fled like all the rest–but it did not dissipate as the others did, maintaining a blurred semblance of shape even as it slid between the two swordsmen and glided through the confused ranks of the German swordsmen, who had no idea how to prevent it. Half-blind or not, Count Szandor still knew how to move in such a way as to deceive the sight of lesser men.

Not dead, Temple thought, *nor even mortally wounded. I doubt that he'll return to Paris for some little while, though, once he's had time to collect himself.*

The candlelight was becoming bright again now, and all the eyes that had closed were opening again, staring into empty space in puzzlement. Sarah Boehm looked at the door of her reception-room, frowning at the unbidden intrusion.

None of them, Temple presumed, had seen the false Sévérin change into his skeletal form and then vanish. They were more than a little surprised to see the true one with a sword in his hand instead of a cane, wearing a completely different costume, while the Marquis de Belcamp's old suit and the vampire's cane lay in an untidy heap on the floor. They were even more surprised, though, by the sight of a warrior monk whose habit bore a huge red cross of Calvary, wound around with thorns.

"Who is this man?" Sarah Boehm demanded of her lackeys, who now seemed somewhat shamefaced by the discovery that no one in the room seemed too be under threat, and obviously had not the slightest idea what had just happened.

"Forgive my lack of ceremony, my lady," the warrior monk said, as he sheathed his improbably large sword. "My name is Malo de Treguern. When I arrived in Miremont just now, in company with Monsieur Sévérin, and we were informed that his double had already been summoned to this house, I realized immediately that vile diabolism was at work, and that I had a duty to discharge."

Temple ran his gaze over the Germans, who had obviously yielded to the sheer force of the crusader's personality in letting him in–although the sight of a man whose double was already in the reception-room must have assisted their decision.

"Where's Countess Marcian Gregoryi?" demanded Robert Walton, looking in rapt astonishment at a blood-red evening gown that was extended on the carpet.

"I'm afraid that she had to go," Temple said, suppressing a giggle that would surely have confirmed his reputation for lunacy had he let it out. "She had a reckoning to meet, for crimes committed 18 years ago–but I fear that Monsieur Vidocq's men will not be able to lay their hands on her."

As he spoke, his eyes met those of Colonel Bozzo-Corona, who was staring at him with an unfathomable expression. "For a moment there, Mr. Temple," the Colonel said, almost as if he too were suppressing a giggle, "I feared that *it was getting dark.*"

Epilogue
When the Dust Had Cleared

"As you can probably imagine," Gregory Temple said to the Comtesse de Belcamp, "Walton and Surrisy were not the only ones who found Malo de Treguern a less delightful dinner companion than Countess Marcian Gregoryi would have been. The man is quite insufferable, and we really could have done without his ranting and raving about entertaining the Devil in our homes and hearts."

"But Treguern's timely arrival did save you from the demon's clutches," the Comtesse observed. She was sitting in her favorite armchair, in the room that had formerly been the Marquis of Belcamp's study: the room in which her husband had supposedly shot himself. The two of them were alone, at her insistence, although Temple fully intended to repeat most of what he had just told the Comtesse to his daughter, in order that she would not think that he was still keeping secrets from her.

"The vampire did not intend to kill anyone," Temple told her, trying hard to make himself comfortable in his own armchair. "He is not the Devil–he is not even evil, in any straightforward sense. He can hardly be blamed for feeling isolated, in a world that regards him with fear and loathing, and for his inability to trust anyone who is not entirely subjugated to his will. He did not come to Paris in search of plunder, this time, but in search of enlightenment–as we all did. It is direly unfortunate, but quite understandable, that he could not imagine any other way to obtain it, without risk to himself, but coercion. There is a certain irony, is there not, in the fact that it was his determination to subjugate his fellow guests as a precondition of negotiation that actually led to his downfall? Malo de Treguern's belated visit to Sévérin's house was lucky, though–as Coco-Lacour remarked, it needed a more powerful friend than Lord Byron or myself to relieve him of his unofficial house arrest."

"Fortunately," the Comtesse observed, "the Restoration has not only restored the King to his throne, but the Church to its former prestige."

"On the other hand," Temple pointed out, "if Vidocq had not stuck his oar in, it would have been the real man sitting watchfully in the inn in Miremont, not the masquerader, when Pierre Louchet went in search of him and I would not have been tricked into playing the Trojan Horse, introducing our adversary into our very midst. The chain of coincidences was too elaborate to enable Treguern to claim all the credit for breaking it. Nor will Treguern's intervention make Lord Byron any more trustful, I fear–although I do believe that he and I had reached a better understanding by the time the party broke up."

"But if what you say is true," the Comtesse persisted, "Malo de Treguern is at least correct in thinking that the vampire really is a supernatural being. If he and his female companion can turn themselves into clouds of dust and vanish into not-so-thin air, then they really are demons of a sort, are they not?"

"Alas," said Temple, "I merely reported what I saw–and that is not the same as reporting what actually happened. As Jean-Pierre Sévérin has now demonstrated to me twice, and a dozen professional card-sharpers have shown me repeatedly, the hand certainly is quicker than the eye. We put far too much trust in our eyesight, Madame de Belcamp, even when we it has been proven to us that it can and does lie to us. It is not our eyes that see, but our minds–and our minds are far more vulnerable to deception than we would like to believe. We have very little idea, at present, as to what the limits of Mesmeric suggestion and induced hallucination might be, any more than we have a clear idea of the true limits of life and death. Sévérin kept the Paris morgue for most of his working life, and saw the dead come back to life repeatedly–but his mind would not believe it, and he insists to this day that he *cannot be sure* of what he saw. And yet, paradoxical as it undoubtedly is, he cannot quite bring himself to *disbelieve* in what he saw on the river on the night when his daughter died, even though he knows full well that it must have been a hallucination induced by the shock of finding her drowned body in the water.

"Frankenstein's *daemon* deduced, rather cleverly, that the vampire could not cope with weight of numbers, because he only has one pair of eyes with which to confuse them, but it is not a simple matter of vulgar arithmetic. The vampire was easily capable of mesmerizing a dozen people at a time, in hospitable circumstances; all he required was some distraction of their attention. It was easy for him to persuade people–including me–to see him as Séverin, while they were expecting to see Séverin...or, at least, not expecting to see someone other than Séverin. In the right circumstances, he could doubtless mesmerize a multitude and make them see something that did not happen. It was a different matter, though, when he was confronted with more than one person who fully expected to see *him*–not necessarily as he is, but as they believed him to be. That was a different kind of challenge. He could have met it, I think–but Jean-Pierre Séverin's hand was far too quick for him, and far too determined. Yes, I *saw* the vampire and his minion turn to dust and disappear–but that was in my mind's eye. It was not what actually *happened*. That, I did not see at all, even though my actual eyes were open."

"Did you say all this to your fellow guests?" the Comtesse asked.

"No. I did not even tell them what I saw. Nor did Jean-Pierre Séverin. Malo de Treguern undertook to shoulder that responsibility single-handed–and what *he* saw, as I have explained, was the Devil vanquished by the strong arm of the Lord."

"Did the others believe that?"

"I doubt that they were as utterly convinced of it as Treguern is. Sarah Boehm and Surrisy were more credulous than the rest, I think. Giuseppe Balsamo probably has a better understanding of what occurred than I have, and might well inform Lord Byron and Walton, now that they have all had the opportunity to get better acquainted. The evening was not a waste of time, you see–it really did build some significant bridges."

"What about the poor old gentleman? He must have been terrified."

"Oddly enough, no. I don't know how old Colonel Bozzo-Corona is–he seemed quite old when I first met him, so I suppose he must be even older than Séverin–but he has obviously seen enough of the world to take everything in his stride. He seemed remarkably undisturbed by the entire experience. Indeed, he seemed strangely delighted by Malo de Treguern's performance–which he appeared to view as a mere performance, devoid of any real significance. He took a polite interest in all the post-prandial discussions, but I don't believe that he will provide Victor Frankenstein with any financial support, if that is what Byron hoped. I think he eventually came to the conclusion that all the talk of resurrection was just as crazy as Treguern's fervent talk of diabolism."

"You have yet to convince me, Mr. Temple," the Comtesse said, dryly, "that the Churchman's talk of diabolism is as crazy as you seem to believe."

Temple accepted the rebuke. "I know that I sound more than a little crazy myself," he said, "and I know that I have quite a reputation for it–but I really am doing my best to sort out the reality from the illusion."

"I don't doubt that," his interlocutor murmured, sympathetically. "What will you do now? Will you try to discover where the vampire has fled, and track him down again?"

"No. To tell the truth, I'd be just as happy if he never raised his ugly head again, no matter how much useful information he might be able to give us on the subjects of life after death and magnetism, were he so inclined–but I suspect that he'll get in touch, when he's recovered from his wound and regained his strength. He has an appetite for enlightenment himself, now. We shall have to hope that he adopts a more discreet strategy next time he makes contact. I shall return to London to wait for news from the *Belleville* regarding Germain Patou's whereabouts. If he and Mortdieu really have found a secure place of refuge in the New World, I shall have to seek him out…if my employers will allow it."

"I might acquire a steam-driven yacht myself," the Comtesse observed. "I rather enjoyed my one brief excursion to the South Atlantic, and the Americas have always intrigued me. If you find yourself without employment, Mr. Temple, I might well be able to step into the breach."

Temple knew what she meant. If the report came back that Germain Patou had found a safe haven, then Henri de Belcamp would make haste to join him– and Jeanne de Belcamp still believed that her place was at her husband's side, in spite of his firm determination that it was not. Alas, it was highly likely that, as soon as Patou's haven became known in Europe, it would immediately cease to be safe, especially for innocents like her.

"Thank you, my lady," he said, but could not help adding, a trifle morosely–for he was, after all, an honest man: "I fear, though, that I might not be much use to you. My powers as a detective seem to be on the wane, and my meager achievements in this present affair have been entirely due to good fortune."

"Your timely warning kept me out of the danger zone," she pointed out, "and you are at least a little wiser now than you were before. You might have been tricked by the vampire, but it was you who brought his eventual nemesis into the affair. But for you, the real Jean-Pierre Sévérin might be in Paris still, his ancient ears ringing with Malo de Treguern's dire warnings, while Lord Byron and Giuseppe Balsamo might have been sucked dry of all their secrets…not to mention the poor old Colonel, although I cannot imagine that he has any secrets to keep."

"Everyone has secrets of some sort, Madame de Belcamp," Temple said, mournfully. "That is one of the reasons why our own minds are so ever-ready to delude us, in pretending so relentlessly that the world is other than it is."

END OF PART FOUR

Part Five of The Empire of the Necromancers, *"Where Zombies Armies Clash by Night," will appear in* Tales of the Shadowmen 6.

Credits

The Tarot of the Shadowmen

Starring:	Created by:
The Famous Five	Enid Blyton
Antinea	Pierre Benoît
Irma Vep	Louis Feuillade
Fantômas	Pierre Souvestre & Marcel Allain
Sâr Dubnotal	Anonymous
James Bond	Ian Fleming
Nero Wolfe	Rex Stout
Harry Dickson	Anonymous
Hercule Poirot	Agatha Christie
Joseph Rouletabille	Gaston Leroux
Tarzan	Edgar Rice Burroughs
Jeeves	P.G. Wodehouse
Madame Atomos	André Caroff
Maigret	Georges Simenon
Dracula	Bram Stoker
Doc Ardan / Doc Savage	Guy d'Armen & Lester Dent
Doctor Omega	Arnould Galopin
The Nyctalope	Jean de La Hire
Sherlock Holmes	Arthur Conan Doyle
Judex	Louis Feuillade & Arthur Bernède
Arsène Lupin	Maurice Leblanc
Nestor Burma	Léo Malet

Written and illustrated by:

Michelle BIGOT lives in Aix-en-Provence and is an established illustrator of fantasy, science fiction and children's books. She has been the main contributing artist to French publisher Les Moutons Electriques's imprint *La Bibliothèque Rouge*, which features heroes and villains from popular literature. She also provided the cover for Brian Stableford's novel, *The New Faust at the Tragicomique*, published by Black Coat Press. This is her first portfolio for *Tales of the Shadowmen*.

The Way of the Crane

Starring:
Kato Hayashi
Madame Atomos

Created by:
George W. Trendle
André Caroff

Written by:
Matthew BAUGH is an ordained minister who lives and works in Lockport, Illinois, with his wife Mary and two cats. He is a longtime fan of pulp fiction, cliffhanger serials, old time radio, and is the proud owner of the silent *Judex* serial on DVD. He has written a number of articles on lesser known pop-culture characters like Dr. Syn, Jules de Grandin and Sailor Steve Costigan for the Wold-Newton Universe Internet website. His article on Zorro was published in *Myths for the Modern Age* (2005). He is a regular contributor to *Tales of the Shadowmen.*

Iron and Bronze

Starring:
Hareton Ironcastle
N'desi
Harry Killer / Zanigew
Antinea
Doc Ardan / Doc Savage
The Wandarobo
And:
The Reaver of Worlds
Blackland
Gondokoro

Created by:
J.-H. Rosny Aîné
based on H. Rider Haggard
Jules Verne & Walter Gibson
Pierre Benoît
Guy d'Armen & Lester Dent
John Peter Drummond

based on H. Rider Haggard
Jules Verne
J.-H. Rosny Aîné

Written by:
Christopher Paul CAREY holds a B.A. in Anthropology, and a M.A. in Writing Popular Fiction. He is the co-author with Philip José Farmer of *The Song of Kwasin*, the third novel in the Khokarsa cycle, a contributor to the anthology *Myths for the Modern Age: Philip José Farmer's Wold Newton Universe*, and the editor of two fiction collections from Subterranean Press. Carey lives with his wife in the Seattle, Washington area, where he works for a publisher of role-playing games and classic science fiction and fantasy novels.

Win Scott ECKERT, a regular contributor to *Tales of the Shadowmen*, holds a B.A. in Anthropology and a Juris Doctorate. In 1997, he posted the first site on the Internet devoted to expanding Philip José Farmer's concept of the Wold Newton Family. He is the editor of and contributor to *Myths for the Modern Age: Philip José Farmer's Wold Newton Universe* (2005), a 2007 Locus Award Finalist for Best Non-Fiction book. He has also written stories for *The Avenger Chronicles* (2008) and *Captain Midnight: Declassified* (forthcoming). He is a regular contributor of Wold Newton essays and stories to *Farmerphile: The Magazine of Philip José Farmer*, and he was honored to provide the Foreword to the new 2006 edition of Farmer's seminal "fictional biography," *Tarzan Alive: A Definitive Biography of Lord Greystoke* (2006). Win's latest book is *Crossovers: A Secret Chronology of the World*, coming in 2010. He is also the co-author, with Farmer, of the Wold Newton novel *The Evil in Pemberley House*, featuring Patricia Wildman, the daughter of a certain bronze-hued pulp superman.

Tros Must Be Crazy!

Starring:	Created by:
Tros of Samothrace	Talbot Mundy
Druid Panoramix	René Goscinny & Albert Uderzo
Astérix	René Goscinny & Albert Uderzo

Written by:
G.L. GICK lives in Indiana and has been a pulp fan since he first picked up a Doc Savage paperback. His other interests include old-time radio, Golden and Silver Age comics, cryptozoology, classic animation, British SF TV, C.S. Lewis and G.K. Chesterton. He is, in other words, a nerd and damn proud of it. He is a regular contributor to *Tales of the Shadowmen*.

May The Ground Not Consume Thee...

Starring:	Created by:
Edmond Dantès (a.k.a. Lord Wilmore, Abbé Busoni, Count of Monte Cristo)	Alexandre Dumas
Noirtier de Villefort	Alexandre Dumas
Renée de Saint-Méran	Alexandre Dumas
Lord Ruthven	John William Polidori
Haydée	Alexandre Dumas
Ianthe	John William Polidori

Written by:
Micah HARRIS is the author (with artist Michael Gaydos) of the graphic novel *Heaven's War*, a historical fantasy pitting authors Charles Williams, C.S. Lewis and J.R.R. Tolkien against occultist Aleister Crowley. Micah teaches composition, literature and film at Pitt Community College in North Carolina. He is currently developing several comics and prose projects. His self-published novel, *The Eldritch New Adventures of Becky Sharp*, in which the villainess of *Vanity Fair* becomes the agent of a Lovecraftian alien race, is now available. He is a regular contributor to *Tales of the Shadowmen*.

The Knave of Diamonds

Starring:	Created by:
Francisco Scaramanga	Ian Fleming
Sir Stephen	Pauline Réage
Carl	Pauline Réage
O	Pauline Réage
Peter Franks	Ian Fleming
Albert Wint	Ian Fleming
Charles Kidd	Ian Fleming

Written by:
Tom KANE was born in 1960, and grew up fascinated by the early space program, old-time radio, comic books, *Star Trek*, classic horror movies, and all the science fiction books he could find at his municipal and school libraries. Currently residing in Illinois, he is single and has no children, but prides himself on being a very indulgent uncle to numerous nephews and nieces. He comes to writing through the New Wold Newton Meteoritic Society, whose members were a big inspiration. This is his first published story.

Perils Over Paris

Starring:	Created by:
Fascinax	Anonymous
Irma Vep	Louis Feuillade
Introducing:	
Phobiarch	Lovern Kindzierski & Alan Weiss

Written by:
Lovern KINDZIERSKI has written for several major publishers in the comic book industry. In 1997, he wrote six issues of the ongoing *Tarzan* series for

Dark Horse, which got him nominated for Best Writer at the following Harvey Awards. After completing his *Tarzan* work, Lovern was invited to write *The Victorian* series for Penny Farthing Press. Amongst other projects, he has written a series of stories in the tradition of the *Arabian Nights* for *Heavy Metal*. These stories have been collected in an album, *Demon Wind*. Lovern is also well known for his award winning colouring of comics and graphic novels. He currently resides in Manitoba with his family and assorted feline freeloaders.

All Predators Great and Small

Starring:	Created by:
Claude Gabriel Dupont-Verdier (a.k.a. Satanas)	Louis Feuillade
Aguilar	Giuseppe Magione & Warren Garfield
Siegfried von Frankenhausen	Miguel Morayta
Eugenia von Frankenhausen (a.k.a. Szandra, Countess Dracula, Countess Alucard)	Miguel Morayta
Hildegarde	Miguel Morayta
José Alejandro Balsamo	Miguel Morayta
Ricardo Peisser	Miguel Morayta
Anna Peisser	Miguel Morayta
Captain Thompson	William Hope Hodgson
Dracula	Bram Stoker
Urania Caber	Philip José Farmer
Josephine Balsamo	Maurice Leblanc
Jillian Blake	Philip José Farmer
Madame Delhomme	Emile Zola
Joseph Bridau	Honoré de Balzac
Baron Kralitz	Henry Kuttner
The Durwards	Brian Clemens
Count Szandor	Paul Féval
Sharita	Gardner Fox
Henri de Belcamp (a.k.a. Serge Dolgolruki)	Paul Féval & Maurice Leblanc
Sara Balsamo (a.k.a. Madame Sara)	L.T. Meade & Robert Eustace
Gorcha the Vourdalak	Alexis Tolstoy
Felina de Valgeneuse	Frédéric Soulié & Alexandre Dumas
The Black Coats	Paul Féval

Léonard	Maurice Leblanc
Madame Koluchy	L.T. Meade
	& Robert Eustace
Larry Parker	Sir Arthur Conan Doyle
Jacob Dix	Fergus Hume
Abraham van Helsing	Bram Stoker
Irma Vep	Louis Feuillade
Introducing:	
Sabine Balsamo (a.k.a. Dr. Ab-salom)	Rick Lai
And:	
Akivasha's Tear	Yutaka Kaneko
	& Robert E. Howard
Yiggurath	H.P. Lovecraft
	& Robert Bloch
Slidith (Draco)	Lin Carter, Peter Tremayne
	& Robert E. Howard
The Great Old Ones	H.P. Lovecraft
The Elder Sign	August Derleth
Charles Loridan's *L'Essence du Dragon*	Rick Lai
Ludvig Prinn's *Les Mystères du Ver*	Robert Bloch

Written by:
Rick LAI is a computer programmer living in Bethpage, New York. During the 1980s and 1990s, he wrote articles utilizing Philip José Farmer's Wold Newton Universe concepts for pulp magazine fanzines such as *Nemesis Inc*, *Echoes*, *Golden Perils*, *Pulp Vault* and *Pulp Collector*. Rick has also created chronologies of such heroes as Doc Savage and the Shadow. He is a regular contributor to *Tales of the Shadowmen*.

The Heart of a Man

Starring:	**Created by:**
Henri Giraud	Agatha Christie
Hercule Poirot	Agatha Christie
Ernst Stavro Blofeld	Ian Fleming
Leo Saint-Clair (a.k.a. The Nyctalope)	Jean de La Hire
Introducing:	
Edouard & Nina Boucher	Roman Leary

Written by:
Roman LEARY was eight years old when a family friend gave him an Ace pa-perback of *Conan* stories. He has been a devotee of pulp fiction ever since. To-day, he is a librarian living in the small town of Washington, North Carolina, with his lovely wife Ana. He is a regular contributor to *Tales of the Shadow-men*.

A Matter Without Gravity

Starring:	Created by:
Lord Edward Beltham	Pierre Souvestre & Marcel Allain
Sherlock Holmes	Arthur Conan Doyle
John H. Watson	Arthur Conan Doyle
Cavor	H.G. Wells
Bedford	H.G. Wells
The Time Traveller	H.G. Wells
Also Starring:	
H.G. Wells	

Written by:
Alain le BUSSY hails from Belgium and studied political and social sciences, before working in human resources for the European division of Caterpillar. Bitten with the fantasy bug as a child, Alain became involved in fandom at an early age and attended the Heidelberg Worldcon in 1970. A prolific writer, Alain has had over 25 novels and 200 short stories published. In 1993, his novel, *Deltas*, the first volume of *The Aqualia Trilogy*, won the Rosny Award, the French equivalent of the Hugo. Other significant works include the heroic-fantasy saga of *Yorg* (1995) and *Equilibre* (*Balance*, 1997), the story of a wa-terworld which is the sole meeting point between mankind and an alien reptilian race.

Madame Atomos' Holidays

Starring:	Created by:
Madame Atomos	André Caroff
Monsieur Ming (a.k.a. The Yellow Shadow)	Henri Vernes
Also Starring:	
Howard Hughes	

The English Gentleman's Ball

Starring:	Created by:
The Phantom Angel	Randy Lofficier
	based on Charles Perrault
Gregor Mac Duhl	Jean de La Hire
Simone Desroches (a.k.a. Belphegor)	Arthur Bernède
Sylvie Mac Duhl	Jean de La Hire
Jeeves	P.G. Wodehouse
Bertie Wooster	P.G. Wodehouse

Written by:

Jean-Marc & Randy LOFFICIER, the editors of the *Tales of the Shadowmen* series, have also collaborated on five screenplays, a dozen books and numerous translations, including *Arsène Lupin*, *Doc Ardan*, *Doctor Omega* and *The Phantom of the Opera*. Their latest novels include *Edgar Allan Poe on Mars* and *The Katrina Protocol*. They have written a number of animation teleplays, including episodes of *Duck Tales* and *The Real Ghostbusters* and such popular comic book heroes as *Superman* and *Doctor Strange*. In 1999, in recognition of their distinguished career as comic book writers, editors and translators, they were presented with the Inkpot award for Outstanding Achievement in Comic Arts. Randy is a member of the Writers Guild of America, West and Mystery Writers of America.

The Most Exciting Game

Starring:	Created by:
The First Mate	Hergé
Sergeant Stebbins	Rex Stout
John F.-X. Markham	S.S. Van Dine
Philo Vance	S.S. Van Dine
Margo Lane	Walter Gibson
Lamont Cranston (a.k.a. Kent Allard, Henry Arnaud)	Walter Gibson
Lois Lane	Jerry Siegel & Joe Shuster
Count Zaroff	Richard Connell & James Ashmore Creelman
Ivan	Richard Connell
Allan Quatermain	H. Rider Haggard
Hareton Ironcastle	J.-H. Rosny Aîné

Lord John Roxton	Arthur Conan Doyle
Sebastian Moran	Arthur Conan Doyle
Lazarus	Richard Connell
The Serpent Man	Robert E. Howard
	& Charles Derennes
Ceintras/de Venasque	Charles Derennes
And:	
The *Karaboudjan*	Hergé
The Cobalt Club	Walter Gibson
The Gun Club	Jules Verne

Written by:
Xavier MAUMÉJEAN won the renowned Gerardmer Award in 2000 for his psychological thriller *The Memoirs of the Elephant Man*. His other works include *Gotham* (2002), *The League of Heroes*, which won the 2003 Imaginaire Award of the City of Brussels and was translated by Black Coat Press (2005), *La Vénus Anatomique* (2004), which won the 2005 Rosny Award, and *Car je suis Légion* (2005). Xavier has a diploma in philosophy and the science of religions and works as a teacher in the North of France, where he resides, with his wife and his daughter, Zelda.

A Root That Beareth Gall and Worms

Starring:	**Created by:**
Miguel de Vega (a.k.a. Miguelito Loveless)	John Kneubuhl
Lecoq	Emile Gaboriau
Raphaël Carot	Maurice Landay
Hector Ratichon	Baroness Orczy
Alejando de la Vega	Johnston McCulley
Jules Poiret	Frank Howel Evans
Isadore Persano	Arthur Conan Doyle
Zorro	Johnston McCulley
"Zee" (a.k.a. Zigomar)	Léon Sazie
Elena de la Torre	Federico Curiel & Alfredo Ruanova
Père Tabaret	Emile Gaboriau

Written by:
Jess NEVINS is a reference librarian at Sam Houston State University in Huntsville, Texas. He is the author of two companion books on Alan Moore and Kevin O'Neill's *League of Extraordinary Gentlemen* and of *The Encyclopedia of Fantastic Victoriana*, a comprehensive guide to 19th century genre literature.

Jess is currently working on *The Encyclopedia of Pulp Heroes*, an exhaustive list of series heroes, in numerous media, published around the world from 1902 to 1945. Jess lives outside of Houston with his wife Alicia and their menagerie of animals. He is a regular contributor to *Tales of the Shadowmen*.

The Dynamics of an Asteroid

Starring:	Created by:
Doctor Omega	Arnould Galopin
Denis Borel	Arnould Galopin
Fred	Arnould Galopin
Tiziraou	Arnould Galopin
Professor Moriarty	Arthur Conan Doyle
Zephyrin Xirdal	Jules Verne & Michel Verne

Written by:
John PEEL was born in Nottingham, England, and started writing stories at age 10. John moved to the U.S. in 1981 to marry his pen-pal. He, his wife ("Mrs. Peel") and their 13 dogs now live on Long Island, New York. John has written just over 100 books to date, mostly for young adults. He is the only author to have written novels based on both *Doctor Who* and *Star Trek*. His most popular work is *Diadem*, a fantasy series; he has written ten volumes to date. He is a regular contributor to *Tales of the Shadowmen*.

The Smoking Mirror

Starring:	Created by:
Jean Kariven	Jimmy Guieu
Inspector Kramer	Rex Stout
Sergeant Stebbins	Rex Stout
The Polarians	Jimmy Guieu
The Denebians	Jimmy Guieu

Written by:
Frank SCHILDINER has been a pulp fan since a friend gave him a gift of Phillip Jose Farmer's *Tarzan Alive*. Since that time he has published articles on *Hellboy*, the Frankenstein films, *Dark Shadows* and the television show's links to the H.P. Lovecraft universe. He is a Senior Probation Officer in New Jersey and a martial arts instructor at Amorosi's Mixed Martial Arts. Frank resides in New Jersey with his wife Gail and two cats. This is his first published story.

The Milkman Cometh

Starring:	Created by:
Joseph Josephin (a.k.a. Rouletabille)	Gaston Leroux
The King of Bohemia	Arthur Conan Doyle
Tevye & Golde Milkhiker	Sholem Aleichem
Ivan Dragomiloff	Jack London
Lieutenant Konstantin Vassily	based on Norman Felton
Illyavitch Couriakine	& Sam Rolfe
Charlemagne Solon	based on Norman Felton
	& Sam Rolfe
General Mikhail Strogoff	Jules Verne
Israel Di Murska (a.k.a. Natas)	George Griffith
Leonid Zattan	Jean de La Hire
Waverly	based on Norman Felton
	& Sam Rolfe
Konrad von Siegfried	based on Mel Brooks,
	Buck Henry, Mike Marmer,
	& Stan Burns
Nat Pinkerton	Anonymous
Erast Petrovich Fandorin	Boris Akunin
Reb Mendel and Yentl	Isaac Bashevis Singer
Motl Komsoyl	Sholem Aleichem
Menakhem-Mendl	Sholem Aleichem
Moisei Moiseyevich	Anton Chekhov
Boris Badenov	based on Jay Ward,
	Alex Anderson & Bill Scott
Sylvia Di Murska (a.k.a. Natasha)	based on George Griffith,
	Jay Ward, Alex Anderson
	& Bill Scott
General Trepoff	Sir Arthur Conan Doyle
Stanislaus Wojciehowicz	based on Danny Arnold
	& Theodore J. Flicker
Andrei Sipowicz	based on Steven Bochco
	& David Milch
Sherlock Holmes	Arthur Conan Doyle
And:	
Kasrilevke, Boiberik and Yehupetz	Sholem Aleichem

Stuart **SHIFFMAN** is a native New Yorker long resident in Seattle, where he attempts to say dry and uncovered in moss. He regrets having to give up the Manhattan apartment on the 101st Floor of the Empire State Building and his autogyro. He is a long-time science fiction fan, winner of the Trans-Atlantic Fan Fund in 1981 and the 1990 Hugo Award for Best Fan Artist, Sherlockian and Wodehousian and has contributed cartoons, illustrations and articles to *The Baker Street Journal* and *Plum Lines and Wooster Sauce*. Stu has written on alternate history and is a member of the judging panel for the Sidewise Award for Alternate History. He lives with Andi Shechter, book reviewer and past chair of Left Coast Crime, in a hobbit hole with too many books.

The Jade Buddha

Starring:	Created by:
Arsène Lupin (a.k.a. Duke of Charmerace)	Maurice Leblanc
Hanoi Shan	H. Ashton-Wolfe
Major Henri de Beaujolais	P.C. Wren
Thibaut Corday	Theodore Roscoe
Denis Nayland Smith	Sax Rohmer
The Si-Fan	Sax Rohmer
The Shin Tan	Henri Vernes

David L. **VINEYARD** is a fifth generation Texan (named for his gunfighter/Texas Ranger great grand-father) currently living in Oklahoma City, OK, where the tornadoes come sweeping down the plains. He has useless degrees in history, politics, and economics, and is the author of several tales about Buenos Aires private eye Johnny Sleep, two (nearly published) novels, several short stories, some journalism, and various non-fiction. He is currently working on several ideas while battling with a three month old kitten for household dominance and the keyboard of his PC.

The Vampire in Paris

Starring:	Created by:
Gregory Temple	Paul Féval
Angela de Kervoz	Paul Féval
René de Kervoz	Paul Féval
Jean-Pierre Sévérin	Paul Féval
Sarah O'Brien, Countess Boehm	Paul Féval

Jeanne Herbet, Comtesse de Belcamp	Paul Féval
Countess Marcian Gregoryi	Paul Féval
Robert Surrisy	Paul Féval
Eugène Fantin	Brian Stableford
"Lazarus"	Mary Shelley
"Guido"	Brian Stableford
Count Szandor	Paul Féval
Suzanne Thompson *née* Temple	Paul Féval
Pierre Louchet	Paul Féval
Robert Walton	Mary Shelley
Richard Thompson	Paul Féval
Giuseppe Balsamo	Alexandre Dumas
Colonel Bozzo-Corona	Paul Féval
Malo de Treguern	Paul Féval
Victor Frankenstein	Mary Shelley
Germain Patou	Paul Féval
Henri de Belcamp (a.k.a. John Devil)	Paul Féval

Also Starring:
Coco-Lacour
Eugène-François Vidocq
George Gordon, Lord Byron

Written by:

Brian M. STABLEFORD has been a professional writer since 1965. He has published more than 50 novels and 200 short stories, as well as several non-fiction books, thousands of articles for periodicals and reference books and a number of anthologies. He is also a part-time Lecturer in Creative Writing at King Alfred's College Winchester. Brian's novels include *The Empire of Fear* (1988), *Young Blood* (1992), *The Wayward Muse* (2005), *The Stones of Camelot* (2006), *The New Faust at the Tragicomique* (2007) and his future history series comprising *Inherit the Earth* (1998), *Architects of Emortality* (1999), *The Fountains of Youth* (2000), *The Cassandra Complex* (2001), *Dark Ararat* (2002) and *The Omega Expedition* (2002). His non-fiction includes *Scientific Romance in Britain* (1985), *Teach Yourself Writing Fantasy and Science Fiction* (1997), *Yesterday's Bestsellers* (1998) and *Glorious Perversity: The Decline and Fall of Literary Decadence* (1998). Brian's translations for Black Coat Press include numerous Paul Féval titles, Paul Féval fils' *Felifax the Tiger-Man*; Jean de La Hire's *The Nyctalope vs. Lucifer* and *The Nyctalope on Mars*; Marie Nizet's *Captain Vampire*; Ponson du Terrail's *The Vampire and the Devil's Son*; and other books by Charles Derennes, Henri de Parville, Villiers de l'Isle-Adam, etc. He is a regular contributor to *Tales of the Shadowmen*.

TALES OF THE
SHADOWMEN

Volume 1: The Modern Babylon (2005)
Matthew Baugh: *Mask of the Monster* - Bill Cunningham: *Cadavres Exquis* - Terrance Dicks: *When Lemmy Met Jules* - Win Scott Eckert: *The Vanishing Devil* - Viviane Etrivert: *The Three Jewish Horsemen* - G.L. Gick: *The Werewolf of Rutherford Grange* (1) - Rick Lai: *The Last Vendetta* - Alain le Bussy: *The Sainte-Geneviève Caper* - Jean-Marc & Randy Lofficier: *Journey to the Center of Chaos* - Samuel T. Payne: *Lacunal Visions* - John Peel: *The Kind-Hearted Torturer* - Chris Roberson: *Penumbra* - Robert Sheckley: *The Paris-Ganymede Clock* - Brian Stableford: *The Titan Unwrecked; or, Futility Revisited.*

Volume 2: Gentlemen of the Night (2006)
Matthew Baugh: *Ex Calce Liberatus* - Bill Cunningham: *Trauma* - Win Scott Eckert: *The Eye of Oran* - G.L. Gick: *The Werewolf of Rutherford Grange* (2) - Rick Lai: *Dr. Cerral's Patient* - Serge Lehman: *The Mystery of the Yellow Renault*; *The Melons of Trafalmadore* - Jean-Marc Lofficier: *Arsène Lupin's Christmas; Figaro's Children; The Tarot of Fantômas; The Star Prince; Marguerite; Lost and Found* - Xavier Maumejean: *Be Seeing You!* - Sylvie Miller & Philippe Ward: *The Vanishing Diamonds* - Jess Nevins: *A Jest, To Pass The Time* - Kim Newman: *Angels of Music* - John Peel: *The Incomplete Assassin* - Chris Roberson: *Annus Mirabilis* - Jean-Louis Trudel: *Legacies* - Brian Stableford: *The Empire of the Necromancers* (1)

Volume 3: Danse Macabre (2007)
Matthew Baugh: *The Heart of the Moon* - Alfredo Castelli: *Long Live Fantômas* - Bill Cunningham: *Next!* - François Darnaudet & J.-M. Lofficier: *Au Vent Mauvais...* - Paul DiFilippo: *Return to the 20th Century* - Win Scott Eckert: *Les Lèvres Rouges* - G.L. Gick: *Beware the Beasts* - Micah Harris: *The Ape Gigans* - Travis Hiltz: *A Dance of Night and Death* - Rick Lai: *The Lady in the Black Gloves* - Jean-Marc Lofficier: *The Murder of Randolph Carter* - Xavier Maumejean: *A Day in the Life of Madame Atomos* - David A. McIntee: *Bullets Over Bombay* - Brad Mengel: *All's Fair...* - Michael Moorcock: *The Affair of the Bassin Les Hivers* - John Peel: *The Successful Failure* - Joseph Altairac & Jean-Luc Rivera: *The Butterfly Files* - Chris Roberson: *The Famous Ape* - Robert L. Robinson, Jr.: *Two Hunters* - Brian Stableford: *The Empire of the Necromancers* (2).

Volume 4: Lords of Terror (2008)
Matthew Baugh: *Captain Future and the Lunar Peril* - Bill Cunningham: *Fool me once...* - Win Scott Eckert: *The Atomos Affair* - Micah Harris: *The Anti-Pope of Avignon* - Travis Hiltz: *Three Men, a Martian and a Baby* - Rick Lai: *Corridors of Deceit* - Roman Leary: *The Evils Against Which We Strive* - Jean-Marc Lofficier: *Madame Atomos' XMas* - Randy Lofficier: *The Reluctant Princess* - Xavier Mauméjean: *A Wooster XMas* - Jess Nevins: *Red in Tooth and Claw* - Kim Newman: *Angels of Musics 2: The Mark of Kane* - John Peel: *Twenty Thousand Years Under the Sea* – John Shirley: *Cyrano and the Two Plumes* – Steven A. Roman: *Night's Children* - Brian Stableford: *The Empire of the Necromancers* (3).

WATCH OUT FOR
VOLUME 6: GRAND GUIGNOL
TO BE RELEASED EARLY 2010

Printed in the United States
142287LV00003B/100/P